GRAEME CUMMING

C000137814

RAVENS
GATHERING

GRAEME CUMMING

To Sue

With love + best wishes

Thanks for the experiences!

Graee

RAVENS
GATHERING

Matador
9 Priory Business Park,
Wistow Road, Kibworth Beauchamp,
Leicestershire. LE8 0RX
Tel: 0116 279 2299
Email: books@troubador.co.uk
Web: www.troubador.co.uk/matador
Twitter: @matadorbooks

ISBN 978 1785899 157

British Library Cataloguing in Publication Data.
A catalogue record for this book is available from the British Library.

Printed and bound in the UK by TJ International, Padstow, Cornwall
Typeset in 11pt Minion Pro by Troubador Publishing Ltd, Leicester, UK

Matador is an imprint of Troubador Publishing Ltd

MIX
Paper from
responsible sources
FSC
www.fsc.org   FSC® C013056

For
Lizzie, who left me in peace to do my own thing
and
Christine Tubb, who encouraged me all those years
ago. I don't know where you are now, but you're
often in my thoughts.

ACKNOWLEDGEMENTS

I would like to thank:

Tony Fyler of Jefferson Franklin Editing – for his help and guidance. If there's still something wrong in here, I'll take the rap for it.

Torrie Cooney – for her patience and creativity in designing the cover.

CONTENTS

PROLOGUE

Drums were beating. They drew him upwards, towards them. His ascent felt slow, laborious, like swimming through treacle. At times, he wondered whether the effort was worth it. But the drums called to him, so he kept on.

Perhaps this was like being born. It seemed strange that he couldn't remember that experience. But he knew pushing was involved. He'd seen enough films and TV programmes to know that. Had it been like that when he was a baby? Did he have to push his way out?

Or was it more like swimming against the tide? He could relate to that. More so than the treacle thing. He must have picked that idea up from somewhere else because, God knows, he'd never had that experience. Swimming in the sea when he shouldn't have, well, that was a different story.

Yes, swimming against the tide. That was more like it. He realised his thoughts were becoming more lucid. Which meant he must nearly be there. He was swimming upwards now, the surface close by, the drums growing louder.

And then he broke through. He was awake.

Oddly, the beating had stopped. In the darkness of his bedroom, he wondered for a moment whether the drums had just been part of a dream. Then he heard something familiar from downstairs. The rhythmic rattle of a latch hitting a strike plate. It was the sound his mother regularly complained about when he came in from playing and didn't close the door properly. Someone had left a door open, and it was swinging back and forth in the night air.

Sitting up in bed, he rubbed the sleep from his eyes. In truth, the sleep was illusory, the pause an unconscious effort to give him a moment to rein in his emotions. And those were wide and varied, covering a range that ran from puzzlement to fear. He realised it must be the middle of the night. The only illumination was the faint glow of a nearby streetlamp through his curtains. So why would his parents leave a door open?

His bed was close to the window, so he pushed the bedclothes back and knelt up, leaning forward to lift a curtain to one side. The street was deserted. Looking to the left, he saw no sign of life. To the right, there was barely enough light to see *anything*. Just one streetlamp 50 yards away, then nothing.

He had hoped a quick look outside might explain everything, but it didn't. Now he had to face the prospect of getting out of bed and negotiating the darkness of the house. And the first thing he had to concern himself with was the crocodile under the bed.

Of course, he knew there wasn't a crocodile there. How could there be? He'd seen them on TV. There was no way they could get upstairs for a start. And they lived in and around water – a lot more than they'd find around here. He only got a bath once a week. In addition to that, though, he'd checked under the bed before he got in it. And the door was closed. Crocodiles weren't noted for their skills in silently opening and closing bedroom doors so they wouldn't disturb sleeping children. So there couldn't be a crocodile under the bed, could there? But logic and rational thought aren't always dominant when your companions are darkness and shadows.

Assuming he managed to outrun the crocodile to his bedroom door, who knew what other terrors lurked in the rest of the house? But he certainly couldn't just stay where he was. His mum and dad would kill him if they were burgled, and then found out he'd known a door was open all the time.

Reluctantly, he began to pull away from the window. Just as the curtain started to fall back into place, he glimpsed something moving at the edge of the darkness. He held the curtain and leaned forward again. A fragment of colour drifted towards him, blown gently along by a light breeze. He watched it for a long moment as it drew nearer. It was only when it passed directly under the streetlamp that he recognised it. A checked handkerchief. It belonged to his dad.

His father was outside. He knew it instinctively. And so was his mum. Crocodile forgotten, he leapt off the bed and raced on to the landing. He didn't stop to check the other bedrooms. He knew he was alone in the house. The door was still slamming, the sound getting louder as he ran down the stairs. His bare feet hardly registered the coldness of the wooden floor as he entered the living room. The front door was at the end of a hallway that opened into the room. As it swung open in the breeze, he caught a glimpse of the street outside before it threw itself frantically at the frame, desperate to close properly.

Before leaving the house, he paused for a second to make sure the snib was up. Obviously he wanted to close the door, but he wasn't going to be stupid enough to lock himself out. Then he was on the pavement, running towards the hankie, which had caught on a nearby hedge . He lifted it off, careful not to tear it. His dad could fly off the handle at the slightest thing. He wanted to put things right now, not make them worse.

When he'd freed it, he realised his pyjamas had no pockets, so he tucked the hankie in the waistband of his trousers. Then he began to run again, heading towards the edge of the light from the streetlamp. There might have been crocodiles out there as well, but already he was aware of bigger fears coursing through him.

Into the darkness. In a sense, it was like the complete reverse of how he'd felt when he was waking up. It was like being plunged into cold water. He slowed for a moment, but wasn't prepared to stop. He wasn't prepared to, but that didn't prevent it happening. His foot pushed into something soft and cold and coarse, and it met resistance, causing him to lose balance. He put his hands out as he fell. The slap of his palms on tarmac left them stinging. The impact on his knees left a tear in his trousers, and the knowledge that he was going to be in big trouble for ruining them.

He reached down to pull the thing off his foot. As his fingers ran over it, he knew the fabric was familiar. It was a jacket his dad wore. It had been lying on the road, and his foot had slipped in under one of the lapels, catching in the opening to the sleeve. Why had his dad's jacket been abandoned? Though underneath that question, he suspected he knew the answer. He realised the apprehension he was feeling now was very strong. He also realised that it was an apprehension that had started even while he was asleep. Which didn't really make sense, but he didn't have time to dwell on it.

His eyes were beginning to adjust to the darkness, and he could make out the outline of the hedge running alongside the road. A little further on, the shape changed and there was blackness instead. He recognised the opening, and knew the track there would take him up into the woods. Strangely, he felt as if he should have predicted that. He put the jacket down carefully under the hedge. It would be too heavy for him to carry, but he wanted it in a safe place, where he could find it later.

When he first started up the track, he could see nothing up ahead. The only light was a small glimmer that came from the road behind him, but his eyesight adjusted quickly.

The next item of clothing was his mother's. A headscarf, it was caught on a low branch of a tree at the side of the track. Further along, he came across her cardigan. Then a shirt, another coat, some shoes, his dad's trousers. Intermittently at first, and then more regularly. Some he recognised, some he didn't. And all the time, he was getting closer to them.

Gradually, he became aware of firelight up ahead. He was well into the woods now, and flames flickered among the gaps between the trees. There were brief glimpses of movement. Shadowy silhouettes.

The apprehension he'd felt on the road had grown even more. Oddly, he knew he wasn't in any physical danger. And yet there was a part of him that expected whatever lay before him to be far worse. In spite of this, he went on, drawn relentlessly forward.

Sounds were beginning to carry now. He could hear voices. The words were indistinct, but the tone suggested a mixture of different emotions. Anger was a strong one. He was reminded of his dad shouting at him when he came home a few weeks earlier. He'd been playing with his mates in the stream, and had fallen over. By the time he made it to the house, he was soaked through, and Dad had been furious with him. The anger in the woods reminded him of his dad, but it wasn't his voice he could hear.

Fear was another emotion he picked up. And shame.

The gaps between the trees were getting wider now as he drew nearer. More clothes lay scattered in his path. And not just outerwear. He'd passed at least two bras and several pairs of underpants – both men's and women's.

Bare skin flashed in the firelight. A part of him wanted to turn and run. A part of him wanted to discover what was happening. And the biggest part of him knew that he had no say in the matter. He'd slowed down now, but still he walked forward, heading inexorably towards the fire.

Overhead, he heard the rustle of wings, and looked up in time to see a large dark bird settle on to a branch in a nearby tree. Its eyes were looking in the direction of the fire. Sitting on the same branch were two more birds. He looked into other trees, and saw the outlines of birds in each and every one of them. Their presence was more unsettling than the idea of a crocodile under his bed.

He was close enough now to recognise where he was. At last he stopped moving. The clearing was only three trees away from him. Near enough for him to be able to see everything happening in it, but far enough back to still be concealed by shadows. No one in the clearing would be able to see him.

On the far side of the fire, he could see his dad. Standing beside him was a tall man he didn't recognise. Long black hair, and a long pale face that seemed to reflect the firelight. As he watched, he saw the long-haired man smile and nod at his dad. His dad's tormented face should have been sufficient warning for him to turn and run. Perhaps he would have done if he hadn't suddenly spotted his mum lying on the ground to his left. He recognised the figure kneeling down in front of her. Not understanding what he was seeing, he glanced back towards his dad.

Dark eyes stared back at him from a pale face.

★ ★ ★

He sat up, panting. His chest heaved as his lungs pumped frantically. Reaching up with trembling hands, he wiped the sweat out of his eyes. Then he hugged himself, holding on tightly until the tremors subsided, and his breathing returned to something approaching normal.

The nightmares were becoming more frequent, more intense. He had no choice now. It was time to do something about them.

PART ONE

HOW TO
WIN FRIENDS

ONE

Farming had been in the family for generations. There were rumours that a great great-grandfather had even had his own land at some point. But that was long before Peter or his father had come into the world. He'd been born into a heritage of working for other farmers. It wasn't a source of great pride, but it put food on the table.

Nigel Salthouse had worked on Lodge Farm since he was a child. His only break from that had been during the war. He could have worked the land, but chose to fight for his country. In the process, he saw parts of the world he would never have dreamt possible. Africa had been where Tarzan came from, though he couldn't recall Johnny Weissmuller spending time in the desert. Burma had felt more like Tarzan's home. Like many old soldiers, Nigel didn't talk about his experiences. But he did come back talking about the opportunities there were, beyond the life he'd been brought up to expect. Mixing with so many different men from so many different backgrounds had opened his eyes to the chances there were in life.

When he finally returned home at the end of 1945, he had great plans. The celebrations that followed his homecoming put paid to them. A hasty marriage didn't cover their tracks, but the miscarriage did. By then it was too late. Nigel had a young wife to support, and that meant working at the only thing he knew how to do. When the children did come along later, he'd felt even more trapped.

He didn't rail against it. The things he didn't talk about were reminder enough that he was lucky to have the life he did. But he was determined to provide his own children with the opportunities he had missed. And he did. The first three were encouraged to look beyond the farm, beyond the village, and beyond the area for their futures. One of them even went to university. Unheard of in the community, let alone the family. But Peter wasn't cut out for that. Not by a long chalk.

Peter was the youngest, by fifteen years. Some might have referred to him as an afterthought, others as an accident. Nigel and his wife were in no doubt that it was a disaster. They'd been approaching a time when their children would have become more independent. In a few years' time, Nigel and Katherine would be able to enjoy more time on their own, doing the things they wanted to do, without having to consider the children first and foremost. After seventeen years of giving priority to others, they were looking forward to being just a little more selfish.

If that had been the sole issue, they would have been more forgiving. Instead they'd been *blessed* – they used the word ironically, though only between themselves – with a crippled child. Nothing too dramatic. One leg three inches shorter than the other, so he would spend the whole of his life limping or wearing specially adapted footwear. It was also safe to say that Peter was never going to scale the heights of academic life. The boy's options were limited. And, although he cursed his son's conception, Nigel still loved him. So when he was old enough to work, he knew the safest place for Peter to be was where he could keep an eye on him. And so another generation of Salthouses came to work the land.

Peter had worked on Lodge Farm since he was sixteen, and Nigel had taught him everything he knew. Which was good, because Nigel had been due to retire and the current owners of the farm needed some continuity. But from Nigel's point of view, it also meant he could teach his son the safest way to do all the jobs.

Like ploughing. Ploughing involved using some very dangerous equipment. It was safe if it was handled correctly, but deadly if it wasn't treated with respect. Peter knew his own limitations, and he was always very careful.

As he drove the tractor up and down the field, he kept a watch all around him. In the past, he'd spotted bricks in the ground that might have damaged the blades of the plough. Where the bricks had come from was anyone's guess. Out here in the country all kinds of things could be dumped in odd places. Apart from potential harm to the tractor or plough, he had also found children playing in the fields, sometimes as young as five. What their parents were thinking letting them off on their own like that, he didn't know. But he'd made sure they were out of harm's way before he carried on. That was how his dad had taught him to plough, and that was the way he did it today, as he did every time.

He'd covered almost a third of the field when something caught his eye. It wasn't too obvious because it was on the other side of the hedge to his right. That field had sheep in it and he'd checked the hedge earlier to make sure there was no gap they could get through. All part of that safe approach his father had taught him. But it wasn't the sheep that caught his attention. Close to the hedge, he saw a head. It was too far away for him to make out any features – or even tell if it was facing this way. Nevertheless, he got the impression that he was being watched. It was unusual, but he didn't see it causing any risks, so he ignored it. Having said that, he'd probably report it to his boss, Bob Lambert, when he got back to the yard.

Reaching the end of the field, Peter stopped the tractor, then raised the plough, watching clumps of soil drop off the blades. Satisfied they were clear of the ground, he turned the tractor, ready to start its next run. Once in position, he lowered the plough again, keeping his eyes on it to ensure it dropped into place as it should do. As the blades cut into the soil, he returned his gaze to the front of the tractor, slipping the tractor into gear as he did. Directly ahead, no more than ten feet away, stood a ewe.

It was unremarkable as sheep go. White face, white body, thin white legs. It was standing side-on to the tractor, its head turned so it was looking in his direction. Peter dropped back into neutral, cursing mildly under his breath.

How the hell did that get into the field? And how did it get there so quickly?

He looked over at the other sheep and saw the head he had noticed a few moments earlier. Perhaps that answered one of his questions. Had the man over there somehow let the sheep through the hedge? The head still wasn't very clear, but he thought it must be a man. Not that it helped to make any sense of the situation, because Peter had checked the hedge. There wasn't even a gap you could widen sufficiently to let an animal pass. A human might be able to climb the tree that stood in the corner of the field, crossing the barrier in that way. But sheep didn't have a reputation for climbing.

As the thought ran through his mind, he glanced at the tree. It was old and dying. No leaves had been seen on its branches since Peter was a boy. They were occupied today, though. Dozens of birds were lined up on them. And their attention seemed to be focused in his direction. Not that they were his concern right now.

Peter double-checked the handbrake, and made sure the gearbox was still in neutral. Then he opened the cab door and climbed down to the ground. The soil on this side of the tractor had already been ploughed, so as he stepped on to it his wellington boots sank slightly. Unlike his other footwear, Peter hadn't been able to get wellies that compensated for his short leg, so at the best of times they were awkward to walk in. His lopsided gait was aggravated by the mud clinging to his boots, tugging his feet up with each step. Behind him, the diesel engine ticked over steadily.

Lodge Farm wasn't a huge concern by modern standards, but it was big enough, and several men worked there. Peter had demonstrated an aptitude for handling farm equipment well, and carrying out heavy tasks. Contact with the animals was limited as other workers were more adept with them. As a consequence, when he did deal with them, he generally found they were quite wary of him, tending to run away when he approached them. So when the ewe turned and moved away, he wasn't too surprised. Though it did seem odd that it didn't rush, and it also kept itself almost exactly in line with the tractor's path. A dozen or more paces on, and Peter had gained a little ground on it. They were about eight feet apart. The tractor was maybe ten feet behind Peter.

For a moment, the change in the engine note didn't register with him. He was distracted by his quarry and the effort it was taking to walk through the mud. He had put an extra few feet between himself and the tractor before he realised something was wrong. Looking over his shoulder, he saw the radiator grille start to move towards him. All concerns for the welfare of the ewe disappeared in an instant.

Turning to the right, he started to lift his foot. His boot was stuck firmly in the mud. Which was impossible. He hadn't ploughed that stretch yet. He might have picked up some mud when he walked through the ploughed part, but that wouldn't be enough to stop him moving. Panicked, he pulled harder and his foot slid out of the wellington. Leaning forward, his stockinged foot landed in the mud and he jerked his other foot clear of its boot. The effort caused him to lose his balance and he landed face down. He knew he didn't have time to take stock of where he was in relation to the tractor. He just had to get himself as far out of the way as he possibly could.

Rising to his knees, he started to move forward again. As he lifted himself further, the front wheel struck him. He was halfway between kneeling and standing when he felt the tyre catch the side of his calf. The impact knocked him down and he was helpless as the wheel rolled over his leg.

The softness of the soil helped. He felt his leg being pushed down into it, which undoubtedly cushioned the effect of the wheel's weight. It didn't stop the sharp cracking sound of bones breaking, though. As the wheel rolled clear, he rolled sideways. He wanted to free his shattered legs from the soil, but they barely shifted. He could only watch in horror as the larger rear wheel came towards him. And behind that were the unforgiving blades of the plough.

TWO

"*He* doesn't look familiar."

Villages have a reputation for being somewhat insular. And the village pub has done more than its fair share in boosting that reputation. *The Major Oak* in Ravens Gathering was no exception. When the bus pulled away from the stop on the opposite side of the road, the landlady was the first to see the stranger it had dropped off.

The half dozen lunchtime regulars followed her lead and looked over their shoulders. Turning back to their beer, they nodded and muttered agreement.

It would be hard *not* to agree. A suntanned face wasn't uncommon among those living on the edge of Sherwood Forest. But if you got it on holiday, it faded rapidly; and if you worked outdoors it might last longer, but usually left a weather beaten look to go with it. One thing you were not going to see from a local, though, was sun-bleached hair. It was safe to say that the man at the bus stop wasn't from these parts.

Norma Fuller kept an eye on him as she pulled David Sullivan his first pint. He hadn't made any attempt to move. Instead he seemed content to simply stand and look around him. From this distance, she couldn't see the face clearly enough to make out any expression, but she got the impression he was just taking in the view. What the view could *be* exactly, she didn't know. The village was pretty much just one long street. A few cul-de-sacs led off that street, but there were no big housing estates, no major businesses. Apart from the pub, the only other places for the villagers to congregate were the church and the Post Office. And surrounding those structures was nothing but farmland and woods.

There were times when she contemplated the limitations of the village and could understand why her ex had given up on their dream of running a country pub.

As David counted out his change on the bar, he nodded to an empty stool. "Bob not in yet?"

"'Aven't you heard?" The response came from a gnarled and wrinkled old man standing round the corner of the bar. Walter had been retired since before Norma moved to the village, and had looked as if he was eighty then. It was possible that this ravaged appearance had contributed to Frank's decision that the country life wasn't for him. There was certainly no doubt that his years as a farm worker hadn't done his complexion any favours.

"Heard what?" David asked. From the offhand way he spoke, it was clear he hadn't heard.

"'Bout young Peter," Walter offered – though it wasn't much of an offering, Norma thought. Tempting as it was to jump in and tell David the news, she knew from past experience that it was better to stay out of it.

"What? The cripple?"

Norma winced inwardly. She knew Peter would be mortified to hear himself being defined in such a disparaging way. She was also shocked to hear David, of all people, talking in those terms.

"Aye." A sly glint appeared in Walter's eye. "Well he definitely is now."

Norma held her tongue.

"What d'you mean?"

"'Ad an accident with a plough this mornin'." There was something almost malicious about the way Walter spoke. She knew he had a dark sense of humour, but this just seemed twisted. "But the Devil loves his own," he went on, though how he could connect Satan and Peter was beyond Norma. "Seems Bob had to go out near where the lad was workin', and he saw the tractor just standin' there doing nothin'. Well, you know what Bob's like. Don't like to see his workers idlin'. So he went to find out what the lad was up to." Walter stopped and took a long draw on his pint. Norma wasn't sure whether all this talk had dried his throat, or if he was just pausing for effect. She suspected the latter, but busied herself straightening bar towels.

"Well get on with it," said David impatiently.

Walter put his glass down and sneered. It was fair to say that the banter at the bar did sometimes cross the line, but Norma couldn't recall such an obvious display of antagonism between these two before. As Walter continued, Norma wondered if he only did so because he was getting so much pleasure from the tale he was telling.

"The tractor 'ad run over the lad's legs, and the plough ripped 'em to shreds." Walter's smirk was barely concealed. "'E's still alive, but it don't look like 'e'll be needing them special shoes any more."

"Hang on!" David said, apparently spotting a hole in the old man's tale. "How could the tractor've run him over if it was standing still?"

"Don't know. Perhaps it'd run into the 'edge."

"Don't be daft! It'd just go through the thing and keep going."

Walter shrugged as if it was of no interest to him, which it probably wasn't. All he seemed to be concerned with were the gory details. As he began to demonstrate. "I 'eard there was blood everywhere. And they'll be picking bits o' bone and flesh off the shares for weeks, I reckon."

Norma couldn't listen to any more. She opened her mouth to say something as Walter continued: "Always thought 'e'd come to a sticky…" But his words tailed off as he stared past her.

As one, everybody in the bar turned to see what he was looking at. In the doorway stood the man from the bus stop.

THREE

The new arrival brought silence to the bar as the landlady and regulars took stock. He was tall, but not tall enough to worry about the low beams. Norma guessed a shade under six feet. His hair came to his neckline and looked clean, so he wasn't a hippy or a greasy biker type. It was more of a surfer look – an impression that was reinforced by his physique. Although he was wearing a leather jacket, and beneath that a plaid, lumberjack style shirt, she could see a strong outline of his chest and no sign of a belly straining over his belt. His jeans clung to his thighs as well, leaving no doubt that he was in great shape. She might be an honorary local, but Norma wasn't averse to looking beyond the village boundaries for male company. And this one would do very nicely. It was just a shame she was probably old enough to be his mother. Still, that wouldn't worry her if it didn't bother him.

"Afternoon, love," she said breezily. "What can I get you?"

As the conversation among the regulars recommenced, she caught the twitch at the corner of his mouth. Amusement at the obvious appraisal he had received from everyone in the room? she wondered. Or…

"Well, that depends on my options." He was standing at the bar now, and looking directly at her. There was humour in his eyes, and something else that she couldn't quite define. The opening shots had been fired on both sides, and there was plenty of scope for banter and double-entendres. Norma was a past master at both, and revelled in suggestive remarks – both giving and receiving. Yet she suddenly felt her enthusiasm drain away. The stranger was playing a part, going through the motions. His response had been smooth, well-practiced. And empty.

"We can start with whether you want food or drink," she suggested.

He nodded slightly, an acknowledgement that the flirting was over. But he kept smiling, so Norma knew he hadn't taken offence at her sudden about-face.

"Or are you just 'ere for directions?" Walter interjected from the corner.

The stranger turned his head to look at him. It was an easy, relaxed movement. He smiled, and Norma could see an even set of teeth. Against his tanned skin, they looked as if they belonged in a toothpaste commercial.

"No," he reassured the old man, "I don't need any directions." His attention returned to Norma. "I take it when you asked if I wanted food or drink, you didn't mean I could only have one or the other?" The smile and the eyes were still playful. It was tempting to offer him "the other", but she knew it would be a waste of time.

"We do serve both if you want them," she confirmed.

"Good." A nod to one of the beer pumps. "I'll have a pint of lager while I'm studying the menu."

"You won't even get through an 'alf looking at the menu 'ere."

This time he ignored Walter's attempts to include

himself in the conversation, though he did pick up on the comment. "I take it your lunchtime offerings aren't extensive," he said to Norma, who had just placed a pint glass under the tap.

"Shepherd's pie or a Ploughman's," she confessed, pressing a button. The glass began to fill.

"Just right for a farming community," he said, though she realised there was no relevance to his remark. It was as if he just felt a need to respond with something that at least sounded witty.

"You want to be careful of the Ploughman's today," Walter said, and Norma could tell that he was looking for an opportunity to retell his story about Peter Salthouse.

"Where do you want to sit?" she asked hurriedly. "I'll bring your drink to you."

As the stranger looked around the room, Walter carried on. "Have you heard about the accident on Lodge Farm?"

Distractedly, the stranger looked at Norma and nodded to a corner near the window. To Walter he said: "Yes I have. Awful, wasn't it?" And before the old man could say anything more, he was moving towards the table he had indicated.

Having turned away from the bar, Norma could now see the rucksack he had over his shoulder. She'd noticed a strap earlier, though it had blended well with the brown of his jacket. The rucksack was a large one though. He wasn't just on a day trip. The bag slid from his shoulder and was dropped casually at the side of the table as he sat down, his back to the wall.

His attention had turned to the street by the time Norma brought his drink to him, offering little

24

opportunity for Walter – or anyone else for that matter – to engage him in conversation. Not that anyone else was likely to get involved. They had long since returned to their own conversations. And David had taken the chance to join two fellow drinkers, so he didn't have to listen to any more from Walter. The old man was standing in his usual spot, nursing his pint and keeping a watchful eye on their visitor.

Against Walter's advice, he had the Ploughman's. Norma wasn't sure if he was making a statement, or just didn't like microwaved food.

He was half way through his meal when Colin Gates came into the pub.

The weekday lunchtime crowd was primarily made up of retired people. Lodge Farm took up most of the land immediately behind *The Major Oak*. Bob Lambert was a man who liked his routines, and tended to work the various parts of his farm at set times on set days. So he would find himself working close to the main entrance every Monday and Thursday. And on those days he had made part of his routine a stop off at the pub for lunch. For a Ploughman's, as chance would have it. But Norma kept that to herself, and hoped that Walter wouldn't remember what Bob was missing while he was at the hospital with Peter.

So, Bob was one of the few exceptions. And Colin was another.

Compared to the rest of the drinkers, Colin was a child – and not just because he was only in his mid-twenties. When Norma had first arrived in the village, he had still been at primary school. Based on his mental capacity, she reckoned that's where he should be now. He wasn't completely retarded, but he was certainly out of his depth if he wasn't supervised.

Most days he stayed at home on his own. His family were all at work, and Colin hadn't found any employment yet. Like most of the village, Norma suspected his parents were reluctant to let him work, because his options were limited. He could work on the land, which would allow him to be relatively close to home. The incident with Peter today was evidence of the potential dangers there. Or he could look further afield. The most likely place to go would be Westfield, a market town about ten miles away. But someone like Colin wouldn't last five minutes in a town. He had a hard enough time here.

Colin didn't so much walk up to the bar as bounce. His legs had a rubbery quality that meant his head seemed to bob up and down as he moved. In Norma's experience, he had two expressions. A broad smile that looked as if it must become painful after a while, and a frown that suggested complete and utter bewilderment. Right now the former was in play.

"Hello, Mrs Fuller!" Inevitably, he still spoke to most of the adults with the respect offered by a young child. If only more of his age group could do the same. His voice was loud. Not so much that you had to tense when he opened his mouth, but you were always aware of him when he said anything, even if it was complete rubbish.

"Hello, Colin. What brings you here?" Not that she needed to hear the answer. It was a little over an hour since the ambulance had raced away from Lodge Farm. She guessed it had taken him that long to get himself dressed properly and walk down to the pub, calling at the

Post Office first to share his excitement with anyone who happened to be in there.

"Yeah, Colin, what d'ya want?" Walter sneered. The words he added were spoken more quietly, but only just. "Ya dipshit."

The familiar puzzled look briefly crossed Colin's face. A lock of brown hair had fallen across his right eye. He reached up and absently brushed it away, and his smile returned as he did so.

"There was an amb'lance," he said excitedly, looking around all the faces near the bar. Presumably he was hoping to see similar levels of enthusiasm so he could share the experience fully. Instead he was met with cold eyes and sneers.

Norma couldn't help but feel sorry for the lad. But once again she knew it would be fruitless to say anything to the others, and they would only look for an opportunity to put the boot into her as a result. Colin, on the other hand, was so simple he wouldn't even understand what was going on. And sure enough, the confused expression was back. Not offended or upset. Just bewildered by it all. So in the grand scheme of things, she reasoned, there would be no benefit to anyone for her to stick her oar in.

"Peter's been hurt." Greg Williams was sitting on a stool at the bar a few feet to Colin's left. He'd turned in his seat so he was facing the lad when he spoke, his voice calm and clear. Greg would often spend an evening playing darts with Peter's dad, Nigel. Like everyone there, he knew that Colin and Peter were the same age. For a moment, Norma felt some relief, expecting Greg to engage with Colin and try to explain why his enthusiasm was inappropriate.

Well, he engaged with him. Colin had turned to face him, head bobbing as he did so. Now he was giving Greg his full attention. "So fuck off, Colin. Go and get back in your cot, or your Wendy House, or wherever you hide during the day, and leave the rest of us in peace, you fucking cretin."

There was a venom in Greg's voice that caused Norma to take a step back from the bar. It was only when she felt the till brush against her lower back that she realised she'd done it. She hadn't heard Greg speak like that in the sixteen years she'd been there.

And Colin hadn't taken it well either. His head was twisting from side to side as if he was searching for something that would explain what had just happened. The perplexity on his face was bordering on fearful. Then a hand appeared on his shoulder, and Norma looked past Colin to see the tanned face she had briefly flirted with earlier. The humour had left without a trace.

"Colin," the stranger said gently. "Sometimes people get very stressed and say things they don't mean. I'm sure this gentleman –" he gestured to Greg – "didn't mean what he just said." He paused and looked meaningfully at the older man on the stool. "Did you?"

In Norma's experience, Greg had never gone this far before. Nevertheless, he wasn't averse to verbal confrontation, and she seemed to recall stories she'd heard of him being involved in quite a few physical confrontations when he was younger. But at sixty-eight and with his weight focused on his midriff instead of upper body, he was in no shape for that kind of activity now. She watched as he licked his lips, and realised how nervous he was.

His gaze flickered from the stranger to Colin and back

again before he nodded. "That's right, Colin," he said, his voice not quite as clear as it had been a few moments ago. "I didn't mean what I said just then."

"And I'm sure you're very sorry, aren't you?" the stranger prompted.

"That's right, Colin," he added hurriedly. "I *am* very sorry."

Reassured by the kinder words and tone, Colin smiled back at Greg. "That's all right, Mr Williams."

Behind Colin, the surfer smiled, though there was still no sign of humour there. He patted the lad on his shoulder. "I think we should get you home, Colin, don't you?"

The stranger led Colin to the door and opened it. She heard him tell the lad to wait outside for a moment. Closing the door, he headed back to the bar.

"How much do I owe you?" The banter was gone now. This was just a transaction.

Norma took his money, gave him change, then watched as he returned to his table to pick up his rucksack. She wasn't the only one. Surreptitiously, every eye in the room was on him as he walked back. He was heading for the door, but stopped halfway there, and turned back to look at them all. Reluctantly, they returned his gaze.

As a group, these men had known each other for many years. In some cases, the relationships had lasted a lifetime. Within that closeness, even where there was antipathy, there was also camaraderie. And with that came a sense of safety that promoted confidence. At that moment, all sense of safety and confidence had gone.

Satisfied he had everyone's attention, the stranger spoke. "I think it's time you found out who I am."

FOUR

Tanya McLean wasn't happy. To be fair, this wasn't unusual, and hadn't been for some time. This afternoon her main cause for complaint was that she had yet again been forced to make a twenty-five mile round trip to pick up some decent groceries. And, having made the journey, she now realised she'd forgotten to pick up some lentils and ginger. She didn't stand a chance of finding that vital ingredient for the curry she planned to make this evening. At least, not without returning to the Sainsbury's at Westfield. The Post Office in the village only stocked the essentials, and even some of those were questionable. The local shops in the nearest villages were slightly better. Long Clayford actually had a mini-mart. But the chances of finding lentils or ginger there were pretty remote. Both at the same time would be damn-near impossible.

This was her main cause for complaint this afternoon. But she was perpetually in a complaining mood, a fact she grudgingly admitted to herself as she walked back across the yard to her car. It wasn't a state she was happy being in. Some people seem to get a real sense of pleasure from moaning. That wasn't something that suited Tanya at all. But, since she and her husband had moved up here from Oxford, things just seemed to have gone from bad to worse. And, as time had passed, every little niggle she would previously have shrugged off seemed to become a major downer for her.

She hadn't been too impressed with the idea of moving north in the first place, but Ian had insisted it presented a fantastic opportunity. It had turned out to be such a fantastic opportunity that he was currently with a bank manager in Nottingham trying to renegotiate the terms of a loan with them so they could afford to maintain the payments. Tomorrow, he would be with another bank manager in Westfield begging for mortgage arrears to be added to a different loan, because there was no way they were going to be able to cover the last three months' payments. It was even questionable as to whether they could afford to pay anything in the coming months. But Ian was fighting for their financial survival, and buying time was the most important thing to do right now.

In the meantime, Tanya could only curse his decision to come here, and look out for her own opportunities. Though the opportunities she was looking for were ways to escape – and not necessarily with Ian for company. She realised that wouldn't be as easy as it could have been in the past. She also knew that it was her own fault she was in the more difficult position. When she'd first married Ian, the house was in his name. With plenty of equity in it, Tanya hadn't been too impressed that he did nothing to put that right. So when they were arranging the move up here, she'd subtly dropped hints about her own insecurity. The result – as anticipated – had been Ian asking if she'd mind becoming a joint owner. It would demonstrate their commitment to each other as husband and wife, he had explained. So she'd got what she wanted. And now she wished she hadn't.

With debts in joint names, she couldn't just walk away. If she didn't have them, it wouldn't be a problem, and the next gullible man would be more than happy to take her on. She knew she was attractive, and she always made the best of herself. Even now. She might have only been to the supermarket, but she was wearing a cream sweater that clung to all the right places, jeans that appeared to have been moulded to her, and five inch heels on black knee boots. Her long dark hair was styled so it bounced gently as she walked. Everything about her appearance was designed to attract attention.

Reaching into the boot of the car, she lifted two carrier bags. They were quite heavy, and another five still lay there. She hesitated for a moment, debating whether to take any more this time and reduce the number of trips she'd have to make.

"Excuse me." The voice came from behind her. It was softly spoken, but not in a prissy way. She guessed he might have lowered it so as not to startle her. Always aware of a potential opportunity, she stayed where she was for a moment or two longer than necessary. Giving him plenty of time to admire the view of her jeans-clad bottom.

Pulling back from the car, she turned.

He was standing about ten feet away, and slightly to her left. He wasn't facing her directly, which suggested he'd probably come up the main track to the farmyard from the village. The same track she'd driven up ten minutes ago. She glanced towards the opening, but there was no sign of a vehicle there. Nor, now she came to think of it, had she heard one. If he'd walked, he must have pretty much followed her off the main road. She couldn't recall seeing

32

him down there, but that didn't mean anything. The mood she was in, she might have missed Tom Cruise.

She was glad she'd seen him now, though. He looked as if he was about her age, early thirties. The surfer look was good, if a little incongruous. She could also imagine him as a ski instructor. Both images reminded her of happier times, when it had been normal to jet off on holiday three or four times a year, and have occasional extra fun while Ian was otherwise engaged. Sometimes he insisted on taking work with him while they were away, so what was a girl to do when she wasn't getting the attention she deserved? Already, she was wondering whether this newcomer might provide her with some welcome distraction.

"Sorry to disturb you." The stranger smiled. He wasn't handsome, but he wasn't ugly either. Blue eyes, even teeth, slightly crooked nose, as if it had been broken in years gone by. More importantly, there was a masculinity about him that she found very attractive. There was also something vaguely familiar about his face.

"No problem," she said. "Just bringing in the shopping."

"Would you like a hand?"

Depends where you plan to put it. She smiled back at him. She was flirty, but she wasn't stupid. He could be an axe murderer for all she knew, no matter how tempting he looked. For now, she ignored the offer.

"What can I do to help you?"

"I'm looking for Patrick Gates. I was told by his son that he was still working here." He added: "Colin," as if she needed further explanation.

Tanya nodded. "That's right. He's working on one of the houses."

The stranger frowned. "Houses?" He seemed confused by her response.

"The development?" she offered, but he just looked back at her blankly.

"I'm sorry. I don't know what you're talking about. I thought he still worked on the farm."

Tanya smiled warmly, amused by the situation. He responded in kind, clearly not taking offence.

"Did Colin tell you that?"

"Not exactly," he admitted. "He just told me his dad was working up at the Sullivans' place. I put two and two together…"

"And got twelve?" Tanya suggested.

A wry smile. "Maths never was my strong point."

"What *is* your strong point?" The words were harmless, but the tone was suggestive.

The smile broadened. "That would be difficult to explain," he said.

"So you'd need to show me?"

"Something like that."

There was a pause in the conversation. She guessed that, like her, he wasn't sure where to go next with this. It had been over a year since she crossed this line, and she suddenly felt apprehensive.

"I take it you don't know about the development," she said at last.

"No. Enlighten me," he invited. There was still a playfulness in his voice, but she sensed he was backing off a little. No doubt he'd recognised that she had done the same.

"We're having some houses built." She gestured to

the opposite side of the yard. A couple of hundred yards from where they were standing was another gateway that led on to a track. About half a mile along that track there had once been some old barns. They were virtually falling down when Ian had bought the farm. Now they were in the process of conversion. Already eight houses had been created, and five more were under construction. Unfortunately, only five of the eight had been sold, and two of those had gone for less than they expected. Hence Ian's meetings with the banks.

"What's that got to do with...Patrick?"

The hesitation was brief, but she was aware of it.

"He's helping Matt. They're working on it together." She saw understanding begin to creep into his expression. "I don't think he could get any other work when the farm was sold."

"Sold to you?"

She cocked her head, then looked down at herself. "Do I look like a farmer?" She was aware that she was taking them back in a direction she'd already shied away from.

"I wouldn't have said you were typical. So what's the story?" He gestured to the farmhouse. "I take it you're not just visiting?"

"Could be."

"Not if you've got that much shopping. Besides, you said 'we' are having some houses built. I take it that means you own the land? I also take it that means there's more than one of you?"

Plus, there's the incriminating evidence of the gold band on my left hand, she thought to herself.

"Been watching a lot of *Inspector Morse*?"

He looked at her blankly. "Inspector…?"

"John Thaw?" she offered helpfully.

"The guy out of *The Sweeney*?"

"Well, yes. But he plays Morse nowadays."

He shook his head. "Haven't seen much TV for a while."

"Been away?" Stupid question really, considering the colour of him. And he must have recognised that from the look he gave her.

"You could say that."

Her reference to his detective work had clearly fallen by the wayside now. Although she did contemplate bringing *Columbo* into the conversation, there was no point really.

"You're right," she said at last. "This is our house. It belongs to my husband and me. We bought the farmhouse and a few extra acres. But most of the land was sold to Mr Lambert at Lodge Farm."

"So that's when he would have lost his job?"

Tanya shrugged helplessly. "I imagine so. It was before we moved here. From what I can gather, the land was sold a few years earlier."

The stranger smiled awkwardly, as if an uncomfortable thought had just struck him. "I'm sorry. I've just realised I must sound as if I'm interrogating you."

"Not at all." And that was true. It hadn't even occurred to her. Now she considered it, she could see that his questions had the potential to be intrusive, but they had felt perfectly natural.

He nodded at her hands. "And your arms must feel as if they're about to pop out of your sockets." He glanced behind her at the open boot. "Let me help you take these in, then I'll leave you in peace."

36

Her reservations about him were gone, though she couldn't have explained why. Well, maybe there was good old-fashioned lust getting in the way of common sense. But she suspected it was more than just that.

"Okay." She stepped aside to let him get to the car. He reached in and lifted the remaining bags out. Slamming the boot shut, she followed him to the kitchen door. "Go on in," she told him when he paused outside. A gentleman? she wondered. Not wanting to be too pushy. She wasn't sure if that was a good thing or a bad thing.

The other carrier bags were on the big wooden table in the middle of the kitchen. They stood on either side of the table, and added to the collection.

"I'm sorry to have troubled you," he said, genuine apology in his tone.

She gave him a warm smile. "You've been no trouble at all. It's nice to get some company for a change."

"Surely your husband doesn't leave you on your own?" The flirtatious look was back.

"He does have other things to attend to as well." She was careful not to overplay the wide-eyed innocent.

"I'd be very careful if I was in his position." *Intentional innuendo?*

"What position would that be?"

A broad grin. "I think we'd better leave it there for now, don't you, Mrs…?"

"McLean. But please call me Tanya."

He reached out with his hand. After the banter, the offer of a handshake seemed almost ridiculous, but she took it. His palm was harder than she expected, as if it was used to manual work. Having said that, it wasn't as coarse as the hands of some of the men who had worked on the development over the past year.

"I'm Martin."

"Martin…?"

"Gates. I'm Patrick's other son."

FIVE

The Barns provided peace, privacy and the countryside right on your doorstep. Every house stood in its own grounds. That was what the marketing blurb said anyway. Close inspection might have suggested that the word "grounds" meant something a little larger than the 1/8th of an acre of land that formed the gardens for each property. It also implied that the houses were detached, but the reality was that each unit was attached to at least one other. Even so, they had been laid out in such a way as to offer the maximum privacy. And with the main road half a mile away, the peace was definitely there. The road through the village wasn't especially busy or noisy anyway, but that only added to the sense of quietness. The only noise you were likely to suffer here would be the occasional aircraft from the small commercial airport on the other side of Westfield or – more likely, though still infrequent – a lively summer barbecue held by one of the neighbours. As only five of the houses were occupied, and three of those by people commuting to London every week day, it was very peaceful.

At mid-afternoon on a Thursday, the only sounds to be heard at *The Barns* were of power tools, hammers, timber being hauled, and the chink-chink-chink of trowels on brickwork. There wasn't even the other familiar sound from a building site: tinny music from a well-worn transistor radio. On this particular afternoon, the builders were concentrating on a garden wall, so things were more quiet than usual. The scrape of metal against brick and the slap of the trowel into the cement mix only occasionally interspersed with muted comments. Neither workman was particularly talkative at the best of times.

They were distracted too. All of the houses faced the woods. The edge was perhaps two hundred yards away. That meant the back gardens were south-facing. Just as importantly, they were not overshadowed by the tree line. All the same, the architects had allowed for the retention of trees on the south side. This would enhance the sense of being in the country, whilst adding to the privacy for each house. All part of the marketing plan.

Matt had spotted the birds half an hour or so earlier. As he worked, he had a habit of pausing every fifteen minutes or so. He would step back for a moment, stretch, and look around him. It eased the strain on his body, and relieved his mind from the boredom it felt when he was involved in work that was especially repetitive. For some time, there had been nothing of interest to see. Suddenly he was confronted with five black birds. They were sitting in the branches of an oak tree at the edge of the woods. And they appeared to be watching the builders intently.

At first, he'd shrugged it off. It wasn't that unusual to see several birds at once. And their apparent interest in the building work was undoubtedly just a matter of timing. He'd simply looked up just as they all happened to be gazing in his direction. That's what he told himself. But he still felt uneasy. More so when they were still in exactly the same position a few minutes later. On this second

40

glance, he realised what kind of birds they were, though he also appreciated that he'd probably registered this on a subconscious level anyway. And no doubt that had added to his uneasiness. When they were still there the next time he looked, he reluctantly nudged Patrick, and made him aware of them.

The older man's reaction shouldn't have come as a surprise, but Matt was still struck by it. Patrick was sixty-two years old, but anyone meeting him for the first time would easily add another ten years if they were asked to hazard a guess. His hair had long since passed on from grey, and was now a yellow-tinged white. The real aging had taken place in his face, though. Decades of working outside in all weathers had left him with a patchwork of creases and lines. Where suntanned skin can often look attractive, Patrick's dry, leathery look simply made him look deathly. When the colour drained from his face at the sight of the ravens, that impression became even more pronounced. And there was real fear in his eyes.

"What does it mean?" Matt had asked.

At first, Patrick had just shaken his head, unable to answer. Instead, he'd loaded his trowel up and turned back to the wall, as if by carrying on with his work, he could somehow make the birds disappear. But they didn't.

"Do you think he's back?" Matt asked after a couple of minutes had passed.

"I don't know." The reply was curt, a hint of anger behind it. Anger hiding fear, Matt guessed. After a moment or two, he added: "It's probably nothing. Just a coincidence." His tone was hardly reassuring.

"Well, do you think we should tell the others?"

41

A sharp shake of the head in response. "What would be the point?"

"We can warn them. If they know in advance, maybe they can do something. Maybe we can all do something together."

"It wouldn't do any good." Patrick was never the best at eye contact. But even for him it was noticeable that he was deliberately looking away from Matt.

"Why not? If nothing else, we could move away for a while."

Patrick's face contorted, a twisted smile that lacked any humour. "If he wants us, he'll get us, no matter where we are."

"You don't *know* that."

"I *feel* it."

And they lapsed into an uncomfortable silence, neither knowing what to say to the other. Neither knowing what they should do. Until the cawing began. It didn't last long, only a few seconds. But the sound tore through them like slashing blades. Terrified, they looked across at the ravens, in time to see them rise from their perches and, in the effortless way that birds do, soar up above the trees, then wheel away and disappear from view.

For a few moments, they watched the treetops, waiting for the birds to come back into sight. When they didn't, the two men felt the tension begin to ebb away, started to hope that it had all been a matter of their imaginations running wild.

The hope was short-lived.

"Hello, Dad."

SIX

Patrick studied the man in front of him carefully. It had been almost fifteen years since he'd last seen his son. He'd been a teenager then, his build slighter, his face thinner and much more pale. The man who smiled back at him now looked very different. Not just his appearance, but also his manner. There was more confidence. Borderline cocky, he thought. Martin hadn't been like that. He'd been quiet. Kept himself to himself. Not that Patrick or the rest of the family had complained. They'd had other things to worry about.

When he'd bought himself an old Volkswagen camper van and started to do it up, they'd been a little surprised, but too distracted to consider the implications. The real shock had been when he announced he was using the van to leave the village. Shock mixed with relief. In his more reflective moments, Patrick was ashamed of that. But as he considered the prospect of his son returning, he understood why he'd felt the relief. He might be his son – his own flesh and blood – but his presence was already making him uncomfortable.

Assuming he really was Martin, of course. He studied the eyes, noted the wrinkles that hadn't been there last time he saw him. Creases that suggested sun – and probably sea. The skin didn't look as soft either. A combination of age and outdoor living. Beard stubble wouldn't have looked out of place, but the face was freshly shaved. He wondered whether that was the norm, or if the lad was just trying to make a good impression. The hair was longer, of course. Another difference. Still, no matter how much he wanted them not to be, Patrick knew that the differences were minor when you considered the length of time he'd been away.

"Hello, Martin." The words came out reluctantly, as if by saying them he was admitting guilt about something.

The lack of enthusiasm in his response was noted. Martin didn't say anything, but he could see it in his eyes. Just a flicker, but it was there.

"How did you find us?" He knew it wasn't the most welcoming thing to say, but that wasn't necessarily a bad thing.

Martin gave a little nod, acknowledging the distance that still lay between them. "Colin told me where you were." He paused, clearly thinking about what he had just said. "Well, kind of."

He was still standing on the track that ran in front of the house. To the left, the track led eventually down to the main road. To the right – the direction from which Martin seemed to have come – led up the hill to the farmhouse and yard. Behind him was an open field and then the edge of the wood. He rested his palms on the top of the partially constructed wall. So far, his focus had been on his father, but he looked at Matt now.

"How's my big brother?"

Matt glanced briefly in his father's direction. Patrick saw and understood the wary look in his eyes. But he had nothing to offer by way of help.

"I'm fine," Matt said. His words were spoken slowly, carefully, as if he wanted to make sure that nothing he said could be misinterpreted. "When did you see Colin?"

"About an hour ago. He was in *The Oak*. Being given a hard time."

"He knows he shouldn't go there," Patrick said defensively.

"Well, I got him out as soon as I could. Took him home."

"You've been to the house?" There was no attempt to keep the suspicion out of his voice.

"Don't worry, Dad. I just saw him to the door. I've not been inside."

Realising he'd gone too far, Patrick back-tracked. "Oh, I didn't mean anything by that. I was just surprised, that's all." Not to mention relieved that he hadn't been in their home. He didn't like the idea of Martin roaming freely around the house.

Martin was moving on though. "He told me you were working on the farm. I assumed you were still working for the Sullivans."

"Not since 1986. David and Paul sold up."

"I heard. Tanya Mclean said Bob Lambert bought the land. Couldn't you have worked for him?"

The reference to Mrs Mclean troubled Patrick, but he didn't pursue it. To do so risked highlighting his concern, and he didn't want Martin to be aware of that.

"Bob's been investing in machinery," he said, unable to completely suppress his bitterness. He'd known Bob Lambert since they were kids. They'd gone to the same school. But that hadn't meant anything to Bob. Business was business, and his view was clear: machinery was much more efficient than labour – it could do more for less money. Occasionally, Patrick was prepared to admit to himself it was probably true. But it didn't make it any easier to come to terms with when you were far enough from retirement age to need a job, but close enough for retraining to be an unrealistic investment of time or money.

"I'm sorry." The words were spoken with feeling. For a moment, Patrick wondered if they were meant, then pushed the idea aside. He had to keep his guard up.

"So have you been working as a builder for the last three years?"

"No. Just the last year."

"It's been tough then?"

Patrick shrugged awkwardly. He didn't feel comfortable talking about his financial situation at the best of times. And certainly not to someone who was a virtual stranger to him. "We got by."

"Mum's working," Matt chipped in. The next generation, who didn't have the same hang-ups about money. "She's got a job in Westfield. Same place as Janet." Patrick watched Martin carefully, looking for any reaction to these references to his mother and sister. None were obvious. "Of course, Janet and I contribute to the upkeep of the house anyway."

Martin cocked his head quizzically. "D'you mean you're still living at home?"

Matt and Patrick looked at each other, recognising that they may have made their first mistake. But it was too late to take anything back.

Shrugging, Matt gestured to the houses around them.

"It's not easy to get on the housing ladder. I'm guessing from your tan that you've not been in the country for a while, so you probably don't know how bad things are here. There's been a housing boom in the last few years. Property's got so expensive in the south, people are moving up here, especially Londoners. Westfield's on a mainline to London, so they can commute to work, and it doesn't take them that much longer than when they lived in the suburbs. For their money, though, they can get a house that's three times as big as what they could get down there. The only problem is that's pushed up house prices round here, and locals can't afford to buy."

There was a lot of truth in everything Matt said. Patrick was relieved to see Martin nodding, accepting the explanation without question.

"Must be cramped," he commented, but didn't wait for any elaboration. "So why'd the Sullivans sell up?"

Patrick answered. "Paul had an accident back in '83. He was careless with a threshing machine, and lost a leg. Probably had too much to drink with his lunch."

Martin raised a questioning eyebrow. "Did he have a drink problem, then?"

Relieved his son was steering things away from the family, Patrick was happy to talk about his past employers. "Just a bit. Still, you can understand it. When you find your dad's killed himself because he's found out your mum and brother-in-law have been having an affair, it can do strange things to you."

"I didn't know about that," Martin said gravely.

"Why should you? You were only a young lad when it happened. It was a real scandal at the time, but nobody talked openly about it much in the village. The Sullivans were good employers. Good people, in fact. It was a real shock to us. So you can only imagine the effect it had on the family." He shook his head as he thought back to those times. Twenty-five years had passed, but he could remember so much of what had happened back then. Too much.

"So Paul's accident prompted them to sell up?" Martin brought them back from the side-track.

"That's right. I think he'd just had enough. The doctors fixed him up, and he can walk okay. He moved to Thornberry, so we don't see him that often. But once in a while, he pops into *The Oak*. You can hardly tell he's limping. So he could've carried on, but I don't think his heart had been in the farm for years."

"But you said he had the accident in '83. Yet you only stopped working in '86."

"That's how long it took to sell. They were hoping to sell it all off lock, stock and barrel. But they couldn't find any takers. Not at the price they wanted."

"Any particular reason why?"

Patrick hesitated a moment, realising he may have moved back into can-of-worms territory. But he knew that if he took too long to respond, he would just arouse his son's curiosity further.

"Just the market, I suppose."

"The booming property market?" Martin's lips had curved slightly upward at the edges. Not quite a smile, but there was certainly some humour. Patrick suspected an element of mockery too.

"There's a big difference between housing and farms,"

Matt said quickly, possibly a little too quickly, but Patrick was grateful for the intervention.

Martin nodded. In agreement? Patrick wondered.

"I'll take your word for it."

Or possibly still mocking?

"So how come you've ended up working as a builder?" It was clear that, in spite of his tone, Martin wasn't going to dwell on any inconsistencies. Hopefully that was a good thing.

"Builder's labourer, really," Patrick said.

"No, Dad," Matt corrected him, "you're a builder."

Patrick looked fondly at his oldest son, reacting naturally to Matt's protectiveness.

"You don't have to make me feel better, you know. I know my role here, and I'm very grateful for it."

Matt opened his mouth to respond, but Martin beat him to it. Cutting to the chase.

"So you're working for Matt, then?"

"On a self-employed basis."

"I'm sure that makes all the difference." It was difficult to tell from his tone whether the remark had an edge to it or not. "But I take it you're running things here?" Martin had turned his attention back to his older brother.

Shrugging, Matt said: "That depends."

"On what?"

"Whether you mean from the point of view of the project management, or as the person bankrolling it."

"Well, as you can't afford to buy your own house, I'm guessing you're not the person bankrolling it."

"A fair point," Matt conceded.

"And, as Tanya's already told me that she and her

husband're having the houses built, I took it as read that managing the project was the highest up the pecking order you could be." There was definitely an edge this time. Martin's voice was tinged with impatience, and possibly sarcasm. Patrick watched him guardedly. The wall was still between them, and he instinctively wanted to keep that barrier there.

Martin raised his hands off the top of the wall, palms up, a gesture of supplication. "I'm sorry," he said, and sounded as if he meant it. "I've been away a long time, and I'm just trying to get up to speed with things here. Things have changed." He gestured to his father. "Last time I saw you, your hair was darker, you were a few pounds lighter, and you were going to work the land until the day you died." A nod to his brother. "And you, Matt. You were working for a building firm in Westfield. JC Construction, wasn't it?"

"JB, but close enough." Although Martin seemed to be making an effort now to lighten things up, Matt wasn't letting his guard down.

A grin from the younger brother. "It has been a while." He paused a moment before continuing. "What I'm saying is... Things have changed. So I'm sorry if I got a bit pushy. You're my family, and I just want to know about you."

Patrick shifted uneasily at that remark. He suspected that Matt wouldn't be too happy at it either. But Matt was younger, his brain a little more nimble.

"You're right," he said, then deliberately looked around him at the bricks stacked up and the tools lying idle. "And that kind of conversation needs time and no distractions."

His brother cocked his head to the right and ran his fingers through the long blond hair thoughtfully. "Okay," he said at last. There was some reluctance, but he seemed to be accepting the implication of Matt's words. "My timing's not good, is it? When would be a good time?"

Never, Patrick thought, but kept it to himself. Instead he watched Matt play acting. The elder son looked at his watch for a moment, then glanced around him again, as if he was assessing how long they would need here. In practice, Patrick knew they could knock off whenever they wanted. They weren't being paid for this work anyway.

Eventually, Matt said: "We really need to get this wall finished today. I can't see that happening for a while yet. Maybe the best thing would be for us to meet up tonight."

"Good idea," Martin said. "What time do you want me to come around?"

Matt's glance at his father was surreptitious, but Patrick was sure it didn't go unnoticed.

"Well, I was thinking of us maybe coming to see you wherever you're stopping," Matt said.

Martin nodded, apparently in agreement, though his words soon put them right on that score. "It's a nice thought. Unfortunately, I don't know where I'll *be* stopping. I had wondered whether you'd be able to put me up –" Patrick hoped to God that his horror at that prospect wasn't showing on his face – "but, as we've already established, things are already somewhat crowded there. So I haven't sorted any digs out yet. Do you know of anywhere in the village?"

"No, I don't." The pub did Bed and Breakfast, but Patrick didn't want to volunteer that information. With any luck, Martin would head to Westfield and find somewhere to stop there.

Martin bent slightly, and reached down for something

hidden behind the wall. As he straightened up, Patrick saw he'd picked up a rucksack. Which gave him an idea.

As he pulled the rucksack over his shoulders, Martin looked at them both in turn. "So what time shall I call round?" he asked.

Matt was hesitating. "How about eight o'clock?" Patrick suggested. "We'll all be in by then, and we'll have had time for a bath and some dinner." He ignored the sharp look from his firstborn. He had a plan forming in his mind.

"Eight it is then." Martin seemed a little put out, but it was only later that Patrick realised he might have expected to be invited for dinner. He raised a hand in a farewell gesture, then turned and walked back up the hill towards the farmhouse.

They watched him carefully until he had disappeared over the rise. At no time did he look back. Nor did this strike them as at all odd.

As soon as they were confident he was out of earshot, Matt turned on his father.

"What the hell did you do that for? Why've you invited him back?"

Patrick gripped his son's shoulder firmly, and leaned in to him. "He invited himself," he reminded.

"Yeah, he did. And I was trying to find a way of keeping him away."

"Well, I've got a way," Patrick said with a grin. "Did you see the rucksack?"

"Yeah. What about it?"

"Why would he be carrying it?"

Matt shrugged. "I don't know. It's a rucksack. That's what you do with them."

"True. But why wouldn't he leave it in his car?"

"Maybe he doesn't have one," Matt pointed out.

"Exactly. And if he doesn't have one, he's going to be stuck if he can't get a bed for the night in the village."

"What do you mean?"

"Well, if he has to stop in town, he's going to find the bus service is pretty limited." They both knew the last bus back from Westfield was at six o'clock, because that was the one Anne and Janet Gates caught back from work. The last bus into the town was at quarter past seven. One of the hazards of living in the sticks.

"Good idea, Dad, but *The Oak* does B&B, and he's bound to try there."

"He is. But what if we have a word with Norma first?"

The penny dropped. Matt looked back in the direction his brother had gone before looking at his pick-up which was parked facing the other way.

"Brilliant!" He patted his father's back. It was both affectionate and congratulatory. "I'll be fifteen minutes. You stay here in case he comes back. If he asks where I am, I had to nip to get some supplies."

Neither of them noticed the ravens return. The birds settled into the shadows, and watched the truck race off, and the older man resume his brick-laying.

SEVEN

After putting the shopping away, Tanya had toyed with the idea of having something stronger, but opted for coffee. The phone had rung as she'd settled down to drink it, and by the time she'd finished arguing with her husband it had gone cold. The temptation for something stronger rose again as she emptied the mug down the kitchen sink. If she thought for a moment it would be possible to patch things up again when Ian came home, she would have headed for the cocktail cabinet. As it was, she realised it might be better to keep a clear head. Whether that would be so she could continue the argument coherently, or drive away later without fear of failing a breath test didn't matter. Alcohol wouldn't be a good idea right now.

What she could be tempted by appeared in the farm yard while she was standing at the kitchen window finishing off her second coffee.

She assumed he hadn't worked out yet that he could get to the village more rapidly by continuing past *The Barns*. He would come out at the edge of the village, but overall the walk was shorter. Not that she was complaining. A good looking bloke, who looked as if he had all the stamina she might need. All right, he came from the village, but he wasn't like the rest of the deadbeats who frequented the local pub. He'd seen there was life outside the village. She couldn't imagine him wasting his time in this backwater. He'd seen the world. Well, some of the sunnier parts of it anyway.

A fling with someone like this could just be enough to help make life bearable at the moment. It could be dangerous, but it would certainly make life interesting. And, frankly, she didn't really feel she had a lot to lose right now.

Martin was halfway across the yard when she came out of the house.

"Did you find him?" She had to raise her voice. They were about thirty yards apart, and he was clearly lost in thought. So much so that he took a couple of steps more before stopping and looking up.

The smile was slow in coming, but it seemed genuine enough. "Hi. Sorry, I was miles away."

She crossed the yard to join him, speaking as she went.

"I could see that. Penny for them?"

Once again, she was flirting. Not her words, but her tone conveyed a level of intimacy they hadn't achieved. Yet.

"Wouldn't be worth the cost," he said, still smiling. He was deflecting her, she knew, but the challenge just added to the fun.

"I could argue that, as the buyer, I should be the one to make that judgement." Before he could respond, she went on: "But I wouldn't dream of being so rude. They're your thoughts, and you're entitled to keep them to yourself if you want to."

She'd reached him now and was standing only a few feet away, her head tilted back a little so she could look into his face. She was a little over five and a half feet, and in her heels was almost as tall as him. This close, though, she still needed to look up slightly.

"Anyway," she continued, "did you find your dad?"

He nodded slowly, hesitantly. The smile had gone now. "Yeah."

"You don't sound very sure."

"It was definitely him," he said, more positively.

"I'm guessing it didn't go too well." Tanya knew she was taking a risk with this comment. But then, she was taking a risk by just coming over like this and talking to him.

The smile came back, but it was a wry one. "You could say that."

"Want to talk about it?"

He gave her a look. "Now?"

She spread her arms slightly, palms towards him. "No time like the present." Catching him glancing around the yard, she gestured towards the house. "I didn't mean out here. We can go and sit inside."

His look became more questioning. "Don't you think that's a little dangerous, Mrs McLean?" She knew the formal address was deliberate, a reminder she was married. And she recognised it for what it was: a request for clarification of her intentions.

Grinning, she said: "Well, as the buyer, I should be the one to make that judgement."

He grinned back. "I'll remember that next time."

She turned to lead him back to the house, but his next words stopped her. "It'll have to be another time, though."

Puzzled, disappointed, and – if she was honest with herself – a little angry, she stared at him. She'd thought he'd understood. Was he stupid, or something? She was offering herself to him on a plate.

He must have recognised something in her expression, because he shook his head apologetically. "I'm sorry, Tanya. I really do have to get on. I'm supposed to be meeting up with my dad and the rest of the family this evening. And, in the meantime, I've got to find myself somewhere to stay." He glanced at his watch. "It's already nearly three-thirty, and I don't know how easy it's going to be to get a room round here. I've been away a long time, so I'm not even sure where to start."

For a moment, Tanya thought she had just made a fool of herself. But listening to him talk, she realised that the situation could yet be salvaged. It might even give her an opportunity to really get back at Ian.

"How long are you stopping for?"

Martin shrugged. "In all honesty, I don't know. Depending on how things go tonight, I could be gone tomorrow morning." He paused, allowing his gaze to wander. It was as if he was taking in his surroundings, and possibly something more. "I doubt it, though," he said at last. "I suspect I'll be around for a few days at least."

A few days, eh? That prospect had plenty of appeal.

"Where were you planning to try?"

"The obvious place is the pub, but I don't know if they even have any rooms."

"They do," Tanya said, "but they'll probably need to know exactly how long you'll be stopping for." She hesitated, pretending to think things over. "You know, Ian and I have been making plans to offer B&B here." Which wasn't entirely true. They'd included it among their lists

57

of options when looking at how to improve their financial situation. But they hadn't taken the discussion any further than that. "We've got an annexe at the side of the house that has a bedroom and its own bathroom." Which *was* true. David Sullivan had used it as guest accommodation when his children came to stay with their families. "We haven't started to offer it, so we don't have any bookings at the moment. If you wanted to, you could use that, and we could treat it as a trial run."

"Well, it would solve a problem for me," Martin said thoughtfully. "But how will your husband feel about it?"

"Frankly, he'll probably just be glad of the money." And he'd be suspicious as hell, but that was his hard luck. "So what do you think?" She was resting a hand on her hip provocatively as she asked the question.

"It's a very attractive proposition," he replied, and she was well aware of his eyes on her as he said it.

"I'm glad you think so." She was surprising herself at her own brazenness. But as she watched his reaction, she knew it was being well received.

They discussed cost as they walked over to the house, and by the time he had sat down at the kitchen table, everything was agreed. The terms she was offering would have been difficult to refuse.

Although she was eager to move things along, she also realised there were some practical issues she had to deal with first.

"Obviously the room isn't ready yet," she explained, "so I'll have to sort it out for you before you settle in." She was quite happy to give Ian cause for concern, but she wasn't going to be too bloody obvious. If he came home to find a stranger in the house, the guest room not made up, but his own bed looking recently used, she might as well suggest he sit and watch her being unfaithful.

"Would you like a drink while I get things ready?" She was already reaching for the kettle as she asked.

"Do you make a decent cup of tea?" he asked. "It's one of the few things I've missed."

Fortunately, she did, and a few minutes later he had a mug filled with a strong, sweet brew. Satisfied that he was settled, she hurried from the kitchen and into the annexe.

Four doors led out of the kitchen. The first was into the yard. Almost directly opposite that was the doorway into the dining room. If you made a left turn as you faced the dining room, you found the door that led into the hallway – a huge open space that led to the sitting room, living room and the way out to the garden. It also contained the staircase to the upper floor. Since they'd moved in, at Tanya's insistence, a lot of work had been done to the house in order to "make it more bearable". The hallway, a dark space made all the darker by the oak beams and the wide oak staircase, had been the final area she planned to change. Unfortunately, the money had run out before they got to that part.

The fourth door was in the same wall as the entrance to the dining room. This one was to the far right of that wall. It opened on to a corridor that led to three rooms. The first of these, on the right hand side of the corridor, was a utility room, though it was rarely used for anything other than housing the many and varied pairs of boots Ian used for tramping around the woods and building sites. Next to that was a sitting room which served no purpose to the rest of the house, but was useful if you were a guest – or if you wanted your guests out of the way. It was furnished with an armchair, two-seater sofa, coffee table, television and a small writing desk. Opposite the door to the sitting room was another door that led out into the garden, so anyone stopping in the annexe didn't need to disturb the rest of the house to come in or go out. Between the entrance and sitting room doors was the final door, which led to the bedroom.

Furnishings in the bedroom weren't lavish but they were comfortable. While work on the master bedroom had taken place, Tanya had demanded that they sleep in the annexe because it would keep them away from the dust and debris. It also meant she still had access to an en-suite shower room and could maintain a suitable distance between herself and the workmen. She might be happy to stray, and even to simply tease other men, but she felt no inclination to put herself in any compromising positions with relatively local tradesmen. Especially if there was a chance her husband would employ them to work on *The Barns*.

So she had spent a few weeks using the guest room in the past and knew it would be comfortable. In spite of the double bed, the large wardrobe with matching dressing table and chest of drawers, the room didn't feel cramped. And the shower room also had plenty of space in it. At a push, they could have installed a bath, though that would have left anyone using it having to practically sidle around the room.

Tanya expected to be less than five minutes getting the rooms ready. She wasn't the most enthusiastic at housework, and tended to do the bare minimum. When they had employed a cleaner, it hadn't been an issue anyway. She, unfortunately, had been one of the first casualties of the McLean cash-flow problems. To be fair to him, Ian did help out. He'd lived on his own for a while before she met him, and had proven to be fairly well house-trained. He could change a bed, wash and iron, point a hoover in the right direction, and even put together a more than palatable meal. Even so, Tanya did miss having someone else to come in and do the more menial work.

And she was disappointed to realise that the guest bedroom and shower room hadn't seen any attention for some time. Keen to make the right impression, she overcame her natural disdain for cleaning, and set about putting things right. By the time she was satisfied that the rooms would pass muster, the planned five minutes had become almost half an hour.

A glance in the mirror told her that her efforts had not only transformed the appearance of the guest rooms, but also her own. In her case, not for the better. Her hair seemed to have lost its bounce, loose tendrils hanging scrappily across her face. She was also aware that her exertions had led to an unwelcome dampness under her arms and elsewhere. Reluctantly, she acknowledged to herself that she was going to need a little more time yet before completing her seduction. And with Ian due back at any time from five thirty, that was going to cut things fine.

Quickly tying her hair back in an attempt to disguise its current shortcomings, she returned to the kitchen. Martin was still sitting at the table. He had found a copy of the local paper and was flicking through it, looking up as she came in the room.

"It's all ready for you," she said hurriedly, and gestured back through the doorway.

"Just the room?" he asked, an eyebrow raised quizzically. A good sign, she thought. He hadn't lost interest during her absence.

"For the moment," she said carefully. "I just need to…" She hesitated. She barely knew his name. It didn't seem quite the done thing to tell him she needed a wash. Fortunately, he misinterpreted the reason for her pause.

"…Slip into something more comfortable?" he suggested. He was on his feet now, walking towards her, bag in his hand.

"Close enough," she agreed.

He stopped in front of her. "Is *that* close enough?" he asked.

"That's not what I meant."

"I know." He glanced at his watch. She noticed it was a heavy one, with three buttons on the side instead of a single winder. The strap was metal – stainless steel, she assumed – and there was a bezel around the watch face. She'd seen similar watches before when she'd been on holiday. Divers, she seemed to recall.

He nodded down the corridor. "Which room?"

She pointed straight ahead. "That's the bedroom." Something flickered in his eyes as she said that, and something stirred inside her in response. "The door to the side is a sitting room, and you can use that if you want it too."

"That's very good of you."

"Will you need long to settle in?"

He shook his head. "Five minutes."

Tanya thought she'd need a little longer herself, but if she kept it to a minimum they might still have time before Ian came back.

"Then I thought I'd take a walk up into the woods."

It took a second or two for his words to sink in. "I'm sorry?" she said at last. Not the best response in the world, but it was all she could manage under the circumstances.

"As I said earlier, it's been a while since I was back here. I thought I'd go and explore some of my old haunts."

"The woods?" She knew she sounded stupid as she said it, but she was still reeling from his sudden lack of interest. Awkwardly, she gestured down the corridor. "What about…?"

He nodded his understanding. "I think we'll be pushing it to get finished before your husband comes home, don't you?"

It was true, she supposed, but she was disappointed that Martin wasn't champing at the bit. Most men would be. Even Ian.

"So I thought I'd take advantage of the remaining daylight, and go for a walk in the woods." He leaned in close to her. "Of course, you could come too if you wanted."

Walking wasn't really her thing, but maybe the woods could provide some other opportunities. "I'll need ten minutes," she said, then she was off to her own room. She didn't see the frown on her guest's face as he watched her go.

EIGHT

Before moving to Ravens Gathering, Ian McLean had driven a Porsche. Life had been good to him – financially, at least. Not that he had been handed everything on a plate. He'd worked bloody hard for over thirty years, so the rewards were more than justified. Some of his colleagues balked at the idea of having such a flash car, worried about what their clients might think.

"They'll be suspicious that we're making too much money at their expense," was a typical comment.

"No," Ian would correct them firmly. "They'll know that we're earning well because we're working hard for *them*. And if you've got clients who're going to be jealous of you for being successful, then you really ought to be looking for a different class of client."

Which was true. He had worked with his clients for years, building up a strong relationship with them all. A lot of them had become friends. He'd attended weddings, christenings, birthday parties and funerals. They all knew he was looking out for their best interests. And they all knew he made his money earning commissions on products he sold them. But they also knew he'd be there providing a service even when there wasn't a product to sell. It was the way he'd always worked, and they were happy with it. Quite a few had made a point of admiring his cars when he came to see them at home or their places of work. No envy. They were pleased for him, he could tell. After all, he'd known them long enough. He knew people, knew what made them tick, knew which buttons to press. Not that he'd abused that. He genuinely wanted the very best for his clients. Sometimes they just needed a little more convincing.

So the Porsche had been a measure of his success. To be fair, it had also been a chance to let his hair down while he still had some. Like a lot of people, he'd come to the realisation that life is the wrong way around. In his teens and twenties, he didn't have the life experience to make the best of his youthfulness. At that time, he'd had the energy and vitality to do anything he wanted to. He just hadn't had the confidence or the experience to know that he could. He also didn't have the money. As he'd aged, and gained the confidence and knowledge that would allow him to do those things, his body had seemed less willing, and he was under no illusion: he knew his looks were fading.

Sports cars are for the young, he'd thought. Yet he hadn't been able to afford anything decent until he reached his mid-forties. Not that he felt old. A combination of squash and running kept him in good shape. He ate healthily – well, most of the time. And his enthusiasm for business kept his mind sharp. But he also felt that the time would come soon enough when getting in and out of something low-slung would become a major operation. His own reactions to seeing older blokes driving around in fast cars informed him as well. It may have been vanity, but he didn't want to be laughed at by younger men who saw him behind the wheel of something shiny, red and sporty.

So at forty-seven, he'd taken the plunge. His hair was only just starting to show signs of grey, and you had to look closely to see it. Which wasn't likely to happen while you were travelling at fifty miles per hour and more. A few more years, though, and it would be too late. In his eyes at least.

Funnily enough, that had been around the time he'd met Tanya. He'd only had the car a couple of months when she came into his life. Not that the car had influenced her – at the outset, at least. She hadn't known he'd got it the first few times they met.

It had been a good time. Business was booming, he was starting to claim some time for himself – holidays, weekend breaks, trying out new sports – and he was enjoying the life of a bachelor after seventeen years of marriage. The divorce had been messy, but he'd managed not to give too much away. Financially, anyway. The kids were a different matter. They hated him even now, and had made it clear that they wanted nothing to do with him. He hadn't been a good father, and he knew it. That didn't make their reaction any easier to bear, but he could understand it. Fortunately, work kept him distracted most of the time.

And Tanya had certainly helped to keep him distracted when he wasn't at work. She was nineteen years younger than him, but he hadn't seen that as an obstacle, and she gave no indication that it bothered her. The constraints of family life had meant that passion and excitement had been in short supply for most of his marriage. With Tanya, rationing wasn't an option. He was bewitched. Still was, even though things had changed.

The Porsche had gone, replaced with a Land Rover. Olive green with a long wheelbase, it was ideal for the farm and for country living generally. If the truth be known, having passed into his fifties, and aware that the amount of grey was beginning to outstrip the brown hair, he also felt it was a more appropriate vehicle to be seen in. Not that Tanya had viewed it that way. She liked the sports cars, and refused to give up her Merc. He hadn't pushed that. Frankly, he had just been grateful that she'd given in and agreed to the move north.

There were plenty of other changes too. Tanya's attitude towards him in recent months was a worry. In the grand scheme of things, he knew that was probably his biggest concern. But the more pressing issue at present was keeping their finances afloat.

When they moved up here, the move into property development had seemed an ideal opportunity. Property prices had been rising rapidly for a few years. His own house on the Woodstock Road had doubled in value in just three years. With prices being significantly higher in the south, he could get a lot more for his money if he came north. An old friend from university had let him know about Forest Farm. He worked for the local council planning department and had been aware of several proposals being bandied about for change of use. It seemed the Sullivans had sold most of the agricultural land off, and were getting desperate to sell the rest. Mark had known Ian was looking to get out of his own business and thought this might be just what he was looking for.

"Property's going up and up, the banks and building societies can't lend money fast enough, and I'm on the inside to help you get the planning permission through. What can go wrong?"

Good question. And the answer, as it turned out, was "quite a lot". Mark had been offered a better job with a different council, so Ian's inside man had gone. To be fair to him, Mark had still given Ian advice on how to get his applications through successfully. Nevertheless, the process had taken a lot longer than expected, so it was eighteen months after they moved to the farm before they were granted the permissions they needed.

On the plus side, property prices were still racing upwards. On the minus side, that meant they had already lost some potential growth. At the same time, the major house building firms were pulling out all the stops, and were throwing up housing estates all over the place. Fortunately, none were being built near Ravens Gathering. But it did mean that the majors were sub-contracting all the builders, joiners, plumbers and other assorted tradesmen to work on their projects. So finding contractors to work on *The Barns* development was also harder than Ian had anticipated.

Eventually, though, work began, and within six months they had built and sold three houses. Buoyed up by this success, Ian ploughed all of the sale proceeds into starting the next tranche of houses.

He had sold the first three houses for £50,000 each. Within a few months, one of the houses was back on the market for £65,000. A part of him wished he'd hung on to them for a few months longer. But he knew he'd made a good profit. More importantly, he knew the potential profit on the next few would be even greater. So he borrowed extra money so he could build some more. After all, interest rates were low, and the profits would more than outweigh the costs.

But then interest rates started to rise. Within a few short months, the rate he was paying on the loan had risen from just under 9% to 16%. The house that had been on the market for £65,000 was withdrawn. The couple who had bought it had clearly hoped to make a quick killing, and realised that wasn't going to happen.

Five of the new houses were completed by the spring of 1989. Two sold for £45,000 each, a long way short of the £65,000-£70,000 he had been hoping for only six months earlier. It allowed him to repay a part of the loan, but the margin wasn't high enough to make a big dent.

Then all enquiries dried up. Interest rates were still rising and property prices were tumbling, two factors inextricably linked. And Ian and Tanya were left with a rising debt and assets they couldn't sell.

It was no wonder Tanya was pissed off with him. He'd persuaded her to move up here, away from the attractions of the south. London, with its theatres and clubs and restaurants. Major international airports – very important to Tanya. Even the temperature seemed to be warmer back in Oxford. That alone was bad enough. But now he'd added insult to injury by making such a mess of the housing development. He blamed himself unreservedly. The fact that so many other people had fallen into similar traps – including the major house builders – was of no consequence to him. His decisions had got them into this position, and he wasn't going to point the finger at anyone else. What he needed to do now was find a way out of it.

Part of the solution required breathing space, though, which was why he had been at the bank today. This bank had advanced the loan for the development. They hadn't yet made any noises to suggest they were concerned about it. The chances were that they had other debts that were more of a worry to them. From their point of view, at least this was secured against the farm. That, of course, was the concern for Ian. So he had called the meeting today because he knew it would look better for him if he was being proactive. By demonstrating to them that he was working on a solution, they would be less likely to focus on him, and more likely to start digging where they were getting no feedback. Banks liked to know their money was safe.

Using his years of experience in the financial services arena, Ian had presented a very effective case to the bank. His reason for being there, he explained, was to reassure them. He pointed to the repayments he had made so far, including the fairly substantial capital amounts paid after the sale of the houses. He outlined the marketing plans he was pursuing, and the partnership agreement he had made with the builders as a means of reducing his overheads. Everything was set out on paper, and a copy had been left with the lending manager to put on his file. His presentation had been professional and confident, although he had taken several very deep breaths before entering the branch.

For the first half of the hour-long drive home, he had replayed the meeting in his head over and over. He knew he couldn't have done a better job. He just hoped it had been good enough.

The second half hour was filled with thoughts of what lay waiting for him when he arrived home. He'd phoned Tanya to let her know how the meeting had gone. His assumption that she would be pleased he was keeping her informed was obviously misplaced. It seemed that it only served as a reminder of the situation he had dragged them into. His years of dealing with people meant that he was able to anticipate most reactions. Clearly, he still had a blind spot where his wife was concerned. What he did understand was that talking to her about it was like prodding and poking at a wound. Or, perhaps more accurately, at a wounded animal – and probably one that was only too happy to claw and bite you in response.

His intention had been to spend a little more time in Nottingham after his meeting at the bank, and he'd told her he expected to be back around five-thirty. Rather foolishly, he now realised, he'd thought he should buy her a gift. The idea was to let her know that he was still thinking about her, even if he was busy trying to sort out the finances. From her heated comments over the phone, it was clear that the gift would be considered an unnecessary expense. So he'd abandoned his plans, and simply headed for home.

When the kitchen door wouldn't open, he briefly wondered if she'd decided to lock him out in a fit of anger. But his key went in easily enough, and he let himself into the house.

The empty mug on the table was unusual. Tanya normally liked the table to be clear, so she tended to leave them in the sink, or put them straight into the dishwasher. It didn't alarm Ian, though.

He called out as he walked through the house, but there was no response. It was puzzling, because her car was in the yard, and she rarely went anywhere without it. The idea of Tanya walking into the village was so improbable it didn't cross his mind.

In a way, her absence was a blessing. He was convinced there would be more confrontation, and having had the tension that came with preparing for and presenting a case to the bank, he didn't really want any more right now. So he headed for the bedroom, undoing his tie, and sliding his jacket off. It had been a stressful day. For now, he'd have a shower, then grab a Scotch and unwind. If she wasn't back in half an hour, then he'd worry about her.

NINE

They had left by the kitchen door again, and walked through the yard. Beyond the gateway, the track went by at a near right angle. If you followed it to the right, after a quarter of a mile you would reach the village's main street. Turning left, you passed between several old farm buildings – barns and stores. Once past those, the track opened out, merging into another yard area that was concreted over. A tractor stood idly up against a barn. Tanya had never seen it used, and suspected the Sullivans had left it behind for the simple reason that it didn't work any more. She had asked Ian about it, but his response had been vague. She guessed he didn't know any better than she did whether it worked or not.

This second yard was bordered by post and rail fencing. At a point in line with the track, the fence was broken by a five bar gate, which was secured with a heavy chain and padlock. At the side of it was a stile.

"Still a public footpath then." It was more of an observation than a question, so Tanya's response was only a slight nod.

Martin led the way, pausing only to make sure she climbed over the stile safely. It wasn't in bad condition, but he must have recognised that she was hardly a regular rambler. Perhaps the near-pristine condition of her walking boots had been a giveaway, she thought to herself. They had only been on her feet once before, when Ian had insisted on giving her a complete tour of the land they owned. She'd sported blisters for several days afterwards, and refused to accompany him again.

As they made their way up the footpath, she was aware of the – to her – unnatural sensation of wearing the boots again. They were flatter than she was used to, and her feet seemed to move a little more freely inside them. She began to wonder whether she would have been better to let Martin go on his own, and save herself the possibility of further discomfort. Especially as he seemed very focused on the walk and his destination, and not on her company. At the same time, she didn't feel comfortable with the idea of simply telling him she'd changed her mind. She didn't want to seem either indecisive or a wimp. So she kept up with him, surprised to find that she was having to take two strides to his one.

In the past, Ian had tried to persuade her to take up running. She had responded that she couldn't see the point. Whenever she saw anyone running, they never looked as if they were enjoying themselves. Ian had tried to explain that, for him at least, it was the sense of achievement that created the buzz, not the running itself. He had also said that, when he was running long distances, he found it helpful to have someone with him to talk to. The conversation took his mind off the running, and the time passed more rapidly. The memory of these words gave her hope.

"So, Martin, would I be right in thinking you've been working abroad?"

"Yes."

It took a moment for her to realise that was it. When she'd met Ian, she had been working in sales. Using her sales training, she identified her mistake: she'd asked him a closed question. She tried one that was more open.

"Where have you worked, then?"

"Here and there." Only marginally more helpful.

"But obviously sunnier climes," she prompted.

They had covered a couple of hundred yards, and now the path led into the woods themselves.

"Sunnier than here," Martin agreed. His eyes were on the route ahead. All of the attention he had paid to her earlier was gone now. She was starting to feel as if she had been duped, though what his game was, she didn't know.

"Are you trying to be deliberately obtuse?" she asked in frustration.

He glanced across at her and grinned. For a moment she saw the playful flirtatiousness that had attracted her in the first place.

"Not deliberately," he assured her. "Just a habit."

"Why?"

"That's a long story."

"It could be a long walk," she pointed out.

"Not that long."

As they continued along the path, the trees closed in overhead, cutting out most of the light. It was still bright enough for them to see where they were going, but the relative gloom made her feel a little more uncomfortable.

"What about you?" he asked suddenly, surprising her.

"Me?"

"Yeah. What's your background? You're not from these parts, are you?"

"Hardly," she said, then realised that she'd been too dismissive. "I'm sorry…"

"Don't worry about it. I'm with you on that. Why d'you think I left? If I hadn't, I'd still be living with my parents, stuck in a dead-end job, and spending my free time propping up the bar at *The Oak*. Everyone in the village would know everything I'd done since I was a baby. Every minor indiscretion used against me at all times."

"Indiscretions?" Tanya prompted.

"Nothing to get excited about," he said. "And that'd be half the problem." She caught a flash of teeth as he grinned again. "So don't think I'll be offended that you're glad you're not from the village. You need to get away from your roots and get a life."

"Is that what you did?"

He hesitated, pondering the question. "I don't know. Maybe I'll find out while I'm here." Another pause, then he reached out and touched her arm. It was a surprisingly gentle gesture. "But you were going to tell me about you."

The path had become an incline now. It wasn't steep, but Tanya was beginning to feel the strain on her thighs. For the first time she could recall, it occurred to her that she was unfit.

"What do you want to know?" she asked.

"Let's start with: 'What's a nice girl like you doing in a place like this?'"

She laughed, both at the question, and her immediate answer: "Trying like hell to get out of it."

"I can understand that. But why come in the first place?"

"It was Ian's idea. He needed something different to do, and this seemed like a good opportunity."

"Something different? Why?"

"I don't suppose you've heard of something called the Financial Services Act?"

"I've been out of the country," he reminded her.

"It wouldn't matter. Most people who've been in the country haven't heard of it. The Government decided, in their infinite wisdom, to regulate the financial services industry. That was a few years ago now, so we got some warning. The regulation itself only came into being last year."

"Regulation's not a bad thing, is it?"

She sighed. It was an old debate that she'd had with Ian too many times over the last few years. "I don't think so. But he's been worried about it."

"Why? Has he got something to hide?"

"Ian?" She snorted at the idea. "God, no! He's as straight as a die. He's driven, of course. That's why he's been so successful over the years. But he's not the sort of person who'll flog anything to a punter just to make some money."

"So what was he worried about?"

"In all honesty, he's never said specifically. I mean, he's convinced it's the thin end of the wedge. He reckons they'll make it compulsory to take exams before long. I think that's a concern. He's fifty-three now." She watched for a reaction, but it was difficult to tell in the half-light. "So I suspect he's uncomfortable with having to sit exams at that stage in his life. I did tell him that I could do that, if we needed it."

"You worked in the same business, then?"

"That's how we met. I was a rep for an insurance

company. I used to call on advisers and try to persuade them to use our products."

"I doubt you had any problems doing that." She was surprised to feel heat in her cheeks. His comment had hit home, and she suddenly felt embarrassed at the memory of the things she had done to get the business. Which was strange, because it had never embarrassed her before. "So you called on Ian?" he prompted.

Still flustered, she took a moment to regain her thoughts. "Yes," she said at last. "And after we married I went to work with him."

"That's difficult," he remarked. "Working together and living together."

You don't know the half of it. She hadn't thought that one through at the time. It seemed like a good idea to allow her to keep a close eye on Ian's finances. But it also meant she was under his watchful eyes more than she'd expected. Married or not, she'd never intended to become a one-man woman.

"It can be difficult," she agreed. "But we made it work."

"And then he decided he didn't want to carry on," Martin reminded. "But you don't know why."

"Not for sure. I just think that, after doing things in a certain way for thirty years or so, he didn't like the idea of change."

"So to keep things the same, he got rid of his business, sold his house and moved a hundred and fifty miles north."

"It does sound ridiculous when you put it like that."

"But who knows what makes us do the things we do?"

She knew the question was rhetorical. They walked in silence for a while, the path winding through the trees but still rising.

"Why did you come to Ravens Gathering?"

"Ian heard about *Forest Farm*, and thought he could make a go of it."

"And what did you think?"

"Honestly?" Even as she asked the question, she knew it was redundant.

"You can lie if you want to, or you could even refuse to answer the question on the grounds you might incriminate yourself." She looked at him and saw the good-natured smile on his lips.

"I thought it was a crap idea."

"You didn't think it'd work?"

"No it wasn't that. To be fair to Ian, I could see exactly where he was coming from. I just thought if he was going to sell up, he'd be taking the opportunity to retire and move abroad."

"I have heard that a lot of southerners think the North is a foreign country."

"We do," she laughed. "And having lived up here for a couple of years, I can't say *my* view's changed."

"Presumably you were thinking of somewhere more exotic."

"I had my eye on some villas in the Costa del Sol."

"I'd have thought you'd prefer the Canaries or the Greek Islands."

"Not to mention the Caribbean. But it seems Ian couldn't even afford Spain. He said if he could have drawn his pension, it might have been possible, but he can't touch that until he's sixty. The stupid thing is, because things have gone wrong here, his pension will barely allow us to exist when he does draw it."

The trees were closing in on them now, and the woods were becoming darker. She guessed it must be around five o'clock. Still more than two hours before sunset. Yet the visibility in here was little better than she would expect after nightfall. She stumbled over a tree root sticking up from the ground. Martin's hand shot out and grabbed her arm just above the elbow, steadying her. When he released his grip, she felt him take her hand gently. It felt safer.

"So, you're stuck here then?"

"Unless you fancy whisking me away," she said.

"I don't think my lifestyle would suit you, Tanya."

And she knew he was right. Her attraction to him was purely physical. If she was looking for someone to rescue her from the mess at the farm, it would have to be a man who had his own car and didn't carry his belongings around in a rucksack.

Up ahead, she could see a beam of sunlight shining down through a gap in the wood's canopy. Martin had obviously seen it too, because he suddenly stopped walking.

"We're here," he said.

TEN

It hadn't occurred to Tanya that there was a destination in mind. Martin had said he wanted to go for a walk in the woods, but he hadn't given any indication that there was a specific part of the woods to go to. For a brief moment, it occurred to her that he might have remembered a special place which was good for taking girls to. Perhaps he'd considered the pending arrival of her husband might be too much of a distraction for him, and bringing her here would allow them to take their pleasures uninterrupted. But his face suggested that was simply wishful thinking on her part.

He was wary. His eyes darted in all directions, taking in everything that lay before them. She looked ahead, curious to see what it was that had attracted him here.

Where the light was brighter, it was apparent that this was because there was an open space among the trees. The edge of the clearing was about a hundred yards away. It was difficult to tell from this distance, but she guessed it must be circular in shape. Possibly an oval. Scattered around it was the usual debris you could expect to find in such a place. Fallen branches, rotting leaves and a handful of wildflowers were accompanied by the ashy remains of a camp fire and, hanging from a branch of one of the sturdier trees, an old car tyre on a rope. Local kids, no doubt, making good use of the recent school holidays. She momentarily envied them the simplicity of their lives. Innocent of danger, free of all cares. *Enjoy it while you can,* she thought.

The path they were on led up to the clearing, and appeared to carry on beyond. Although there were no obvious hazards, Martin squeezed her hand gently and said: "Stay behind me and only walk where I walk." Before she had a chance to respond, he was moving forward. He still kept a grip on her hand, but let his arm fall back so she would follow him. Unsettled by his words and manner, she watched his feet, and tried her best to put hers exactly in his footsteps.

His caution was unnecessary. They reached the edge of the clearing without incident. He stepped aside as he entered it, allowing her to move next to him.

"Do you want...?" she started, but he raised his free hand to her face, his expression leaving her in no doubt that she should keep quiet. Frustrated, but still unnerved by his sudden seriousness, she resigned herself to waiting for him to decide when to tell her what was going on.

Apparently satisfied there was no immediate danger to them, he took a tentative step forward. He was still holding her hand, so Tanya came with him, feeling as if she was being dragged along. His next steps were equally cautious. Each one was punctuated with a few seconds' pause, before he moved on. Tanya found herself searching the trees that surrounded them, not really knowing what she was looking for. And that was the part that was both scary and ridiculous at the same time. Fear of the unknown, and the growing suspicion that she was having the piss taken out of her. She was even beginning to wonder if this was some

82

elaborate game Ian had arranged just to wind her up. Not that he was that malicious, and she didn't think he had the imagination to do it even if he had been.

Nothing was moving among the trees, either at ground level or up in the branches. There was no sign of anyone stalking them, nor of any wild beast roaming the woods.

The clearing itself was, she guessed, about thirty feet in diameter. Now she was in it, she could see that it wasn't a perfect circle, but it still seemed more circular than oval. The trees that bordered it were evenly spaced, the gaps between them wide enough for half a dozen or more people to pass through side-by-side. She didn't recognise the type of tree. Her interest in the countryside being less than passing, she couldn't have told anyone whether they were silver birch, Scots Pine or giant redwoods. What she did know was that they were big. The trunks looked to be about six to eight feet across, and the lower branches were at least head height.

Apart from the ash that took up a square foot or so near the centre, the floor of the clearing was a carpet of fallen leaves, a mixture of browns and greens. Some of the leaves had obviously been there longer than others. Occasional sticks of wood and fallen branches were scattered about. The tyre swing was over to the left, hanging perfectly still in the late afternoon air.

They stopped in front of the remains of the fire. She looked up at him questioningly. Without the heels, it was a bit more of a strain on her neck.

He must have recognised something in her expression, realised it was time to explain himself. She saw him open his mouth, hesitantly, but definitely with some intent. Behind her she heard something rustle.

Perhaps it was her nerves, wound up from the tension Martin had created with his seemingly paranoid approach of the clearing. Or maybe it had simply added to the strain she'd been feeling lately. Whatever the cause, she found herself whirling round like some frightened kid. Her eyes were all over, searching for the source of the sound. Nothing was obvious to her. Not in the half-light, at least.

Another noise. To her left this time. It wasn't quite the same. The rustling was there, but it was followed by a brief and barely audible *click-click*.

"What was…?"

Even as she turned, she felt a strong hand cover her mouth, and a muscular arm cross her chest, pulling her back against a firm body.

"Quiet!" The voice was low, but there was no mistaking the warning in it.

Her eyes had widened in shock, but she did as she was told. What she had felt before was nothing compared to the fear she was experiencing now. She could feel her heart pumping, her ears filling with a dreadful roar that she knew must be coming from inside her. Ahead of her, high up in the branches of the tree she was facing, a shadow suddenly moved.

"Phhu…!" The sound was involuntary, and distorted by the hand over her mouth.

Against her ear, warm breath and an animal hissing. She got the message. *Shut the fuck up!* Swallowing hard, trying to regain some control over her own breathing, she watched the tree. She didn't want to see whatever it was up there, but she knew she had to.

You've nothing to fear but fear itself.

She forced the mantra through her head, not sure where it was coming from, but grateful for it all the same. It was true. Martin, the sadistic bastard, was doing his damnedest to terrify her. That was all. He'd brought her up here, pretended to be worried about what he was going to find as they got nearer, and then used the first noise they'd heard as an opportunity to put the fear of God into her. Well, fuck him! She'd find whatever it was he was trying to frighten her with, and when she could see it, she'd know there was nothing to be scared of.

Her eyes gradually adjusted to the dull light. About half way up the tree, she could see a darker patch against the silhouette of the branches. It was difficult to tell from this distance, but it looked to be a couple of feet high, maybe half a foot or more across, with what looked like an 'X' shape crossing its body. The top ends of the 'X' looked sharp and stopped several inches above... A head? She couldn't be sure, couldn't make it out clearly. Then it moved, and she saw it for what it was.

The 'X' wasn't an 'X' at all. The ends she had seen, both top and bottom hadn't even been attached to each other. They were completely separate branches, two of them, large ones from a tree that stood further back. More importantly, the shape of the moving object was easier to define now. She had judged the height correctly. The width was harder to assess because, as it moved, it raised its wings slightly, which made it look much wider. She couldn't recall seeing a bird this size before – not outside a zoo anyway.

It had blended into the shadows because it was completely black. Even now, it was difficult to make out its features. In a way, she was relieved that she couldn't see its eyes, although she felt sure they were gazing directly at her. A silly idea, she thought. But she couldn't get it out of her head.

Very gently, the hand covering her mouth turned her head to the right. She kept her eyes on the bird for as long as she could, but gave up when it became too uncomfortable. As she did, she became aware of more movement from her right. Again, it came from the branches of a tree. Because she knew what to expect this time, she was able to see the bird more readily. This one was perfectly still, its head facing her.

Apparently satisfied that she had seen what he intended, Martin used his hand to steer her head back in the other direction. She watched the second bird for as long as she could, before turning her attention back to the first. Both creatures were fascinating to her. And, even though they were strangely creepy, knowing what they were had alleviated her fears. They were only birds, after all.

Before Martin had grabbed her, she'd heard two noises, and they had come from the positions of the two birds. Because of that, she was expecting the rotation of her head to stop when it was facing the second bird. When his hand maintained its momentum, she was puzzled, but not resistant. There didn't seem any point in trying to put up a fight. He was clearly much stronger than her, and he was very much in control of the situation. It even crossed her mind that this might be some kind of kinky sex game he liked to play. If so, she wasn't interested. Always happy to experiment, but not if it meant giving someone else complete control.

The reason for turning her further was quickly apparent. A third black bird was perched in the branches of another tree to her left. She hadn't heard that one.

"Can I trust you to stay calm?" The words were spoken softly, his mouth still close to her ear.

Very slowly, she nodded.

"I'm sorry if I frightened you. I just didn't want you to panic."

Well, that worked!

"I'm going to let you go in a moment. Take your time, and look around you."

Again she nodded, letting him know that she understood. And she felt his grip loosen as he stepped back from her. In spite of her concerns about him trying to scare her, this latest development gave her cause to re-assess what was happening. A few minutes ago, she would probably have stormed off back to the farm. Even then she hadn't felt threatened by him, wasn't concerned that he'd suddenly attack her. She just wanted to let him know that she wasn't impressed with his behaviour. And that he'd be looking for another place to stop tonight.

But now she was curious. So she did as he asked, and as she let her gaze drift around her, she saw that there were more birds. Perhaps a dozen or so, perched among the trees that stood on the edge of the clearing. And yet more were arriving, swooping down through the gap overhead and landing on branches that overlooked them.

The birds weren't threatening, yet the sight of them all coming together in this dark and isolated spot was unnerving. Tanya reached a hand out towards Martin, and was relieved to feel him take it. She felt him move in behind her. After the uncertainty she'd experienced with him in a similar position only a few moments ago, she recognised the irony of her reaction. His closeness offered security.

"You know what they are, don't you?"

ELEVEN

During thirty years or so of working long, hard hours, there had been many days when Ian had come home feeling completely drained. He knew it wasn't just the hours he put in. Because he took his work seriously, wanting to make sure he did the very best he could for clients, very often he felt a lot of tension building up. The tax office, for example, had cut-off dates for certain things. Naturally, the fifth of April was always a stressful time, but there were other times too. He always managed to meet the deadlines, but he generated a lot of sweat, and gave his blood pressure a hard time in the process.

When he came home, though, he was able to switch off. There were certain things that worked, little routines he used to get himself into the right frame of mind. To start, he had to have a shower. When he felt the water flowing over his body, it was as if it was washing all his troubles away. Very often he didn't feel physically dirty, but he certainly felt as if he'd been cleansed when he stepped out of the cubicle. After towelling himself dry, he padded out of the en-suite bathroom.

Some comfortable clothes would be next. Light and loose, giving him a sense of freedom. When he opened the wardrobe, he reached in for a favourite pair of cotton trousers. He didn't need to look for them because he knew exactly where they'd be. Except they weren't. The hanger was empty.

He was side-on to the wardrobe. A chest of drawers was facing him, and he'd been about to pull one of the drawers open so he could get some fresh socks out. Confounding the researchers, he was an accomplished multi-tasker. With his clothes kept in the same places at all times, it had been easy to develop a habit of producing his clothes in very short order. Surprised at finding the empty clothes hanger, he hesitated for a moment. The interruption to his routine was confusing him.

Very slowly, he turned to face the open wardrobe and studied its contents carefully, occasionally shifting a jacket or shirt to one side to get a clearer view of the adjacent clothing. But the trousers were gone. For most people, it probably wouldn't have been much of an issue. He recognised that himself. It was just so unusual for the trousers to not be there. They'd only come back from the dry cleaners a week ago, and he hadn't worn them since.

What was more puzzling, though, was that he realised one of his jackets was missing as well. It was thick tweed, ideal for wearing in the autumn when he went for walks. Ordinarily, he wouldn't have noticed it wasn't there. Not at this time of year. If he hadn't been searching for the trousers, its absence would have passed him by completely.

A more thorough check told him there was a possibility that a couple of shirts were missing, but they could very easily have been put in the laundry basket, and be anywhere between that receptacle and the utility room waiting for him to iron them. Out of curiosity, he wandered back into the bathroom and checked the basket. Nothing resembling the missing clothes was in there.

Shrugging to himself, he returned to the bedroom, found another pair of trousers and started to dress. He'd ask Tanya about it later.

The next stage of winding down was a glass of whisky. It was especially effective if he could find something to watch on the television while he sipped it. Nothing too challenging – and certainly nothing serious. Comedy, action or adventure were ideal. It didn't matter whether it was a film or TV programme. They helped him escape to a different world. If there was nothing suitable on the box, he had a collection of videos he could pick from. Some comedy in recent years didn't seem all that funny. He didn't get the so-called 'alternative' comedy. To his way of thinking, the alternative to comedy was…well, *not* comedy. But there was still plenty of material out there that appealed. When it came to the action and adventure, the video options were quite limited. Not many of the TV series he liked were available on video yet, which was a shame when he wanted to watch some in the late afternoon and early evening. Films were more plentiful, but not so practical. At that time of day, he'd probably have to break off at some point to have dinner or help in its preparation.

Drinks were kept in a cocktail cabinet in the dining room, so headed there first. He had to pass through the kitchen to get to it. As he did, he was vaguely aware that the door leading to the annexe was ajar. While he poured himself a Scotch, his mind drifted between considering what to put on the TV and wondering where his jacket and trousers had got to. In a sense, this lack of focus was part of the process of relaxing.

Returning to the kitchen, he glanced again at the partially open door. It wasn't a conscious thing, but he was aware enough to realise afterwards that his subconscious might have already started to connect some dots. The words 'utility room' floated briefly across his mind, shadowy echoes from his earlier thoughts. He had been about to turn right towards the hallway and, beyond that, the living room. Instead he stopped. It would only take a moment to check the utility room. That might just solve the mystery of the missing clothes, then he could settle down and enjoy an episode of *Cheers*.

One of the shirts he was looking for was on a hanger, suspended from a hook screwed into an oak beam in the ceiling. There were several hooks scattered across the four beams that supported the ceiling. He had never been sure what the Sullivans had used them for, but Tanya found them useful for the laundry. Apparently it cut down on the amount of time she spent ironing.

There was no sign of the other missing items of clothing, so he came out of the utility room and into the corridor. As he turned to close the door, he noticed the door to the guest bedroom was half open. On another occasion, he probably wouldn't have thought anything of it. But with the other strange things happening – Tanya's unexplained absence, the missing clothes – this additional inconsistency grabbed his attention.

They did generally keep this part of the house closed up, especially when the heating was on. Tanya begrudged all of the little economies he was asking for, but he knew that the collective effect could mean a big saving overall. And he knew that deep down she realised it too. Which was why she generally went along with his requests.

A part of him considered going back to his bedroom first. During the course of his negotiations with the Sullivans, they had discussed a range of different aspects of farm life. Although Ian and Tanya wouldn't be farming, living in a farm house about half a mile from the village, there were certain experiences they could have which were significantly different to the lifestyle they had been used to. Foxes, for example, weren't rife in Oxford. And you needed to learn how to deal with them. Like a lot of people who enjoy watching action and adventure films, Ian had never contemplated actually using a firearm himself. Buying the shotgun had been a real wake-up call. His life was changing dramatically.

The gun was kept in a locked cabinet in the bedroom. Tanya wasn't happy about it being there, but the alternatives were even less appealing. She didn't want it in the kitchen or other living areas, and the hallway wasn't secure enough. She also accepted that, if they were going to be so remote from the rest of the village, there was an increased risk of them being broke into at night. If that was the case, it was pointless having their primary means of defence on a different floor, or even a different bedroom.

Ian's thoughts of retrieving the shotgun were fleeting, though. This was the real world, not some suspense thriller. Whatever the explanation for the guest room door being open, it was hardly likely to involve a psychopath waiting for him with a long knife. It was more likely that Tanya would be down there. He couldn't guess what she'd be doing, but the last thing he'd want to do is confront her with a gun barrel. Things were strained enough.

Still, he was cautious. He didn't march straight in. Instead, he paused at the doorway and gently pushed the door open. As his view into the room widened, he saw a rucksack on the bed. It was leaning at an angle, like it had been dumped there by someone in a rush. He knew it didn't belong either to him or to Tanya. They'd never bought one, and there was no possibility in his mind that Tanya might have suddenly acquired an appetite for outdoor living.

There was no other obvious sign of occupation. Not from the doorway in any event. He stepped inside, still cautious, and carefully looked around the bedroom and en-suite. A damp sheen in the sink and a crumpled hand towel were the only other indications that anyone had been there recently. But who was it? And why were they here?

As he returned to the kitchen, he mulled over those questions. But no answers were forthcoming. Suspicions perhaps. About Tanya. He had no evidence that she had been unfaithful to him over the years, but that didn't stop him having his concerns. She was nearly twenty years younger than him. She was beautiful, and sexy, and very physical. He had no doubt that other men would find her attractive – and probably pursue her. The doubts were about whether she would respond to them.

Surely she wouldn't bring a lover into the house, though? The thought horrified him. He had his suspicions about her, and they came with a familiar gnawing in his stomach at the thought of her being unfaithful.

A year after they'd moved here, she had decided to return to work, and had got a job as Marketing Director for a firm in Westfield. Soon after starting there, she'd begun to spend a lot of time working late and attending meetings that needed her to have overnight stays. It had been agony for him. His jealousy had known no bounds. Wondering what she was up to – and with whom.

Many times he'd wanted to confront her, to find out whether his suspicions were true. He was afraid of the answer, though. And he was afraid of losing her.

Then she'd left the firm. He'd sold the first few houses, and they seemed to be making some money at last. She'd told him she could be of more help with the development. Her reasoning didn't really make sense, but he wasn't prepared to question her. In part, he didn't want to show her how vulnerable he felt. He also didn't want to hear the truth about the reasons for leaving the company.

The familiar insecurities crept over him, as he wandered through the kitchen. He was going to get that Scotch, see if that helped. As he passed the window, movement in the yard caught his eye, and he looked out. Tanya was coming towards the house. Beside her was a tall blond man. Ian felt his guts twist as he realised they were holding hands.

TWELVE

The walk back from the clearing was uneventful. That didn't mean Tanya felt any more comfortable.

"What happened back there?" she'd asked when they'd been walking for a while. A look back had told her that the clearing was hidden from view, and there was no sign of any birds following them.

"I don't know." Martin shook his head thoughtfully.

"But you were expecting it."

"I don't know what I was expecting."

"But something?"

He stopped walking and looked warily around them. She wasn't sure if he was genuinely worried, or just trying to keep her scared. In fairness, it didn't really matter. She'd been unnerved by the appearance of the birds. And now she had something else to consider.

"Yes. I was expecting something."

"Crows?"

"I doubt it. They were too big."

"Ravens then?"

He shrugged. "I don't know. I really don't." He sounded as if he was almost as bewildered by the incident as she was.

"I've never seen birds like that. Not gathering together like that, anyway. It was like something out of a Hitchcock film."

Martin shook his head, clearly unable to verbalise any coherent response to that. "I don't think you need to worry about being attacked by them..."

"Probably not, but *you* scared me bloody shitless!"

"Seriously, Tanya, I don't know..."

"*Anything*? Do you know anything *at all*?"

She was looking up at him, trying to see what was going on behind his eyes, but was thwarted by a combination of the fading light and his apparent unwillingness to return her gaze.

"Probably not enough," he said eventually.

"But you know something. What is it?"

"You wouldn't understand."

"I'm guessing from the way you said that, you're not planning to give me a chance to, either. Are you?"

He glanced around them, searching for something. She was frustrated with him, and that made her annoyed. But she was also still frightened. The birds had continued to gather, landing in the branches of the trees like an audience arriving. To watch a performance of some kind – a play or a sporting contest? At first she had tried to keep a count of them, assess how many there were. Within minutes, she'd realised it was an impossible task. There were too many of them. Easily dozens, possibly over a hundred. And they had continued to take their places as Martin had guided her out of the clearing. For all she knew, there could be hundreds of them by now.

Martin had been expecting something. His behaviour had told her that, and now he'd admitted it too. She wouldn't have said he was frightened, but he was certainly on edge. The light shining down through the trees had been all but blotted out by the ravens descending through the opening. Things always seemed worse in the dark. She knew that from her childhood, going to bed after listening to her parents arguing. Afraid it would mean they would split up. Lying in the dark and imagining the consequences, all too terrible for her to bear. And when they had eventually gone on to separate and divorce, it had been terrible – but not as bad as it had seemed in the darkness.

In the clearing, with the ravens perched all around them and the light virtually gone, fear had become an intrinsic part of her being. She had felt it building up inside her. Until Martin took her hand, and led her away.

Now the fear had abated, but she was aware of the darkness creeping into the woods. She checked her watch. It took a moment or two in the half-light, and she was surprised to see it was nearly ten past six. How had all that time passed? She didn't want to be here at night, and the sun would set in little more than half an hour.

"I'm obviously not going to get much more out of you right now," she complained. She tried to sound annoyed, but wasn't able to mask her apprehension. "We might as well go."

Without thinking, she reached for his hand, and was comforted to feel it grasp hers. For the first time since she'd met him, she stopped thinking of him as a potential lover. As they walked back to the farm, it was like being held by her father.

THIRTEEN

"Take a deep breath," Ian murmured to himself. He had stood well back from the window, but was watching Tanya and the stranger covering the last few yards to the kitchen door, safe in the knowledge that they couldn't see him. The last thing he wanted was to expose himself for the coward he felt he was. Tanya had little enough respect for him these days. Seeing him virtually hyperventilating wasn't going to help matters.

He did as he'd instructed himself to do. Inhaled deeply through his nose, filling his lungs with air, before letting it all out slowly. He only managed it twice before the door opened. It wasn't enough to mask his nerves, he knew. But he hoped it would cover some of them.

"Oh, Ian!" Tanya said as she stepped into the room and saw him standing by the table. "You made me jump!" And she did look startled. Or was he being generous? Was it guilt?

Swallowing, he opened his mouth to speak, but then the blond man appeared behind her. He smiled at Ian, but there was an underlying shiftiness about him. Again, it could be guilt. Or was he trying to hide something? Maybe both.

Stepping past Tanya, the stranger came towards him, hand outstretched, and nowhere near Tanya's. "Pleased to meet you, Ian."

Without thinking, Ian raised his own hand in response.

As he did, he realised what a fool he was about to make of himself. But he also realised that if he suddenly withdrew the hand, it would seem even more foolish. So they shook, the husband and the lover. It made his insides curl.

Having closed the door, Tanya was making her way to the dining room. "I need a drink," she said sharply.

Ian glanced at the tumbler he'd put down on the table. She wasn't the only one. He felt an urge to snatch it up and drink it in one swig.

"Where've you been?" he called after her as she disappeared. The other man had stepped back, but was still standing in front of him. Their eyes had locked briefly, but Ian didn't feel he had the strength to stare him down.

"Up in the woods." The reply was distracted. Much as Ian was. Which was why it took him a second or two to register what she'd just said.

"*Where?*" he said incredulously. For a moment, his fears about her infidelity were lost behind the near impossibility of what he'd just heard.

Footsteps could be heard coming from the wooden dining room floor. "The woods," she said again before appearing in the doorway. The expression on her face was challenging, as if she wanted him to ask her why she had gone to the woods, when she had refused to go with him at any time in the last three years. The very fact of that challenge was enough to convince Ian he needed to avoid it for the time being.

She looked over at the stranger, and raised the tumbler she held in her right hand. It was filled with a clear liquid that he took to be gin. She hadn't had time to add tonic. "Do you want a drink, Martin?"

Martin? Martin? He didn't recall a Martin being mentioned before, so this wasn't likely to be an old work colleague or university friend who just happened to call in.

Martin was shaking his head. "No thanks." He gestured to the sink. "Perhaps a glass of water, if that's all right." His questioning gaze passed between the two of them.

Well, he was polite, Ian thought. He'd give him that. A handshake, a humble request for water and not a raid on the drinks cabinet. Was that meant to throw the cuckolded husband off the scent?

"Help yourself," Tanya told him. "The glasses are in the cupboard above the drainer."

Ian didn't know whether to commend him for making himself at home so quickly, or rage at him. His indecision took away his options.

"You won't believe what we've just seen." Tanya pulled a chair out and sat at the table. She looked at Ian expectantly. He wasn't sure what she was expecting: for him to look at her wide-eyed and beg her to impart her wondrous news, or for him to simply sit down. He opted for the latter, and she took it as the equivalent of him having done the former. "We've seen the reason for the village getting its name."

It was fair to say that she still had the ability to surprise him. He acknowledged that to himself as he gazed back at her in bewilderment. Was this just an elaborate distraction technique, he wondered.

As his brain fought to process this apparently off-the-wall revelation, he was aware of Martin sitting down as well. He sat with his back to the hallway, while Tanya had hers to the dining room and he, Ian, was facing her.

Clearly not happy with the response she was getting

from her husband, Tanya turned to Martin. "Tell him," she urged. "Tell him what we saw." Ian realised that there was something different about the way she was talking. One of the great attractions Tanya had always held for him was her energy and enthusiasm. It had waned in recent months, though he could understand that. Even so, she seemed to have a natural inclination to be forceful in her words, voice and actions. Some of that was coming across now, but Ian recognised that there was an edge to it somehow. He couldn't put his finger on it but, for the first time since he had spotted the pair of them in the yard, he stopped thinking about himself and how he was reacting, and began to consider her.

"It was probably nothing," Martin said dismissively.

"That's not what you said on the way back."

"I've had a bit more time to think. I probably over-reacted." There was something about the way he spoke that Ian found unconvincing.

The look on Tanya's face suggested she was thinking along the same lines. But instead of arguing with him, she turned to Ian. "*I'll* tell you then."

He wasn't sure whether she was too wrapped up in her experiences in the woods, or if he was managing to hide his feelings better than he thought. Whatever the truth, she seemed oblivious to any concerns he might be showing about her turning up with this stranger in tow. Oddly enough, as she related her story, the concerns about Martin's designs on his wife – or, more importantly, hers on him – started to fade. And, as she explained in vivid detail about the appearance of the ravens, he became so engrossed in her words that any jealousy or suspicion rapidly disappeared.

It was certainly very strange. Ian had spent many hours – probably the equivalent of weeks over time – roaming through the woods. It was one of the great pleasures he'd gained from moving up here. The knowledge that it was his own land, and he could walk for miles on it was a great satisfaction to him. When Tanya described the clearing, he knew exactly where she meant. He'd seen the tyre swing himself several weeks ago, and the remains of the fire. His initial reaction had been one of annoyance, though he recognised that it was fuelled in part by concern for the kids that had lit the fire. What if it had got out of hand? What if it had spread and they'd been hurt? He'd had a strong urge to cut the tyre down. That'd let them know he was on to them. Hopefully it would make them wary of coming back and doing something stupid again.

When he'd calmed down, he'd realised he was over-reacting. He was thinking like a father – something he wasn't used to. But he thrust that idea away, afraid of where it might take him. Instead he focused on the positives. Hadn't he lit fires in woods when he was a boy? No one had died then. They hadn't even burnt their fingers on the matches. It was all part of growing up. And if there was an accident... Well, things like that happened in life. And if it didn't happen here, it could just as easily happen somewhere else. In centuries past, it had been part of Sherwood Forest. The forest might be a fraction of the size it had been, but there was still plenty of woodland in these parts.

So he'd left things as they were, and hoped the kids would come back and enjoy themselves out in the fresh air instead of sitting at home watching TV. He'd also mentioned his findings to anyone he bumped into in the village. It wouldn't do any harm for the word to get around, and for parents to be a little more attentive. Then he'd made a point of walking up that way at least once a week in the meantime.

So he'd been up at the clearing only a few days ago. No sign of ravens, though. It did briefly cross his mind that Tanya might be making it up. Especially when she went on to explain that she had felt so frightened she'd needed to hold Martin's hand for comfort as they walked back. Was that just an excuse? Her face suggested not, and he clung to that hope, pushing all thoughts of infidelity from his mind.

Getting to his feet, he went round the table and sat at her side, his arm around her shoulder, holding her tightly. "I'm sure Martin's right. It was probably just one of those quirky things that happen. When you've had some time away from it, the chances are you'll wonder what the fuss was about."

She looked up at him, and he knew his words could have been misinterpreted. She was still processing them, so he had time yet. He leaned in, pressing his lips to the side of her head. They were just above her ear, close enough for her to hear him clearly.

"I love you, Tanya. I won't let anything hurt you." He squeezed her for emphasis, and was surprised to feel her hand stroke the back of his.

"Thank you, Ian." She pulled back and smiled at him. "Now, I suppose you're wondering who our guest is."

The tenderness of the moment had passed, but Ian was grateful for it all the same. He looked expectantly at Martin, although he knew it would be Tanya who explained things.

Which she did, of course. He felt himself torn again by his emotions. Annoyance that Tanya had made a decision to let the room without consulting him; relief that they would receive some income from the transaction; surprise that Patrick had another son; and gratitude when Martin offered to take them to the pub for something to eat.

"It's getting on a bit now," he told them. "It sounds like you've both had a trying day. You've been good enough to offer me a place to stay, and it seems like the very least I can do." He looked Ian in the eye. "I really am very grateful for your hospitality."

Perhaps, Ian thought to himself, I've misjudged him. There had been times recently when he'd wondered if he was becoming paranoid. He glanced at the clock on the wall. It was almost seven o'clock and he was feeling hungry. Outside, it was growing very dark.

FOURTEEN

When Matthew returned from *The Major Oak*, he and Patrick had tried to focus on their work, but it soon became clear that neither of them could concentrate. If they carried on as they were doing, they realised they'd have to knock the wall back down and start from scratch. So they did the sensible thing: they packed up and went home.

Colin was excited. An ambulance and the return of a long-lost brother were almost too much for him. Twice they had to steer him to the bathroom before he had an accident. It was like dealing with a small child. Frustrating. And all the more so because you want them to have the best life they can. Unfortunately, the best life Colin could have would fall way short of anything they could possibly hope for.

They learnt very little from him. The vague references to his meeting Martin at the pub gave no clues as to what had been said between them. Of more concern was what Colin might have told Martin. The chances were that he had said nothing of consequence, but they couldn't be sure. There was no indication that Colin had experienced the verbal abuse Martin had referred to.

That was to be expected. Most of the time it went straight over Colin's head – and the rest of the time it was forgotten about ten minutes later. Just like a child that falls over and hurts himself. The shrieks of pain suggest a red hot blade has sliced into him, yet minutes later he can be playing happily with his Lego or Matchbox cars as if nothing has happened. So it was with Colin – whether the pain was physical or emotional. In a sense, it was to be welcomed. The lad didn't suffer the anguish others might if they were subjected to the same levels of regular abuse. But it also meant that he didn't know enough to avoid it happening again.

"Do you think I should go down to *The Oak* and find out what happened?" Matthew asked his father during one of Colin's toilet breaks.

Patrick shook his head. "No. You might bump into Martin."

"Norma said she'd tell him she had no rooms."

"That doesn't mean he won't be there. He might decide to stay until the last bus, and the pub's as good a place as any to stop."

Technically, the licensing hours were such that the pub should have closed between two-thirty and six, but Norma often kept it open throughout the afternoon. It was quiet, and the locals didn't cause any trouble. The police turned a blind eye on the very odd occasion they passed through the village. Some coppers liked a pint outside of normal hours, so it was useful to keep a few landlords and -ladies onside.

Norma had been happy to go along with Matthew's request. She hadn't been very happy about Martin's behaviour at lunch time. Though she sympathised with his defence of Colin, she also recognised that he wasn't likely to stay around, whereas the people he'd upset in the pub were. The most important thing was to keep the punters happy.

But it was one thing to tell him he couldn't have a bed for the night. Quite another to bar him from the pub altogether. So Matthew realised that it was possible his brother *could* be in the pub. He didn't pursue that idea any further.

Anne and Janet came in from work just after six. It wasn't unusual for Patrick and Matthew to be back before them, but when they spotted dinner on the table as well, they clearly knew something was wrong.

FIFTEEN

Outside it was already getting dark. In the barn it was gloomier still. That was good. He liked it that way. It made him feel comfortable. At home.

The farmhouse had been an option. When he arrived earlier in the day, he had considered using it. But there were things he would need to conceal, and the barn offered much more opportunity for that. From what he had seen of the farm's residents, they were unlikely to even wander in the direction of the barns, let alone come along and inspect the contents. Not like the Sullivans. They were real farmers, and probably spent more time on the land or in these outbuildings than they did in their home.

He was disappointed about the Sullivans. He'd hoped they were still living here. They'd been such good sports when he was last in the village. He smiled to himself. It wasn't an attractive smile. In the wrong company, it could be terrifying. A fact he was well aware of.

The McLeans were a different matter altogether. They were soft, bound only by the material trappings they had acquired. It would be too easy to break them. No challenge at all. He doubted he would even bother with them. They provided a place to rest. A place to hide things. That would be their main purpose. He did contemplate using the woman. She was attractive, and she knew it. He was in no doubt that she was used to getting her own way. There would be significant entertainment value in having her squirm as he used her body to satisfy his needs, and made her realise that she wouldn't always get her own way. He hadn't completely dismissed the idea yet, but having studied her for a while today, he wondered whether she might actually be aroused by him physically abusing her. If she felt that in only a small way, it would defeat the object.

Overhead, there was a rustling noise. His sharp eyes pierced the darkness and he saw the ravens. Thirteen of them perched on a beam in the roof. They waited patiently, occasionally shifting uncomfortably.

His arrival in the village had been noted. Whether the villagers fully appreciated the implications of his arrival was yet to be established. But it wouldn't take long. No more than a couple of days. By then it should be time for him to move on. He had important work to do while he was here, and that work would start soon.

He had business to attend to in the village tonight. It had been years since he was last here. They had felt his presence before. They would feel it again this time.

SIXTEEN

"How's Peter?"

It was a question on a lot of lips, but Norma got it in first.

Bob Lambert had just walked in and was standing at the bar. Medium height, slightly overweight, and with a mop of curly hair, light brown, but generously sprinkled with grey. His ruddy face looked strained. He'd obviously been home and changed before coming here, but his clothes must have been selected because of their proximity rather than their coordination. Green Barbour jacket over a purple jumper and black shirt, the tail of which was covering the front of his jeans. It wasn't a stretch to imagine that the buttons of the shirt were probably not lined up properly either.

He shook his head despondently. "I don't know. I had to leave him there. His mum and dad are at the hospital, but there was nothing I could do." He looked sheepish as he added: "And the cows needed milking."

Norma smiled reassuringly. "No one'll think badly of you for dealing with that. Least of all Peter."

"It doesn't seem right, though." He glanced around the pub. It was busier than it had been at lunch time, though still quieter than Norma hoped it would be later. "I can't say it seems right being in here when Peter's still in Intensive Care."

"What can you do, though?" Norma pointed out, partly to continue with her reassurance, but also to improve the chances of him staying and buying a few drinks. She was already pushing a glass up to the optics, ready to give him his usual tipple. "If his parents are with him, that's all he's going to need. Having you hovering in the wings is just going to make him more anxious."

"If he's even aware."

"That's nothing new." Apart from regular trips to the Gents, Walter hadn't moved since lunch time. He was still in the corner of the bar, and yet again he was cackling to himself.

"Ignore him," Norma said quietly as she placed the whisky in front of Bob.

"I have been for the last forty years," Bob told her. "I'm not likely to change now."

"Is he in a coma then?" Gregory Williams asked. He was further along the bar, perched on a stool. Like everyone else in the pub, he had taking a keen interest in Bob's arrival. "I mean, you said: 'If he's aware'."

The farmer looked witheringly at him. "Don't be daft. He's had his legs run over. Or is that where you keep your brain?" He gestured in the general direction of Gregory's thighs.

"'Bout right," someone said, raising a few chuckles.

Ignoring the laughter, Bob turned to take in his audience properly. When he was sure he had their attention, he spoke again. "Peter's lost both his legs. They're keeping him sedated to block out the pain, and I reckon he's just been unconscious most of the time because he's lost a lot of blood." Norma watched him as his eyes roamed around the bar. He clearly wanted to get his message across. "I've seen a lot of shit over the years, but nothing like this. Believe me, you wouldn't want to have to see it." He glared in Walter's direction. "And I don't want to hear anyone making fun out of it either."

Walter grinned back at him, the gaps between his teeth giving him a macabre appearance. He didn't say anything, but his eyes mocked all the same.

Scowling, Bob turned back to the bar and took up his drink. He was tense, and it wouldn't take much to set him off, Norma reckoned. She added a measure to a fresh glass and put it in front of him. "Have this one on me," she said. It was an investment. If he drank, it'd soothe his nerves. Then he'd calm down and stay for a few more.

The pub had two entrances. One was at the side of the building, to the right of the bar as you stood facing into the room. This was the door you used if you came in from the street, as Bob just had. It was only a few steps away from the pavement. If you arrived by car, it was more likely you'd use the door at the back of the building, which led straight in from the car park. That door was just beyond the corner of the bar where Walter was sitting.

She assumed it was because she was preoccupied with Bob that she didn't notice anyone come in through the back door. It was only when she heard a polite cough that she realised someone else was at the bar. Instinctively, she turned towards the new customer, the smile forming on her lips faltering as she recognised him.

Adam Hawthorn was tall. She guessed nearly six and a half feet. He had sandy-brown hair that was long enough to cover his ears, but didn't come anywhere near his shoulders. It lay flat on his head, strangely lifeless and yet not unattractive. He was slim, carrying no sign of extra weight. His jaw was strong and quite long. Not square, but borderline rectangular. He wore a canvas jacket, jeans and a loose fitting shirt. It was difficult to tell his age. He could be anything between thirty and fifty.

It wasn't that she didn't like him. She just didn't see him that often and always felt there was something odd about him. He rarely came into the village, and she couldn't recall when she'd last seen him in the pub.

Her recovery was quick, and the smile returned easily. Fortunately, he didn't appear to have noticed. Nor did he seem to be aware of the interest his presence was causing among the regulars. It was surreptitious, but it was there all the same.

"I'll have a pint, please, Norma." He didn't have a loud voice, or a quiet one. It seemed very neutral. Like his accent really – or lack of one. Although she knew he lived locally, she didn't know if he came from these parts originally or if, like her, he was an outsider.

She gestured to the three pump handles. "Any preference?" Inside, she felt uncomfortable. There was obviously something about his presence that was making her feel that way. But she hid it well, keeping her smile in place as she asked him.

He paused, studying the options carefully. It was almost as if he was unfamiliar with the process. Eventually he gestured to the nearest pump. "That'll be fine," he said at last, giving her a shy smile.

Pulling the pint felt awkward. Under ordinary circumstances, Norma would use the time to have a chat with a newcomer. It was a good chance to get to know a bit about them, make them feel welcome, and gauge whether they were likely to spend much money while they were in. Instead, she found herself watching the beer dribbling into the glass and wishing it would hurry along. An occasional glance up at Adam was as close as she got to dialogue. The fact that the noise level in the pub had also gone down since his arrival made her feel even more self-conscious.

When she finally handed him his pint and he'd paid, it was a relief to see him wander over to a table in a quiet corner of the bar and sit down.

For the next few minutes, she was distracted by customers who needed refills. Each one seemed to use their moments at the bar to ask about the visitor. They didn't come right out and say anything. They would just give her an inquiring look and roll their eyes in the direction of the corner table. And her response was equally silent but expressive. Like them, she hadn't got a clue what Adam was doing here.

Because the more she thought about it, the more convinced she was that Adam Hawthorn had *never* been in *The Major Oak*. Certainly not in the sixteen years of her tenure.

Adam was from a farm just outside the village. Norma had never had cause to visit the farm, and didn't know anyone else who had either. For that matter, she had no recollection of even seeing it. She just knew it was out there somewhere. For most of the time, the farm and the Hawthorn family were largely forgotten about. On the very rare occasions when they put in an appearance, talk did start, and it could last for a few days. But interest would dwindle, and they slipped from people's consciousness.

Now their consciousness had been provided with a reminder, though, Norma could be confident of how much talk there would be for the next few days. And she could understand why. Unlike the other three farms, theirs appeared to be run only by the three members of the Hawthorn family – Adam, his wife Jennifer and his sister, Claire. The lack of outside help only served to make them more of a curiosity.

So they were a strange bunch, and she couldn't help wondering what had brought Adam in tonight.

A glance over at the table, and she could see he was leaning back against the nearest wall, apparently staring into space. His height made him an awkward looking figure, his knees bent upwards, his shoulders well clear of the back of the chair. The pint was virtually untouched, as if he had no real interest in it.

Around the bar, conversation had picked up a little. The regulars seemed to be getting over their initial reaction to his arrival. She couldn't help but compare it to the incident at lunch time. The quiet descending over the pub when Martin Gates had come in. Odd really. Two similar instances in the same day. A bit like buses. You wait for one for ages. She wondered when the third might turn up.

At seven o'clock, her barman, Andy, arrived. "Good day?" Andy asked her as he nodded greetings to a few familiar faces.

"So-so," she said distractedly.

He took an order and started to pull a pint. "Heard about the accident at Lodge Farm?"

She saw Adam's head lift slightly. He suddenly seemed to pay more attention to the people around him.

"I think you'll find everyone has," Norma told him. She gestured towards an unusually dressed figure. "Bob's over there. He'll give you chapter and verse on it when he's had a few more whiskies."

"Bit buttoned up at the moment then?"

"Yeah, but you know what he's like. Makes out he's got the weight of the world on his shoulders at the best of times. Get some drinks down him and he'll lighten up."

"Not exactly light entertainment, is it?" Andy pointed out.

"No." She made a discreet signal towards Walter. "Not that everyone sees it that way."

Andy nodded his understanding. "I'll keep an eye on that. Don't want any trouble."

She hesitated at that, wondering whether to mention what had happened at lunchtime. Then the decision was taken from her hands as the back door opened again and Martin Gates walked into the room.

SEVENTEEN

"It's like *The Slaughtered Lamb* in here."

Martin looked at Ian. "Like what?"

"*The Slaughtered Lamb,*" Tanya repeated for him, shaking her head. "*I* didn't have a clue what he was talking about the first time he said it."

"You make it sound like I say it all the time."

"Only when you come in here, or if you're talking about having been in here." She seemed to be speaking patiently, but Martin was aware of tension beginning to return.

They'd been in the pub for five minutes now, and were sitting at the table Martin had used earlier. Drinks were in front of them, and food was ordered. The evening menu was only marginally less limited than at lunchtime, so it hadn't taken long to reach decisions about what to eat.

"Well put me out of my misery," Martin prompted. "*The Slaughtered Lamb?*"

"Haven't you seen *American Werewolf in London?*" Ian seemed almost incredulous at this idea.

"*American* what?" Whilst he had nothing against cinema, he wasn't exactly a connoisseur.

"…*Werewolf in London,*" Ian repeated.

"In the film," Tanya went on briskly, "two Americans go into a pub on the Yorkshire Moors called *The Slaughtered Lamb,* and when they do everything suddenly goes quiet.

All conversation stops, and the locals just stare at them."

Martin grinned and nodded. Tanya might be fed up with the comparison, but hearing it for the first time, he completely understood where Ian was coming from. He let his gaze drift around the bar, taking everything in. The locals were talking to each other again, but it was very subdued. There hadn't been complete silence when they first came in, but the drop in volume had been almost tangible.

"And much as I find it irritating that Ian keeps coming up with the same comment time and again," Tanya continued, "I have to agree with him. It was just like this the first time we came in. What would that be now, Ian? Three years?"

"Close enough. It nearly put us off moving."

"*You*, dear. It nearly put *you* off moving. I didn't want to come to this dump in the first place." Martin noted that her complaint was not loud enough for any of the other customers to hear.

Ian looked down, clearly stung by her words, and possibly embarrassed at being spoken to like this in front of a stranger.

Their table was circular, and they were seated in a triangular formation, so each of them could see the others without turning their heads. That said, Martin was aware of Tanya looking directly at him while her husband's attention was on his navel. He wasn't sure how he felt about that. For now, he didn't really want to confront it either.

"Surely things must have changed since you moved here," he said.

"You're joking. You saw what it was like when we came in."

"I thought that was because of me."

Ian looked back up. "But I thought you were Patrick's son."

"I am. But I've been away for a long time." He caught the landlady looking at him, and smiled back at her. She moved her head as if she was simply scanning the room, pretending not to notice. "My reception at lunchtime was pretty similar."

"Looks like we're all outsiders then," Tanya suggested. Or was it more a case of her being suggest*ive*. There was definitely something still there in her eyes.

"Give it time," he said. "They'll grow to accept you."

"What about you?"

"I doubt I'll be here long enough." And he didn't want them to pursue that, so he shifted the conversation to Ian. "You said it nearly put you off, but I take it there were still plenty of attractions. Tanya told me you'd moved up from Oxford. I've never been, but I understand it's a nice part of the world."

"It is, yes. But I needed a change."

"You definitely got it here." Tanya's bitterness was barely below the surface.

Ian's eyes flickered towards her, but he continued to speak to Martin. "I did think it'd be nice to settle in and become part of a local community."

"And it hasn't worked out that way?"

"Like Tanya says, we're still outsiders. You can see what it's like here. Surreptitious looks, no eye contact, and a sort of no-man's land between us and them."

Until he said it, Martin hadn't realised, but Ian was right. There was a definite gap between them and anyone else in the bar. The distance to the nearest other customer was around five feet, and the same space applied with a number of people so there was a theoretical corridor that arced its way around them.

"The thing is, it's the same in the Post Office, and even in the street. People cross the road when you're approaching, or rush to get in their cars, anything just to be off the street by the time you get near."

"You don't think you're being paranoid, do you? They might just be shy." Martin was playing with him. He knew exactly what Ian was talking about. "Besides, that's village life. Most of the people who live here have never lived anywhere else. They don't know any different, and anything that *is* different can be quite scary to them."

"I know what you're saying. And I did come prepared for it to a certain extent. But I never expected it to be this bad. There's something else as well." He hesitated, and Martin watched him apprehensively as he searched for the words. "It's not just about *us*. I think it's something to do with the farm."

"The *farm*?"

"It's got a history."

"A history nobody bothered to tell us about until after we'd bought the bloody place," Tanya put in. "I still think we should sue the estate agents. It could be our way out."

"We don't have a leg to stand on," Ian said with a firmness Martin suspected was truer to his character than the comparatively subservient role he seemed to play with Tanya.

"So what…?" Martin started to ask, but was interrupted by the barman arriving with two plates of food.

"Steak and chips?"

Ian gestured to the empty space in front of him.

"Scampi and chips?" Which went to Martin, before the young man darted back to the kitchen to collect Tanya's food.

"What are you having with *your* chips?" Martin asked drily.

"I know, it's bloody limited here, isn't it?" But she smiled at him, in spite of her irritation. He had to admit, it was a very attractive smile.

When the barman was sure they had everything they needed, he left them to their meal. Satisfied he was out of earshot, Martin went back to the question he'd been about to ask.

"What's this about the farm having a 'history'?"

"I assumed you'd know," Ian said, between mouthfuls of what he later described as cardboard rather than meat. "Unless you've been away for twenty-five years."

"I was young when I left, but not that young. I was eight twenty-five years ago. I left when I was eighteen."

Ian gave him a puzzled look. "Surely you know about the suicides then?"

EIGHTEEN

"Suicides?" Martin was careful to keep his voice down. He didn't want to attract any unnecessary attention. "How many?"

"Two."

"And these happened twenty-five years ago?"

"Well, one of them did. The other was a couple of years later."

Martin hadn't realised there was tension building up in him until it started to ease. "When I spoke to my dad this afternoon, he mentioned that one of the Sullivans had killed himself. I hadn't realised there was more than one."

"Oh yes. Husband and wife. Him first and then her, both in the same house."

Unexpectedly, Martin felt the tension coming back. There was something about the scenario that seemed familiar. He just couldn't put a handle on it yet.

"What else do you know about it?"

Ian took a long look around the room while he chewed on his meat. As he did, Martin realised the story must also involve the living, and he was checking to see if any of them were present. Apparently satisfied they were safe, he swallowed and started talking again.

"Maybe you'll remember Phil Sullivan?" It was more a question than a statement, so Martin shook his head. The name was vaguely familiar, but as his dad had worked on the Sullivan farm since before Martin was born, that was only to be expected. "What about David or Paul?"

"Only because my dad mentioned them this afternoon."

"They owned and ran the farm until I bought it. But they inherited it from their dad, Phil. He killed himself in nineteen sixty-four. Shotgun, apparently. Both barrels."

"That's enough detail," Tanya complained. "I *am* trying to eat, you know." She looked at Martin. "He watches too many films," she explained. "Just loves the blood and gore."

"Any idea why he did it?"

Another furtive look around the bar, then Ian leaned forward and spoke even more quietly. "Apparently, he found his wife in bed with their son-in-law."

Something prickled in Martin's head.

"How do you know this? If the locals won't talk to you."

"They seem to be a bit more talkative in Long Clayford and Thornberry."

"Try any of the other villages and you'll find they're a *lot* more talkative," Tanya added tartly.

"If we're going out for a pub meal, we tend to go elsewhere," Ian said awkwardly. Martin guessed he didn't want to seem ungrateful for his offer of a meal in *The Major Oak*. He chose to ignore it, and let Ian deal with his own hang-ups.

"To be honest it seems even stranger that people from other villages are talking about it. I'd've thought the Sullivans would have kept all this to themselves, wouldn't you?"

Ian shrugged. "I don't know. I can only tell you what

I've been told. Maybe it came from the police? They're not noted for keeping things as quiet as they should be. And it's a juicy piece of gossip."

"Unless you have to live in the same house," Tanya pointed out.

"What happened to the wife and son-in-law?"

"Don't know about the son-in-law. The rumour is that he disappeared."

"Suspiciously?"

"Probably not. If I was in his shoes, I'd just want to get as far away from here as possible."

"I'll second that…"

They ignored her.

"What if it was true love?" Martin doubted it, but nothing could be discounted.

"She was old enough to be his mother," Ian pointed out.

"Stranger things have happened," Martin commented, but Ian didn't bite.

"True enough," he acknowledged. "I doubt we'll ever know what really happened to him. But we know what happened to her. She was the second suicide. Nineteen sixty-six."

"Shotgun?"

"Overdose. The general consensus was that she couldn't live with the guilt of what she'd done. To her husband. Her daughter. Even her grandchildren."

"Jesus!" Martin said it softly, but with feeling. At first he'd thought only of the sexual triangle between husband, wife and lover. Ian spelling it out like that made him realise just how far-reaching the damage had been.

"From what I can gather, the experience had an impact on the whole family. David and Paul found their mum and brother-in-law standing over their dad's body."

"In a state of undress." Tanya seemed to enjoy the scandalous aspect of that.

"Was it definitely suicide?" Martin was thinking of how it would look to the Sullivan sons.

"Apparently, the initial suspicion *was* that he'd been killed by his wife or the son-in-law."

"Rumour is that some people still think it's the case," said Tanya. Definitely liking the scandal, Martin thought.

"That may be the rumour," Ian said patiently, "and there may be people who do think like that, but I've been told on several occasions that the police found enough evidence to support the suicide theory."

Martin mulled it all over for a few moments, before saying: "I know it must have been a shock to find his wife with the other bloke. But, even if it *was* his son-in-law, it's still a bit extreme to top yourself, isn't it?"

"I agree. But I'm sound of mind – "

"That's a matter of opinion."

" – and who knows what state he was in? He might have had a load of other things on his mind, and this was just the last straw."

"You're right," Martin nodded. He forced a smile. It was time to leave this for now. He didn't want to raise any suspicions. "We'll never know the truth, will we?"

"Not at all. But it doesn't help when you live there." Ian dropped his cutlery on to the plate with a clatter. He hadn't cleared it, but Martin couldn't blame him for leaving the gristly bits of meat or the world-weary peas.

Martin checked his watch. It was already eight o'clock. He didn't mind keeping his family waiting, but he didn't want to make it too long. He'd wait until Tanya finished eating, and then go. In the meantime, he would take the opportunity to dig a little more. "What are you saying? The house is haunted?"

Ian chuckled as if at a private joke. "Hardly. Don't worry. Your sleep won't be disturbed by any bumps in the night."

Maybe not bumps. Martin glanced at Tanya, but she was concentrating on the remains of her chicken.

"No," Ian went on, "it's just the reputation the place has. It was on the market for nearly four years before we bought it. I assumed it was going for a song because of problems in farming. Now I know it was because no one wanted to live in a house where two people had killed themselves."

"Is that why the Sullivans wanted to sell? Because of the property's history?"

"If it is, they waited a long bloody time," Tanya pointed out as she put her cutlery neatly together on the plate.

"It might have been a part of it," Ian said thoughtfully, ignoring his wife's comment. "But they obviously needed something extra to push them to do it." He hesitated, once again casting an eye around the bar. The room had filled a little more while they were eating, but he clearly didn't see anyone he needed to be careful of. "Paul had an accident."

"Do you know, we've even had people telling us the farm's cursed," Tanya said irritably. "And Paul losing a leg in an accident with a plough was just more evidence of the curse."

"Surely it's an occupational hazard," Martin ventured. "I mean, I don't think it's an everyday event, but there's a lot of dangerous equipment on farms, so accidents are bound to happen, aren't they? I'm sure we had a couple of serious injuries while *I* was living here."

"You're probably right. But it obviously doesn't stop the rumour-mongers."

"And rumours don't help to sell houses," Tanya added.

It was time to leave, but Martin paused for a moment to study Tanya. When he first met her, he had been struck by her attractiveness. There was a sophisticated sexiness about her, and he could still see it. On the outside. But now he could also see the cold and bitter woman inside.

NINETEEN

From the outside, *The Major Oak* was beginning to show signs of wear. Even in the orange light from the nearby streetlamps, it wasn't hard to see paintwork peeling and the cracks in the rendered walls. The windows that looked on to the street were low down, sills below knee level for even the shortest of adults. To the left of the building was the opening that led to the side door. A light fitting had been fixed just above the doorway, but the bulb had blown a while ago, and no one had got around to replacing it. About twenty feet beyond the door, the driveway opened out into the car park at the rear of the property. Exterior lights were still working at the back of the pub, and some of it spilled out to provide some illumination for anyone coming in or out through the side door. Nevertheless, the length of wall between the door and car park was filled with shadows, and it was very easy to simply lean against it and blend in.

In spite of his height, Adam Hawthorn had the ability to blend in anyway. When Martin Gates had come into the pub with the McLeans, none of them had noticed the tall man sitting quietly in a corner of the room. Nor had they been aware of him watching them. And listening.

His cue to leave was when Ian McLean dropped his cutlery on the plate. The pint on his table was barely touched. He hoped Norma wouldn't take offence. He didn't like alcohol. Ordering the beer had seemed like the most appropriate thing to do in a pub, but he knew he'd been clumsy. Not really knowing what to ask for, he'd stumbled over his request, and he knew that had drawn more attention to him than he'd wanted. Leaving an almost full glass would have the same effect. If he had to do it again, he'd be better to settle for a soft drink. Fortunately, his mistakes had been made before Martin arrived. Getting attention from the landlady was regrettable, but not damaging.

Summer had passed, yet the evening was still warm. He didn't know how long he'd have to wait. Probably not long, but at least he wouldn't be shivering if it did take a while. About five feet beyond the doorway, the wall turned in slightly. The rendering masked the brickwork, of course, but Adam guessed that if it was exposed it would be obvious that this junction was where an extension had been added to the building at some point. Regardless of its reason for being there, it provided useful additional cover for anyone who didn't want to be noticed.

As he'd expected, his wait was no more than ten minutes. During that time, one person had left the pub, and three others had gone in, none of them aware they were being watched.

The second person to leave was Martin. Adam watched him walk the few yards to the street, then turn right. Once he'd disappeared from view, Adam gave him another thirty seconds before stepping out of the shadows.

The main street through the village curved away to the right a little further along. The Post Office was just around the bend, and several hundred yards beyond that was the entrance to *Forest Farm*. Adam was pretty sure Martin's destination lay further than that.

By the time he reached the road, Martin had disappeared from view. Between the pub and Post Office was an opening that led up to the Lodge Farm nursery and farm shop. It was a wide track, big enough to comfortably allow two vehicles to pass each other. To one side of that was a field that had once been used for pasture, though Bob Lambert seemed to use it simply as a buffer between the rest of his farm and the main road now. It was possible Martin could have hidden himself in that entrance, or against the hedge that bordered the field. He could be lying in wait for Adam.

But he wasn't – not that Adam had expected him to be. By the time he had him in his sights, he was already striding past the entrance to the McLeans' home, clearly in a hurry.

Adam crossed the road. A terraced row was on that side. If Martin did happen to look back, he might assume the lone figure was heading for one of those. Being diagonally opposite also gave Adam a better view.

It had been over a hundred years since the Sullivan family had first owned the farm. In those days, farming machinery was limited and they'd been much more reliant on manual labour. Farm workers generally had accommodation provided. A row of cottages had been built on the street. The land had originally been owned by the farm, and it was possible to access the farm from behind the cottages. Just before you reached the first one, there was a driveway that ran along the side of it, then curved round to pass behind all four. It provided access to each of the houses as well as parking spaces. And at the very end was a gate that opened on to a footpath that could be taken up to the farm house and the accompanying outbuildings. Adam knew all this because he'd spent time exploring every part of the village. Usually at night, when no one else would know he was around.

Opposite the farm cottages was St. Peter's. The old church was set well back beyond the graveyard, and half-hidden by trees. That was where Adam was aiming for.

Martin reached the farm cottages, and stopped in front of the third one along. Adam had reached the end of the row of houses on the other side of the road. Beyond that was a children's play area. The swings and slide were hidden in the darkness, the nearest lights coming from the last house in the row – a distance of at least a hundred yards. The vicarage garden bordered the play area, though high hedges obscured its view. No doubt it also saved its windows from flying cricket balls or other similar projectiles.

Adam continued to walk. On the other side of the church there was a *cul-de-sac*. He didn't want to go that far, but if Martin glanced his way he would have to carry on and double back later.

But Martin stood facing the front door of the cottage, apparently oblivious of anyone – or anything – else around. Adam could only guess at what was going through his mind. Apprehension, uncertainty… fear?

There were no vehicles on the road. At that time of night, there rarely was. Ravens Gathering wasn't used as a thoroughfare much. The only traffic would be people either travelling to or from the village, and most of those going out would have left earlier and wouldn't be back till much later. There weren't many visitors.

The lack of traffic meant that there was almost no background noise. A laughter track could be heard dimly from one of the old farm cottages. Edith Lacey, Adam recalled. Deaf as a post and unwilling to admit it. So she'd have the TV on full blast, and wouldn't be able to hear the neighbours complaining. Other than that, the only sounds were of leaves rustling gently above the graveyard. When it came, then, the knock on the door was startling, even though Adam was expecting it. The thick timber vibrated against Martin's fist and sounded hollowly across the street, its echo lingering.

By now Adam had passed the play area and drawn level with the vicarage. He was almost behind Martin. Another twenty feet and he'd reach the gate to the church yard. So far, he didn't seem to have been spotted.

As the sound of Martin's knock died away, the ensuing silence seemed even more pronounced. Adam had time to cover another ten paces before the door opened. Light shone briefly out on to the street, then it was gone, the only trace that it had been there was the echo of the door shutting firmly against its jamb. Adam glanced over to make sure Martin had gone in, then a further check for anyone else that may have strayed out into the night. Satisfied he wasn't being watched, he passed through the gate and into the shadows of the grave yard.

Once inside, his pace changed. The erect stance that had accompanied his apparently casual walk transformed into a low crouch as he darted between gravestones, hurrying to find a suitable place to carry out his surveillance. He didn't know how long Martin would be in the cottage, so he needed to be reasonably comfortable. Naturally, he also needed to maintain a clear view of the cottage, as well as the driveway – just in case he decided to leave from the rear of the house. There was a possibility, of course, that Martin could return to the farm house using the footpath, but at this time of night that would be foolhardy. There were too many things he could trip over or walk into, and if he seriously hurt himself he could find himself out there all night, and possibly well into the day before anyone found him. It wouldn't kill him, but Adam couldn't think of a good reason why anyone would take the risk.

Halfway between the gate and the hedge that bordered the vicarage, Adam came to a tall and broad headstone. In the limited light available, he could only vaguely make out its shape. He reached out and ran his fingertips along the top. It stood almost shoulder high – so nearly head high on most people – and he guessed at around four feet across. It was squared off, with no intricate details carved into it. As he stepped around it, he knew he would find another length of the same stone laid across the grave itself. He didn't need to touch this to know the inscriptions were already fading and the edges chipped. Phil Sullivan's grave. It could be coincidence or irony, he thought to himself as he settled down. The coldness of the stone seeped up through the denim of his jeans and into his buttocks. Leaning against the headstone so that the rest of him was concealed from the street while his eyes peered around it, he reasoned that it was more likely to be fate that made this the perfect spot.

A lot of people find graveyards disturbing. Most probably because they find death disturbing. Adam wasn't troubled by such ideas. He was very comfortable with death, and had no problem with using a grave for these purposes. In spite of the cold in his behind, he was also very comfortable with the possibility of spending several hours here if he needed to. Not that he expected to be that long. An hour at the outside, he reckoned.

But it wasn't activity from the cottage that attracted his attention first. It came from the vicarage.

A door opened. It wasn't loud, but in the still night air and with all of his senses on alert, Adam heard it clearly. The main entrance to the vicarage faced the church, and he was in no doubt that this was what he had heard open. But there was no light. Even through the hedge, he should have seen fragments of light coming from the hallway. The door closed, and he heard shoes crunching across the gravel driveway, heading towards the road.

He was here to watch over Martin Gates, and yet his instinct told him this was just as important. The vicar, Simon Cantor, was a man who followed routines. And leaving his house at this time on a Thursday night wasn't one of them.

Very carefully, Adam raised himself into a crouch, then started to make his way between the graves to the wall that bordered the street. As he did, he continued to listen to the footsteps on the other side of the hedge. He looked for signs of movement as well, but the hedge had been grown over many decades and was very thick.

The footsteps stopped, and Adam froze, wondering if he had made some noise that had alerted the other person. It took him a moment or so to realise that they hadn't stopped walking, they'd just stepped off the drive. Cautiously, he moved forward again, his eyes darting all around, looking for anything else that might be out of place. But all the time coming back to look at the Gates cottage in case Martin suddenly appeared.

When he reached the stone wall, he hesitated only a second before raising his head and peering out. A hundred yards away, a tall lean figure was walking along the middle of the road, heading towards the centre of the village. From the way he carried himself, he looked as if he thought he owned the place. Adam couldn't help thinking there was more than a grain of truth in that.

TWENTY

Fifteen years can make a difference, but not in all ways. His mother looked older, more like seventy than sixty. Grey hair where it had once been blonde. Shorter too, so there was no hiding place for the crow's feet or the sagging flesh around her neck. Her dress sense did nothing to help. Martin thought he even recognised the cardigan she was wearing.

Surprisingly, his sister Janet didn't look much younger. She was only a few years older than Martin, but she could have passed for his mother with only a minor stretch of the imagination. The hair was still blonde, but it hung lifelessly just above her shoulders. Her face told a story of long hard hours and little prospect of respite. She wore jeans and a shirt that looked as if they may have been in fashion, but on her they were shapeless. It was no wonder she was still living with their parents. He couldn't imagine she had the get up and go to strike out on her own, and looking as she did it seemed unlikely she'd have her pick of men.

The house hadn't changed much, though. The same TV stood in the corner by the window. The window itself was covered by the thick red velvet curtains he had hidden behind as a child, oblivious of the fact that his feet were sticking out where Matthew and Janet could see them. It seemed as if it had taken him years to realise why they found him so quickly. Strange, the memories that came back to him.

Like sitting on his mum's knee in the big armchair where his dad sat now. He didn't know how old he had been, but he guessed no more than two or three. Just a phase they had gone through. Enjoying the warmth of the fire as they watched *Andy Pandy* and *Sooty* on the tiny black and white TV set they'd rented.

He suspected the carpet was different, but it was difficult to tell in the dim light. The fact the room was cramped, with furniture covering most of the floor, didn't help much either. Although he couldn't identify any new items, he didn't remember it being so crowded in here. Then again, most of his memories were from his childhood, when he was smaller and the whole world seemed like a much bigger place.

Or maybe it wasn't just the physical confines that made him feel like this. There was an almost palpable hostility. Not from all of them. Colin was clearly delighted to see him, although Martin couldn't for the life of him think why. He'd only been nine when Martin left, and that was in physical terms. Mentally, he'd been barely an infant. It was a wonder the lad could remember his older brother at all.

When he'd opened the door, Matthew had looked annoyed. He didn't say anything, but it was clear he wasn't happy Martin had turned up. His dad looked much the same when he came into the living room. He guessed the fact that he was late had made them hope he wasn't going to come. He didn't sense quite the same from his mum or Janet. They were wary rather than unfriendly. Regardless, it was uncomfortable.

Colin had been sitting on the floor in front of the TV, legs crossed like a six year-old. When he saw Martin, he jumped to his feet and rushed over.

"Martin! Martin!" His excitement reminded Martin of his own behaviour as a small child. He looked at Patrick, the big man watching him carefully. It was hard to believe that he'd worshipped this man. He'd known instinctively when it was time for his dad to come home from work, and would watch from the kitchen window. As soon as he walked through the gate into the back yard, Martin would dash outside and run into Patrick's waiting arms. Good times. Long gone.

Clutching Martin's arm, Colin pulled him across the room to the table. It was pushed against the back wall, but there were four dark wooden chairs around it. Janet was already sitting at one of them. It had its back to the wall and was facing into the room. Martin was conscious of her drawing back as he came closer. Although it was tempting to add to Janet's discomfort by picking the nearest chair to her, he realised that would be unnecessarily confrontational. It wasn't time yet. He steered Colin to a chair on the opposite side of the table, then sat down. Colin sat down on the floor next to him, his eyes fixed on Martin's face.

Ignoring his younger brother, Martin looked at his family. Matthew had remained leaning against the door that led back out to the hall and stairs. His dad's chair was facing the TV, so he was sitting at an awkward angle, almost wedged into a corner of the chair as he looked across his right shoulder to see his middle son. A two-seater sofa was pushed against the wall opposite the fire, and his mum was sitting at the far end of that. He could see that she was relieved he hadn't come to join her. Not that Colin had given him a choice. Still, he suspected he would have played it safe anyway. It was a small room, but they'd managed to space themselves out as much as possible. Martin didn't kid himself that this was going to be the warmest of family reunions.

In all honesty, he couldn't say he'd been looking forward to this meeting. He knew it wouldn't be easy, but he also knew they needed to talk. The main difficulty was knowing what needed saying. But it was also hard to know who he should talk to first. In one sense, the easiest option was to talk to the only person who was pleased to see him. Unfortunately, Colin didn't strike him as having much capacity for conversation. He did offer a way in though.

Martin rested a hand on his younger brother's shoulder, a gesture that made Colin sit up straighter and smile more broadly. "I can't believe how grown up you are." His gaze switched between his parents as he spoke. At that moment, he wasn't too concerned about their effect on his brother.

"He was only nine when you left," Patrick pointed out.

"True, but he…" Martin hesitated.

Patrick glanced at his youngest son's oblivious smile. "He's done well," he conceded, "all things considered."

"Still needs some looking after, though." He didn't even attempt to make it sound like a question.

"If you're talking about what happened in *The Oak*, well…" He looked across at his wife. "We do our best, but sometimes it's just not enough. You can't protect your children forever."

Martin decided to keep his thoughts on that subject to himself for now. "How does he get on at work?"

"He doesn't." Matthew had clearly decided he needed to be included.

"Must be a strain."

"We manage."

"I suppose it helps that you work in the village."

For a moment, Matthew's lips tightened. "It helps, yes." There was an edge to his words that left Martin wondering.

"How is the work up at the farm?"

"It's work." Matthew shrugged.

"It's funny, I always got the impression you'd want to move away. When I came back I half expected to find out you were working down south, or even abroad." Martin made the comments lightly, but they prompted the response he was looking for: tight lips again.

"Sometimes life doesn't turn out the way you expect," Matthew said carefully. "But that has nothing to do with Colin." The last remark was unnecessary – which said plenty.

Rather than pick up on it, Martin turned to his mother. "And you're working too now?"

Anne's eyes were reminiscent of those of a rabbit caught in headlights. She stared back at him for several uncomfortable seconds. It was tempting to help her out and start talking just to fill the silence, but Martin resisted.

Finally, she gave a slow nod. "That's right."

The idea of his mother working still seemed alien to him. Throughout his childhood, she had been at home, looking after the children and making sure the house was clean and tidy, and that food was on the table when it should be. Even though that had been more the norm in the sixties, and attitudes had changed during the seventies

141

and eighties, he still couldn't imagine his father wanting his wife at work. He had no doubt they must be facing hard times financially if he was prepared to let her go. Which didn't make sense. Even without his mum working, there were three others who were out at work and bringing money into the household.

"Where are you working?"

"Griffin's," she said. There was no hesitation this time. Perhaps she was getting into her stride. He decided he'd try to keep things easy for now.

Shaking his head, he said: "Never heard of them. Are they a new company?"

A quick glance at Patrick before she answered. Martin didn't see his reaction, but assumed he must have indicated it was okay to carry on.

"I think they've been around for about ten years or so. Since you…" She faltered for a moment, dropping her eyes. "They started up after you left. That's why you won't have heard of them."

Martin nodded his understanding, turning to his sister as he did so. "And you're there too, I gather."

The sudden shift of focus was intentional and had the desired rabbit and headlight effect. Janet's mouth repeatedly opened and closed as he smiled at her patiently. No sound came from it for several moments, and again he had to restrain himself from sparing her the awkwardness.

Eventually either the Gates genes or instinctive mimicry kicked in as she nodded and said: "That's right," her tone identical to her mother's.

"What do Griffin's do?" He kept his attention on Janet for now.

"They're a wholesalers."

"Do they wholesale anything in particular?"

"All kinds of things really. Clothing mainly, but there're other things too." As with her mother, once she'd started, the responses came a little easier.

"And what do you do there?"

She shrugged dismissively. "Nothing much. Just general help in the warehouse. Packing cartons for shipping, unloading new stock when it comes in, that kind of thing."

Martin had to agree with her initial assessment: nothing much. So his sister's income probably wasn't fantastic, but it would still be more than helpful when added to his dad's and Matthew's.

"Are you doing the same, Mum?"

Although Anne wasn't caught out quite as much as last time, he knew he still had her off-balance. The pause was short, but there, and the nod was jerky and awkward. "Er... yes."

"Must be nice to spend so much time together," he commented.

Again a nod. "It is. Yes."

"What about you, Dad? Is it good to be working with Matthew?"

Patrick was more prepared than his wife or daughter had been. He must have been watching the way Martin was playing with them, because he appeared to be expecting a question. Just not this one particularly, though he could see where it was heading.

"I do, yes. Matthew's been very good to me and your mum. He's given up a lot to help us with Colin." He gestured to his youngest child, who beamed back at him when he heard his name. "And he supported us financially when I lost my job at the farm." He gazed directly into Martin's eyes, the challenge in them plain to see. "I'm a very lucky man."

His words and their implications caught Martin out. He leaned back in his chair and adjusted himself as if he had become uncomfortable and needed to change position on his seat. He wasn't sure how well he covered himself. He suspected not very well from the glances that passed between Patrick and Matthew.

"I can see that you are," he replied eventually. He let his gaze pass over everyone in the room. There was a definite closeness between them. It was something he hadn't experienced for a long time. And it was something he couldn't imagine he was going to feel again with these people. There seemed little more to be gained by prolonging this meeting. He needed time to think now, to consider whether he should pursue things with them or simply move on.

Standing up suddenly, he didn't know whether to laugh or be upset at the reactions from his family. Both his mother and sister flinched, while his father and elder brother seemed to tense as if they were preparing for a fight. On the floor beside him, Colin simply looked up at him in puzzlement.

"I'd better get on," he said, tapping his watch. "It's well past nine, and I've got a bit of a walk yet."

"Walk?" Matthew asked suspiciously.

"Yes, I'm stopping up at the McLeans' house. And as it's my first night there, I don't want to be getting in too late and disturbing them."

"First night?" Patrick's expression made it clear that he regretted the question as soon as it came out.

"Well, I don't know how long I'll be stopping, but Tanya and Ian have said I can stay as long as I want." Which wasn't true, but there was no harm in giving them something else to gnaw on. And from the looks that passed between his parents and older siblings, it had the desired effect.

TWENTY-ONE

Question Time had just started. Tanya couldn't understand why Ian watched it at the best of times. She had no interest in politics, and bearing witness to a bunch of overgrown schoolchildren arguing about things that seemed of little or no consequence to her was clearly a pointless exercise. And the mood Ian was in, she couldn't see that he'd be getting any benefit from it tonight.

She was allowing herself to be subjected to the programme for the simple reason that she wanted to be around when Martin came back. Under other circumstances, she would have made her excuses and gone to bed. That would allow her to, at the very least, *pretend* to be asleep when Ian joined her. Their sex life was pretty limited these days, and her enthusiasm for it had long since disappeared. They were in a rut on that front, and her needs involved a lot more excitement. Having to endure Ian laying on top and going through the motions was almost less attractive than watching Peter Sissons refereeing a bunch of idiots who seemed to think they were demonstrating their intellect by scoring points off each other.

Tonight, though, her curiosity about Martin was stronger than her aversion to political debate or to the risk of Ian's advances. To be fair, she felt pretty safe on the advances front, as Ian had been very introverted since they'd come back from the pub. He'd made an effort while they were out, and even tried to prolong things by getting another round of drinks after Martin had left. But by the time they were in the car, he'd gone very quiet, and since then had only spoken if he needed to. She knew the symptoms. It was pathetic really. He pretended everything was all right, but bottled up all of his worries because he was afraid of appearing weak. The reality was that, if he actually opened up about his problems and talked about them, she would think more of him. Instead, he was going to stew on them, make himself and everyone else around him miserable, and achieve nothing until he admitted to himself that he did need to talk. In the meantime, Tanya would just have to guess what was troubling him.

Unfortunately, at the moment, there could be any number of things. Obviously there were the money worries, and she was pretty confident that was a large part of it. She knew he was also concerned about the building work at the cottages. Matthew and Patrick were doing the work for nothing at the moment. True, they'd been promised a share of the profits in exchange for that work, but until the houses were complete and – more importantly – sold, that was as good as thin air to them. If Ian couldn't renegotiate their loans, there was a strong chance that the properties would be repossessed, which would mean the builders had worked for nothing. That wouldn't sit well on Ian's conscience. On the other hand, because Matthew and Patrick had no other income at the moment, if other work was offered to them, they could very well drop the cottages and move on. That would leave Ian with no way of finishing the building work off, which meant he wouldn't have anything to sell. On that front, it was all a very fine balancing act. If he misjudged anything, the whole thing could fall over.

At the same time, she knew Ian was aware of how strained their relationship had become recently. That could well be preying on his mind. Martin's presence might not have helped, though he seemed to have accepted things quite well. He'd been very friendly while they were at the pub. But that didn't necessarily mean anything. She knew from experience how his mind worked. He knew that jealousy stemmed from insecurity and, to him, insecurity would be a sign of weakness. There could very well be an internal battle going on right now as he fought to control any such feelings. He would be reasoning with himself, methodically listing all the reasons why he shouldn't feel jealous or insecure. Completely ignoring the fact that he could rationalise as much as he liked, but emotions and rationality rarely have anything in common. And while he did all of that, he would pretend that he wasn't remotely bothered.

Whether it was any or all of these things – or even if there were other issues Tanya wasn't aware of – right now she knew her husband was a boiling mass that was trying to keep itself sealed. Any time soon, one of two things was going to happen. If they were both lucky, he would have to crack the seal and let some of the steam out to ease the pressure. What was more likely was that there would be an explosion. As she sat back in her armchair and surreptitiously studied him, a small part of her wondered if the explosion might come in the form of a heart attack.

She couldn't help thinking that a coronary might solve a lot of problems. Having been a financial adviser for so many years, Ian was a great advocate of life insurance, and always felt it was important to lead by example.

On the TV, a familiar face was droning on about something Tanya was convinced would have no impact on *her* life. Ian appeared to be taking an interest, but she knew he was miles away. She glanced in the direction of the hallway, wondering when Martin would be back.

He was another strange one. It crossed her mind that maybe she was attracted to odd blokes, but she quickly dismissed that. Her last fling had been with someone who she thought was very normal. Married, but bored like her. He'd been just ready for some excitement, and she'd been very happy to give it to him.

But Martin was quite different. He'd been very flirty with her when they first met, and yet it seemed that, as soon as she became more serious about the opportunities they could have together, his manner had changed. The term 'all mouth and trousers' came to mind, but she sensed it wasn't that. Nor did it seem to be a concern about what Ian might think. There was something else, and that intrigued her.

Not that it was likely she would get to the bottom of it tonight. Even if Ian was asleep, she wouldn't be stupid enough to try and get Martin into bed. *That* would have to wait until tomorrow. But she might be able to find out some more about him. She glanced at her watch. It was almost quarter to eleven. If she was going to find out some more, it wasn't going to be a lot.

As if on cue, she heard a door close in another part of

149

the house. She was surprised at how tense she suddenly felt.

"That must be Martin." Ian was on his feet before she had a chance to react. It was almost as if he'd been waiting for their guest. "I'll go and see if he wants a nightcap."

On the one hand, this meant that she didn't have to come up with any excuses to bring Martin in, Tanya realised. At the same time, it seemed strange that Ian should be so enthusiastic. All she could do was sit still and wait for them to come back to the living room. In the meantime, a member of the audience was asking for the panel's views on how the Poll Tax was working out in Scotland. As it wasn't due to be introduced in England until next year, this question was yet another irrelevance to Tanya. Fortunately, she was saved from further boredom as Ian came back with Martin in tow.

"I'll get the drinks," he was saying. He gestured to an armchair. "Have a seat." Picking up his empty tumbler, he turned to leave the room again. "Do you want a refill?" he asked Tanya.

She glanced at her glass, which was less than half full. Again she was aware of feeling uncomfortable about Martin. There was something not quite right. For once, she thought she'd play it safe. "I'm fine for now. I'll see how I feel when I've finished this."

When Ian had gone, she looked at Martin properly. His chair was angled slightly away from her, but he'd adjusted his position so he was virtually face-on to her. She couldn't help thinking how attractive he was. Yet there was nothing in his expression to give her any indication of what he was feeling – about her, or anything. *Play it safe*, she reminded herself.

"How did it go tonight?" she asked.

"Not a joyous reunion," he said. His tone gave nothing away either. No disappointment, no upset, no irony. Nothing.

"How long is it since you last saw them?"

"I left in June nineteen seventy-four."

"I suppose you've all changed a lot in that time."

He smiled, but there was no humour in it. "Not as much as you'd think."

She was still wondering how to react to that when Ian returned with two half full tumblers.

"I thought you said a *small* nightcap," Martin said as he took his glass.

Ian smiled back at him conspiratorially. It was a look that made Tanya feel uneasy. "That's nothing. We'll have that down us before we know it." He sat back in his own chair and raised his tumbler as if giving a toast. "You might even want another before you go to bed. Cheers!"

It looked like Ian was settling in for a long night, which didn't seem right to Tanya. He had an early start tomorrow. A meeting with another bank. And he'd want a clear head, so why was he talking about drinking more after this one?

Martin had raised his glass in response to Ian's, and was smiling agreeably back at him. She felt distinctly excluded, and couldn't understand why. After all, *she* was the one who'd brought Martin into the house. *She* was the one who'd offered him a place to stay. But now wasn't the time to find out. It would inevitably mean arousing Ian's suspicions, and while she had no qualms about hurting him, she wanted out of the marriage on *her* terms. Tomorrow morning, when Ian was out, she could talk to Martin and find out what was going on.

"Do you mind if I turn the telly off?" Ian asked her. Too politely? He must know the programme bored the pants off her.

"Not at all." She smiled sweetly at him. Was that *too* much? She took a gulp of her gin and tonic. Or was she becoming paranoid? "I think I'll leave you two after all. It sounds like you need some *Man* time, and I need my beauty sleep."

It was an innocent enough comment, but almost guaranteed to result in protestations that beauty sleep was completely unnecessary in her case.

"Fair enough," Ian said distractedly, switching the TV off.

"Have a good night," was all Martin had to add.

Not sure whether to be offended, annoyed, suspicious or concerned, Tanya finished her drink.

TWENTY-TWO

The gate clattered against the post. The breeze had developed into a strong wind, snatching the gate from his grip. It wasn't like him to be caught out like that. Further evidence that he was distracted. He cursed as he caught the gate in his hand – probably too late. Chances were that the noise would have been heard from within the farmhouse.

Carefully, he eased the gate closed, and turned to face the house. A low light seeped out at the edges of the blind in the kitchen window. Too low to come from the kitchen itself. He suspected it came from one of the living rooms. Moving with his usual stealth, he crossed the yard, reaching the door in a few strides. He rested his hand on the knob for a moment, listening for any sound coming from inside. If he really strained his hearing, he could make out a low muttering. Definitely further into the house. Perhaps they hadn't heard the gate after all.

Gripping the knob, he turned it and was surprised when the door opened. A cold gust blew past him, rattling pans that he knew were hanging up from one of the beams in the kitchen. The muttering stopped. He stepped inside quickly, closing the door behind him. The key was in the lock. He turned it.

Tentative footsteps had replaced the low voices. He recognised the tread on the wooden floorboards in the hallway that lay beyond a half open door on the other side of the room. There was no point in using stealth now, he realised. He flipped the nearest light switch as he moved swiftly across the kitchen. They almost collided as they reached the doorway at the same time.

"Why's the door unlocked?" he demanded. He should have been angry, but he'd found from experience that anger was very difficult to maintain with the woman he was looking at.

Jennifer Hawthorn's hair was light brown, almost to the point of being blonde. Her olive skin and bright blue eyes contrasted with her hair to give her an exotic appearance. Undoubtedly in generations past there had been mixed parentage, but exactly what that mix was would be impossible to establish. She was five feet five and a half inches in height. She wouldn't try to round up to five and a half feet, but she wasn't prepared to negotiate on that extra half inch. From some people, that pedantry would be irritating. From Jennifer it was endearing.

Inevitably, he found himself staring at her, drinking in her beauty. After so many years – decades even – of being together, he was still very grateful to have her as his wife. And even more grateful to see his love for her reflected in her eyes. How lucky was *he* to have earned the love of this amazing woman?

She reached out and put both arms around him, pressing herself against his body. "I'm sorry," she said. And he knew she understood that his concern was for her safety. "We just thought it would be easier for *you*." Then she pulled back and looked up at him, her brow creased with worry. "There isn't any danger is there?"

As she said this, he was aware of movement to his right. Adam looked over at his sister, who had just come out of the sitting room. The pair of them had obviously been waiting for him in there. Her expression was very serious, questioning.

There was no easy way to break it to them.

"He's here."

PART TWO

FEEL THE FEAR

ONE

Going with Martin for the walk in the woods had clearly taken its toll. Tanya wasn't used to that amount of exercise or fresh air, so she'd fallen into a deep sleep almost as soon as her head hit the pillow. She had no idea what time Ian had come up and joined her. When she looked at the alarm clock after being woken up by the creak of the wardrobe door, she was surprised to see that it wasn't yet quarter past seven. And from the relative liveliness of his movements around the bedroom, she guessed he'd already been up for a while. She'd pulled the duvet over her head and pressed the right side of her head into the pillow, hoping that with one ear incapacitated she'd minimise the disturbance.

Inevitably, she couldn't go back to sleep, but at least her waking was a more gradual process. And, as she woke, she started to think.

Ian's meeting with the bank was scheduled for ten o'clock. This meeting was only in Westfield, so he didn't need to leave until 9:15. She knew plenty of people who would leave it until 9:30. But she also knew that Ian would be ultra-cautious. He'd want to make a good impression, so he would give himself extra time, then wait around outside the bank until a couple of minutes to ten. That way he'd be confident of being punctual... which always seemed to help in his negotiations.

The question was: what was he doing up and about this early? He always showered and ate breakfast before dressing, so she knew he must have been up no later than 6:30. By the time she'd reached this point in her thinking, she could hear him gargling. She lifted the covers half-heartedly to look at the clock again. It wasn't even 7:30 yet. But gargling meant he was almost ready, which meant he'd be leaving within the next five to ten minutes.

Whatever his reason for going this early – and she could think of several – it began to dawn on her that she was being presented with a fantastic opportunity. At the very least, the meeting with the bank would last half an hour. It could very well go on for a lot longer. And if it started late – Ian might be punctual, but bank managers generally weren't – it could be well past eleven before he left. But even if she assumed the worst-case scenario, he wouldn't be back at the farm before 11:00. And if he was gone by twenty to eight, that gave her over three hours in the house with Martin. Curled up under the duvet, she allowed her fingers to wander just as her mind did.

Only to be interrupted by the mattress sinking at the side of her. Guiltily, she snatched her arm back, disguising the movement by lifting the covers from her head.

"Sorry to disturb you." His voice was soft, little more than a whisper. "Just wanted to let you know I was going."

She forced a smile. "I'm sure it'll go well," she said, and she meant it. If anyone could handle the money side it was Ian. More importantly, if anyone could handle the *people* with the money, he could.

He nodded an acknowledgement, though he didn't

look as convinced as she thought he should. "I'll see you later." He didn't attempt to kiss her, for which she was grateful. Instead, he just stood up and left the room. She heard him on the stairs, and for several minutes there was some movement downstairs. Eventually, she heard the kitchen door open and close. All the time, listening carefully, willing him on, and forcing herself to wait for him to go. Much as she wanted to jump out of bed, she knew she couldn't be too hasty. Even after she'd heard the door close, she strained her hearing, waiting for the sound of the Land Rover starting.

She didn't like the vehicle at all. Ian would argue that it was practical for getting around on the land, and in the countryside. But Tanya wasn't interested in practical. She wanted sleek lines, distinctive colours, and an engine that made heads turn. The engine was the only advantage the Land Rover had as far as she was concerned. Not because it sounded good, but because it was loud and distinctive. It acted as an early warning system if she was doing something she shouldn't be. Fortunately, it had served this purpose on only one occasion so far. But it was equally good at clearly announcing its departure so she knew when the coast was clear.

Which it did for her thirty seconds after the kitchen door closed. She listened to the engine noise rise in volume as Ian warmed it up, then the pitch changed as he set off, and moments later it was fading away as he drove out of the yard and turned on to the track.

Less than a minute later, she was in the shower.

★ ★ ★

By ten to eight, she was at the bottom of the stairs. In spite of her experience at seducing men, she had hesitated over her preparations. Her entrance had to have an effect, and that meant getting her appearance right. Different men found different things exciting. Tanya was quite capable of catering to all tastes, from the near-virginal look to the complete slut – and had the exciting memories to prove it. Working out what would do the trick was normally easy enough, but Martin was difficult to read. In the end, she'd decided to keep things relatively simple – a silk kimono-style dressing gown that came no lower than mid-thigh. It clung to her body, leaving any onlooker in no doubt that she was naked beneath it.

The wooden floor of the hallway gave way to cold quarry tiles in the kitchen. A glance out the window and into the yard confirmed Ian hadn't returned while she was in the shower. Not wanting her feet to freeze, she hurried to the other side of the room. She didn't mind the cold, but was thinking ahead, and didn't want to give Martin a shock when she climbed into his bed – not that kind of a shock anyway.

Fortunately, the floor in the annexe hallway was carpeted. At the end of it, she could see the bedroom door was slightly ajar. Inviting, perhaps? A part of her wanted to savour the anticipation, but there was also some apprehension. In spite of her previous successes with members of the opposite sex, she still had some doubts as far as Martin was concerned. The lack of time was a bigger driver, though. She might have until eleven before Ian returned, but he would be expecting to find her showered, dressed, breakfasted and the washing up all done. If she was going to make the most of this opportunity, she didn't have time for hesitation.

Pushing the door open, she stepped quietly over the threshold. It would be good to sneak into his bed while he slept. She had a whole range of ways she could gently – erotically – wake him up. Even as this thought was filtering through her mind, she realised her plans might be thwarted.

His bedclothes had been pushed back. The sheets were still rumpled from where he'd lain, and the pillow showed the indent his head had made. She glanced towards the shower room. The door there was half open, the only light coming through was from the small window in there.

It crossed her mind to climb into the bed. *That* would be a surprise for him. But something didn't seem right. There was no sound, not running water or even the splash of urine flowing into the toilet bowl.

Crossing the room, she popped her head into the en-suite. It was empty.

A minute later, she'd established he wasn't in any of the other rooms in the annexe. Within five minutes, she knew he wasn't anywhere in the house. Irritated and frustrated, she returned to her bedroom. She'd worked up an itch that needed scratching. Lying back on the bed, focusing on her own needs, she didn't consider where Martin was or what he was up to.

TWO

"We didn't 'ear anything," John Payne said, shaking his head. "Not that we'd've been listening out for it…" He tailed off, clearly at a loss for words. It was obvious the man was still in a state of shock.

He was standing behind the counter. In front of him was the tiered confectionary display, an array of chocolate bars and sweet packets that reminded Brian Oakes of his schooldays. Only six years ago, yet a wholly different way of life. Long gone were the visits to the newsagents on his way home from school, a ritual that seemed as if it would last forever. A selection of goodies at least as wide-ranging as the one Payne was resting his hands on the back of. And yet he'd found himself still buying the same things every day: Opal Fruits and a finger of Fudge. Sickly sweet and all the better for it. These days he'd be more likely to stop off at the pub on his way home.

Brian glanced around the shop. It wasn't a big place. Apart from the counter there was a single shelving rack in the middle of the floor, as well as shelves on the walls either side of the store. The windows were directly opposite the counter, and stretched floor to ceiling, giving a clear view of the row of houses on the other side of the street. The goods on offer were the usual mish-mash of things you'd expect to buy in a village shop: magazines, tinned food, breakfast cereals, bread, a limited supply of fresh vegetables. He looked again. Well, maybe *fresh* was optimistic. Without looking at the price tags, he knew everything would be over-priced, but they were only likely to be bought in an emergency anyway. Under those circumstances, he supposed you wouldn't mind paying over the odds. So he couldn't understand why there were two customers in right now actually filling their shopping baskets.

When he turned back to look at Payne, he was unsurprised to see that the shopkeeper's face gave no indication he'd been aware of the young constable's lack of attention. Mrs Payne was another matter. She was standing in a boxed-off area to the right of the main counter. This was the official face of the Post Office. The expression on *her* face made it clear that she wasn't suffering from shock. He got the impression she wanted the bastards who'd stolen their van strung up and left alone with her and a baseball bat for half an hour.

Nodding towards the two customers, Brian said: "It would be helpful if we could talk about this without any interruptions. Is there anyone who could help out while I take all the details off you?" He pulled his notebook out as he spoke, hoping they'd get the message that he was taking their situation seriously – and so should they.

The chances were that they were probably impressed that he was there at all. They'd reported the van stolen at eight o'clock this morning, and it was only ten-thirty now, a fast response for a case like this, especially with them being out in the sticks. Not that he was inclined to tell them, but the only reason they were seeing him this soon was the fact that he was already due to visit Lodge Farm this morning. Although it wasn't expected that the gruesome accident yesterday would lead to accusations of criminal action, the injuries had been sufficient to warrant a referral by the hospital to the police. Conscious of the need to stay within budgets, the Desk Sergeant had told Brian he might as well pull this one in while he was in the village.

Behind the counter, John Payne hadn't budged or changed his expression. Mrs Payne, on the other hand, was leaning through an opening at the back of her cubicle. Brian realised he hadn't noticed it before. It reminded him of a serving hatch his grandparents had between their kitchen and dining room. Watching the postmistress, he let his gaze fall to her bottom, which was pushed out towards him. *Nice arse*, he thought. She pulled her head back and turned towards him. *Shame about the face.* He guessed she might have been attractive once. It was difficult to tell how old she was. Whatever age, she hadn't worn well. Her hair was blonde, but shot through with grey. Face pasty and creased with wrinkles. He couldn't even be generous and call them laughter lines, because there was no sign of good humour. There was just a weariness that emanated from her.

Not that her husband looked much better. His age was easier to guess. Brian would put him in his mid-fifties. Silver-grey hair, thick-set and thick-jowled, his complexion ruddy in a manner that spoke more of a fondness for alcohol than the great outdoors. The large, dark-rimmed glasses served to make his eyes look small and sunken in his fleshy face.

A door in the Post Office cubicle opened and Mrs Payne's head poked round the side of it.

"We can't leave the shop unattended. My daughter'll be here in a moment to look after the till, but we'll need to stay close in case she needs any help."

That seemed okay to Brian. He just didn't want interruptions from the customers if they decided they wanted to pay for their shopping. A glance at their baskets did make him wonder how they'd managed to find so much to buy in this place. And they were still perusing the shelves.

The sound of a door opening brought his attention back to the counter area. The door in question was behind the counter and on the opposite side to the Post Office cubicle. He watched as a young woman emerged cautiously, her eyes cast down shyly. If this was the daughter, Brian could see why he'd thought Mrs Payne might have been attractive when she was younger. Her features, even from this awkward angle were clearly those of her mother. The rounded nose, the wide mouth, the pale skin with freckles dusting her cheeks and nose. Her hair was long and loose. As she moved, it was almost as if she used it to hide behind.

"Come on, Helen!" Mrs Payne said impatiently. John didn't even seem to be aware she was there. Apparently startled by the sharpness of her mother's voice, Helen jumped a little, her shoulders rising, her right hand briefly coming into view. Nodding, her lips moving in a silent apology, she hurried past her father and into the cubicle. A moment later, he saw her settle on to the stool behind the desk. Light reflected off the glass screen, obscuring his view of her. Still, there was something…

"Right!" It was Mrs Payne, closing the door behind her. "Let's get on with this, shall we?" Without the door or the bandit screen in the way, he heard her voice for the first time and realised she wasn't a local. He wasn't very good with accents, but he knew a strange one when he heard it.

Pushing her husband ahead of her, she moved out into the shop. John Payne was shaking his head in disbelief, though Brian was pretty confident this wasn't because he was being shoved around. He guessed the shopkeeper accepted that as a normal part of his life.

As they came to a stop in front of him, Brian could hear John muttering: "Why would they do that?"

"What do you want to know?" Although he suspected he'd need to use kid gloves with John Payne, there was clearly no need for that with his wife.

He fought back a sigh, and raised his pen. "I know your husband has already given some details to my colleagues at the station, but I always think it's best to hear it from the…" He hesitated as he glanced up to see Mrs Payne's bared teeth. "…source," he finished lamely. "Perhaps you could tell me everything from the beginning." He looked at each of them in turn, though that was more on the off-chance that he might see some reaction from John than any expectation he might contribute anything verbally.

"Just so unnecessary…" His voice tailed off as his eyes seemed to focus on a spot just over Brian's shoulder. The policeman knew there was nothing there.

In contrast to her husband's ramblings, Mrs Payne spoke clearly and precisely. Her tone gave him no cause to doubt her annoyance at the theft of the van, but she was clearly not affected by it in the same way as John.

"Something woke us up in the night. There was a scraping sound."

"Like something being dragged?" Brian suggested, wanting to give his notes more clarity.

"No, like fingernails on a blackboard."

He looked up sharply, but she ignored him.

"It actually sounded as if it was coming from the bedroom window, though obviously it couldn't have been as it's upstairs and there's no way to get up to it. Still, when it's the middle of the night and it wakes you up, you don't think straight, do you?" She didn't wait for an answer. "It was scary, though. Like something from a vampire film."

Brian had a flashback to a film he'd seen: a deathly white teenager with barely concealed fangs floated outside a bedroom window demanding to be let in. He had to make a conscious effort not to shiver. Fortunately, Mrs Payne was oblivious to this as she carried on.

"We were both frightened by it, though *he* probably wouldn't admit it." Brian couldn't help thinking that John Payne looked as if he'd be hard pressed to hide being frightened. "So we did the only thing we could. We pulled the covers over our heads and tried to pretend it wasn't there." She spoke in a very matter of fact way, yet she was talking about acting like a child afraid of the monster in the cupboard. "It must have worked eventually because the alarm woke us. Don't remember falling asleep, but I do remember the bloody alarm going off." She smiled at that. It didn't last long, but Brian caught a glimpse of a different woman for a moment, a woman who *had* enjoyed a sense of humour once. "Anyway, we came downstairs for breakfast, and it was gone."

"The van?"

"Well of course the van. We haven't reported anything

169

else stolen, have we?" The sarcasm seemed to thicken her accent, and he recognised it as Welsh, though identifying which part of Wales would always be a gap in his skills.

"I'm sorry, Mrs Payne. I just want to make sure I don't miss anything important. It doesn't pay to make too many assumptions." Not sure she was convinced by his explanation, he went on: "So how did you know it was gone?"

"Well, it wasn't there," she said, looking at him as if he was a complete idiot.

"What I meant was, what were the circumstances in which you discovered it wasn't there?" *Honestly, some people needed spoon-feeding.*

Not looking particularly satisfied, Mrs Payne said: "The van's always parked just outside the kitchen window. When we came into the kitchen, we could see it was missing."

"And what did you do then?"

"John went outside and had a good look around. There was no sign of it." She gestured in the direction of the driveway that ran alongside the shop. "You can go and have a look yourself if you don't believe me."

"I wasn't suggesting that I didn't believe you," he assured her, starting to wonder if both husband *and* wife were a bit light in the marbles department. Trying to keep her on track, he carried on with his questions. "Was there anything of value in the van itself?"

"No. We use it for picking up stock from the wholesalers, and the last time we were there was the end of last week. It's been empty for days."

Ordinarily, he would ask what type of van it was at this point, but he didn't want to be subjected to more sarcasm. Instead he checked his notes. "I see it's a navy blue Sherpa. Nineteen eighty-four model." As he confirmed the registration number with them, he was aware of one of the shoppers heading for the counter. Mrs Payne cast an anxious glance in the direction of her daughter.

"No need..." John muttered. "Evil..." He shook his head slowly, marvelling at something he didn't seem likely to share with them.

Choosing to ignore him for the moment, Brian asked Mrs Payne: "Have you had any similar incidents in the past?"

"No."

"Anything unusual happened recently?"

"No."

From her attitude so far, he'd expected her to give him some stick over this line of questioning, but she was distracted, her eyes flickering rapidly back and forth between him and the counter. The customer, an old woman – Brian guessed she must be at least eighty – had lifted her basket on to the counter top at the side of the cubicle. Helen had disappeared from view, and the door was opening.

"Do you count what happened to Peter as being unusual?" The question came from behind him, taking him by surprise. Turning, he saw the second customer. She was a lot younger than the first one, probably about the same age as his mum – fiftyish. Not bad looking if you liked the older woman. Brian didn't particularly, but he was happy to take a look. And she was certainly easier on the eye than Mrs Payne.

"Peter who?" he asked.

"Peter Salthouse. He was badly injured by a plough yesterday."

Oh, *that* Peter.

"Well, I'll grant you that was unusual," he said, "but it was an accident."

"Are you sure it was an accident?"

That stopped him in his tracks. No one at the station had suggested anything untoward had happened. He made a mental note to check in with them before he called at the farm.

"You may have a point, and I'll take it into account. Even so, I was thinking more along the lines of things going missing, strangers being around, that kind of thing."

"Patrick Gates's son." The woman said it as if she'd experienced a sudden revelation.

"I'm sorry?" He was beginning to feel as if he was making enquiries in Wonderland. Out of the corner of his eye, he saw Helen putting some cans into a shopping bag for the elderly customer. It was just a glimpse, but something there seemed surreal as well. Before he could take a proper look, his attention was caught by Mrs Payne's strident tones.

"What do you mean, Norma?" she was asking. There was concern in her voice. Brian had been standing almost directly between the two of them, but she had stepped around him so she could look at the customer properly.

"Not Matthew or Colin," Norma said, as if by way of explanation.

"Martin?" The name was spoken in a hushed tone, which surprised Brian.

Norma thought for a moment. "Yes, I'm sure that's what he called himself."

Before he started to feel like a Wimbledon spectator, Brian decided to re-enter the discussion. "Who's Martin? And what's so unusual about him?"

"Well, he just turned up yesterday. From what I've heard, he's been gone from the village for a long time. I don't think anyone expected to see him again."

Mrs Payne had turned to her husband and gripped his hand. Her anger had been replaced by something else. Fear? Maybe that was too strong a word for it, but this news had obviously shaken her. Though what comfort she thought John could offer her was beyond Brian.

"Has anything else happened since he turned up?"

"Apart from Peter nearly dying under a plough?"

"Are you seriously suggesting…"

"Who knows? But he's been in my pub twice already and you could have cut the atmosphere with a knife both times."

"A knife…" John muttered.

Brian had hoped he could ignore Payne's ramblings, but there was something quite painful in the way he had spoken. "Are you all right, John?"

The shopkeeper looked up at him through watery eyes. "How can I be all right?" He sounded astonished at the question. "After what they did to Charlie?"

That sense of the surreal struck him again. As he collected his thoughts, he let his gaze run around the shop. Behind the counter, Helen was closing the till. The old lady was lifting her bag down. It caught on the corner of the display where the mints were. Helen reached forward and helped to release it. And seeing her hands clearly for the first time, Brian thought he really must have fallen down the rabbit hole.

"What's happened to Charlie?" Norma asked, bringing his attention back.

"Who *is* Charlie?" His training must have kicked in, because he hadn't consciously thought the question.

"He's their dog, a black lab."

He looked at John and it finally dawned on him that his distress had nothing to do with the stolen van. Something else suddenly occurred to him. Earlier on, John had said they hadn't heard anything. And yet his wife had talked about the scary sounds at the window. He'd assumed John was talking about the van and had just been confused.

"What did they do to Charlie, John?"

But the shopkeeper just shook his head, unable to say the words.

"You'll have to see for yourself," Mrs Payne said. Her voice was tender now as she held her husband's hand, comforting him. "He's at the back of the house."

Brian found the dog covered by an old blanket. He'd left the others in the shop. The form beneath the blanket didn't look particularly dog-shaped, but then he didn't have a lot of experience of dead ones. Bending down, he lifted a corner and peered under it. Bluebottles buzzed out and back in again. The smell that came out with them caught in the back of his throat. He wrinkled his nose and pressed his lips tightly together. It didn't make much difference.

Lifting the blanket hadn't really allowed him to see much. Just the pads on the base of a paw. They looked as if they'd been cut. Blood was smeared across them. Standing up, he lifted the blanket aside so he could see properly.

And immediately regretted it.

THREE

Martin had grown used to constant sunshine. He'd lived in the Canary Islands for the last ten years, and before that he'd travelled around the Med, going where the work was. The camper van he'd bought and fixed up had lasted long enough to get him to Rhodes before it gave up the ghost. It had served its purpose – a means of transport, and a place to sleep, so he didn't have to pay for accommodation. He had money, but he didn't have loads of it.

In those early years, he'd lost count of the number of times people had expressed their admiration for him. "That's such a brave thing to do," they'd say – or words to that effect. "Just leaving home and hoping for the best. What if the money runs out?"

That wasn't an option. He found work wherever he went. It didn't matter what it was, or how badly paid. He could save money by sleeping in the van, but he still had to eat. As for bravery? He hadn't felt brave. When you don't have a choice, bravery doesn't come into it.

But he'd settled into the new life, and it had served its purpose. Shortly after the van died on him, he'd been offered the chance to help crew a yacht. The owner had retired and was sailing wherever the fancy took him. He'd arrived in port with some friends, but they'd abandoned him for some reason. Martin never found out for sure, but after a week of listening to him bragging about how he'd made his money, he had a pretty good idea why. When they moored at Puerto del Carmen, he followed their example.

It was the beginning of November, and the temperature was in the high seventies. The Med had been warm, but not that warm. He'd stayed. Not in one town – or even one island – for long, but he liked the climate, and he rubbed along well enough with the locals, including all the other ex-pats who had settled there. For variety, he occasionally joined sailing trips to Morocco or, if he was feeling particularly adventurous, up to Madeira. But he had everything he needed. A place to sleep – always plenty of choice on holiday islands – enough work to allow him to feed and clothe himself, and heat.

He'd expected it to be colder here in England, but the weather was more tolerable than he'd anticipated. The clouds were few and far between, and there was no breeze today. Not that he was reliant on the weather to keep him warm. He'd been walking for the last four hours and had already stripped down to a T-shirt, his jumper tied around his waist.

This morning he was getting his bearings. He'd made his presence felt in the village yesterday, though whether that was a good or bad thing, he wasn't sure. Today, he needed to remind himself of the lay of the land. He usually had a pretty good sense of direction. You needed it when you were at sea, but the advantage there was having the sun to guide you. In the woods, it wasn't always easy to see.

He'd started in the clearing again. When Ian had quizzed him last night about what had happened, he'd offered to show him.

"But that was this afternoon," Ian had said. "What are the chances of it happening again in the morning? I've never seen anything like that."

"The ravens'll still be there," Martin assured him.

So they'd gone together first thing. Ian had explained about his meeting, so he'd have to go early or wait until the afternoon. Martin was happy with early. He knew he'd got a lot of ground to cover. They'd travelled most of the way in the Land Rover. Ian had taken a different route that meant the walk was shorter. More importantly, it meant he could head straight off for his meeting.

This time, Martin didn't go right into the clearing. He remained ten feet or so outside its perimeter. As he'd predicted, the trees were filled with ravens, and more arrived while they were there. There was an eeriness about the scene. He sensed that Ian was aware of it too. The pair of them stood quietly for more than five minutes, just absorbing what they could see.

When it was time for Ian to go, he seemed to do so reluctantly. Martin knew they would talk about it again later.

They'd hit it off well last night over their whisky. That had surprised him. The meal at *The Oak* had been pleasant enough, but he hadn't really gained much of a sense of his unwilling host. He realised now that the reason for that was Tanya. With her out of the way, a different Ian emerged, and Martin found that he liked him. He hoped it wouldn't be necessary to cause him any pain.

Left alone, he'd started walking. He took no obvious direction. At times he meandered, picking up trails when he came across them. Sometimes he would emerge from the woods. If there was a pathway, he might follow it. If not, he would walk along the tree line until he came to a hedge or fence and use that as his guide for a while. In either case, he would be drawn back to the wood before long, and within it he would pass randomly from one side to another. By doing this, he was able to explore the land that lay all around the village.

When he crossed from one side of the main road to the other, he made sure he was on the western edge of the village. A few yards to his right was a T-junction. The signs showed him which way to turn for Thornberry and Woodhead. He ignored them. Instead, he re-entered the woods and used them to conceal his route as he circled around the other side of the village.

The countryside around Ravens Gathering was still dominated by trees. Sherwood Forest was generally considered to be about ten miles south of here, but in times gone by it had covered a large part of the county, and even stretched up into Yorkshire. The woods around the village had undoubtedly formed part of Sherwood at some time in history. Trees had been felled to make way for farmland or housing since mediaeval times. So the village was effectively surrounded by the wood.

It was shortly after eleven when Martin reached the other end of the village, crossed the road again and began to circle back. At that point, he'd guessed he might be another couple of hours before he returned to the farmhouse, and he was becoming aware of the fact that he hadn't had breakfast yet.

Half an hour later, he stumbled into a different farmyard.

Naturally, any landowner makes sure there are boundaries clearly marked out. Martin had been ignoring these markers – even barbed wire fencing – as he'd walked. The reality with farm land is that there is generally a lot of it. As a result, the chances are that you can cross it at many times of day without seeing a soul. Very often even cattle will steer clear of you. So he hadn't really been too concerned about what he considered to be his minor acts of trespass. He just made sure he kept far enough away from the buildings to be out of sight. Until he found a farmyard where he wasn't expecting one.

He was caught out because the farm house and farm buildings had been built in a natural bowl in the landscape. There were three openings in the surrounding slopes. One presumably led to the main road, a second must have gone out into the farmland itself, and the third led into the woods. That was the one Martin was on. It curved downwards, concealing the presence of the farmyard until the last possible moment. The instant Martin could see the yard, anyone in it would be able to see him well enough to make out his features.

Motion attracts the eyes, so he stopped moving as soon as he realised his mistake. Very slowly, he turned his head, taking in the view in front of him.

During his childhood, he had spent hours roaming through the woods and across the farmland that surrounded the village. He thought he had seen every part of it. But he'd obviously overlooked this one, because it didn't look remotely familiar.

To the left was the farm house, a large red brick building. From this angle, he could see two sides of it, so he could gauge the depth as well as the width. The house could accommodate a big family, possibly two. Unlike Ian and Tanya's place, the farmhouse didn't have a wall around it separating it from the rest of the buildings. Whoever lived here was clearly happy for work and home to merge into one.

Scanning to the right, Martin saw some single story outbuildings about twenty yards away from the house. They were painted white, but he could tell they were made of breeze blocks. He guessed they might be storerooms and possibly a small workshop. Further along there was a barn. One of the doors was open slightly, but he couldn't see inside. Beyond the barn were some stables. The doors faced the farmhouse. There were four of them, two of which had the top half open. He could see shadows shifting inside, though whether they were horse or human he couldn't tell.

So that meant there were three possible places from which he could be spotted: the stables, the barn, or from inside the house. But there was no reaction to his presence. Everything seemed perfectly still. It was almost too quiet.

He counted to a hundred twice, but no one came out to challenge him. They were either waiting for him to make a move, or they weren't bothered by his presence.

His intention this morning had been to explore, but without getting too close to the locals. This was new territory, though. As he watched for signs of life, he decided he should have a look around. The worst that could happen was that he'd be asked to leave. He could live with that.

So he walked into the yard.

The shadows *had* been horses. They poked their heads out so he could pat them when they spotted him. He wasn't an expert on horses, but was surprised to see they were in such good shape. He might have expected to see healthy animals that were good for riding along bridleways and country lanes, but these looked more like racehorses. And friendly too. They were obviously used to being well treated. Stroking their necks was oddly soothing – Martin hadn't realised he was so tense – and it was something of an effort to tear himself away.

His next port of call was the barn. It was clearly used for storage. To the right as he came in, there was a collection of equipment that he guessed must be for attaching to the back of a tractor. He recognised a plough, but the rest was a mystery to him. The tractor itself was parked alongside them. It looked like it had seen better times, its red paintwork faded almost to orange, the seat cracked and worn, which was hardly surprising as there was no cab to protect it. Martin guessed it must be even older than he was.

The other side of the barn was piled high with crates filled with vegetables. The earthy smell was strong, but not unpleasant. They looked like they were waiting to be collected and delivered to a local market or a wholesaler. He walked to the back of the barn, curious to see what else might be hidden away. But there was nothing. The barn was less than half full.

He expected the other outbuildings to be locked, but they weren't. As he'd thought, one of the doors hid a workshop. The tools seemed antiquated, but had clearly been looked after. They were displayed in an orderly manner. Every hook had something hanging from it; shelving was in convenient reach of the two workbenches;

any sets of tools were placed together and organised in order of size.

Two more doors revealed storage for grain and seeds of various types. A fourth door led to an outside loo. He stared at the polished dark wood seat for a moment. He couldn't recall having seen a square one before. The high level cistern was clearly ancient, but appeared to be in excellent condition. What with this and the old tractor, it looked as if the place belonged to a farmer who was well past his prime. Perhaps the reason he hadn't been disturbed was because the old duffer was too deaf to hear him.

There was just the house to look at now. Not that he was planning any breaking and entering. He just wanted to have a scout around, which took him only a couple of minutes. There was no sign of life inside. The kitchen door was partially open. He saw the table in the middle of the room, and stepped inside to take a closer look. Bowls and plates were set out haphazardly. It wasn't clear how many people would have been catered for. Maybe three or four. There were six chairs around the table, and four of them were pushed back carelessly from it. A half-eaten apple lay on its side, the exposed flesh a light brown colour. In a bowl, a pear was in a similar state. A loaf of bread sat in the middle of the table, the knife still embedded in it where it was being sliced. Nearby a slice lay on a plate, bites taken from it. At the closest edge was a mug, two-thirds full, its contents disguised by a thin creamy film across the top. Three tumblers were scattered amongst the crockery, only partially filled with water. The rims smudged where they had been drunk from.

This was breakfast, and whoever was eating it had been interrupted.

Martin looked around the kitchen, searching for the crocodile. He stepped back outside. There was nothing there either. The place was deserted.

Across the yard, he heard one of the horses moving around in its stable. It was the only sound. No birds, no breeze rustling nearby trees, not even a car on the road. He realised that was the key. The road wasn't busy, but there would be the occasional vehicle. Certainly more than one every fifteen minutes, and he'd been here for longer than that. He couldn't hear anything because they were surrounded by a natural barrier. The grassy mounds that formed the bowl around the farmyard kept most noises out.

Smiling, he recognised that he'd allowed himself to be spooked. This was one of the most tranquil spots he'd ever been in. And the fact that the people who lived here had been disturbed could have been caused by anything. Granny had fallen and been rushed to hospital; a farmhand calling for help with cattle that had broken through a fence; the realisation that they were simply late for something. True it was odd that they'd left the house unlocked, but sometimes these things were forgotten about in the rush. He knew things weren't right in the village, but he couldn't assume everything he experienced was connected to it.

It was time to move on. He couldn't honestly say his curiosity had been fully satisfied, but he'd have to make do for now. Crossing the yard, he headed for the opening that he guessed would take him across the farm. He didn't want to go back the way he'd come, and he had no desire to return to the road.

At the stables, he stopped to stroke the horses.

They nuzzled him playfully. For a few moments, he let everything else slip from his mind. He had no real experience with horses. They'd been around during his childhood, but only those ridden around the lanes by a select few of the villagers. He'd never ridden one, or even helped out in stables. Yet he felt drawn to them, and enjoyed the warmth they showed him, with no requirement for him to give them anything back other than the palm of his hand as it ran up and down their necks. It would be very easy to just stay here and share time with these wonderful animals.

Even as he became aware of that idea, he heard a sound behind him. Footsteps. Turning, he saw a tall woman walk out of the barn. She was about fifty yards away, so it was difficult to tell, but he guessed she was almost six foot. Her hair was long and dark and tied back in a ponytail. She wore a work shirt, jeans and boots he would normally have associated with a labourer. Yet she walked with an elegance that belied her masculine attire. He caught only a glimpse of her face before she headed for the house. That first, brief impression suggested she was in her thirties. And attractive. Not in the sexy, sophisticated way that Tanya McLean was. Nor did he immediately think of her as a classic beauty. But there was definitely something about her...

She obviously hadn't spotted him, though. And as she had just emerged from a building that had been empty only minutes earlier, he pushed any thoughts of attraction from his mind as he began to wonder how that had happened. It seemed judicious at this point to conceal himself. The edge of the stable block was only a couple of feet away. Patting the nearest horse in a gentle goodbye, he moved around the corner, glancing back to make sure she hadn't turned and seen him. She hadn't, but two more people were coming out of the barn. Two men this time.

Ducking out of sight, he didn't see the taller of the two men look in his direction and smile to himself.

FOUR

Driving back from his meeting, Ian was feeling pleased with himself. The bank manager *had* been caught on the hop by his promptness. Together with Ian's confident manner – accomplished through years of practice – he'd been easy to persuade of the merits of the renegotiated loan. He had at least three months of breathing space. It wasn't enough to allow him to sit back and relax, but it would be one less distraction so he could focus on the important job of getting the cottages built and sold – or finding another solution to their problems.

Not that he could do anything practical about that until he was home. With the worry about the bank out of the way, he allowed himself to reflect on his conversation with Martin the night before. He'd expected it to be awkward, especially when Tanya showed no signs of going to bed before their guest returned from visiting his family. Her decision to leave them alone had made it easier. Even so, in spite of his many years of experience of dealing with people, he still wasn't sure how to tactfully go about accusing someone of having a fling with his wife.

Martin broached the subject first.

"It must have seemed strange seeing Tanya holding my hand."

Ian hadn't realised that either of them had been aware

he was watching them when they crossed the farmyard. His experience told him to keep his mouth shut and listen.

"Who was the band that sang When You're in Love With a Beautiful Woman?"

Dr. Hook, Ian thought. The nail had been hit squarely on the head.

"I used to listen to those words and wonder what it would be like to feel all that insecurity and jealousy." Martin seemed to be gazing into space as he said this, a rueful half-smile on his face. "Still wonder sometimes." His focus returned to Ian. "I'm guessing you *do* know what it's like." He paused, but must have realised that Ian had no desire to interrupt him. "She *was* genuinely disturbed by what she experienced in the clearing. I think she just took my hand because she needed to feel comforted." His smile broadened, but it was an awkward one. He shrugged, and that didn't seem very natural either. "I'm not sure *I* was the right person to offer comfort, but I was the only one there at the time."

He glanced towards the door, as if expecting Tanya to storm in and confront them over talking about her behind her back. The door, slightly ajar, didn't move. Ian had heard the familiar creaks of the floorboards overhead, and knew she was well beyond earshot.

"If you *are* concerned about me being here, I will understand," Martin had continued. "It's too late for me to find anywhere else to sleep tonight, so I'd prefer it if you let me stay till morning. But I can be gone first thing."

His candour was disarming, and Ian had felt his reservations diminish. He knew it would be impossible for them to disappear altogether. As the song said, you watch your friends and you look for lies. He hadn't caught her out yet, but he had his suspicions. And there was no guarantee that Martin was telling the truth. But as they talked, he felt more at ease with their guest, and when he went on to describe the events in the clearing, Ian was intrigued. Which was why they'd arranged to leave early in the morning so he could see for himself.

And it *had* been very spooky. Ian had walked through the woods many times, often passing through, and occasionally even stopping in, the clearing. There had never been anything out of the ordinary there before. No strange sights, no palpable sensations. This morning, it had been like visiting a completely different site. The layout was identical. Nothing had altered physically, apart from the congregation of birds. Yet he felt as if it was his first time there. Much as he wanted to be able to explain that to himself – let alone anyone else – he couldn't.

Leaving to go to his meeting had been harder than he'd imagined. There was something about the place that he felt drawn to. But he was also aware that it must be similar to the way a rodent is hypnotised by a snake. He was drawn to it, yet it felt threatening.

As he wound the Land Rover through country lanes, that thought seemed preposterous. Overhead, the sun was shining down. Nearing the village, on either side of him, the ever-present trees had given way briefly to open farmland. In the distance a herd of cows stood idly looking around themselves. All was well with the world. Deep inside, though, he knew he'd felt something that suggested all was *not* well with the world.

Turning off the road and up the track that took him

home, it occurred to him that maybe it wasn't the clearing. The other common factor for both Tanya and him had been that they had Martin with them. That thought didn't stay with him for long. As he pulled into the farmyard, the police car parked outside the kitchen gave him something else to think about.

FIVE

Everybody tempts her, according to the song. And at least since they'd moved up here, that's what Ian had felt was happening. It stood to reason, then, that a man in uniform would have Tanya positively drooling so, as he entered the house, Ian was preparing himself for the worst. Instead, he was confronted with a very irritated wife standing with her arms folded across her chest and an expression on her face that would leave no one in any doubt that she was not happy about them being there.

Sure enough, the officer was hardly movie star material. As he introduced himself, Ian took in his appearance. He guessed he barely made the minimum height requirement. Not that he was short, but with a burgeoning waistline he certainly didn't come across as particularly imposing. In his early twenties, the tightness of his uniform didn't bode well for his future health prospects. With short-cropped ginger hair and a more than generous sprinkling of freckles that gave his face an almost orange hue, Ian could understand why the officer's physical limitations had outweighed the potential attraction of the uniform.

They were all standing. Tanya had clearly not offered a seat or any other form of hospitality.

"Been here long?" Ian inquired casually, pulling a

chair out from under the kitchen table. As he sat down, he gestured for the others to join him.

The constable nodded his thanks. "About five minutes. I was just explaining why I was here to Mrs McLean."

"Apparently, they think Martin's stolen a van and murdered a dog." There was something about Tanya's tone that made Ian wonder if she hoped their guest might be guilty. He looked at her questioningly, but she seemed not to notice. Or possibly chose not to. She remained standing.

Constable Oakes introduced himself properly, and relayed his experiences at the Post Office. He finished by explaining: "I'm not here to make any accusations against anyone. But the information I was given at the shop suggested the possibility of a link between the incidents last night and Mr Gates' arrival in the village."

"Of course, Officer." Unlike his wife, Ian felt there was nothing to be gained by antagonising the Police. Due deference would at least help to rebuild any bridges Tanya might have broken down. Though from the appreciative glances Oakes gave her, Ian wondered if he might have underestimated how much a man will put up with from an attractive woman. "What can we do to help?"

He had got on well with Martin, both last night and this morning. But he had no real reason to defend him, or to be confident that he wasn't guilty of any crimes. Not that he had any reason to consider him guilty either. But it was clear that the only appropriate thing to do here was cooperate.

Oakes had been referring to his notebook while he was talking. He turned now to a blank page. "Can you account for his movements at all last night?"

"Any particular time?"

"I can't confirm anything specific because I don't want to lead you in any direction."

"Fair enough." As the first time Ian had met Martin was on the cusp between afternoon and evening, he started there. Although Tanya didn't add anything to his comments, he occasionally looked to her if he was unsure if he had recalled everything correctly. Her only confirmation was a curt nod.

When he'd finished, Oakes read back through his notes for almost a minute. The silence was uncomfortable. Ian briefly wondered whether it was a deliberate psychological strategy, but from his assessment of the constable so far, he guessed he was just a slow reader – and probably a slow thinker as well.

Eventually, Oakes looked up.

"You said he left the pub sometime between eight and eight-thirty."

"That's right. I wasn't keeping track of the time, but I would imagine it was around quarter past. I know he was going to be late for…" What was it? An appointment? It suddenly struck Ian how odd this meeting of the Gates family seemed. "…his family reunion."

"And then you didn't see him until quarter to eleven?"

"Or thereabouts." Ian didn't want to be pinned down on a time that he genuinely wasn't sure about.

"And you think he was at his parents' house in between times?"

"That's what he told us. I assume you'll want to check that with them anyway."

"Of course, sir."

"Well if it's any help, I know his father and brother will be working on our development at the moment. I'll happily show you the way myself."

Oakes looked up from his notes, apparently incapable of concealing his suspicions. *Columbo*, he wasn't. "His father and brother *work* for you?"

"It's more of a partnership at the moment," Ian said, immediately wondering why he felt he needed to explain himself. At the same time, he understood that Oakes was making all kinds of connections in his head that would probably take him nowhere, but could lead to some awkward conversations and unnecessary revelations.

The policeman bent over his notebook and scribbled furiously for a few moments. When he'd finished, he read back what he'd written, pausing once or twice to make corrections. Satisfied at last, he continued with his questions.

"What time did you go to bed?"

"As I said, Tanya went to bed shortly after Martin came back. Martin and I went at the same time. I'd guess around twelve-thirty."

"And you *know* that Mr Gates went straight to bed?"

Ian smiled his most disarming smile. "Short of following him into his room, how could I know that for sure?"

"Wouldn't you have heard him?"

Realising that a demonstration might be more effective than words, Ian showed Oakes the layout of the house. When they returned to the kitchen table, there was a long silence as yet more laborious notes were made. Eventually, the policeman looked up again.

"Would it be possible for him to have left the house without disturbing you?"

"Probably. The kitchen door can usually be heard from our room, but I honestly don't know whether we would hear it in the middle of the night. But he also has the door right next to his room." Even as he said it, he realised it sounded as if he was making a case for Martin to be the culprit. That didn't seem right, but the truth was that he could have gone out and come back and they would have been none the wiser.

"So he could come and go as he pleased?" Ian nodded his response. "But he was here first thing this morning?"

"Yes. I was up just after six, and I saw Martin for the first time about six-thirty."

"And did he look as if he might have been up in the night?"

"He looked the way I would expect anyone to look first thing in the morning. Bleary-eyed and hair all over the place."

"So if he did go out, he'd have had to do it between twelve-thirty and six-thirty?"

"I'd have definitely heard him if I'd been up, and if I was him I'd want to wait for me to settle down, so it's more likely the window's between one and six."

"I'll be the judge of that," Oakes said, and made some more notes. He looked thoughtfully at them again. Ian looked over at Tanya, who rolled her eyes. For the first time in ages, he thought they might be sharing a joke.

"So he would have had to walk down to the village, kill the dog, steal the van and hide it somewhere, and get back here – all within five hours. It's plenty of time, but where would he hide the van?"

"We're in the country, officer. There are loads of places." Ian smiled as he realised that maybe Oakes was not as stupid as he looked. He wanted Ian to come up with the answer himself. Obligingly, he did so. "He could even have hidden it in one of our old farm buildings. Do you think we should check?"

Tanya stayed in the house. The area around the outbuildings was muddy, and she didn't see any need to go out there and spoil her shoes. Nor did she see any point in changing into wellies when there was no need for her to be involved anyway.

Having been dressed for a meeting with the bank manager, Ian did need to retrieve his boots from the Land Rover. The delay clearly left Oakes feeling impatient but, by the time they had walked up to the old barns and stores, the policeman looked as if he was wishing he'd had the foresight to bring some alternative footwear.

The buildings were set out in a square. The side that bordered the track was open, with the buildings forming the other sides. Facing them as they turned into the yard was an old hay barn. The supports held up a solid roof, and beneath that were the remnants of a few old hay bales that had been there since before Ian had bought the farm. Apart from that, the space was empty, unused, giving a clear view across a field beyond and then the inevitable tree line.

To the left and right were brick built structures that stretched back around fifty feet or so. The bricks on the left hand building were interrupted with several doors, mainly at ground level, but at either end there were stone steps leading up to doors on the first floor. Beyond the doors were the remains of workshops and store rooms. The timbers upstairs were rotten, making it almost treacherous to try to traverse any of the rooms up there. On the ground floor, although the rooms inside would be big enough to hide a vehicle, the doors weren't large enough to allow access.

Which left the building on the right hand side. This was as long as the other one, but only had two sets of doors in it. The nearest was a standard size, large enough for a person to pass through, but certainly nothing bigger than that. Further along were the larger doors, tall enough and wide enough to allow a combine harvester to pass through. Most cars or vans would probably only need one of the doors open. Ian knew that the building was empty, which was why he never locked it. He reached for the handle of one of the doors and heaved back on it. In spite of it having been neglected for a few years, it swung open easily.

Side by side, the two men entered the building. There was no van. But it had been there. Even before he opened the door, Ian had known that. The tyre tracks in the mud outside had been fresh.

SIX

It took a while for him to regain his bearings. Having stumbled into the *Marie Celeste* of farms, only to discover an empty building had somehow concealed at least three people, his focus had been purely about getting out of there. So, as he did his best to remain undetected, his attention was on the exit rather than where that exit would take him. And where it had taken him was, perhaps inevitably, into fields that he didn't recognise. Taking his cues from the position of the sun – which wasn't ideal in the middle of the day – he gradually made his way in the general direction of the village. Fortunately, the fields he traversed were filled with crops rather than cattle, so he didn't have to deviate simply to bypass herds of animals. Instead, he worked his way steadily away from the farm yard, keeping close to hedges so he could easily hide himself if the need arose.

Predictably, he encountered the woods again before entering different farm land. It was a fairly narrow strip, taking him only five minutes or so to pass through. Then he was out in the open again.

The layout of the fields had changed a little, but the land angled downwards in a way that was familiar to him. He recalled playing up here when he was a kid, during the long summer holidays with nothing to do. He hadn't had many friends even when he was popular. It was a small village, and finding children his own age was a challenge in itself. But he hadn't always been up here on his own. The memories were very clear. Wandering aimlessly, sometimes carrying a makeshift picnic (sandwiches in tin foil, an old squash bottle filled with a fifty-fifty mix of *Kia-Ora* and water, and – if you were lucky – a Kit Kat), sometimes with only the clawing hunger in your belly to tell you it was time to go home. Rolling down the sloping grass, and sometimes running down it – until your velocity was greater than your legs could cope with and you fell or sprawled, or even dived, the sudden pains from various parts of the body eclipsed by the hilarity of it all. Keeping yourself hidden if there was any sign of a farmer. The older lads talked about farmers carrying guns, and every now and then those rumours were borne out with the sharp cracks heard in the distance. Martin knew the sounds came from shotguns because his dad had told him. Of course, as a child, he didn't realise that farmers only used the guns for shooting vermin. In a way, that was a good thing. It would have spoilt the adventure for the kids who roamed across farm land.

As this particular stretch was so distinctive, he knew he was now on what he remembered as *Wharton's Farm*. During his conversation with Ian last night, though, he'd learnt that *Lodge Farm* had acquired that land as well as the land from the Sullivans. Bob Lambert was clearly focused on building up his farming empire.

With sufficient distance between himself and the unexpected farm yard, he was able to relax and go over his experience there in his mind. There had definitely been no one in the barn when he'd gone inside. As far as he could recall, there were no hidden doors or trapdoors. He was sure the tractor and farm equipment hadn't concealed anything. The crates of vegetables were too heavy to be pushed casually to one side, so he couldn't imagine there was a hideaway either behind or beneath them. So how had three people managed to come out of there?

No matter which way he looked at this puzzle, he couldn't find a solution. And for the next hour or so, as he worked his way across Lodge Farm and then back through the woods, he thought of little else. Even the temptation of a return to the clearing couldn't take him away from those thoughts. Instead, he decided to get back to the McLean house. It was well after one o'clock and he was sure Ian would be home by now.

He pondered whether he should tell Ian about the empty barn. It might not be wise because it might mean explaining what he was up to. But Ian was clearly very intelligent and, he suspected, insightful. It was possible he might be able to come up with an answer that had yet to occur to Martin. He was still considering this as he climbed over the stile and began to walk down the track from the wood. He ignored the old buildings on his left. Ahead of him, the track passed the gateway to the farm yard and about thirty yards beyond that it angled downwards as it took you to the village.

As he entered the yard, he saw a car approaching the gateway on the opposite side, coming up from the cottages his dad and brother were working on. He stopped for a moment, surprised to see the blue light on its roof. He had known it was a possibility the police would have to become involved, but he'd thought it would take longer. Perhaps things were going to move faster than he expected.

SEVEN

Tanya had plenty of questions.

What the hell have you been doing in our barn? What the hell are you doing in the village? Where the hell were you this morning? Are you responsible for killing the bloody dog? Did you cause the fucking birds to come to the clearing? Who the bloody hell are you?

They lacked subtlety, but subtlety was never her strong suit. Even so, she kept the questions to herself. She might lack subtlety, but her survival instinct was full to the brim.

Once she'd been told about the tyre tracks, she'd assumed he wouldn't be back. From what she'd learnt from Ian and PC Plod, it sounded as if Martin must have stolen the van last night, hidden it in the barn, then retrieved it after Ian had gone to the bank. She probably wouldn't have noticed the sound of an engine on the track. Especially if it was covered by the sound of the shower, or – a guilty thought – a light buzzing noise.

So when Plod had asked Ian to take him to where Matt and Patrick were working, it hadn't crossed her mind that being left on her own would be a problem. Until she saw Martin crossing the yard. Then her instincts told her to get out of there quickly. And she was already getting up from the table when the door opened. Fortunately, just as it did, she saw the police car roll into view.

"I see you've got visitors."

His tone was casual. He'd left the door open behind him as he came close to her. She felt his palm briefly touch her shoulder, then he was past. Was he telling her to sit back down? Was it meant to reassure her? Yet again she was confused about the messages he was giving out. And his calmness was at odds with the evidence that seemed to point to his guilt. Her mind in turmoil, she only realised that she'd sat down again when her husband came into the room.

He gave her a concerned look, and she was surprised at how grateful she felt. It hadn't occurred to her for a long time that he might care for her. Nor had it occurred to her that she might need someone to care for her. She tried to convey with her eyes that she was all right. He seemed to get the message.

"Hi Martin." He was looking past her as he spoke. His voice was steady, relaxed. Playing to his strengths again.

"I see you've brought company." Martin's response coinciding with Plod coming into view.

She'd taken an instant dislike to the copper when he'd arrived earlier. If she was honest with herself, in part it was because he was a singularly unattractive man. At the sight of the police car coming into the yard, instead of wondering what bad news this heralded, she'd immediately fantasised about a man in uniform. PC Oakes wasn't great fantasy material. But she was also irritated by his lack of finesse. Ian was a people person. He handled his fellow humans with a care and tact and dexterity that she realised she'd taken for granted. Plod, as she'd begun to think of him within minutes of his arrival, struggled at times to find the words he wanted to say, and when they came to him, they were used like a blunt instrument. And then there were the surreptitious looks he kept giving her. At least, he clearly thought they were surreptitious. But he might as well have been wearing a T-shirt with the words "Get yer tits out!" emblazoned across it. A part of her recognised her double standards. She liked to know she was getting male attention: she just preferred it to be attention from attractive males.

In spite of the fact that they had a suspected thief and dog murderer in the kitchen, yet again his gaze fell on her cleavage. She regretted not taking the opportunity to go and change into something less obvious while the men were out. Fortunately, he remembered his reason for being there after a moment or so.

"Mr Martin Gates?" he asked formally. She half expected him to start reciting his arrest speech, rights and all.

Martin came back into her line of sight as he moved towards the officer, hand outstretched. "That's right. And you are?"

Plod ignored the proffered hand, glancing down at his notebook as he volunteered his name, albeit reluctantly. Martin glanced at both Ian and Tanya as he took his hand back. He seemed to be amused by the officer's attitude.

"Mr Gates, could you explain your whereabouts last night?"

"Any particular part of last night?"

"From the time you left Mr and Mrs McLean at *The Major Oak*."

As Plod was still concentrating on his notebook, Tanya guessed that Martin's playful shrug was for their benefit.

"Well…" He looked thoughtful, as if he was dredging

his memory. Somehow, Tanya didn't think that was likely. "I don't know what time I left, but I know I was late. I'd agreed to visit my family around eight o'clock, but it was nearer half past by the time I got there."

"But you went there straight from the pub?" Plod's eyes flicked briefly up to meet his.

"There aren't many distractions in this village." Surprising her, he flashed a flirtatious grin at Tanya.

"Shall I take that as a 'yes' then?"

"Yes." His tone suggested that he was chastened by Plod, but his face told a different story.

"So you arrived at your parents' house around eight-thirty?" Pedantry was clearly Plod's forte.

"Around then, yes."

"And how long did you stop for?" Plod's eyes lifted again. This time they stayed there. It was clear that this question was more important than the others.

"I don't know, officer." Martin must have recognised the sudden interest. He sounded more serious himself. "I haven't seen my parents, or my brothers and sister for nearly fifteen years. It was quite an emotional experience, and the time just passed."

"Well, would you say you were there for twenty minutes, half an hour, an hour? Longer?"

"I really don't know."

Plod nodded, though Tanya got the impression it was to himself.

"What did you do when you'd finished visiting your family?"

While they'd been talking, Martin had moved over to the sink and was leaning back against it. Now he folded his arms across his chest. Classic defensive gesture. Tanya looked for Ian's reaction. Although there was nothing overt, she could see he was watching Martin more closely.

"I came back here," Martin said.

"And what time did you come in?"

He shook his head uncertainly. "I don't know."

"You don't seem to know much, do you, Mr Gates?"

"As I said, I had a very emotional night. Keeping track of time wasn't high on my list of priorities."

"What *was* high on your list of priorities?"

Martin stood upright at this, his arms slowly unfolding and dropping to his sides. At first glance, it seemed a fairly relaxed stance, but Tanya got the impression he could explode into action in a heartbeat. With his eyes back down at his notebook, it was unlikely that Plod was aware of this. At least not until Martin spoke, a hard edge to his voice that she hadn't heard before.

"I think you need to tell me what all this is about."

Looking up, Plod stared at him for a few moments. He didn't seem to be intimidated, but there could be any number of reasons for that.

"I'll come to that in a minute, Mr Gates. But first I'd like you to answer my questions."

"And if I don't?"

"Then I'll have to ask you to accompany me to the station."

"Which is where?"

"Westfield."

He pondered this, and clearly decided that wasn't a route he wanted to go down just yet.

"Go on, then."

A long look at the notebook to remind himself where he'd got to. Then: "Any idea when you arrived back here last night?"

"No. But I'm sure you've already checked this with my hosts, so perhaps you'd like to enlighten me."

Ignoring Martin's response, Plod asked another question: "So you don't know what time you left your parents' house, and you don't know what time you got back here?" He paused a moment before ploughing on. "As you've said, I have checked with Mr and Mrs McLean, and they tell me you returned here around quarter to eleven."

"Well I'm glad that mystery's solved."

Plod bristled at the sarcasm. Tanya got the impression that he'd like to take Martin back to the station, get him in a cell and give him a good kicking. Instead, he made do with grinding his teeth.

"The problem, Mr Gates, is that your father and brother tell me you left their house around nine-thirty. Now I haven't tried walking it, but I can't see how getting from the main street to here can take more than twenty minutes. Which begs the question: what were you doing for that hour and a quarter?"

"Walking."

"Walking?"

"Walking."

"It would be helpful, Mr Gates, if you were a bit more cooperative." He'd dragged his eyes away from the notebook and was staring fixedly at Martin. Even so, Tanya had the impression that he was uncomfortable with the eye contact.

"I found the meeting with my family upsetting," Martin said reluctantly. "So I went for a walk."

205

"Where?"

A shrug. "I really couldn't tell you. I just needed to clear my head, so I wandered around."

"Aimlessly?" The suggestion was almost derisive.

"You could say that."

"Did you see anyone?"

"Not that I can remember."

"So no one can vouch for you."

Martin smiled, but Tanya couldn't see any humour in it. "No." He hesitated, and Plod waited for him. "Is this where you tell me what it is I've done and arrest me for it because I haven't got an alibi?"

"No, sir. This is where I ask you where you were at lunch time yesterday."

Ian had been watching Martin closely for the last few minutes, but Tanya saw his head snap round to Plod when he heard this. All three of them were curious about this turn of events.

"I was at the pub. Why?"

"What about before you went to the pub?" He clearly had no intention of answering any questions just yet.

"I was on the bus from Westfield. When the bus dropped me off, I went into the pub." The irritation Martin had been feeling was growing now, and his voice reflected that.

"What time did you get off the bus?"

"At a guess, I'd say around twenty past twelve."

A pause as notes were made.

"I take it you'll be checking this with the driver, then?"

"Yes." Plod finished writing and looked up again. "So you didn't get off the bus earlier?"

"No."

"You didn't come out to the village earlier and then catch the bus at its previous stop?"

"Why the hell would I do that?"

"I thought this was about the incident at the Post Office." Ian was looking concerned as he said this, though Tanya wasn't sure whether his concern was about Martin's guilt or the apparent tangent the line of questioning had taken.

Plod looked across at him. "I'm involved in two investigations."

Tanya was only just behind Ian in understanding. The look on Martin's face suggested he was with them too.

"Are you suggesting Martin was involved in the accident on Lodge Farm?"

"It hasn't been established yet whether it *was* an accident."

"Bloody hell! Please tell me you're just taking the piss." This from Martin.

"Why would I do that, sir?"

"Honestly? I haven't got a fucking clue. But are you seriously suggesting that, in the twenty-four hours or so that I've been back in the village, I've already seriously injured Peter Salthouse and carried out some other crime at the Post Office? And what am I supposed to have done there? Robbed it with a sawn-off shotgun?"

It was interesting to note that Martin was happy to show his anger, and yet it still seemed to be restrained.

"I'm not suggesting anything, Mr Gates. I'm just trying to…"

"What? Eliminate me from your enquiries? What is this?"

Ian stepped forward, putting himself between the two men. His whole demeanour emanated calm. Tanya recognised the approach. She'd seen him handle tensions between employees in the same way. "There are reasons why you're being asked these questions, Martin." His hands remained at his sides. Non-threatening. "Something's been found on the farm."

"What?" Martin seemed genuinely perplexed, but she could see that he was responding to Ian's manner.

A glance back at Plod. "Have you got any more questions, or can we tell him?"

Reluctantly, the policeman shook his head. "No more questions."

So Ian explained about the missing van and the tyre tracks in the yard. As he did, Martin bowed his head, listening intently. Because they were standing, Ian and Plod wouldn't have been able to see his face at all. From her sitting position, Tanya could see it, and was surprised at his expression.

EIGHT

Friday night, and there's a younger crowd in the pub. Lads in their twenties. Unsurprisingly, the females in this age bracket are few and far between. They want the bright lights of the town, not the boorish behaviour of a bunch of blokes who haven't got the gumption to extend their horizons beyond the boundaries of the village. Not that they'll be here all night. Sometime between nine and nine-thirty, a group of them will head off to Westfield. But they'll stick to the same few pubs they always go to, then head into a club. They'll probably keep drinking till they can barely stand, hoping along the way they'll get lucky with some bird who's desperate enough to take them on. With very few exceptions, they'll fall into a taxi at the end of the night with ambitions thwarted by their own lack of charisma. At least, that's how Norma sees it. Her customers provide her with a reasonable living, but that doesn't mean she's not allowed to have an opinion of them.

By seven-thirty, they've started to drift in. By eight-thirty, she reckons pretty much all of the young males in the village are propping up her bar, playing darts or waiting to use the pool table. Fags dangling from their mouths in a way they think makes them look cool and sophisticated, pint glasses being waved around as they emphasise the points they want to make. Dickheads, the bloody lot of them. Anywhere else, she'd expect them to grow up soon, become aware of how stupid they look. Not here. She's seen it before. The youngsters of ten years ago are still acting in the same way. They just come in a bit later because they've got to wait until their kids are in bed. And they'll stay in the village. They might still want to go into town and try their luck, but most of them are too frightened of what their wives would do to them if they found out. Not that Norma would encourage them to put it about. But she finds their hypocrisy distasteful. They spend their evenings eyeing up any half-decent female and making lewd remarks about what they'd like to do to them. But none of them would have the nerve to even attempt to do anything about it.

The older customers will also be in. Some of them already are, but most will turn up after nine, hoping to avoid the youngsters. She has no doubt they were the same in their youth. They just won't recall that they too would have splashed beer around, or flicked fag ash into other people's drinks, or been so pissed they couldn't tell the difference between normal conversation and shouting raucously at their mates.

Just another typical Friday night at *The Oak*.

Or so she was beginning to think until Ron Dakin came in.

To be fair, Ron's presence wasn't untypical. He didn't come into the pub as often as some of the lads, but he would be in at least once or twice a week. It was also fair to say that he didn't generally go into Westfield with them unless he was feeling particularly adventurous.

He was a nice lad, and he mixed well with his own age group and most of the other regulars. His proficiency with a pool cue had also earned him a place in the team. At twenty-four, he was the youngest. The rest of the team ranged in age up to sixty-two. An unlikely combination, but it seemed to have worked. They were currently the title holders in their league, and already looking forward to the new season.

What made this all the more gratifying to Norma – and, she was sure, to most of the other regulars – was that Ron was a mute. He communicated with a kind of sign language that was universal. With the exception of his father, Derek, no one else had bothered to learn sign language properly, so Ron improvised and made sure everyone around him knew what he meant. He had a ready smile, and a sense of humour that often caught people out.

Seeing him arrive, Norma was already pulling his pint for him as he approached the bar. He grinned at her and nodded his appreciation. When he had his drink, he headed off to the pool table, greeting the people he met along the way with a nod.

Norma was reaching for a clean glass to provide Walter with a refill when she heard a raised voice.

"He-llo!" The word was spoken very slowly and sounded as if it was being deliberately exaggerated. There was an audible reduction in the chatter going on around the bar. Norma searched for the owner of the voice. It sounded like Neil Thatcher, one of the lads at the pool table.

For several seconds, there was no follow up, then she heard the same voice, and this time could see that it *was* Neil.

"What's up, Ron? Cat got your tongue?"

To Norma's horror, this was accompanied by laughter

from the lads standing nearby. Through a gap in the crowd, she could see the back of Ron's head, which was twitching from side to side. She could only imagine what he must be thinking.

"Come on, Ron, speak up." Another voice, but she couldn't identify this one. Not that it mattered, because more joined in.

"What's that you say?"

"Come again?"

"You're going to have to speak louder than that."

The lines were feeble attempts at humour, but they seemed to be getting the laughs. More importantly, they seemed to be hitting home. Their target was backing away, his glass wavering in his hand, the contents slopping over the sides and on to the floor.

Norma couldn't help but compare this to the previous lunchtime when Colin Gates had come in and been taunted. Although that wasn't acceptable either, it was kind of understandable. Colin wasn't a regular in the pub, wasn't part of the crowd. But this was different. There was no obvious reason for his friends to suddenly turn on him like this.

Andy was working the bar with her again tonight. Whereas Norma was frozen in place, stunned at the shock of what was happening, Andy was already out from behind the bar, and heading towards Ron.

"Come on, Ron, you can speak louder than that." Neil Thatcher again. Clearly, neither variety nor originality were among his strengths. But that didn't make the words any easier to take. Ron suddenly turned, the motion half-emptying his glass. As some of the beer splashed on to his hand, he glanced down as if he had just become aware of it. He leaned over and put it down on the nearest table. Still considerate, not wanting to cause any more mess than he had to. Andy reached him as he began to move forward. His offered hand was slapped to one side as Ron pushed past him.

"Go on, you cunt! Run off home to your other freaky mates!" From Neil again. Norma flashed him a look, but he ignored it, watching Ron until he disappeared through the door.

For a long moment, silence fell over the pub. Uncomfortable glances were exchanged. Awkward attempts were made to sip from glasses. Then a cue ball cracked against another, and everything returned to normal.

Back behind the bar, Andy gave her a bewildered look. She didn't know what to say. Then two strangers walked in and the spell was broken.

As she prepared their drinks, she studied them both. Surreptitiously, of course.

The man on the right had dark hair, long enough to cover his ears and most of the back of his neck. His eyes were blue, similar to Paul Newman's. Though that was as far as the resemblance went. His face was thin and long, a narrow nose only adding to the effect. Underneath his thick round-necked jumper, his body looked appropriately slight. Bony wrists and hands protruded from the sleeves. Even the thick hair that covered the backs of his hands did nothing to hide his skinniness.

Beside him, his companion was quite different. His head was completely hairless, and from what little more of his flesh she could see, she guessed the rest of him must be in a fairly similar state. A thick neck supported his head. He wore an open-necked shirt, and she couldn't imagine he'd ever be comfortable in one that was buttoned up. No matter how large the collar size, it would be a tight fit. As, indeed, was the rest of his shirt, bulging as it did over his arms and chest. He reminded her of one of the stereotypical henchmen from a 1960s spy movie, only bigger. He wasn't as tall as Adam Hawthorn, but you certainly knew he was there.

Stereotyping was clearly inappropriate, though. From their appearance she would have expected them to ask for hard drinks: Scotch – either neat or on the rocks – or maybe *Jack Daniels*. Whisky of any kind would have fit with her expectations. Not orange juice. The grateful smiles also surprised her.

Not that she had long to dwell on it. The moment they had their drinks, she was presented with a pint glass by Walter. As she started to refill it, she glanced up to see where they went, and noted they were heading towards a table close to the door.

In the meantime, the few men standing at the bar had resumed the conversations they'd been having before the outburst from Neil Thatcher and his mates. Already, darts was underway again. A young lad was thumping the cigarette machine. She guessed he was after twenty *Rothmans* because that drawer always stuck.

All of this was taken in as she attended to Walter. It was as if nothing had happened. Were she and Andy the only ones who'd seen what had happened? Or were they hallucinating? She glanced across at him, but he was already busy again.

It briefly crossed her mind to go and find Ron, make sure he was all right. But he would probably be home by now. Of course, that could mean his father, Derek, would be down soon. Quite rightly, he'd want to know what had gone on. Then again, there *was* only Derek at home. Ron's mother had died a long time ago. Certainly before Norma moved to the village. There was another son, but Steve lived at the other end of the village. She rarely saw him, so didn't know whether he'd be around to look after Ron. Derek might feel it was more important to stay at home and look after his son. Norma could only hope he took that option, because she hadn't got a clue what to tell him.

When the door opened ten minutes later, she assumed the worst. The group of regulars milling about blocked her view, so she couldn't tell who it was for sure. Then he was at the bar, and she felt her heart sink.

"I'll just have a pint of lager," he said, his voice level. There was nothing in it to show how he was feeling.

"Any particular…?" She gestured to the different taps.

"Doesn't matter. I'm not a connoisseur."

He turned to look round the bar area while she drew his pint. She thought he was looking for someone. Didn't know who. He'd seemed happy enough with his own company yesterday lunchtime.

Yesterday lunchtime. The last time a customer had been picked on. And she realised that was why she'd felt so bad when she realised it was him. Twice in two days she'd seen one of the less fortunate of the villagers being treated like shit. And Martin Gates had been close by both times.

Even as she thought it, she dismissed it as irrational. He'd actually stopped things getting out of hand with Colin.

And he'd not even been here when the lads had started on Ron. Still, as she'd told the policeman this morning when he'd come back from inspecting the dog, there was something happening in the village. And it seemed to have started when Martin turned up. The funny thing was, from Linda Payne's reaction, it was as if whatever that something was, it was something she'd been waiting for.

Just as she placed the glass in front of Martin, two other men arrived at the bar.

"You timed that right. Were you waiting for me so I'd get the first round in?" The tone was humorous, not at all out of place in a pub, where taking the piss was not only accepted, it was almost mandatory. But neither Patrick nor Matthew seemed to appreciate the joke.

"We can buy our own." Patrick was abrupt to a point well beyond rudeness. Norma couldn't help but wonder what it was that Martin had done to cause his father and brother to want so much to be without him.

She half-expected him to protest and insist that he buy their drinks. It was part of pub etiquette. Instead, he shrugged, winked at Norma conspiratorially – though she had no idea why – and headed towards the window and an empty table. Father and brother followed him a couple of minutes later.

Convinced that things couldn't get any stranger, within a few minutes Norma realised that you could never assume anything, when she turned to find Adam Hawthorn smiling down at her.

NINE

"You wanted to see us." It was both a statement and a question. The fact that Matthew said it at all spoke volumes.

If he'd understood his feelings, Martin would probably have hidden them. But he didn't know whether to be saddened, dejected or angry. So he hid his confusion instead.

He'd been down to the cottages this afternoon. You could hardly say the policeman had been satisfied with his answers earlier, but he had nothing he could pin on Martin, so after another twenty minutes of fruitless questioning he'd gone. Five minutes later, Martin had been out the door and on the way to see his father and brother. He hadn't expected them to want to talk to him there and then. But he was left stumbling over his words when they said he wasn't to come to the house again. Their agreement to meet him in the pub this evening was clearly a reluctant compromise on their part. And Matthew's words now underlined the fact.

Glancing round the pub, Martin reflected that this was hardly the ideal environment for the conversation he wanted to have with them. That needed privacy. Even though the other people in the pub seemed to be otherwise occupied, it wouldn't take much to grab their attention: a slightly raised voice, a badly chosen phrase – or a grown man crying.

As he scanned the room, he noticed two men sitting near the back door. The man with the bald head was scanning the room. It seemed to be a fairly innocent activity, as if it was simply idle curiosity. Indeed, it could well have been, but Martin wasn't so sure. He recognised him from his visit to the apparently unoccupied farm this morning.

Very briefly, the man's eyes flickered to his right. Martin followed his gaze and saw two more people he recognised from the farm.

The tall man was moving away from the bar, looking for a seat. Behind him, the woman he'd also seen at the farm came into view. They both seemed to attract some attention. It was supposed to be surreptitious, but he guessed none of the regulars had any experience of surveillance work. Still, he could understand why they were so interested. Both the man and the woman were striking. Obviously their height made them stand out, but there was more than that. They seemed to exude…something. He didn't know what, couldn't put his finger on it. But they certainly had a presence about them.

And the girl. Well, he was struck once more by her appearance. Not exactly girl-next-door, but no beauty queen either. He struggled to find the right words for her. *Something* came to mind again, and he knew it was more than inadequate. The way she moved was so natural – why wouldn't it be? There was no awkwardness, no self-consciousness. Even in a room that was devoid of any other female, where most women would be very aware that they could be the centre of male attention, whether they wanted it or not, she seemed to be completely oblivious of the interest she was provoking.

They found a table close to the back door, and began talking animatedly as soon as they sat down. Martin felt a pang of envy.

"I wouldn't bother if I were you." It was Matthew again.

"Just looking," he replied, hoping he sounded as nonchalant as he wanted to.

"If that's the case, you might as well take your time. You won't see her again."

He looked at his brother. "Why do you say that?"

"She's a Hawthorn. They live out on the edge of the village. *Kindness Farm.*"

Not Marie Celeste *Farm then*, he thought wryly.

"They don't come into the village much. Last time I saw her must be at least five years ago."

"So you're saying I'll need to stay for another five years to see her again?"

That comment brought sharp looks from both of them.

"I wouldn't bother," Matthew said. "Even if they do come into the village, they don't mix."

"Keep themselves to themselves?" Martin couldn't help but smile as he said it. "They probably fit in very well here then."

From the stony looks he got from them, his sense of humour clearly wasn't catching.

"*Kindness Farm*? That's an odd name, isn't it?"

"Never thought about it, to be honest. It's just always been there."

"And when it's always been there, you don't notice," Martin finished for him. Then added: "But I don't remember it."

The expressions on their faces told him they weren't bothered whether he did or not.

"You wanted to see us," Matthew repeated. Martin was pleased to note that, this time, there wasn't quite as hard an edge to his voice as there had been before. Perhaps the distraction of the Hawthorn girl had worked to his advantage.

"We need to talk."

"So you said, and that's why we're here."

"I mean, *really* talk. Somewhere a bit less public."

The glances that passed between Matthew and Patrick told him that they weren't comfortable about that.

"Why do you think that's necessary?" It was still Matthew doing the talking. His father seemed to be happy to take a back seat for the moment.

"More importantly, why do I get the impression you think it's a bad idea?" Martin kept his voice low, but the emphasis on his words was firm enough for the others to recognise his frustration. And, again, he could tell that this only served to make them more wary. Patrick obviously didn't want to commit himself to any comment. Matthew just looked at him, unseen cogs spinning furiously inside his head.

Silence is uncomfortable. Even when there's the background noise of chatter, clinking glasses, and balls cracking against each other on a pool table. That silence stretching out between a small group of people can still feel very awkward. But Martin was okay with uncomfortable and awkward. He let it sit there, waiting for the first one to break.

It turned out to be Patrick. "It was a bad idea for you to come back."

"Any particular reason why?"

More exchanged looks, another silence, though briefer this time.

"You've been away for a long time…" Matthew taking up the reins again. But his voice tailed off, as if he recognised the irrelevance of his own words.

"You're right. I have. And it's not exactly been the welcome of the Prodigal Son, has it?"

"What do you expect, Martin? You disappear for fifteen years. No letter, no phone call. Not even a post card to let us know you're alive. And then you turn up unannounced. Did you think we'd just greet you with open arms?" Matthew had also managed to speak quietly enough not to attract any attention from anyone else in the pub.

"No I didn't. But I also didn't expect to be shunned."

"Shunned? We're here now, aren't we?"

"Grudgingly," Martin pointed out, "and only to stop me from going to the house. Because you two are here, but no one else. My own mother doesn't even want to see me."

"That's not true."

Martin was surprised to hear what sounded like genuine hurt in his father's voice. Both he and Matthew looked at Patrick, waiting for more of an explanation. But nothing came. He just shook his head.

"Come on, Dad," Martin urged. "You've got to give me more than that." He waited a few seconds for a response, but with none forthcoming, he decided to push harder. "Let's face it, considering you're my parents, neither of you really wanted me around. Why do you think I left?"

Patrick looked down at his pint, apparently deep in thought. He shook his head again after a few moments.

"That's not true either," he said, his eyes still focused on the beer. There was a tremor to his voice that hadn't been there before.

"So explain that to me."

"I can't."

"Why not?"

Still apparently unable to face him, Patrick shook his head for a third time. "I just can't." Abruptly, he stood up, his pint untouched on the table. He looked at Matthew. Martin saw pleading in his eyes. His brother responded to it, standing as well.

"Please tell me this is a joke." Martin wanted them to know he was exasperated, and made sure that came across in his tone.

Matthew gave him a shrug. It was the closest to empathy he'd experienced since he'd first seen them. But that was all he gave away. Patrick had already turned and was heading for the door.

"We need to talk." But even as he said it, he knew he was wasting his time. Matthew was following their father, and this opportunity was slipping through his fingers. He could call out. He could make a scene. But that wasn't what he wanted, and it wouldn't help his cause. Instead, he watched the pair of them push their way through to the door.

Frustrated and angry, Martin looked down at the three untouched pints on the table. He didn't know whether to drink them and drown his sorrows, or hurl them at a wall and hope it would ease some of the tension he was feeling.

He compromised, and decided to drink some of his own beer.

TEN

Norma was beginning to think she'd fallen into an episode of *The Twilight Zone*, or *Hammer House of Horror*. First there was the incident with Ron, which had been horribly disturbing, if only because it was so out of character. Much as she looked down on the lads in many respects, she had to acknowledge that their insistence on including Ron in their group had been admirable over the years. It would have been quite easy for them to exclude him without being especially rude about it. His limited communication skills would have provided all the excuse they needed. But they'd gone out of their way to make sure he was part of the group.

In any pub, there is banter and piss-taking, and sometimes it can even seem abusive. Ron had been part of that, both giving and receiving. But the viciousness displayed tonight had been well beyond anything you might consider acceptable. She couldn't help thinking about the comments being made yesterday about Peter Salthouse. And then the abuse heaped on Colin Gates. Something was definitely not right here.

Like the two strangers. It was possible, of course, that their presence was just a coincidence. But it was hard to believe that there was no connection with the events of the last two days. Of course, what it all meant was impossible to guess. She thought back to the Post Office this morning, and wondered whether the conclusions she and others had jumped to could have been off the mark. Could it be that Martin's return to the village was the coincidence, and these two newcomers were the culprits?

And then there'd been Martin's arrival in the pub tonight, together with the uncomfortable exchange between him and Patrick. It looked as if they had some serious talking to do, but no more than fifteen minutes had passed before Martin was sitting alone with three barely touched pints in front of him. She didn't know what was going off in the Gates family, but her curiosity was being seriously tested.

As if that wasn't enough, for the second night in a row, Adam Hawthorn had been in. No awkwardness over the purchase of a pint this time. He'd asked for two orange juices. The second for the girl accompanying him. There was something vaguely familiar about her, but Norma couldn't recall where or when she might have seen her before. They seemed to attract the attention of the strangers as they crossed to a table. Then again, the girl's presence automatically attracted attention from a large percentage of the room anyway.

Her head filled with so many thoughts, Norma worked on. As she did, she was briefly aware of Martin Gates leaving, but it was another ten minutes before she had a moment's pause. When the opportunity came, she cast her eyes around the room. It wasn't nine-thirty yet, so no one had left for town. In fact, as far as she could see, the only people who were missing were Adam, his girlfriend and the two strangers.

ELEVEN

Downing three pints had been an attractive prospect. He wasn't happy about the way he was being treated by his family, but he was also curious about the two men at the bar, especially when they ignored the Hawthorns. That was really weird. He watched them sit on the opposite side of the pub, barely a glance passing between the two tables. But there was a glance. Very curious.

It was tempting to stay and watch them, find out what they were up to. But half way down the first pint, Martin reminded himself of his plan for tonight. Although he was frustrated with the responses from his father and brother, in reality he hadn't expected the meeting to go well. So his intention had always been to follow them back to the house. A pub wasn't the place for the conversation he needed to have. And whether they liked it or not, he was determined to have it.

So he'd left the pub and gone after them. He guessed they'd been gone for three or four minutes, which was more of a head start than he'd intended to give them. And when he reached the road, sure enough they were out of sight. He jogged the hundred yards or so to the bend, and saw they were already past the Post Office and would probably be home in less than a minute. Annoyed with himself for leaving it so long, he picked up his pace. He was wearing trainers, so hopefully they wouldn't be alerted by the sound of him running.

If they managed to get inside the house before he caught them, there was no guarantee they'd open the door to him. He knew he needed to catch up before they were off the street.

Between the bend in the road and his parents' cottage were the shop, the track up to the Sullivan Farm and the first two cottages in the row. By the time they reached the first of the cottages, he was close to the Post Office. As they passed the front door of the second, the shop was behind him.

He was beginning to think he might just make it. They might still be in the process of closing the door by the time he got there, but as long as the door wasn't completely shut, he could push his way in. At least, that was what he was thinking. Until the two men from the pub appeared in front of him.

They emerged from the opening to the farm track, only ten yards or so ahead of him. Surprised, his initial reaction was to slow down. When they stopped directly in his path, he assumed they were just as surprised as him. Recovering from the shock, he stepped off the pavement so he could pass by. The bald man was nearest to the road. He moved to block Martin. The move was fluid, almost balletic. It was also very effective.

The road was wide enough for two cars to pass, so Martin knew he should be able to get past this man easily enough. He should be able to get past both of them with ease. But even as the bald man stopped moving, he became aware that the other one was also in motion.

Martin had been in fights before. He didn't like them, and would avoid them if he could. But when you're a stranger in a strange land, sometimes you couldn't. And when you don't come out of them too well the first couple of times, you realise you need to learn from your mistakes. So he'd gone out of his way to learn, and the first thing he'd learnt was how to identify when you're under threat. He was under no doubt about that right now. The second thing he'd learnt was how to work out whether the prospective opponent knew what they were doing. From the coordination between them, he felt confident these two knew exactly what they were doing. The third thing he'd learnt was to establish whether he should fight or run.

Up ahead, he could see his father and brother at their front door. Matthew was turning the key in the lock. Even if he could get past these two, he wouldn't reach the house in time now. So if he chose to fight, there'd be no point if his sole objective was to continue with his plan to confront the family. He turned his attention back to the two men.

The man on the road was a similar height to Martin. In the street light, it was difficult to tell, but Martin guessed he was in his forties. He wore jeans and walking boots. The boots could cause some damage if used appropriately. His companion was shorter, maybe five foot eight. He too had jeans on. Martin couldn't tell whether he was wearing black trainers or boots.

More important than their appearance was their stance. Both men could fight. They seemed to be quite relaxed, but were keeping their bodies deliberately loose, allowing themselves the flexibility they might need. If he gave them the reason.

His father and brother entered the cottage, neither looking back in his direction. Had they not heard anything, he wondered. Or had they set this up?

Anger and frustration rose up in him again at that last thought. Was that the case? Had they decided he needed to be given a physical incentive to leave them alone? Just like the three pints had seemed appealing to him a few minutes ago, going up against these two offered some attractions too. Whichever way the fight went, there were benefits. He could use his fists and feet to let off some of the steam building up. Or the pain from the beating would take his mind off the other pain he was feeling.

But neither would resolve anything.

He took a step back. Neither man moved, just watched him. He couldn't read anything in their eyes. Couldn't tell if they wanted simply to intimidate him or were itching to give him a good hiding.

Another step back. Still no reaction. It looked like it was just intimidation, then. He might get away with turning away now and going back the way he'd come. Perhaps to the pub for a while. But he wasn't prepared to risk that yet. They were still too close. He wouldn't have time to react if they decided to attack him while he had his back to them.

Taking another step, he started planning his retreat. A couple more paces would put him a comfortable distance from these two. The question then was what to do when he turned away. Should he walk manfully back to the pub, or should he run for it? The latter option had its attractions. He wasn't worried what they would think of him. And if he was running, he'd get away quicker. But he also knew that with the rush of air past his ears and the pumping of blood around his body he wouldn't hear them coming up on him as easily if they gave chase. And they looked fit enough to catch him.

He started to lift his foot for another step.

"I think that's far enough."

The voice came from behind him. Spinning around, he found another two people facing him. The Hawthorns. The tall man looked over Martin's head and nodded, a gesture towards the two men behind him.

"Are you going to come quietly, or do my friends here need to help you?"

TWELVE

Having the police around had been unsettling. And Martin's reaction hadn't been any more reassuring. When Oakes had left, there'd been a long uncomfortable silence. Then he'd announced he was going out.

The way he said it and stormed out put Ian in mind of his teenage son, Danny. Not that he was a teenager any more. Danny must be… Oh, twenty-four now. A wave of regret washed over him as he contemplated the fact that he had to think hard to recall his son's age. Now wasn't the time to dwell on his past mistakes, though. With an effort, he pushed the thoughts aside and turned to Tanya.

"What do you make of that?" he asked.

He wasn't looking for a meaningful response, so was surprised at her answer. "He's hiding something."

"What, apart from the van in our barn?"

"I'm serious, Ian." She'd moved closer to him, and reached out with a hand, resting it on his forearm. He was suddenly aware of how vulnerable she looked.

"Tanya, what's wrong?" He'd removed her hand to allow himself to put his arm around her. It felt strange, after such a long period of coolness between them. But he knew it was the right thing to do, and she'd leaned against him for comfort.

"You couldn't see his face."

"What do you mean?"

"When you were telling him about the van. He had his head down."

As she said it, he'd replayed the scene in his mind. She was right. He and Oakes had been standing up, but Tanya had been sitting close to Martin. She would have been the only one to see his face.

"What happened?"

Her hand slipped into his, and gripped it tightly. "He was frightened."

★ ★ ★

They didn't go out much these days. Finances were a constraint, but so was the fact that they hadn't built up a circle of friends since they moved up here. Even if they had the opportunity, neither felt inclined to leave the house unattended.

As evening passed, they waited. The television was on, but neither of them were watching it. They were too distracted, listening out for the kitchen door – or the sound of a van coming into the yard. They even talked to each other. At one point, Ian reflected that maybe something good had come out of this situation.

In recent times, they had taken to sitting separately. Ian had his armchair and Tanya had hers. To sit on the sofa was clearly too much of a risk for either of them to take. It invited companionship. But that was what Tanya had done when she first came into the living room, a gesture Ian had acknowledged by joining her and leaving his hand free for her to hold if she wanted.

Considering the years they'd been together, it was awkward. But he was aware that they both welcomed it too. In Tanya's case, he knew she was afraid. But, more than that, he suspected that feeling was aggravated by her awareness that it was she who had brought Martin into their home. He didn't have any answers that could reassure her, so he satisfied himself with offering unspoken comfort.

As it grew later, and more likely that their guest would return, Ian would have liked Tanya to go to bed, out of the way. Then he could talk to Martin without her around. He had already worked out that Martin was more comfortable one to one. But he also knew that she wouldn't be happy about being on her own. She needed company for now. He contemplated asking her to leave when Martin did come in. Contemplated it, but didn't say anything. His fears had nothing to do with dog murderers and van thieves. They were about rejection. For tonight, he could hold her hand and be close to her. His own uncertainties lay snugly with their relationship, and he was afraid of what he might find if he faced that head on.

It was after midnight when they heard the engine. It didn't stop running, just idled for a few seconds, then they heard it rise in volume again as it went away. A moment later the kitchen door clattered open and closed again.

Squeezing his wife's hand, Ian stood up. He gestured to her to stay where she was. This was his compromise. He was going to head Martin off and talk to him in the kitchen. That way, he didn't have to risk rejection.

The kitchen was empty when he got there. A light shone in the passageway that led down to the guest room.

By the time he reached the doorway, he could see the bedroom door was closing.

"Martin?" He was relieved that his voice didn't sound too wary.

The door opened again, and a weary figure appeared, his face drawn, almost pale.

"You okay?" Ian asked tentatively.

His houseguest gave him a wry smile. "Not really."

"Want to talk about it?"

A shake of the head. "Not really." Then he made a show of looking at his watch. "I'm sorry I'm so late. It's very inconsiderate of me. I hope you haven't stayed up just for me."

Ian opened his mouth to reply, but suddenly found he didn't know what to say. He had lots of questions to ask. After all, he'd been thinking about them all afternoon and evening. But Martin looked completely shattered, ready to collapse. Maybe now wasn't the time.

"We should talk in the morning," he said eventually. It wasn't perfect, but at least he was making it clear that he wasn't going to ignore the situation.

Leaning against the doorframe, Martin nodded his understanding. "We will," he assured him. Then he raised his hand in a parody of a wave, and disappeared into his room.

"Let's hope so," Ian murmured to himself, as he turned to go back to Tanya. She wasn't going to be very happy about the continued uncertainty. He just hoped he could convince her of what he'd just seen. They weren't in any danger from him tonight. That man was in no fit state to do anything other than sleep.

THIRTEEN

Sleep was the last thing on Martin's mind. He wanted it. His body would have welcomed it. But his mind was elsewhere.

A myriad of thoughts tumbled around his head. The reason for coming back to the village fluttered in and out as he pondered over what he should do. When he'd left Gran Canaria, he didn't have a clear plan, but he did know what he wanted to achieve. More sleepless nights hadn't been on the list.

He didn't try to sleep. There was no point. He knew from years of experience that the harder he tried, the harder it was to drop off. The best he could hope for was some rest. So he allowed his body to gradually relax, starting at his extremities, methodically easing the tension out. To a point, anyway. It was impossible to let it all go. When certain images flashed across his mind; when the memory of sensations scampered over his flesh; when the voices played back in his head, then the tension crept up on him. Unnoticed at first, until he'd realise that his fists were clenched, or he was grinding his teeth. The process would begin again. Fingertips and toes to start, followed by his hands and wrists, his feet and ankles. Slowly letting his body relax once more.

It was a cycle he would repeat all night. He knew that

in advance. At some point, he might sleep, probably for only minutes at a time. If he was lucky, it might stretch out to half an hour. That had been his past experience. Somehow, he doubted he would be fortunate enough to achieve that tonight. Nightmares had kept him awake before. Memories of a distant past. Or so it had seemed. Those had been sufficient to leave him troubled, spending his nights staring into the darkness and wondering how things had gone so badly wrong.

This was different. The distant past didn't seem so far away. Perhaps he'd confused distance in miles with the passage of time.

With his return to Ravens Gathering, he'd hoped to lay some ghosts to rest. It seemed that there were more phantoms than he'd imagined. Maybe even poltergeists. Certainly his encounter with Adam Hawthorn had left him battered and bruised.

Moonlight filtered through the edges of the curtains. Shadows stirred across the bedroom wall. He knew it would be possible to see all kinds of shapes among them. There was no point in trying to. Not unless he planned to get no rest at all. He closed his eyes.

Sometimes that was worse. At least the things you could see were a distraction from your thoughts. They didn't take your mind off things altogether, but they could blur the edges. He tried to focus on his fingers and toes again. It worked for a while. Then he knew he had to open his eyes. Another cycle. Another technique he'd developed over the years.

There were times when he got up. Whenever he rented a new room or apartment, he tried to get one with a table.

That hadn't always been the case. But he'd realised that, when sleep was impossible, it often helped if he could write down all the things that were going through his head. As if, by putting those things on paper, he was physically extracting them from his mind and laying them out. It was like taking an engine apart when it wasn't working. With all the component parts laid out on the ground, you could see them all clearly. You could find the part – or parts – that were causing the problem, fix them, and then put them all back together again. But he'd found that sitting on the edge of his bed, hunched up over a notebook didn't help that process. A table or a desk was better.

On many occasions, he'd spent an hour, or more often two, writing frantically, pouring his thoughts, his troubles, his fears out on to paper. Then he'd crawl back into bed and sleep like a baby. He knew instinctively that no amount of writing would help him tonight.

At night, with no distractions, minor concerns could become major problems. And putting those problems into black and white could provide perspective. Right now, he knew he already had perspective. Minor concerns and major problems would be welcome right now.

So he turned to the question that kept surfacing. Should he leave?

He'd expected trouble. Hell, he'd planned on it. But he hadn't expected it to take this form. And he hadn't anticipated the direction it would come from.

It was clear that his family didn't want him back. Not that he'd intended to return for good. But they obviously wanted him out of their lives as rapidly as possible. A few hours ago, he'd been ready to press them for answers, wanted to know why. Now he wasn't so sure he did. It wasn't worth all this aggravation. Police, accusations, threats against him. And more.

Oh, yes. Much more.

But he didn't want to dwell on that. If he left in the morning, he wouldn't have to.

The luminous dial of the alarm clock told him it was after two. Nearly five hours before sunrise, at least six before the first bus left the village. He could be in Westfield by nine. On a train by half past. Out of the county before ten. He hadn't planned his departure, but he was still pretty confident he could be out of the country by mid-afternoon. If he hired a car rather than relying on public transport, he might even be flying by midday. It wouldn't be a cheap exit strategy, but money wasn't his main motivation right now.

So he could move quickly. He just couldn't start moving yet.

And yet... There was part of him that didn't want to run. Demons were there to be faced. Perhaps he should do just that. Because one day he might have to do it anyway. Running away from them would only defer it.

He let out a long breath, surprisingly noisy in the still of the night. Focus on the extremities, he told himself, conscious of the tension rising inside him again.

Then he heard another noise. Louder than his breathing. It was coming from outside.

At first he tried to ignore it. Kidding himself, he reflected later. Pretending it wasn't there, that it had nothing to do with him. It was only when he became aware of the tremor in his hands that he knew he had to make a decision.

It was an engine. Diesel by the sound of it. Distant, but getting closer. It wasn't noisy. If he'd been asleep, it wouldn't have disturbed him.

Twenty to three, the clock told him. Since coming to bed, he'd been wanting to get up. Now, when he knew he really had to, his only inclination was to stay exactly where he was.

The engine was moving away now. Still close, but it had passed the house. Steeling himself, he pushed the duvet back. It took a few seconds before he could bring himself to sit up. A few more until his feet touched the floor. But then momentum took over. Jeans, sweatshirt and trainers were quickly pulled on, then he was out into the hallway.

It might have been because he'd moved out of the bedroom, but he couldn't hear the engine any more. He hurried. He'd been afraid to act, but now he was up he didn't want it to be in vain.

The kitchen, like the rest of the house, was in darkness. He paused long enough to recall where the table and chairs were. It would have been better to allow his eyes to adjust, but he didn't have enough time. He headed for the door, guessing where the furniture was, and giving it a wide berth. The key was in the lock. He turned it, grimacing as the inner workings of the locking mechanism ground together. It was unlikely it would be heard by whoever was responsible for the engine, but he didn't want to disturb anyone in the house.

During the day, with all of the other background noise, the sound of a door knob turning would go unnoticed. In the dead of night, it was a different matter. Martin winced as it squealed under his hand. As he pulled the door inwards, he glanced over his shoulder. He was looking for any sign that he may have been heard – the dim glow of light from upstairs, perhaps. Instead, he found the silhouette of a man only a couple of feet behind him.

FOURTEEN

"What the hell's going on?"

Martin had been bracing himself, expecting the shadowy figure to lash out or grab him by the throat. Somehow, he couldn't imagine Ian doing that. Recognising his voice, he felt the increased tension ease a little. Faint movement caught his eye and he reached out to catch Ian's arm.

"Don't!"

"Why the hell not? What are you hiding?"

"Us. From whoever's outside."

Something in his tone must have struck a chord with Ian, because he relaxed his arm, let it fall away from the light switch he'd been stretching for.

"What are you doing up?" Martin asked.

"I thought I heard something, so I came down to investigate."

Someone else having trouble sleeping then.

"So what's going on?" Ian continued.

"I don't know for sure. I heard an engine outside." He hesitated for a moment, unsure how much he should tell Ian. Time was against him, though, so he made a decision. "After what happened today, I wondered if it might be the van coming back." It was a plausible enough answer, he reckoned.

"What were you going to do?"

"Go out and have a look. If it is the van, we can call the police."

"I'll come with you." He said it without missing a beat. "Let me just grab some boots and a coat."

"I'm not sure we've got time for that..." But Ian was already half way across the kitchen, heading for the annexe.

In a way, he was relieved about the delay. It might mean they were too late, which could be a good thing. After all, with Ian involved now, there was an additional risk to going out and confronting the driver of the vehicle.

But the delay was brief. Less than half a minute later, Ian was back with him, a Barbour jacket and wellington boots on. The prolonged time spent in the kitchen had given Martin's eyes time to adjust, and he could make out more. He could even see that Ian was still wearing pyjamas under his coat. Not ideal clothing if they met up with resistance.

They opened the door carefully, keeping the noise to a minimum. The rubber soles of the trainers and wellies barely made any sound as they crossed the yard.

The engine had either stopped before they came outside, or moved on to another place. If he hadn't already heard it, he might have doubted himself. At night, it's possible for sounds to appear to come from directions other than where they've originated. So he did wonder if perhaps the engine noise had carried from the main road. Maybe it was just his imagination working overtime.

As they headed towards the gate, Martin thought he caught a glimpse of something moving on the track running past the entrance to the yard. It was close to the hedge that ran along the opposite side, so it was indistinct – it might

241

even have just been part of the greenery swaying under the night breeze. The low clouds overhead didn't help, cutting the moonlight to a minimum. Ian didn't comment on it, which made Martin think he was probably imagining things.

When they reached the gate, they leaned over the top of it, looking up and down the track for any signs of activity. None were apparent.

Leaning in close to Ian, Martin said: "Let's go."

They opened the gate as quietly as they could, then made their way carefully up the track. If there was someone up at the barn, it was possible they could come back this way, so Martin pulled them to the side nearest the hedge. It offered more shelter and shadow, and would be easier to hide against than the brick wall on the other side.

Well, that was the plan. Until a gap in the clouds passed under the moon, illuminating the whole track and leaving nowhere to hide. Instinctively – though on reflection rather stupidly – they pressed themselves further back against the hedge. Thorns caught on their clothes, snagging the fabric. Fortunately, none penetrated the skin.

Feeling like a prisoner caught in a searchlight as he made a break for it, Martin turned his head from side to side. Perhaps similarly to the prisoner, he was looking to see if anyone had spotted him. What he saw instead was the backs of two men. They were next to each other, and walking down the track, away from the farm. Because of the angle of the track, he could only see them from the waist up. And, almost immediately, even that view diminished as they gradually descended.

He looked at Ian. Unlike Martin, he hadn't reacted

as if he was afraid of being caught. He was taking the opportunity to look in the direction they were going, and then at the track in front of them. Martin hesitated, wondering whether to tell him or not. He glanced back, but the figures had already disappeared. The decision was made for him.

"Look!" It was Ian, voice low.

Martin followed the direction of his finger. Although it had been sunny here since he'd arrived, he had noticed signs of recent rainfall. The more sheltered paths and tracks still had puddles and pools of dirty water, especially those that were filled with ruts and holes. A few yards ahead of them, just beyond one of those puddles, there was a clear imprint of a fresh tyre track. Not that Martin needed any further evidence. He nodded at Ian.

"We'd better get this over and done with." He knew his words and tone must have seemed odd, even without the puzzled look Ian gave him.

Safe in the knowledge that no one would be waiting for them now, he moved out into the centre of the track and started walking. Ian followed. The walk to the outbuildings took less than a minute.

"Which one is it?" Martin asked.

Ian pointed to the two large doors.

"I'll let you open it," Martin told him.

"Thanks." There was more than a touch of irony, but Martin ignored it. He knew they were both safe for now. Whoever opened the door would be in no more danger than the other. It was just more practical for Ian to do it. He knew what he was doing.

Hesitantly, Ian pulled on the door. As before, it opened

easily. He tried to peer in through a narrow gap, but Martin knew there wouldn't be enough light. He grabbed the edge of the door and pulled it open as wide as it would go.

"Is that the one?" he asked.

Nodding in response, Ian was looking around the rest of the barn, searching for the person who had brought the Sherpa and left it there.

FIFTEEN

By dawn, the outbuildings were sealed off. Crime scene tape was stretched across the track from just above the gateway into the farmyard. The yard itself was filled with all manner of vehicles, and more were parked further down the track, blocking off any access from the village. Police cars, both marked and unmarked, had arrived first. Because the roads were empty at that time of night, they hadn't needed to use sirens, so their arrival had been low-key. The chances were that they'd gone completely unnoticed.

Even the later arrivals at the party had managed to be discreet, a fact for which Detective Inspector Collins was grateful. He was in charge of the police operation, and knew he would be the one who had to deal with this problem locally. The more fuss there was, the harder his job was going to be.

Joint military and police operations weren't commonplace, and certainly not out in the sticks. Dealing with the IRA was more likely to be an issue in London or possibly the other big cities. A small village in North Nottinghamshire hadn't tended to attract the attention of terrorists. Nor did it seem a likely place for any other military intervention.

Two olive green Bedfords were parked by the opening to the square where the outbuildings stood. One of them had reversed in, and from the farmyard gate you could just see the front of it. The other stood a little further up, its tailgate open, the canvas flap rolled up. Half a dozen soldiers were sitting inside. They looked bored and uncomfortable. Like Collins, they were probably feeling somewhat disgruntled at being dragged out in the middle of the night. Unlike Collins, he guessed they were also frustrated at having nothing to do for the moment.

They looked to be young lads, no older than twenty-five. At that age, he'd have wanted action and excitement. Saw some too when he worked for the Met. But that seemed like a lifetime ago. Back in the day when every copper he knew wanted to be Jack Regan. And God knew there had been plenty of opportunities to behave like that. Certainly he'd had his fair of share of violent exchanges with the London low-life. Too many.

Which was why he didn't share the young squaddies' frustration that nothing was happening. With any luck, that's the way it would stay. And if it didn't stay that way, he definitely didn't want to be around when these would-be Rambos started letting off steam with their assault rifles.

What was more disturbing to him was the van that was currently hidden from view. He had been standing outside the barn when it arrived. It was now parked with its back to the barn doors. The gap between the two sets of doors had been sealed off with heavy plastic sheeting, but that hadn't prevented him from seeing the suits the men inside were wearing. The squared-off head covering was distinctive enough to reinforce his impression that the Army were taking this situation very seriously.

That had been several minutes ago now, and the Colonel in charge had made it abundantly clear they didn't want any coppers around. Whether that was because they were concerned to minimise casualties, or because they had something to hide was up for debate. But bearing in mind that, if anything went wrong, they'd only be a few hundred yards away, Collins doubted very much he'd be any safer in the farmhouse.

He pushed that thought aside. It wasn't one he wanted to dwell on too much. Not with a wife and teenage children waiting for him at home.

Inside the house, his DS – Les O'Neill – had tactfully taken over the lower floor. The dining room was to be used for interviewing the witnesses, who'd been separated. Fortunately, there were suitable rooms for them to be held in until it was their turn to be seen. Collins couldn't help a wry smile when he realised that Mrs McLean had been allocated the kitchen. No doubt O'Neill was thinking about all the mugs of tea that would be needed before long. He just hoped Mrs McLean was too shell-shocked to realise what the DS was up to.

The guest, Gates, was staying in a room in the annexe, so they'd made sure he couldn't get anywhere near that. Mr McLean had been put into the small living room in the annexe, and Gates was in the main living room.

There was nothing to suggest that any of them were involved in this yet, but Collins wasn't taking any chances. The witnesses needed to be kept apart in case it turned out any of them were involved. He didn't want to give them the opportunity to get their stories straight. Having said that, they'd had twenty minutes from the time of the 999

247

call to the first officer's arrival on the scene, so this was damage limitation.

Predictably, the kettle was on. Mrs McLean appeared to be in something of a daze. She was filling mugs from a teapot, but looked as if she wasn't really conscious of what she was doing.

"Cuppa, Guv?"

It was O'Neill. No doubt the other witnesses were being watched over by a couple of DCs he'd managed to drag out of bed. Looking at Mrs McLean, Collins understood why O'Neill had pulled rank. Even pale with tiredness and shock she was an attractive woman. In times gone by, Collins might well have acted with similar self-interest. He wondered if he was just getting too old.

Shaking his head, he declined the offer. "Not now. Let's get on with the statements, shall we?"

He'd been going to thank Mrs McLean for her help, but she'd barely been aware of him. With other policemen coming and going through the kitchen, that was hardly surprising. Although the Army wanted them clear of the barn, Collins had insisted his officers be allowed to move freely in all other areas nearby. He suspected it would be impractical to cover all of it effectively, but wanted to preserve as much as possible in case a fingertip search needed to be carried out later. But they'd only been out there for two hours, and the military for three quarters of an hour, so they were still getting themselves organised. Using the farmhouse as a command centre, it was inevitable that there was still plenty of activity here. Two uniformed constables were currently in the kitchen, apparently just waiting for their cups of tea.

Collins jerked his head, indicating that O'Neill should follow him into the hall. Clutching his mug, the DS did as he was told, but not before instructing one of the PCs to stay in the kitchen. They couldn't afford to leave Mrs McLean on her own.

"Who do you want to see first?" O'Neill asked when they were beyond earshot.

This was a question Collins had been mulling over for ten minutes or so. Ordinarily, he'd have jumped into the interview as soon as they'd secured the area, but the military involvement had added a new dimension he hadn't anticipated, so standard procedures had been put aside until he was forced to come back to them. There was no obvious order for him. He should probably start with either of the two men who claimed to have found the van. In a sense, which one they chose was academic. Still, there was something odd about the house guest.

"Let's have Gates in," he said, then left O'Neill to sort that out while he went into the dining room.

The dining room wasn't huge. A table for six fit in it comfortably – dark, shiny wood and matching the drinks cabinet and sideboard that stood against the wall opposite the doorway. But any more furniture in the room would have made it cramped. The end of the table faced him as he came in. A chair stood at either end, two on each of the sides. A notepad and pen had already been placed on the table. Someone had been efficient in his absence. Probably O'Neill.

Moving to the right side of the table, Collins shrugged his overcoat off and draped it over the back of a chair. He sat down, pulling the notepad towards him. As he picked up the biro, he was aware that he was already shifting into a different gear. He'd been the Army Liaison Officer, he'd been the Guv. Now he was the Interviewer.

O'Neill appeared in the doorway with Gates. Collins had seen him only briefly earlier, and then hadn't had an opportunity to speak to him. That initial glance had given him a perception that he now realised was wrong. It was mainly the long hair and tan, but he'd got the impression that he was younger, probably early twenties. There was, though, also something about the way he walked. An athletic, easy motion that was certainly more common amongst the young. Even as he came into the room, Collins recognised that this was a man used to activity. It was difficult to be sure under the thick shirt he was wearing, but it also looked as if he was quite muscular. Not in an Arnold Schwarzenegger kind of way – he wasn't *that* obvious. But it did leave Collins wondering what he did when he wasn't visiting Ravens Gathering.

"Mr Gates." He stood up and offered his hand. Gates' handshake was firm, but he clearly didn't feel the need to make an impression with a bone-crusher. He gestured to the chair opposite. "Please sit down." As Gates took his seat, Collins nodded to O'Neill. "Would you sit with us too, Les." First names. Keeping it informal for now.

"Well, Mr Gates, first of all can I thank you for contacting us." He spoke naturally. Being in the interviewer mode, he knew he should trust his instincts, and right now they were telling him this needed to be a chat and not an interrogation. "And can I also apologise for having to restrict your movements for the time being. As I'm sure you must have gathered, there's more to this incident than a stolen van."

Gates nodded his understanding, but Collins felt there was something a little guarded about his response.

"I'm Detective Inspector Collins," he went on. "My colleague here is Detective Sergeant O'Neill. I believe your name is Martin, is that right?"

Another nod.

"Do you mind if I call you Martin?"

A shrug this time, but accompanied by a few words. "Might as well." He sounded resigned to it rather than truculent.

"I bet when you hear people saying 'Mr Gates' you look over your shoulder for your dad, don't you?" He smiled at his little joke, but the look on Gates's face told him he was far from amused. "Anyway, let's move on. What I want to do right now, Martin, is just go over with you what happened this morning."

"I assumed you would."

"So… Would you like to go through it all from the beginning?"

"How far back do you want me to go?"

"Well… What made you go out to the barn in the first place?"

Gates hesitated for a moment. That wasn't necessarily a sign of guilt or of a lie coming up, but Collins was aware of it, and waited to see how it would pan out.

As it happened, the story he told seemed realistic. Realistic in the sense that, although the explanation seemed plausible, it also incorporated enough inconsistencies to suggest that, like most people, he didn't remember everything exactly as it happened. The events that seemed to occur out of sequence, the pauses as he thought carefully before going on, even the moments when he asked aloud, "Or did that happen later?" before going on to the next part of his story.

Nevertheless, there was something Collins didn't feel was right. As Gates talked, the policeman wrote, his eyes rising and falling between the interviewee's face and the notepad. He didn't know what was wrong, but his instinct told him to be very careful.

When Gates reached the point where he'd found the van, Collins interrupted.

"Can I ask a question?" Not that he waited for a response. "From the comments you made earlier, I gather you've only been in the village since the day before yesterday." He paused, his expression a study in thoughtfulness. "How did you know it was the stolen van?"

"I didn't. Ian did. But one of your boys had found tracks leading into the barn yesterday when he was round investigating the theft. So it would've seemed a bit coincidental otherwise."

"Fair point," Collins said amiably. He looked over at O'Neill. "Who was the officer dealing with that?"

"Oakes, Guv. He's been contacted. We're expecting him out here soon." There was a twinkle in his eye that suggested Oakes hadn't been too impressed at getting a call. Well, that was tough. If he'd wanted regular hours, he should have gone to work for a bank or the council.

"I'll have a word with him when he gets here." This was said as much for Gates' benefit as O'Neill's. If he'd said anything that might contradict what Oakes had to say, now was the time to come clean. He turned his attention back to Gates. "Now, where were we?"

"I was telling you that we'd found the van."

"Ah, yes. Go on."

"Well, we found the van and came back to the house to phone you guys."

"Right. And this would have been...?"

"I don't know. Maybe around four o'clock."

"That'd fit in with our records, Guv."

And yet Collins had a feeling Gates was lying.

"Then you just waited for us to arrive?" he prompted.

"Yeah. Ian went and got Tanya up, but apart from that, there was nothing else to do. We've all seen enough telly to know you leave crime scenes alone, so we weren't going to go back."

"There was also the danger of the thief coming back, of course," Collins added, as if the thought might not have occurred to Gates otherwise. There was no reaction to his words. Gates just continued to watch him from across the table. It was as if he was waiting for something. Maybe he hadn't asked the right questions yet. He looked down at the notes he'd written. "Can I just go back to something you said earlier? You were disturbed by the sound of the engine. And you got up almost straight away. Why was that?"

Gates looked puzzled. "How do you mean?"

"Well, you made it sound like it was unusual. You seemed to be saying that's why you got up."

"It was."

"It was what?" When this was met with a blank look, Collins helped him. "It was unusual, or it was the reason you got up."

A flicker. Subtle, but not too subtle for an old pro. He'd realised where the question was leading. And he'd realised that he might have made a mistake.

253

"I meant, it was the reason I got up." A pause. He wasn't sure whether to elaborate, but clearly felt he had to. "And the reason, just to clarify, Inspector, was that the interrogation your constable subjected me to yesterday was still playing on my mind." Interesting, Collins thought. He's decided to go on the offensive now. "So when I heard the engine, I wondered whether it was the van."

"Bit odd, though, don't you think?"

"Odd?"

"Well, for a stolen van to be brought up here one night, then taken away, only to be brought back again. Doesn't that seem odd to you?"

"The whole bloody thing seems odd to me. But then I've not had a lot of experience of stolen vehicles."

That was interesting too. Was this a case of protesting too much?

"So you got up straight away," Collins went on. "And you went straight out. Weren't you worried about bumping into whoever was in the van?"

"Of course I was."

"Well why didn't you just phone it in?"

"Because I didn't know for sure that's what I'd heard."

"So you went out in the dark, unarmed, just to check it?" He managed to stay just on the right side of sounding credulous.

"Inspector, have you ever done something in the heat of the moment, and when you looked back on it later you realised you'd been a complete bloody idiot?"

More times than he cared to think about, if the truth were known. And a lot of them while he was on duty.

He nodded. "I take your point." But there was

something else he wanted to cover. As he glanced back at his notes, he was aware of voices elsewhere in the house. They weren't raised, as such, but the volume had suddenly become louder. Before he had a chance to ask O'Neill to go and find out what was happening, there was a knock on the door. Someone opened it without waiting for a response.

Predictably, the man standing in the doorway wasn't one of his. The three stripes on the sleeve told Collins his rank. "I've got orders to move everyone away from here, sir."

"You do know I'm carrying out a police investigation here, don't you?" Even as he said it, he knew he was wasting his time. Under the circumstances, the Army were the ones who were really in charge.

"The Colonel said to tell you he wasn't going to force you to go, but the specialists have arrived and they'd prefer it if the farm was cleared."

And, frankly, so would I, Collins thought to himself. He smiled at Gates. It was best to keep things amicable for the time being. "It looks like we'll have to finish this elsewhere." Turning back to the sergeant, he said: "It'll take a while to get my men together. Can you ask the Colonel to give us half an hour?"

"I'm sure that'll be fine, Inspector." He turned to go, but Collins called him back.

"Sergeant! What about the rest of the village?"

"That's taken care of, sir. There's no need to worry about it." The soldier threw a glance at the civilian. Collins got the message. The village would just have to risk it.

SIXTEEN

The all clear didn't come through till early afternoon. From one perspective, that was bad news for Collins. It meant he couldn't let his officers loose on the farm, and he was desperate to start a search for evidence. On the other hand, it gave him a good excuse to detain the witnesses without formally treating them as suspects.

Before starting his interviews with them, he wanted to talk to Brian Oakes about the enquiries he'd made yesterday.

Almost inevitably, Oakes hadn't received the message about the withdrawal from the farm, and had been greeted by a hostile group of armed men. So by the time he arrived at the station, he was clearly disgruntled.

It's not uncommon for older, more experienced officers to watch the young bloods at work and curse them, whilst at the same time being reminded of themselves when they were first starting out. They're faced with a combination of irritation and nostalgia. Irritation at the lack of ability, and nostalgia for those days when they had been so full of energy and determination to be the best they could. Where Brian Oakes was concerned, there was only the irritation, and that was escalating into something approaching annoyance after forty minutes of watching him laboriously trying to make sense of his own notes.

And not once did the dozy idiot ask what all the fuss was about.

When he was satisfied that there was nothing useful he was going to learn, Collins sent Oakes to get the notes typed up while he started with the witnesses.

He'd told them he wanted to take statements, but what he really meant was he wanted to interrogate them, and he did. At length. He did it in a friendly manner – he chatted, he smiled, he looked for opportunities to make a joke. But he also made copious notes, and he went back over things with them, "just to make sure I've got this right…"

McLean had responded well. Collins was sure he understood what was going on, but was happy to go along with it. He had the air of a man who had nothing to hide.

Mrs McLean was different altogether. She'd clearly recovered somewhat by the time Collins sat down with her. All of the interrogations were held in his office. He felt that the formality of an interview room might have put them on their guard. Of course, the office itself wasn't without formality, but he'd softened that by arranging the chairs on one side of the desk. For all of them, this was helpful. In Mrs McLean's case, having no barriers between them had obvious benefits, and O'Neill certainly took advantage of them. And, in her somewhat refreshed state, she was clearly willing to take advantage of *that*. Her sitting position, and every adjustment she made to it during the course of the interview, was carefully considered. Every time she had to stop and think about an answer to a question, she tilted her head back and angled it slightly away from them. She knew what to do to make herself look good. Collins wasn't immune to her charms, but he was a student of human behaviour, and that interest distracted him enough to avoid falling into any of the traps she was laying for them. O'Neill, on the other hand, was jumping gleefully into them, and seemed quite happy to impale himself on the spikes.

Collins was fascinated by the manipulation. As he carefully went through his questions with her and found nothing suspicious in her answers, he couldn't help wondering why she did it. The behaviour suggested she might be trying to hide something by diverting their attention away from what she was saying and on to her. By the end of the interview, though, he was confident this wasn't something she was doing because of the circumstances. It was just what she did. She needed attention, and took every opportunity to get it.

They saved Gates till last. It was a deliberate choice by Collins. His impression from the early morning meeting had not been good, and the feedback from Oakes also gave him cause for concern. The interviews with the McLeans had provided a further opportunity to unearth more so he had something else he could use, but nothing obvious had come up.

By the time O'Neill led Gates into the office, the McLeans were on their way home.

The three men sat down in a loose triangle. Collins ran a weary hand through his thinning hair. Although he was nearly fifty, his hair was still very dark, almost black, but his widow's peak was becoming more pronounced. His sharp features, softened only slightly by the weight he'd put on over the last couple of years, gave him a hawkish appearance. If anyone looked at a photograph of him, they could easily assume he was a mean spirited and possibly even a bitter man. There were times when that impression was useful to cultivate. If a good cop/bad cop routine was required, Collins was already typecast. It was a testament to his character, though, that he could dispense with that image very rapidly, as he'd already demonstrated in the interviews with the McLeans.

He looked tired now, partly due to the early start. But he was deliberately overplaying it for Gates's benefit. It didn't do any harm to make the witness think you wouldn't be paying proper attention.

"Sorry for keeping you waiting, Martin." Collins gave a short sigh. Not too obtrusive, but enough to be noticed. "It's been a long day for us all and I'm sure you just want to get back to the farm."

"It's safe to go then?"

"Oh yes. The van's been removed."

Collins made a big show of checking his notes, even though he'd read them thoroughly before asking for Gates. After a moment or two, he looked up. His head was shaking slightly, his face registered puzzlement.

"I'm sorry about this, Martin. It's been that long since we last spoke, I've forgotten where we were up to."

Gates made a show of checking his watch. "Well it *has* been over eight hours." He made no attempt to hide his annoyance.

"Have you been treated okay?" The question was filled with concern for his wellbeing.

"Yes, fine," Gates said impatiently. "Now can we get on?"

"Of course."

And they did. Slowly, methodically, Collins went to

work. At first, Gates came across as defensive, which he'd expected after the feedback from Oakes. But gradually the barriers came down, and they even shared a few smiles along the way. Even so, after an hour and a half, Collins felt he'd learnt little more than he already knew. He also felt sure that, in spite of the rapport they'd built up, Gates was keeping something from him. Unfortunately, feelings alone weren't enough to detain him further.

"Well, Martin," he said brightly, covering his disappointment, "I can't think of anything else we need to cover at the moment. So I'll let you get home and get some rest." He hesitated for a moment, clearly pondering something. "Not that the farm is your home." He made the remark as if it was a puzzle to him. "In fact, where *is* your home, Martin?"

It was Gates's turn to look thoughtful. "That's a good question, Inspector," he said at last. "Technically, I have an apartment in Gran Canaria, but the rent on that's only paid to the end of the month. After that, I could be homeless." The idea seemed to amuse him.

"Do you think you'll move back to the UK?" Conversational, not interrogative.

"I doubt it."

"Can't say I blame you. Bloody lousy weather."

"More like a bloody lousy family."

"Aren't they all?"

"Mine's in a class of its own."

A chuckle from Collins. "Are they *really* that bad?"

"I'd be here all day telling you," Gates said. "And you've got bad guys to catch." He gave Collins a meaningful look. "Unless you think I'm one of the bad guys."

"In all honesty, Martin, I can't rule anything out at this stage. But I would struggle to see how your family problems could have anything to do with a stolen van."

"Especially not a stolen van with a bomb in it."

And not just any bomb, Collins thought, but he kept it to himself. He stood up and stretched out his arm. As Gates responded in kind, Collins gestured to the door with his free hand.

"Obviously, you'll need to sign the statement, and we've got to get that typed up first. Sergeant O'Neill here will make sure you've got somewhere comfortable to sit while you're waiting. But as soon as that's done, we'll have a car take you back to the farm."

"Thanks." Gates turned to the door.

"Oh, and one more thing," Collins added before he opened it. "It's likely that we'll need to have another chat with you over the next day or two, so I'd appreciate it if you didn't head back to the Canaries."

"Do you want my passport?"

"Just your cooperation will be fine."

Martin nodded his agreement and allowed himself to be steered out of the room by O'Neill.

When O'Neill returned a few minutes later, Collins was sitting behind his desk reading through the notes he'd made. They would be needed for typing up the statement, but he obviously wasn't in a rush to let Gates go yet.

"What do you think, Guv?" he asked after closing the door.

The DI looked past him to make sure the door was closed. Within CID only a handful of officers knew how serious this enquiry was, and he was pretty confident they'd be forced to sign some paperwork concerning the Official Secrets Act before long.

"I haven't got a clue what to think, Les. All three of them are hiding something. I just don't know what it is. And that's not helping us to find out how a van containing a device stolen from the Atomic Weapons Establishment ended up in a barn in Sherwood Forest."

SEVENTEEN

Tanya was tired, but restless at the same time. The police enquiries yesterday afternoon had been disturbing enough for her, but the events overnight and today had left her with a mixture of emotions. Being told you have a bomb only a few yards away from your home was hardly an everyday event. To be ordered to leave your home because of it threw yet more feelings into the mix. Fear of death or injury, combined with frustration and anger at being told what to do, and having no choice about it.

Ian hadn't been much help either. He'd just gone along meekly with whatever the police or the soldiers said. Why didn't he argue with them?

As she wondered that, she knew that there wouldn't have been any point in arguing. And she also knew that Ian would have recognised that, and saved his energy for more important things. But she hadn't wanted rational and considered thinking. She'd wanted some action. Someone to show they'd got a bit of life in them.

Even though she was still concerned about what he was up to, she still preferred the way Martin had behaved yesterday with the Plod. It probably wasn't very productive, but at least it showed there was a spark of life in him. Whether he'd shown the same spark this morning, she couldn't tell. When Ian had come up to the bedroom,

Martin had been busy downstairs. She thought she'd heard him talking to someone, but couldn't be sure. While Ian sat on the bed and talked to her, she'd heard him go outside again. She'd only been vaguely aware of it. Ian was telling her that they'd found the missing van in the barn. That they were going to phone the police soon, but Martin had to do something else first.

"What? What's he got to do?"

He'd shrugged, unsure what to say to her.

"It's him, isn't it? He's the one who stole the van. He's covering his tracks, isn't he?"

But he'd shaken his head very firmly. "No. It isn't Martin."

"Well what's he up to then?"

Instead of answering, Ian said: "Look, we need to give him some leeway."

"Leeway!" Her voice had risen, and he responded by lifting his hands and waving them downwards, indicating she should do the same with her volume.

"We need to tell the police that we only found the van…" He glanced at the alarm clock. "…around four o'clock."

She followed his gaze. "It's not even half-three yet."

He ignored her protest. "Martin needs a bit more time."

"For *what*? Has he got another dog to butcher, or is he going to see if he can catch some of those bloody ravens, so he can sacrifice *them*?"

At five o'clock in the afternoon, she still didn't know what Martin had been up to. Ian either didn't know, or wasn't telling. He'd given nothing away when he'd returned to their bedroom this morning. Instead he'd stressed that he hadn't time to explain, that he needed her to back him up. By the time he'd convinced her to do that, Martin was back in the house and on the phone. She could hear his muted tones as she dressed.

And when Ian had finally led her down the stairs, they had only a few minutes before the police arrived. Then Ian and Martin had taken the officers to the barn, and after that all hell seemed to have been let loose. Lots of sitting around on her own. You couldn't really class the police officers as company. She'd hardly seen Martin or Ian over the next several hours. They were kept apart at the house, they were driven to Westfield in different cars, and they were taken to separate offices within the police station.

There were times when she'd been tempted to tell the detectives her husband and lodger were up to something. But her annoyance at being treated like a common criminal more than balanced out that urge. And, even though she'd always enjoyed male attention, there was something unusually distasteful about being ogled by men who were supposed to be investigating a serious crime. Especially one in which her own life could have been threatened.

So she'd held out. Hoping to get some answers from Ian and Martin when they got home.

But the answers hadn't come. Once the bomb had been removed from the site, the police had been allowed back on the farm. And when Tanya and Ian were dropped off at the house, it was to find it still occupied by officers who were searching for evidence. Evidence of what, they weren't prepared to disclose, though it wouldn't need *Inspector Morse* to work out they were going through the process of "eliminating the McLeans and their house guest from their enquiries". Or not, as the case might be.

When she'd first gone into her bedroom, it had briefly crossed her mind that they might have been burgled in their absence. Drawers had been left half open, clothes had been dropped on the bed or floor, their hangers lying loosely nearby as if they'd been deliberately separated. Ornaments were scattered haphazardly across the surfaces on which they'd previously stood so neatly. Whoever had carried out the search had been given orders to do a thorough job as rapidly as possible. Finesse wasn't part of the job description.

On reflection, burglars might have been preferable. At least they'd have taken what they wanted and gone. Instead, her most private areas had been breached by strangers, but strangers who were still in the house. And from the looks exchanged between a few of them, she knew they'd found things even Ian didn't know were hidden in her drawers. Being judged by those bastards made her feel ashamed – even though she knew she had nothing to be ashamed about. And then there was the anger she felt knowing they'd been pawing through her underwear. More conflicting emotions. Adding to the confusion in the same way that she didn't know who to be angrier with: the police for invading her privacy, Martin for being the cause, or Ian for persuading her to cover for him.

To make matters worse, because the police were still searching the house, it was impossible to talk to Ian properly and try to find out exactly what had happened in the early hours of the morning.

They could have left the police to it, but she didn't feel happy about that. Not that she was overjoyed at the prospect of staying close by where they could let their eyes drift over her, imagining her wearing some of the more adventurous underwear they'd come across. Or maybe the videos in their heads were playing images of her using some of the toys they'd found. And they'd definitely found them. One had been left in the middle of the bed, a far from discreet message for her.

Under other circumstances, she'd have perhaps enjoyed letting a police officer catch a glimpse of some of her private items. It might have been fun to pick one of them out and tease him. It wasn't unheard of for her to offer tantalising hints of what she was wearing underneath a skirt or blouse, or to "accidentally" show a little more leg or cleavage than might be expected. The knowledge of what that could do to a man was exciting. But it was also on her terms. She was in control. This was different.

As well as the police, there were still soldiers around. None of them were in the house, or even in the yard. But they'd seen the olive coloured Land Rovers and a lorry still parked up by the barn. And they could hear them intermittently. No idea what they were shouting about or why the occasional clattering noise was happening, but in their own way she guessed they were being as thorough as the police.

Not that she could blame them. Another conflicting thought. She was pissed off at the intrusion and disruption. But at the same time, she knew she'd be just as annoyed if they'd simply taken the bomb away and then buggered off without bothering to check the area, either for more bombs or for evidence so they could catch whoever was responsible.

Which made her think of Martin. What the hell *was* he up to?

She'd expected to find out from Ian, but as soon as the police left the house he was out the door and jumping into his own Land Rover. The timing was deliberate. She knew that. As he crossed to the yard, there were still police cars manoeuvring to make their exit. At least one of them was only moving out to join the Army vehicles. An officer had already told them there would be a police presence on the farm for at least another couple of hours. If she caused a scene, they might well decide to stop in the yard – or even come back to the house. More frustration, then. He'd made some comment about going to check how Matthew and Patrick were getting on. But she wasn't sure if that was just an excuse for him to go in the opposite direction to the police.

Now, an hour or so later, she was feeling angry and confused, frustrated and bitter, frightened and embarrassed. And lonely.

The bedroom was tidy. It had been therapy of sorts. At times, her discoveries of what had been unearthed had left her mortified. But she'd ploughed on, gradually restoring order to the room, and hoping that deep down some order would start to be restored inside her.

When she heard the kitchen door open, she assumed it would be Ian. She hadn't heard him drive into the yard, but with military vehicles still moving around outside, she could easily have missed his Land Rover.

A part of her wanted to storm down and demand answers. Another part of her wanted to be held tightly and reassured it was all over. Either way, she needed to be with him. Her head and heart in turmoil, she trudged down the stairs. Martin was waiting for her.

Strangely, she felt relief. With the tension between her and Ian recently, although she needed him to come home, she also dreaded it, not knowing how he'd react. Or how she'd react to him. For months, she'd known the marriage was dead. But that didn't make dealing with it any easier. Ian not being there meant she didn't have to face up to that for a while longer.

Martin was standing just inside the kitchen. He looked expectant. She assumed he must have heard her coming down.

"How are you?" There was a certain wariness about the question. As if he wasn't sure he wanted to know the answer. Oddly, she could relate to it, and it reassured her.

"I've had better days." Her voice sounded weary, and she realised just how exhausted she suddenly was.

He smiled at her, his own tiredness obvious. "Haven't we all?"

Stepping to one side, he gestured to the table. "Want to come and sit with me?"

"Why would I want to do that?" For a moment, she was transported back to two days ago. When they'd first met, they'd been playful and flirty. She'd enjoyed that, and she was sure he had too.

"Keep an old man company?" he suggested.

"*Are* you an old man?" She'd moved closer, as if she was going to sit at the table.

"I definitely feel it at the moment."

Only a foot or so separated them. She stopped and looked up at him. Far from looking old, he seemed like a child. The tiredness he was feeling had stripped some of his protective layers away. Instead of the cool surfer dude, the real Martin was showing through. All signs of confidence were gone. Wariness and uncertainty prevailed. Her anger towards him slipped away. Instead she just wanted to be close to him.

"Will you hold me?" she asked.

He studied her cautiously.

"I won't bite," she assured him.

Then he grinned. "Unless I ask nicely?"

EIGHTEEN

Sex hadn't really been on his mind. But seeing her like this, aware of her proximity, he felt himself stir. He reached out and touched her face. His fingers glided down her cheek, the softness of her skin exciting him.

She looked up into his eyes, and her expression only served to arouse him further.

His intention had been to talk to her. There were things he needed to say. But perhaps this was a situation where actions would speak louder than words.

He dipped his head down and kissed her. Her lips didn't part immediately, but that didn't bother him. He knew they would and, sure enough, moments later he was enjoying the warmth and wetness of her mouth. It spurred him on. His arms slipped around her, pulling her against him as he thrust his hardness into her stomach.

Coming up for air momentarily, he noted the dilated pupils and felt his own excitement rising. Then he was pushing her against the wall, reaching frantically down for the hem of her skirt. Kissing her again, his lips crushed harshly against hers. Lust had taken over. She was his now, and nothing was going to stop this happening.

There had been moments over the last couple of days when he had thought about this. In his heart, he'd known this moment would come. But the time hadn't seemed right. And he'd had other things to do, which meant leaving her out of the picture while he got on with his plans.

But those plans were almost complete. Very soon he'd be able to leave. There might have been another opportunity later, but now just seemed the right time to act.

Her skirt was pulled up around her waist now, and his fingers were pulling aside the flimsy fabric that lay between them and her sex.

She bucked against him, and he pushed her back, letting her know he was in control. He knew she wasn't used to having someone else in charge. That knowledge alone was stimulating.

As he pressed into her, he left a gap between them, enough space for his free hand to access her breasts. The contact with the outside of her shirt was brief, then he was tugging at the buttons, virtually ripping it open. Creamy flesh was exposed. The lacy underwear was no match for his fingers. He caught a nipple between thumb and forefinger, squeezing it. She gasped into his mouth.

His other hand had found what it was looking for. Fingers pushed roughly into her. She wasn't ready for him yet, but it wasn't something he was going to dwell on. This was animal passion, not a physical declaration of love.

In a way, this position he'd manoeuvred them into was uncomfortable. To lie down with a woman was probably the most practical way to do this. But it was boring. The impracticality, the uncertainty of what they would do next and how it would work, that only added to the stimulation.

As did the possibility they might be seen. Anyone coming close enough to a window would be able to see them. The married woman with her breasts and legs exposed. No doubts at all as to what she was doing with her house guest.

Slipping his fingers from inside her, he grasped one of her hands and placed it over his crotch, holding it there long enough for her to get the message. Then he felt his zip being lowered. Her other hand reached for his belt. Satisfied that she would do what he wanted, he pulled her underwear aside and ran his fingertips over her. The jolting reaction told him all he needed to know about the state she was in.

He felt his trousers open and her hand hesitate.

"Take it out," he told her, his voice heavy with the excitement. Then he was kissing her again, thrusting his tongue on to hers.

The soft warmth of her hand sent an intense thrill through him. In part it was the physical sensation, but it was more a result of the knowledge that what they were doing was wrong. Regardless of how good or bad her marriage was, she had made a commitment in the eyes of God, and now he was doing everything he could to tear that commitment apart.

Both hands moved beneath her skirt now and he tore through lace, letting the ruined garment fall to her feet. He cupped her buttocks and lifted her slightly, pressing her back against the wall for support. A glance at her face revealed the shock in her eyes. He grinned, fired up by the spontaneity, the ferocity of his actions. Then he was pushing forward, his groin rising to meet hers.

Remarkably, and apparently to her surprise, his aim was true, and he was immediately sliding into her and savouring the soft dampness around him. Holding her tightly between himself and the wall, he drove himself in and out, taking her roughly and urgently. She gasped and shrieked as he did so, her responses only serving to arouse him more.

He was distracted briefly by movement to his left. He glanced over and smiled. Many things could energise him. Most of them involved other people's pain. He fed off their suffering like a vampire feeds on blood. And to a husband there is very little more emotionally painful than watching your wife being taken by another man.

His climax was one of the most intense he had experienced in a long time.

NINETEEN

Fourteen hours had passed since Collins had been roused from his bed. His own office didn't have windows, but he'd caught a glimpse of daylight when he'd ventured out to the loo, so he knew it was still fairly early. Even though the unsocial hours went with the job, sometimes they could be hard to accept, especially with a family at home. Not that they'd be waiting for him – from past experience, they knew better than that.

It was tempting to knock off early and leave it until tomorrow. The phone calls from the Ministry of Defence seemed to have slackened off. At one point, he'd been getting demands for updates every fifteen minutes. But since he'd patiently pointed out to them that every minute he spent talking to them was a minute less he could spend on his investigation, they'd tailed off. It was nearly an hour and a half since the last call. And bearing in mind the way the Civil Service worked, that probably meant they'd reached the end of their working day, so were unlikely to call again before nine in the morning, especially as it'd be a Sunday. Besides, their main concern had been retrieving the device. And as far as he'd been able to tell, they weren't missing any more of them.

He smiled at his own flippancy. The situation this morning had been deadly serious. There were a lot of people at the farm who'd been wishing they were elsewhere, and that was on the basis that it was just an 'ordinary' bomb. For those in the know, the reaction was stronger. The first instinct for Collins had been to gather his family together and jump on the first long-haul flight he could, but those thoughts hadn't stayed with him for long. He was pretty sure that, if the bomb *had* gone off this morning, it would have been long before his plane took off. Besides, if there was fallout, how would he know where it'd end up? Before Chernobyl, he'd assumed that if anything went wrong in Russia it wouldn't affect the UK. Even now, he refused to eat lamb in case it came from Wales.

Self-preservation aside, at heart he was a copper, and a bloody good one. Not because he was a budding Sherlock Holmes – and definitely not a Starsky or Hutch: those days were long gone. What made him good was his determination to get to the truth and nail the bad guys. There was plenty of injustice in the world that he couldn't do anything about. So if he came across a situation he could do something about, he would. It was why his wife put up with the long and unsocial hours, the time he spent away from her and the boys. He knew that, and he was grateful to her. It was also why he wasn't ready to leave the case alone just yet.

There was something not right about it. Not that there should be *anything* right about a nuclear device being stolen and then left in the back of a van in an old barn on the edge of Sherwood Forest.

The what-ifs were endless. What he really needed was evidence to point him in the right direction. But the evidence about the theft itself was being gathered by the

Royal Military Police's Special Investigation Branch, and it was doubtful anything meaningful would be released by them. The MoD would want this hushed up as much as possible. Alarming the general population was one thing, but this was bloody embarrassing.

So all he had to go on was at this end, and that wasn't much. His boys had been given limited access to the van when it was found and the Army had taken it with them when they'd left.

Their departure from the farm had been surprisingly discreet. Roadworks had been contrived to block civilian access to that end of the village, and they'd used the track that passed *The Barns* to leave the farm. The military presence wouldn't have gone completely unnoticed by the locals, but its scale and significance would pass them by.

What was less impressive about their departure was the complete inability to preserve any evidence they'd bothered to leave behind. In manoeuvring off the main track to pass through the farm yard, lorries and Land Rovers executed three point turns that churned up any imprints from feet or tyres.

Physical evidence was sadly lacking, then, for either CID or SIB. Which left him with witness statements. The three he'd taken earlier, and what appeared to be a random collection of statements from other villagers, the latter relating to the theft of the Sherpa. It seemed PC Oakes had been busy the previous day. Not particularly methodical, but busy.

Collins had several folders on his desk, together with an A4 notepad. Three sheets from the pad were divided into columns. Each of the columns had jotted headings:

Dog, Sherpa, Post Office and *Gates* were on the first sheet. As he'd read through the statements, he'd tried to find patterns in them. If there was anything referred to in more than one statement, he'd cross-referenced them, with each heading representing a different pattern or theme. And for each heading there was a separate folder containing copies of the statements that referred to it. He'd almost worn out a path to and from the photocopier.

O'Neill wouldn't have had the patience for this. He could do the paperwork, but only as much as he had to. This wasn't required paperwork, though. This was the methodical, plodding analysis that Collins felt was necessary to make progress. Very often, it wasn't finding the clues that was the hard part. It was eliminating the clutter around them.

The dog, for instance. Was that important, or a red herring? Its death had been brutal and violent. As well as statements, the file with the word "DOG" written neatly across the tab contained a series of photographs. Collins wasn't an animal lover, but that hadn't made the images any less sickening. Still, how did that fit in with the theft of a nuclear device?

Another puzzle was the references he'd seen to a growing tension in the village in the past few days. A Mrs Fuller had commented on the number of arguments she'd witnessed, and the increasing instances of bullying in the pub she ran. If it had just been her report of this, he would have dismissed it. But there had been another statement referring to the pub bullying, and a further two referring to the "tensions" building up around the village in general.

This issue was also cross-referenced to another heading

he'd jotted down on the second sheet of A4: *Disabilities*. Because the bullying seemed to have been directed at people who were disabled, either physically or mentally. One of them had even been Martin Gates's brother (cross-referenced to the Gates file). Although it wasn't bullying, Mrs Fuller had also commented on remarks made about Peter Salthouse. It had taken only a couple of phone calls to establish that Salthouse was also disabled. Along with Ronald Dakin, that made three disabled people in the village. Not outstanding in itself, but there was something else nagging at him.

It took him nearly ten minutes to find it. A photocopy he'd asked Brian Oakes to take of his own notes. A single word, jotted at the side where the margin might have been. *Deformed*.

He picked up the phone.

Oakes did his best to be helpful, but his pissed-off tone was predictable. More concerned about the case, Collins ignored it.

"You've written the word 'deformed' in your notebook."

"Yeah." As if it was the most natural thing in the world to have done.

"Can you tell me why?"

"I don't understand. How's this important? I thought you were trying to find out who'd stolen the van?" Oakes was still oblivious of the true nature of the case, and Collins had no intention of enlightening him.

"I am," Collins said patiently. "And I'm sure this means nothing, but it was a random word in your notebook, and I just wanted to eliminate it."

At the other end of the line, he heard a long breath

being let out. He guessed it was supposed to signify either exasperation or indignation, but he wasn't really bothered. Whatever Oakes was feeling was *his* problem.

"It was nothing to do with the investigation. Or the statement I was taking down."

Not that it was much of a statement, Collins thought, glancing at the notes on the rest of the page.

"Humour me," he said.

"Well, I was in the shop." Something Collins already knew, but he maintained his patience. "And we were talking about the van being stolen. When I say 'we', I mean the owners of the Post Office…"

"Mr and Mrs Payne," Collins reminded him helpfully.

"Yes… Mr and Mrs Payne. And then there was the other woman…"

"Mrs Fuller."

"I'll take your word for it. I didn't talk to her for too long."

"I'm sure. But what about…"

"Oh, yes. I'm coming to that." A brief pause, presumably while the young PC collected his thoughts. "Actually, if I remember rightly, we'd moved on from talking about the van, and they were talking about odd things happening in the village. You know, like the tractor accident the day before. That Fuller woman made it sound like it'd been more than an accident, by the way…"

"I can see that from your notes. What about the 'deformed' bit?"

"Oh, God, yeah. That was horrible." There was another pause, possibly for dramatic effect. Collins reined in his frustration and waited. "It was the daughter."

Collins scanned the notes, flicking through other pages for an indication of what Oakes was talking about. "Daughter? What daughter?"

"The Paynes' daughter. It was her hands." Another pause, and this time Collins was starting to feel a rising sense of anticipation. "They were horrible."

"In what way?" He could tell that, in spite of his irritation at being disturbed while he was off-duty, Oakes was clearly beginning to savour the story, and Collins didn't have time for this.

"They were deformed."

"I'd already guessed that. How were they deformed?" Not that the answer to that really mattered. There was something more important that was occurring to him.

"Well, she only seemed to have a thumb on each hand. There weren't fingers, as such. It looked like she just had one lump where her fingers should have been. As if they'd been – I don't know – melted together. You know how mittens look? A bit like that, only thinner, as if there were only two fingers there."

"And were both hands the same?"

"As far as I could tell."

Collins thought for a moment. "Okay. One last question. How old would you say she was?"

"About my age, I suppose. Early twenties."

More reading. Scanning statements and looking at reports. He found some of what he wanted in the incident report about Peter Salthouse. His date of birth. 23rd June 1965. That made him twenty-four. The statement from Norma Fuller referred to Ron Dakin and Colin Gates as young men. More specifically, it said that Colin was only in his mid-twenties. And the Payne's daughter was in her early twenties.

Odd, that. Four disabled people in a village, even the size of Ravens Gathering, wasn't unusual. But four of a similar age? Surely that was more than just a coincidence?

He dropped his pen and sat back, rubbing his eyes. It was interesting. But was it relevant? He couldn't see how it could be. Not unless there'd been some kind of nuclear fallout in Sherwood Forest twenty-odd years ago. That thought made him hesitate, but he pushed it aside. He was only thinking that because of the stolen bomb and his thoughts about Chernobyl earlier. In any event, it was unlikely that a nuclear disaster would result in only a handful of victims.

No, it was time to look at the other links.

He took a break. Coffee and a pee. It was nearly half past seven now. The CID office was quiet, the minimum staff on duty. Budget cuts again.

Only slightly refreshed, he returned to his desk. He picked up the folder marked 'Gates'.

Perhaps it was the tricks of the brain again, but he was drawn to the brief references to Colin first. Another copy of the statement by Norma Fuller and a comment by another resident who Oakes had interviewed. By coincidence, that resident had been in the pub when Colin had been abused, so her story was corroborated, though there was nothing in Oakes's notes to indicate why he had picked on this particular resident. The final reference to Colin was in a statement from the other brother, Matthew Gates. According to the accompanying notes, Oakes had spoken with him and his father after seeing Martin. Matthew had also made reference to the incident in the pub, but suggested that Martin might have been behind it. Collins re-read the other two statements to make sure he'd understood them correctly. Both indicated that, far from starting the abuse, Martin had put a stop to it.

So he studied the rest of Matthew's statement, ignoring the comments about Colin. Then he reviewed the father's statement. Both were filled with remarks that were damaging to Martin. They had expressed no surprise at Oakes's suggestion – Collins guessed it wasn't a particularly subtle suggestion – that Martin may be implicated in the theft of the van. He didn't need a degree in psychology to understand that Martin was the black sheep of the family.

Unfortunately, although his family had been more than willing to put him in the frame, his alibi from the McLeans was enough to keep him out of it for the time being.

He made a few more notes. Sipped the cooling coffee.

The contents of the 'Gates' folder were spread out in front of him. The statements from the father and brother; the statement from the person who'd witnessed Colin's bullying; Martin's own statement, which he could practically recite by now; photocopies of Brian Oakes's notes from his interviews at the Post Office. That was where Martin first came into the picture. He read it again. Because he was tiring, it was tempting to skim it, but he knew if he was going to do that he might as well go home and start again in the morning.

It struck him that Mrs Payne had seemed even more disturbed at the news that Martin was back in the village.

He wondered what the history was there. Was he the black sheep because he caused a scandal by screwing Mrs Payne before he left? He guessed from the notes that she was probably in her fifties, but fifteen years ago she'd have been in her thirties. Wasn't it every teenage boy's dream to get off with an older woman? He smiled wryly to himself. Or was that just how he'd felt when he was that age?

And then there was Norma Fuller again. She had plenty to say on the subject of strange things happening in the village. It was her comment that had thrown the spotlight on Gates. But she'd also referred to other things. Peter Salthouse's accident, the tension and friction in the village, and even the appearance of another stranger…

Another stranger? He sat up and drank the last of the coffee as he re-read the tiny handwriting. It was little more than a scribble, which was probably why he'd missed it before. There were a couple of words there that he realised now were names, though he hadn't read them as such before.

He spent two minutes flipping through the files, looking for a particular statement. He was sure it wasn't there, but he wanted to double check. Satisfied he was right, he reached for the phone. The reception from Oakes wasn't any warmer.

"I need to ask you about Hawthorn and Kindness."

"What?"

"The full written statement doesn't refer to it, but your notes mention someone called Hawthorn. Mrs Fuller brought him up."

"Is that the woman from the pub?"

"Yes."

"What did she say about him?"

"That's what I'm asking you. It looks as if, after you'd discovered the dog, you spoke to her some more."

"Oh, yeah, that rings a bell."

I know what I'd like to wring. But he kept the thought to himself.

"And that's where you've jotted down the name Hawthorn."

"Oh, is this the bloke from the farm?"

"You tell me." He let it slip out without thinking. Wincing, he braced himself for the backlash. It wasn't that he was worried about the relationship. He was the superior officer, after all. It was just that he wanted Oakes to cooperate willingly. The last thing he needed right now was a stroppy copper with a chip on his shoulder.

Fortunately, Oakes must have realised what an arse he was making of himself. "I'm sorry, sir," he said quickly. "Let me think."

That'd make a pleasant change.

"Yeah. She mentioned a farmer. I'm pretty sure that's who you're talking about. The farm had a funny name, though."

"Kindness?" Collins offered. He guessed Oakes hadn't been paying attention when he mentioned the name earlier.

"Yeah, that's it. Bloody odd, don't you think?"

"Yes. What's even odder is the fact that I can't find a statement from anyone named Hawthorn."

There was a hesitation, but Collins sensed it wasn't only from the PC thinking. "You know, *that* was bloody odd too."

"What was?"

"Well, I did look for the farm. Although the real fuss

seemed to be about this Gates bloke, I wanted to visit this Hawthorn chap and get a statement from him. But I couldn't find the farm."

"What?" Collins said incredulously. "How can you miss a farm?"

"I know. It's ridiculous, isn't it? But I tell you, sir, it wasn't there."

Five minutes later, Collins had an Ordnance Survey map spread out on his desk. It was a few years old, but he was sure it would be current enough. *Forest Farm* was clearly marked on the map, though he suspected the boundary represented the pre-McLean days. So too were *Blackthorn Farm*, *Lodge Farm* and *Wharton's Farm*, but there was no sign of *Kindness Farm*. From the directions Oakes had been given, he'd expected it to be on the eastern side of the village, but the map showed only forestry.

As if things weren't strange enough, how could a whole farm disappear?

TWENTY

Night had fallen by the time he returned to the house. The kitchen was illuminated only by the light that came through from the annexe. Hours had passed since he'd left the farm. He hadn't intended to leave Tanya on her own for so long. But there were things he had to do, and they'd been more time consuming than he'd anticipated.

Still, he hadn't expected to walk in on this.

Martin's jacket was lying on the floor, discarded carelessly. His shoes lay nearby, the jacket separating them. One lay on its side, the other upside down. They'd clearly been kicked off, and possibly in a hurry. Tanya's boots had been abandoned in a similar manner.

He leaned back against the door, letting out a loud sigh. Suddenly he was very weary. It had been a long night, and a long day. And now this. The betrayal he'd suspected would happen one day – if it hadn't already. But he'd grown to trust Martin. For reasons he couldn't properly explain to himself, he'd felt confident Martin wouldn't do this to him. Perhaps he should've paid more attention to the reactions from Matthew and Patrick. Having said that, the most telling responses had been this afternoon. By then it was probably too late.

The Barns had been his first port of call when he'd gone out. His explanation to Tanya had at least been partly truthful. He wanted to see how they were getting on. But he also wanted to find out how much they'd seen this morning. After all, military vehicles had been driving up and down past the houses, so they couldn't have been oblivious to it all. Ever practical, he was also thinking ahead. There may be a major investigation happening at the moment, but in time things should return to normal. What he wanted to know was whether today's events would have an impact on the already difficult task of selling the houses when they were finished.

There was no one at the site when he arrived, so he spent a short time looking it over to see how they were progressing. As ever, the workmanship was good, though the pace they were working at seemed slow compared to the last time he'd been to visit. It was only as he was returning to the Land Rover that he realised his mistake. In all the confusion of the day, he'd forgotten it was Saturday. If they had been up to work, the chances were they'd have only put in half a day.

They were at home when he called in. He'd never been past their front door, and Anne Gates didn't invite him in this time either. Waiting on the doorstep while she went to retrieve her son, he could hear the TV in the background. A steady even voice reciting something he couldn't make out. The football results, he guessed.

Matthew ambled down the hallway. Ian hoped the puzzled look on his face was a good sign.

"Evenin', Mr McLean."

It was only a little after five, so Ian wasn't sure if the greeting was intended to remind him that it was a bit late to be calling.

"Matt." He nodded his own greeting. "Sorry to call at this hour. I don't know if you're aware, but we've had some trouble up at the farm."

Shaking his head, Matthew's puzzled expression became more intense. "Is it something to do with Martin?"

Good question. Ian pushed that thought aside, saying only: "I doubt it."

But Matthew picked up on the lack of conviction in his voice.

"What's he been up to?"

Ian smiled good-naturedly. "Really. Nothing."

Turning his head, Matthew called back into the house. "Dad! Come here a minute."

A moment later, Patrick Gates lumbered into view, his pools coupon in one hand and biro in the other. "What is it?" He obviously didn't like being interrupted, but the curiosity in his voice suggested he'd recognised something in Matthew's tone.

"Have you heard about anything going on up at the farm?"

"What, the Sullivans' place?"

It seemed that the Sullivan family had owned the farm for as long as anyone in the village could remember. Ian had long since given up on it ever being referred to as "the McLean place". He pasted a smile on his face to reassure Patrick that he wasn't offended by his remark. Though from Matthew's grunted "Yeah," it seemed that neither of them had spotted the potential for offence.

"What's he done now?" There was no doubt in Ian's mind which "he" Patrick was referring to.

"Er, nothing as far as I'm aware," he said, surprised at how defensive he sounded.

Both men looked at him sceptically.

"He's trouble, you know," Patrick said. His tone was very matter of fact. "You should get shot of him as fast as you can."

"Why do you say that?" Ian was shocked that a father could be so cold towards his own son, and his question was as much a reaction to that shock as it was a need for the truth.

But Patrick's response was even more disturbing. He stared at Ian for a long moment. It was as if he was trying to read whatever was going on in Ian's head. Then he flapped a hand, the pools coupon making the gesture seem more pronounced than it really was. "Get shot of him," he repeated, but there was viciousness in his tone this time. "He'll be the ruin of all of us."

Matthew had turned to look at his father. Ian couldn't see his face properly, but something clearly passed between the two men. Looking down, as if ashamed, Patrick turned away and disappeared back down the hallway.

There was an awkward silence on the doorstep for a moment. Ian opened his mouth, wanting to fill the void with words, but still searching for something appropriate. Matthew beat him to it.

"I'm sorry you've had trouble, Mr McLean. I hope it all sorts itself out." Then he was closing the door.

As he returned to the Land Rover, it struck him that neither man had been particularly interested in what the trouble at the farm had been. A more suspicious person might have assumed they already knew what it was. But they seemed to be more concerned about their own family problems. And it was clear that Martin was central to those.

Pushing away from the door, he started to cross the kitchen, steeling himself for what he was going to find. Unwanted images flooded into his mind. Limbs intertwined, naked flesh, thrusting and grunting. He'd always had a vivid imagination. When he was a child, he'd excelled at English, and his teachers had told him his imagination was a gift. Right now, it felt like a curse.

Maybe this was what Martin had done before he left the village, he thought. Fucked the wrong women; brought shame on his family.

He stepped into the corridor. The door at the end was pushed over, but not completely closed. Light shone around the edges. It wasn't bright, so Ian guessed it must be coming from the bedside lamp. He couldn't hear anything. Hope rose within him, but it lasted only a moment. There may be no sound, but that didn't mean nothing had happened. It was after eight. He'd been gone for nearly four hours. Plenty of time for them to…

The thought was unbearable. It was tempting – so very tempting – to just walk away. But he fought the urge, moving forward purposefully. The floor was carpeted, so they wouldn't hear him coming. He expected it to seem like an age before he got there, and was almost disappointed to find himself only a few feet away from the door. His pace slowed as he edged over the final foot or so. Then he was resting his hand on the door frame.

Last night, in the darkness, not knowing what he was going to find, he had been frightened. The possibility of finding someone who was capable of mutilating and killing a dog had filled him with fear. But he'd fought that off, determined not to show it in front of Martin. Not that

Martin had seemed sanguine about the exercise. This was different, though. Out on the track, he'd faced the risk of physical harm. This was going to be much worse.

Taking a deep breath, he let the air out again as quietly as he could. There was still no sound coming from the bedroom, and he didn't want to warn them of his presence. But he needed the deep breathing, needed to regain some control.

Very slowly, he pressed his fingers against the door, gently pushing it open.

He'd been wrong about the light. It was coming from the shower room. The bedroom itself was illuminated only by the light that shone from that room and the corridor. Martin lay on his back, angled across the bed as if he'd just dropped there. His eyes were closed, and his chest was rising and falling in a steady rhythm.

Ian stepped quietly into the room. There was no indication that Tanya was there. He checked the shower room in case she was hiding, but it seemed that Martin had been in there then come out and collapsed on the bed.

As Ian headed back for the corridor, Martin continued to sleep. Still wearing the clothes Ian had last seen him in.

TWENTY-ONE

There is a school of thought that says, if you believe in God, you must believe in the Devil. Simon Cantor had never fully subscribed to that idea, though he could understand the rationale behind it. Many of his colleagues within the Church would be able to put forward a well-structured argument for it. And the chances were that some of the more forceful in their beliefs would incorporate that argument into some of their sermons.

Simon, on the other hand, was less convinced. His faith in God was unquestioning, though he liked to think he was open enough to appreciate why others might have strong doubts. The atrocities that had been perpetrated throughout history by man against man were enough to give any person with a brain pause for thought. Ironically, the colleagues who believed strongly in the presence of the Devil would point to such events as evidence of Satan's existence rather than it being cause to have no faith in God.

But those individuals were fighting against a growing apathy towards religion. And their strongly held views would only alienate their parishioners. Or so Simon thought. It was more important to him that they keep the church doors open, and a part of keeping the doors open was to keep minds open. Starting with those of himself and his colleagues.

He'd been the vicar at Ravens Gathering for six years now, and had been adopting the open mind policy there throughout that time. It was hard to point to any definite results he'd achieved with it. The people who turned up regularly for Sunday services were pretty much the same as they'd been when he'd started. The couples who married in his church might make an effort in the weeks running up to and just after the service itself, but he couldn't think of any long-term converts. Even the grieving, who might seek solace in the idea that their loved ones had gone to "a better place", showed little interest in the help a man of the cloth might be able to provide. Still, he'd told himself many times, there was no rush. After all, God wasn't going anywhere.

Some people who are trying to sell a product, will do so on the basis of fear, rather than on the merits of the product itself. So a disinfectant might be sold because it will save you from the deadly germs you leave around the house, or a brand of beer should be drunk because you don't want to be ostracised by the "in crowd". When Simon did get those rare opportunities to talk to parishioners, he certainly didn't feel that scaring them was a useful way of making them believe in God. So talking up the Devil wasn't part of his sales pitch. Besides, how could he talk convincingly about an evil that he didn't believe existed?

At least, that was how he felt two days ago. Now, he could probably put a compelling argument forward.

Huddled in a corner of the living room in the vicarage, he watched as his tormentor dressed. The blue trousers were fairly lightweight, particularly in comparison to the tweed jacket he was putting on. It was odd that he wore no underwear or socks, but compared to the other experiences Simon had gone through over the last forty-eight hours, this barely registered on the strangeness scale.

A three-piece suite filled a good part of the room. The two armchairs formed the ends of a loose rectangle whose other sides were made up of the large, ornate fireplace, and the three-seater sofa. The space in the middle was empty, unless you counted the sheepskin rug that lay before the hearth.

Sitting down on the chair nearest the door, the other man pulled on a pair of old walking boots. Simon knew they were too big, but that didn't seem to bother him. His method of tying laces seemed to involve wrapping them around his ankle and tucking the loose ends into the top of the boots. While he did that, Simon looked at his wife, Jessica. The upper half of her body lay across the sofa, her knees resting on the floor. She wasn't completely naked, but the scraps of material that covered parts of her body were only remnants of the clothes she'd been wearing before she was raped.

Simon had been helpless. Not that he was physically restrained. But he'd seen what this man – this monster – was capable of, and knew any attempt to stop him would lead to a level of violence he'd never previously imagined possible. And it had been impossible to look away. Something compelled him to watch. In a perverse kind of way, he hoped it was something within the human psyche – the thing that draws us to ghoulishly look on at the aftermath of a car accident. He hoped for that because, in reality, he was afraid the stranger had somehow reached out with his mind and forced him to do it.

Jessica's eyes stared across the room at him, where he was crouched against the wall at the side of the fireplace. The eyes stared, but they didn't see anything. He wanted to reach out to her, hold her, reassure her that everything would be all right. But he knew it wouldn't.

The night before last, this man had invaded their home. Since then, he'd taken control of them both, using them for his own ends. At first, they'd assumed it was just going to be a burglary, an unpleasant and frightening experience in itself. But things had developed, and it rapidly became clear that this was not going to be over in a few minutes or even an hour or so. Worse still, there was a cold menace that emanated from their intruder.

In part it came from his appearance. He was tall and thin. At first, Simon had assumed the thinness went hand in hand with boniness. But in the intervening period he'd had the opportunity to study him at closer quarters, and the narrow limbs were well covered in muscle. His skin was pale, almost white, contrasting sharply with his black hair, which hung limply down to his neck. And from his pallid face, dark eyes stared out, intently taking in everything around them. That intensity was enough to unnerve anyone.

But, while appearances can be deceptive, actions can't.

Within minutes of his arrival at the vicarage, the pale man had forced them down into the cellar, a damp chamber they never used. As far as Simon could recall, he'd only been in it twice before: the first time when they came to view the property in anticipation of moving in, and the second time just after they moved in, when he'd decided they'd never want to use it. But that evening, he'd been

296

forced to spend a couple of hours down there, which was unpleasant enough without the thought that your house was being burgled.

When the door had been opened, only Simon was let out. A stolen glance at the kitchen clock had told him it was already past two in the morning. Then he'd been taken to the Post Office. Over the years, he'd patted Charlie's head many times. He couldn't honestly say he had enormous affection for the dog, but Charlie had been a recurring presence in his life. Though he doubted that the Labrador's suffering, or the pale man's obvious delight in it, would have been any easier to bear if he'd never met the dog before. From the moment the torture began, Simon knew he was in the presence of real evil.

His callousness was further underlined by the fact that Jessica wasn't released from the cellar until this evening. She'd been left there without food or water for almost forty-eight hours. For most of the time she was in there, Simon was helpless to do anything about it. Somehow, as if he'd been hypnotised, he felt he was completely under the pale man's control. The only assistance he'd been able to provide had been the few times he'd been locked in there with her. Even then all he could do was hold her, hoping their closeness would be reassuring. He doubted it had been. And as he looked into her vacant eyes, he knew any reassurance would have been a lie anyway.

The pale man stood up and nodded towards the door. It was time to leave.

Very cautiously, Simon got to his feet. He'd learned that the pale man didn't like sudden moves. The bruises he could feel on his legs, arms and torso were evidence of that. If the pale man didn't need him right now, Simon was convinced he'd already be dead.

As he made for the door, he tried to look at Jessica, but his head wouldn't turn. Passing his captor, he was aware of a tear trickling down his cheek. He wasn't sure if it was born from frustration or the fear that he may have seen his wife for the last time.

Outside it was dark. The curtains had been drawn in the house, so he hadn't been aware of the time of day. They crossed the gravel drive and headed straight to the entrance to *Forest Farm*. Through the haze of his tiredness, he tried to recall how many times they had been to the farm in the last couple of days. The first time had been after they took the van from the Post Office. He'd been expecting them to drive away from the village, so he'd been surprised when he was directed here. They'd left the van and returned to the vicarage, Simon assuming that his part in whatever the pale man's plans were must be over. On reflection, there was a major flaw in this thinking, he'd realised. The pale man couldn't drive. It seemed he needed Simon for that if nothing else. And sure enough, just before daybreak, they were off again.

The purpose of the return to the vicarage was never explained. Simon was given no explanation for anything that had happened. He could only guess that the pale man had taken the opportunity to rest. Something Simon would have liked the chance to do himself but, even without the recurring images of the mutilated dog or the fear of what their fate was with this man, it would have been impossible to settle and rest in the dank confines of the cellar.

Their journey to Berkshire had been disjointed for a

number of reasons, not least of which was his own lack of navigational skills. The pale man certainly didn't know how to get there, and the detail on the road map they'd found in the van just seemed to confuse him more. So they'd strayed off the most direct route, and even found themselves in Wiltshire and Hampshire before finally getting their bearings. There had also been the moments when Simon had thought there might be a chink of goodness in his captor. His own weariness had threatened to overcome him on a couple of occasions, and he'd been instructed to pull over and rest. It was only when he was roughly woken up that he realised the rest was only to ensure they reached their destination in one piece.

They'd arrived at the edge of Aldermaston village by late afternoon, at which point he'd been allowed to sleep again. When he woke up, it was dark. But he wasn't given a chance to think, just drive.

Three men died that night. Their murders were deliberately slow, their suffering maximised. And Simon was made to watch each one. But before they died, those men helped to load the equipment into the van. Simon didn't know what his cargo was, but he could guess.

The return journey was easier. It seemed that the pale man had gained a sense of direction, and the M4 was relatively easy to find, leading them to the M25 and M1. Motorways were a comfort blanket he was glad to make use of. The ten hours it had taken to reach Aldermaston was cut to four hours on the way back.

By the time they were walking back down the track to the vicarage, Simon had been ready to collapse. Which was what he had done when he was pushed into the cellar. He'd been aware of Jessica beside him, so he doubted he'd done more than dozed, but exhaustion overcame him again and the time simply passed.

Little more than an hour ago, the cellar had been opened, and this time they were both allowed out. To think, he'd been relieved that Jessica could leave her prison.

Unlike his wife, Simon had been fed and watered sporadically over the two days, but only enough to allow him to serve his captor's purpose. Bearing in mind the fate of his wife, he wondered whether his captor had much more use for him. And when his usefulness expired, he had no doubt that his fate would involve tremendous suffering. As he trudged up the track to the farm, he wondered whether he had been wrong all along. Was he now in the company of Satan?

TWENTY-TWO

Being held by Martin had brought a mixture of emotions for Tanya. For the first time she could ever recall, she'd lost control. Her life to date had always been about staying in control. When her relationship with Ian had started, she'd always made sure she held the balance of power. Sex, of course, was her biggest weapon. She presented herself to him, let him taste the forbidden fruits, and from then on he was hooked. And he knew he had to keep her happy if he was going to continue to enjoy those fruits.

She played to her strengths and, always, she looked to build on them.

Things had changed though.

First there was Martin. And last there was Martin. In between there was the small matter of a stolen bomb being found in her back yard, and even that might have been something to do with Martin.

Having been confined to this backwater for the last few years, to meet someone who wasn't like one of the locals had been exciting. And he seemed to be attracted to her as well. But then the promise of his flirting had simply died away. He'd intrigued her, offering something different, and yet remaining an enigma.

The power shift had been gradual, but she realised now that it was all in his hands. Even though she knew in her heart he had no interest in her either sexually or romantically, and even though she was sure he was keeping things from her about the stolen van, still she wanted to be with him. Her anger, her sense of betrayal, her frustration and embarrassment from earlier had all combined to leave her weakened, and desperate for him to take care of things for her.

And when he put his arms around her, she surrendered willingly.

For a few moments, there was hope. The physical need she felt for him was intense, and feeling his hands on her back, she'd been convinced her wait was over. Instead of lust, though, she felt tenderness. He stroked her, soothed her, made her feel cared for. Which was a strange experience for her. Not that Ian didn't demonstrate his caring for her. But his expressions of caring tended to involve gifts and treats and words. On a rational level, she knew he genuinely did care. What she felt with Martin, though, was different. He didn't have to say anything. She could just feel the warmth and love emanating from him. In a way she couldn't have imagined possible from anyone, let alone this surfer dude who liked to piss off policemen, villagers and family members alike.

He had taken her to bed. But not for sex. He'd simply sat on the edge of it holding her hand until she fell asleep.

The sound of the kitchen door had woken her up.

She was alone. Even though the room was in darkness, she could sense there was no one else with her. Ordinarily, she was slow to waken when she'd been asleep. But the door had disturbed more than her sleep. Worried that it might mean Martin was leaving, she took only a few moments to clear her head and get up.

Out of habit, she hesitated before going downstairs. Her hair was undoubtedly a mess. It always was when she first woke up. Though she knew that how she looked wouldn't matter to Martin, the importance of her appearance was so ingrained in her that she took a rapid diversion into the shower room. The light made her wince when she pulled on the cord. Blinking, she inspected herself in the mirror. The damage wasn't too bad. A quick brush through was enough to tide her over. The eye makeup was tolerable. She certainly didn't have time to carry out a full repair job.

Since she'd been woken by the door closing, there had been no obvious sounds from downstairs. Inevitably in a house as old as this one, there were creaks and groans all the time. Those were just part of the background. Sometimes they were made by someone moving around, other times it was just the house itself.

As she went out on to the landing, she strained her ears, listening out for anything that might indicate whether Martin was still in the house or not. She hadn't turned any more lights on, afraid that if he was leaving, it might spur him on. At the foot of the stairs, she could see the only light was a dim glow coming from the kitchen.

Of course she realised almost immediately that the glow was only passing through the kitchen. It originated in the annexe. She stepped through the doorway, more uncertain of herself than she'd ever been. What if Martin had already gone? And if he hadn't, what was she going to say to him anyway? Plead with him to take her with him? Or ask him to spend the night with her in the knowledge that it would never be repeated?

A small shadow appeared at the doorway to the annexe,

but rapidly grew bigger. He was coming towards the kitchen. She braced herself, hoping to God she'd know what to say when she saw him. And then he was there. But it was Ian, not Martin.

His whole body seemed to twitch when he saw her. She'd startled him. A combination of guilt and a sudden awareness of her own fragility made her empathise with him in a way she couldn't remember having done before. She opened her mouth to apologise, but he raised a hand to stop her, then closed the door behind him.

"I didn't want to disturb him," he explained, gesturing beyond the door.

All the pieces fell hurriedly into place. Martin was still here. It had been Ian closing the kitchen door that had woken her. She felt relieved Martin hadn't left, and shame because she was feeling that in the presence of her husband. A husband, incidentally, who seemed to be just as concerned about Martin as she was.

"Is he…?"

"Asleep, yes." In the shadows of the kitchen, he peered at her as he drew closer. "And I'm guessing you were too. I'm sorry if I woke you."

She waved the apology aside. Or was it the reference to her having been asleep? Obviously the quick brush of the hair hadn't been enough.

"Don't worry," she said, and was surprised at the tenderness in her voice. She reached for him and gave him a hug. "It's been a long day for all of us."

At first, he was rigid in her arms. She couldn't blame him. After the way she'd treated him in recent months, to be greeted with affection must have felt strange to him.

304

But after a few moments he relaxed, and she was surprised at how pleasurable it was to be held by him. Not in the thrilling and sexy way she'd always thought would mark out the pleasure of being with a man. Instead she was filled with an affection and warmth that felt alien to her. Alien, and yet more right than she could have possibly imagined. Which left her even more confused. Because she might have understood it if this had been Martin. He was new and brought something different with him. But this was Ian, who she'd been in a relationship with for six years.

It was Ian who pulled away first. He looked at her closely. "Are you okay?"

"I don't know," she admitted, surprising herself. "I thought I was, but..." She tailed off, not sure if she could explain how she felt.

Ian smiled at her warmly. "Have you eaten?"

She shook her head.

"Why don't you go and freshen up. Have a shower, it'll help to waken you up a bit. I'll make us a meal while you're up there, and when you come down, we can have a talk."

Something she would have hated to do normally. And yet, somehow, his suggestion felt right to her. Maybe it was because of the warmth she was feeling towards him. She thought it was more likely to be something else, but she was having some difficulty in identifying what that something else was.

"Good idea," she said eagerly and squeezed his hand.

"What would you like to eat?" he asked.

"Whatever you like." She smiled at him, and knew from his expression that he was both puzzled and delighted. It crossed her mind that she may be building his hopes up only to shatter them. But she didn't think so.

Playing along, he made a show of giving some thought to the question, before saying: "You know, we haven't had breakfast yet. What about eggs, bacon, sausage, mushrooms…"

Not ideal for keeping her trim figure, but just right for this occasion.

"Don't forget the tomatoes and fried bread," she grinned, giving him another hug. "I'll be ten minutes."

"Well I'll be at least twenty," Ian told her, "so take as long as you need."

When she glanced back as she headed into the hallway, he was still watching her, his face a picture of amused bewilderment.

He had been right, she realised as she went up the stairs. She always needed a shower in the morning to wake herself up properly. It might seem bizarre after such a long and arduous day to be planning anything other than catching up on sleep, but there were things she and Ian needed to talk about. On his side, he needed to open up to her about why he'd been gone for so long. On her part, she needed to explore these new-found emotions with him.

The alarm clock told her it was almost nine-thirty. Smiling at the idea of a cooked breakfast this late in the evening, she almost skipped into the shower.

As the water poured down her body, her brain was running wild, thoughts leaping all over. She wasn't consciously looking for an answer, but with such a profound change, it was inevitable she'd be wondering why she felt so different. As far as she could tell, nothing had changed within Ian. Okay, there was his secretiveness last night and this afternoon. But if that was going to have any effect on her it should have been a negative one.

It was when she'd stepped out of the shower and was towelling herself that it occurred to her. She was looking for why Ian made her feel the way Martin had. But maybe it was nothing to do with the way they made her feel. Maybe something had changed within her.

Still puzzling over that, she walked into the bedroom. She was dabbing at herself absent-mindedly with the towel as she tried to follow that line of thought. The explanation was eluding her. Strangely enough, the best person to help her with it was Ian. He was very logical and methodical, but understood a lot of the complexities of the human mind, so was well-equipped to guide her to the solution. Previously, she would've fought shy of talking to Ian about something like this because she'd have been afraid of giving him too much power over her. This time her concern was about him. What if, in helping her, he found out how she'd felt about Martin? What if it revealed to him the countless affairs and liaisons she'd had over the years? Having discovered an affection for Ian, the last thing she wanted to do was hurt him.

She pushed those thoughts to one side. There was nothing constructive she could do about them tonight. Not when there were soldiers all around the farm and a bomb had been found hidden there. It was just a relief that they'd managed to move it away, take it back where it had come from.

Dropping the towel over the arm of a chair, she turned towards a chest of drawers. And felt something hard ram into her stomach.

307

TWENTY-THREE

No one was left in CID when he went through. The few that were on duty had been called out to a domestic incident that had escalated into something much more tragic. Or so he learned from the Desk Sergeant. Which meant he either had to wait until tomorrow morning, or he could go out looking by himself.

In a way, it helped to make the decision. The reality was that, whilst the missing farm was strange, there was nothing to link this oddity to the case. So if he'd been accompanied by another officer, there was always the risk of ridicule. And big and tough and experienced as he was, he didn't react well to having the piss taken out of him. Particularly when he was feeling tired.

This gave him the opportunity to go and have a scout around by himself and, if it turned out to be of no relevance, he didn't have to report it to anyone.

To give himself even more leeway, he told the sergeant he was going home. It wasn't a lie. He was. It was just that he was going the long way.

He smiled at that thought as he approached the edge of the village. It was completely dark now, the sun a distant memory, and the white background of the *Ravens Gathering* sign reflected his headlights dully. Ahead and to his right, he saw a dark opening and slowed down, wondering if that was the place he was looking for. The streetlights were still a quarter of a mile away, so it was difficult to see clearly. But as he drew level and looked along the track, he could see a wooden signpost for a bridleway, and beside that a black and white sign with the image of a Friesian painted on it. Beneath the cow were the words *Whartons Farm*.

Gently pressing his foot down on the accelerator, he moved forward. There was no other traffic on the road, so he didn't rush. With no one to see him, there was no one to be worried about his apparently suspicious behaviour.

But he was in the village before he saw any other places to turn off the main road. A cluster of houses that was too small to constitute an estate, then *The Major Oak* and opposite that the entrance to *Blackthorn Farm. Lodge Farm* appeared shortly after on the same side as the pub, but Collins already knew that if this phantom farm existed, he must have gone past it. He turned the Cavalier around and headed back out of the village.

It was strange really. Back in Westfield, the streets would be busy. Saturday night was for letting your hair down – in whatever way was right for you. For a lot of people it would be the pubs and clubs. At nine o'clock, it wouldn't be buzzing just yet, but it'd be well on its way.

Not Ravens Gathering, though. So far, he hadn't even seen anyone out walking their dog. There was light in the pub, and shadows cast on the windows, but he didn't get the impression it would be heaving.

As the streetlights faded in his rear view mirror, he kept his speed at thirty. He didn't want to be going so fast he'd miss anything. But when five minutes had passed, and he could see the lights of Long Clayford ahead of him, he knew he'd gone too far. He gently picked up speed and headed into the village to turn around again.

This time, there were other cars on the road. Just two, and they were both heading in the same direction as him. The roads were narrow and winding. Unsure whether they were patient, sensible drivers, or lairy idiots who'd rather risk their lives than be a minute or two late, he increased his speed until he could find a suitable place to pull over and let them pass. And the suitable place was the entrance to *Whartons* Farm again, so he knew he must have missed what he was looking for. He reversed into the opening and turned back towards Long Clayford.

Unlike in the movies, being a good detective isn't the result of being a maverick with an estranged wife who loves you but hates the job. Nor is it about kicking in doors and being able to put a car into a one hundred and eighty degree turn while reloading your handgun. There are many different facets to a good detective. Some have their strengths in particular areas. But one of the most important things a detective has to possess is patience. It may be something they need as they piece together the jigsaw of a crime scene, or read and re-read statements as they look for a common thread, or they may simply end up driving up and down a dark road at night as they search for an entrance to a farm that may or may not exist.

Collins clocked up over thirty miles travelling back and forth between the two villages that lay less than four miles apart. Thirty miles, and fifty minutes. And then he saw it. A narrow gap in the trees to his right as he headed once more in the direction of Ravens Gathering. He was coming out of a bend in the road. His speed had dropped this time to around ten miles an hour. He knew he was taking a risk. It was pretty well established that the incidence of drink-driving in rural areas was greater than it was in the town. In large part, it was because the police had to concentrate their efforts in the more built up areas. After all, that was where most of the people were. So if you were going to take a chance when you were over the limit, there was a strong likelihood you'd get away with it out here. Any drink driver coming along this road tonight would more than likely not realise the Cavalier was there until it was too late. And he'd certainly not have the reflexes to brake in time. Of course, there were also the dickheads who didn't need to get some alcohol in their system to drive like lunatics. He banked on it being too early for the drinkers, and played the odds on the others. Fortunately, the odds worked in his favour.

There was no sign announcing the presence of a farm. Nor was there a gatepost, or any other indication that this break in the trees was anything of significance. But the combination of his speed and the angle at which the headlights caught the trees made Collins realise that the opening was a little too regular in shape to be a natural development.

Out of habit, he indicated, even though there was no one around to see the lights flashing. He drove into the gap, and felt a warm glow of satisfaction as his headlights illuminated a rough, but well used, track. It curved away to his left, disappearing from view. He stopped the car, letting the engine tick over as he considered what to do next.

The reality, of course, was that he hadn't achieved anything yet. All he'd done was find a track that led off the main road. Where it led to was still up for debate. And there was also the very strong possibility that, even if there was a farm at the end of the track, there would be nothing to suggest its presence had anything to do with the events at *Forest Farm*. In truth, there wasn't any decision to make. He just had to get on with it. Letting out the clutch, he cautiously followed the curve of the track.

Back on the road, the light had been limited. Here, with trees on either side and branches cutting out any illumination from the moon or stars, there was nothing to guide him other than his headlights. And even they seemed to have dimmed, the beams dropping away only a few feet ahead. He drove slowly, alert for any sharp bends or suicidal woodland creatures.

Even though he was watching out for them, he was still surprised to see both at different times. The squirrel appeared first, the headlights catching it as it stood stock still in the middle of the track. He eased the brake on gently, so there was no sudden noise to startle the creature – or alert any nearby humans. It was only when the car stopped completely that the squirrel decided to move on, glancing briefly over its shoulder as it went. Amused more than anything, Collins carried on, and almost missed the sudden turn to the right ten feet further on. A very wide and sturdy looking tree trunk showed up in the lights suddenly, and his amusement turned to gratitude. If he hadn't slowed for the squirrel, he was pretty sure he wouldn't have had time to stop before hitting the tree.

Without the hindrance of darkness, he estimated later that it would probably have taken him little more than a couple of minutes to cover the length of the track. On that first attempt, it was closer to seven. But eventually, it opened up into a farmyard. To the right was the house, with the outbuildings both directly ahead of him and on the left. He parked next to a Land Rover, which stood outside the house.

Dim lights shone through curtains in a couple of downstairs windows, but no one answered the door when he knocked. Not even on the fourth attempt. He turned his attention to the outbuildings. Lights were fitted to some of the buildings, sitting just above the doors to them. They cast a dull glow, creating shadows just beyond their reach. But they were bright enough for someone to find their way around the yard without tripping over anything.

His footsteps sounded unnaturally harsh as he explored the yard. It took him a minute or so – a very long minute or so – to adjust to it. The sensation was reminiscent of the times he'd arrived home in the wee small hours, and been desperate not to disturb anyone. It seemed that the harder he tried to be quiet, the noisier he became. The key would rattle in the lock, the creaky floorboards catching him out because they seemed to have moved, and the door hinges would need oiling. Yet, at any other time, those sounds wouldn't be a problem. Nor were they to his sleeping family. It was just him being more conscious of them.

None of the doors he tried were locked. If nothing else, there was a strong case for sending a crime prevention officer out to visit them. He had a look around the workshop and storerooms. Nothing of interest in those. The barn was interesting in that it housed a tractor and some other farming equipment. Like a lot of men, his curiosity could be aroused by the sight of anything mechanical. From a professional point of view, it was meaningless though. When he approached the stable, he was again reminded of those early mornings returning home. He wanted to look in, but didn't want to disturb the inhabitants. Fortunately, he didn't, but as he headed back towards his car, he did wonder why he'd bothered to make the effort.

From one perspective, the trip had been a waste of time. He'd found no one, nor had he seen anything suspicious. Well, that wasn't strictly true, because it did seem odd to him that the place was deserted. He could partly understand it. Why shouldn't they go out on a Saturday night? But if they did, surely they'd have locked up. Wouldn't they?

He was opening the car door as that thought passed through his head. Triggering another thought. If the outbuildings were unlocked, was it possible the house was too? He hadn't tried the handle when he'd knocked earlier. When he tried it a few seconds later, it opened. With no squeaks. Just when he could have done with one.

After all his years of policing, it still didn't feel right to him when he entered someone's home without their consent. Sure, he could justify it if the need arose. *No sign of life, lights on in the house and the Land Rover parked outside. Wanted to make sure everything was all right.* But being able to justify it and feeling comfortable with it were two different things.

The door opened on to a kitchen. It was smaller than the one at *Forest Farm*, but still twice the size of his own. The fittings looked old but cared for. A tea towel had been dropped carelessly on to the table. It too had seen better days. A washing up bowl was filled with soapy water, the handle of a saucepan sticking up Excalibur-like from within it. Dishes were stacked next to the sink, waiting their turn. Whoever had been in here had been disturbed.

Collins hesitated in the doorway. Someone had been disturbed. Was he about to walk into a crime scene? Because if he was, he really needed to call the station and get some back up. If he did, though, and it was just a case of the person washing up getting called out for something unexpectedly... Well, that had happened to him often enough, and it wasn't always the job. Maybe they'd had a call from a teenager who needed a lift. That was definitely something he could relate to.

No, he decided. He should go on in.

But that was as far as he got. Somewhere in the yard, he heard movement. Hinges creaked, then footsteps. He turned to look, and saw a group of people emerging from the barn.

How the hell...? He'd been in there less than ten minutes ago, and there'd been no sign of anyone. Automatically he started to retrace his steps in his mind, wondering if he could have missed something when he'd gone into the barn. Nothing came to him.

As he searched his memory, he was also watching them. The barn door swung shut, and then they were heading towards him. A combination of distance and lighting meant they were silhouettes more than flesh and blood. But the shapes were not just humanoid. Each of them was carrying something. It was difficult to tell for sure, but he thought he recognised the objects being carried. He'd been involved in tackling armed robbers when he'd been in the Flying Squad. Shotguns and pickaxe handles had been commonplace in those days.

He glanced towards his car. It was about thirty feet away from him. The group coming across the yard were not much further away. He wouldn't have time to make a run for it. And he suddenly realised that, with the light from the kitchen behind him, he was an easy target.

TWENTY-FOUR

A scream tore its way into Martin's consciousness. The deep sleep he'd been in vanished, his eyes flicking open immediately. Later, he would realise that his instantaneous reaction was no more or less than he had become used to over the years. So many nights had been interrupted by his dreams.

Without thinking, he was on his feet and into the corridor. As he entered the kitchen, he caught a flash of movement in the main hallway. Even as he registered that, he heard heavy boots running across the wooden floor. Instinctively, he knew it was Ian. Just as he knew it was Tanya he could hear screaming.

Ian had twenty years on Martin, so reached the bedroom door only moments ahead of him. He was opening it as Martin hit the landing, and had come to an abrupt halt when he caught up.

The scene that greeted them was surreal.

A large picture window ran across the wall opposite the door, and beneath it were two chests of drawers. An armchair was angled into the corner, a towel draped over it.

To Martin's left was the king-sized bed, and beyond that fitted wardrobes flanked a dressing table and full-length mirror. Bottles of perfume and a set of brushes stood at the back of the dressing table, and a padded stool was tucked under it. The furniture filled most of the wall, but at the far right was the open doorway to the en-suite.

Tanya was standing at the foot of the bed. She was completely naked, and apparently oblivious of the fact, which seemed strange as the curtains were wide open. Under ordinary circumstances, her privacy might not have been an issue, considering how far away they were from the rest of the village. But there were still half a dozen or more squaddies wandering around outside.

Her nudity wasn't the surreal part, though. The curtains had been drawn earlier. Martin knew that, because *he'd* drawn them. Now, it looked as if someone had tried to tear them down. Curtain rings had been pulled loose from the rail – shiny glints on the duvet were evidence of where some had landed – and at least half of each curtain was now draped over the chests below them. The drawers themselves looked as if they'd been pulled out by someone who'd been given ten seconds to find something hidden inside them. There were three drawers in each chest. Two were pulled about half way out. Another was teetering precariously, only around a centimetre of it still inside the chest. Two more had been hurled across the room, one landing on the bed, the other shattered against the wall above the headboard. The last one was at an angle on the floor in front of the chest. If Tanya had been standing where she was now, it must have struck her.

The alarm clock and two paperbacks were no longer on the bedside table. He'd noticed the books earlier. One of them was a Stephen King he hadn't read. So he knew they'd been next to the alarm clock. All three were now scattered on the floor in front of the armchair.

He took this all in as he entered the room with Ian. Tanya looked at them both desperately. Her screams had stopped before they started up the stairs, so he guessed all of this had happened at least twenty seconds ago. She still made no effort to cover herself up.

"What happened?" Ian asked, moving forward.

As he did, Martin continued to look around, searching for clues as to what might have caused this damage. He was also conscious that he should look anywhere other than at Tanya. He didn't want to embarrass her, or Ian – or himself, for that matter.

But even as Ian reached the end of the bed, the light fitting in the room began to sway, casting shadows where previously there had been none. All eyes flicked up to it, and as they did the wardrobe doors burst open. The interior of both wardrobes was split into two halves. The top part stored the hanging clothes, the bottom held more drawers. Each wardrobe had two columns of drawers in them. Shirts, jackets, trousers and dresses swung outwards as if caught in the suction of an enormous vacuum cleaner. Only the hangers gripping the rails provided the traction to keep them in place.

Not that either Martin or Ian had time to dwell on the clothes. The drawers from the wardrobe blasted out as if they'd been fired from cannons. Fortunately, the lower ones crashed into the side of the bed, but the four from the top row cleared the mattress and hurtled towards them. Martin leapt backwards into the doorway, Ian lunged at Tanya, pulling her down to the floor. The drawers smashed into the wall. Two of them splintered, the others showed more resilience. Socks, handkerchiefs and underwear scattered across the carpet.

"What the hell...?" Ian shouted angrily, but he was cut off by the unmistakable sound of splintering glass.

Martin's brain told him it must be the window, but his ears told him it was coming from a different direction. He leaned forward, taking a peek into the room. What he saw sent him cold.

"For God's sake stay down!" he yelled at Ian. "And keep Tanya covered."

The splintering became a loud crack as the mirror shattered. Martin ducked back on to the landing as lethal slices of glass flew across the room. From his vantage point, he could see Ian was lying on top of his wife. Fragments fell on him, a few on his back, more on his legs. Because of their position, they escaped the worst of it. The wall facing the mirror was hit by three chunks at least a foot long. One shattered on impact, the others landed with such force they embedded themselves in the wall. The light from the swinging bulb reflected off the pieces of mirror sending a myriad of shining light sparkling across the walls and ceiling.

Watching the broken glass scattering across the room, seeing coat hangers lose their fight and clothing flying out of the wardrobes, hearing the screams from Tanya, and not knowing where the next barrage was going to come from, Martin crouched in the door frame. He'd hoped to God this wouldn't happen. But he realised now there was no way of escaping it.

PART THREE

A BRIEF HISTORY

ONE

In 1979, Martin had flirted with a Spanish girl. She was a waitress in a bar he was working at. The flirting wasn't going anywhere. It never did. He'd learnt that already. Somehow the chatting up came easily to him. He could flash the smile, make them laugh, get close to them. But then everything would cool. His enthusiasm would suddenly dry up. It was fear that did it. Fear of what, he wasn't sure. Maybe it was just a fear of being found out.

He decided on a couple of occasions to face his demons – not that he knew what those demons were exactly. But he knew facing them would involve putting himself on the line, and he guessed that the line involved following through. So when his interest in a girl began to wane, he forced himself to do just that. They got as far as her bedroom before he vomited. It wasn't the most promising start to a relationship, but she was surprisingly understanding about it. Martin wasn't, though. He hadn't felt unwell before they got to her room, so he knew there was nothing physically wrong with him.

The experience with the second girl was equally disastrous. He wasn't ill, but he couldn't perform for her. She blamed the alcohol, allowing him to save a little face. He'd only had two beers all night.

From then on, he resigned himself to a life free of

intimate relationships. He didn't understand why he responded so badly, but he decided it was better to accept it and move on than to spend his life agonising over it.

So when he flirted with the Spanish waitress, he knew it wasn't going anywhere. The problem was, she didn't. More importantly, nor did her boyfriend.

One night after work, the boyfriend confronted Martin in a side street outside the bar. He'd brought two friends with him. It was past two o'clock, and there were still a few party animals on the streets, but most were preoccupied with finding their next drink or the nearest gutter to throw up in. No one took any interest in the exchange between the lone English barman and the three local boys.

Martin was twenty-three. He'd learnt that intimate relationships were something to walk away from, but he was still inexperienced in many other aspects of life. Because he kept to himself most of the time, his communications skills were limited. There are two sides to communication: getting your message across and understanding the message being put across to you. Most people focus on the first and ignore the second and Martin was no exception. He didn't want to listen to what the boyfriend had to say. And initially he ignored the threat posed by the extra numbers. He'd seen the three of them together in the past and assumed they just happened to be out as a group. When the warnings were made verbally, he was already annoyed enough to kick back. He knew he could handle himself. He'd already had two stints working the doors on nightclubs. He also thought they were just making a lot of noise. But he misjudged it. Misjudged it to the tune of three nights in hospital and four weeks off work.

His injuries weren't life-threatening, and nor did they

leave him with any lasting damage, but they very easily could have done.

Like his experiences with girls, he'd learnt when to walk away and when to keep his mouth shut.

Confronted by the Hawthorns and their two friends on the main street of Ravens Gathering, his thoughts had flashed back to that experience with the Spaniards. Back then, he could have walked away. He knew immediately that he didn't have the choice this time. And it took him only a moment or so to realise that fighting his way out of the situation wasn't a viable option either. Even if he discounted the girl – and he wasn't a hundred percent sure he could do that – he was outnumbered, and he'd already seen enough to know that at least two of them knew what they were doing. The pursuit of his family suddenly seemed less pressing. So he came quietly.

The ride in the Land Rover was short in distance and communication. Martin was wedged between the two men on the back seat. During the short walk to the car, he'd heard them called Mason and Croft. No first names were mentioned.

Mason was the bald one. His bulk made the journey less comfortable than it might otherwise have been, but at least he tried to press himself up against the door as much as he could, otherwise it could have been a lot worse. Croft sat on Martin's left and his slightness meant he didn't need to give up any space to Martin. Both men were silent as they left the village.

Nor did the Hawthorns have anything to say. They sat up front, the man driving, both of them apparently intent on the road ahead.

Martin didn't see the opening. When the Land Rover suddenly turned off the road, he thought they were heading for a collision with the trees that lined it. His vocal reaction offered some light relief to his fellow passengers. As the headlights flashed across more trees and lit up the track in front of them, both Mason and Croft laughed out loud. Under the circumstances, Martin should have felt as if he was being derided, but he didn't.

A few moments later, they were pulling up outside the farmhouse he'd visited earlier in the day. The driver looked over his shoulder.

"Welcome back," he said. In the low lighting, Martin couldn't see his expression, but he thought there was warmth and humour in the voice.

Ten minutes earlier, he'd been looking to take flight. Now he was curious to find out what they wanted with him.

They entered the house through the kitchen. The driver led the way, his sister following him. Mason gestured for Martin to fall in behind her as he and Croft took up the rear. While Martin may have felt curious, they were clearly still not taking any chances with him.

From the kitchen they crossed a narrow hallway. It was fair to say that the Hawthorns' living accommodation wasn't as comfortable as that of the McLeans. The simple wooden door they passed through had a latch instead of a doorknob. He hadn't seen one of those inside a house since he was a child. On the other side of the door was a living room. Unsurprisingly, it was snug, especially with six people in it.

The sixth person was a woman Martin hadn't seen

before. She was medium height, her light brown hair hung to her shoulders, framing her slightly rounded face. By the time Martin was in the room, she was next to Hawthorn, her hand resting on his forearm. It was an endearing gesture that offered reassurance.

As he was jostled gently by the two men entering the room behind him, he looked closely at Hawthorn. What did *he* need reassurance for? There were five of them against Martin. What danger could *he* pose to them? Hawthorn wasn't giving anything away.

Mason touched Martin's arm from behind and used it to guide him to an armchair.

There were several chairs in the room. Two armchairs and a two-seater sofa had been pushed back against the walls. He could tell that, because the imprints on the carpet showed where they normally stood. No doubt they'd been moved to allow the extra chairs in from the kitchen. He recognised them from his visit this morning. All of the furniture looked as if it had seen better days. The seating arrangement was a loose circle, with the chairs pressed close to the walls, and a very small gap in the middle.

To be seated was to be vulnerable, but Martin didn't see that he had any choice. At the same time, his concern about having physical violence visited upon him had severely diminished. So he took his seat.

Hawthorn nodded. "Thank you. I hope you'll forgive us for the way we've gone about bringing you here."

Before Martin had time to consider how to respond to this, the others began to take their seats. As they did, Hawthorn introduced them.

"John Mason is the one who has spent the last few

minutes literally as your right hand man." Martin almost smiled as the bald man sat down in the other armchair. It looked as if he was taking the role of right-hand man to heart. "Your other guardian is Ed Croft." The use of the word guardian jarred, but Martin didn't have time to consider it as the dark haired man sat almost directly opposite him in one of the kitchen chairs. "My sister, Claire."

For most of the time since they'd picked him up, he had seen little more of Claire than her back. As she sat down in the other kitchen chair, he was able to appreciate her at close quarters for the first time. His earlier impressions were confirmed. Usually when he saw an attractive woman, he would be relaxed, chatting comfortably with them and before long the flirting would start. Here, he experienced something remarkable. Apprehension.

On his left was a wall, and against that the sofa. The other woman sat at the far end. "This is my wife, Jennifer." Then Hawthorn sat next to her, less than two feet away from Martin. He looked directly into Martin's eyes. "And I'm Adam Hawthorn."

"How do you do," Martin said drily. "Now, would you like to tell me what I'm doing here?"

Adam didn't pause. He continued to look at Martin as he spoke.

"A lot of strange things have happened in the village over the last couple of days, Martin. And we know you're linked to them."

TWO

"Go on."

Adam had paused, waiting for a response. He seemed disappointed that Martin was giving nothing away, but he didn't waste time dwelling on it.

"You don't seem very surprised."

"Let's just say that you aren't the first to suggest it."

"The inquisitive policeman?"

Martin nodded. "Not that he worked that out for himself. I don't think he had the brains for it."

"One of the villagers, then?"

"Probably more than one."

During the course of this exchange, Martin had deliberately not focused on Adam. He wanted to see how the others reacted as well, so he allowed his gaze to drift around them all. They appeared pretty relaxed now the talking had started, but were clearly intent on what was being said. It looked like none of them wanted to miss anything. Claire seemed to be watching him more closely than the others, but that may have been wishful thinking on his part.

"Did he say why they thought you were involved?"

"Not specifically. I think it was more about me being the new boy in town and it coinciding with the problems you've all been having.

"You've not really been made very welcome, have you?" Adam sounded regretful, as if he wished there was something he could have done to prevent that.

"I didn't realise you'd been taking such an interest in me."

"We're just doing our job."

"And what's your job?"

Adam smiled and nodded. "We'll get to that."

"What do you know of the village's history?" Claire interrupted. Adam glanced at her and sat back, letting her take over.

The sudden change of tack put Martin in mind of a police interrogation. It made him wonder if he was dealing with a team of undercover cops. He decided to roll with it, and see what happened. Besides, it meant he could focus more on Claire.

"Not a lot. I left the village when I was eighteen, and history wasn't a big priority for me at that age." *It's not really a priority for me now,* he thought.

Claire studied him carefully for a moment, apparently considering what he had just said – but there seemed to be something more. "It's not really a priority for you now, is it?" she said.

He *had* thought he was giving her his full attention. He was wrong. The word perfect recitation of his own thoughts focused his mind in a way he hadn't thought possible.

"That's true," he agreed, his tone guarded.

She smiled knowingly at him, and went on: "What do you remember about nineteen sixty-four?"

Well it wasn't ancient history, but he supposed it was history of sorts. "I was eight years old, Claire. How much do you remember from when *you* were eight?"

"Quite a lot, but we need to focus on you, not me."

In spite of his earlier apprehension, old habits kicked in. "I'll be happy to focus on you, Claire."

Something flickered behind her eyes. He couldn't identify it with any certainty, but he knew he'd seen it. The moment passed quickly, though, and she smiled politely at him.

"We *all* need to focus on you, Martin." She made a fleeting gesture with her hands that somehow managed to take in the rest of the room. "So tell us anything you can recall from nineteen sixty-four."

Put in his place, he sat back and thought about it, but all he could think was: *I was* eight. When he'd been questioned by the copper that afternoon, he'd just been annoyed. He'd certainly had no intention of being helpful. Tonight, he tried harder. It crossed his mind that it might be because he wanted to impress Claire, though that would go nowhere for either of them. Even so, he did seriously consider her question. Besides, something about that year did ring a bell. But it wasn't a distant memory. It was more recent than that. Even so, he kept coming back to the same response.

"I can't remember anything specific to that year. I remember getting a new bike for Christmas, and passing my cycling proficiency test. I remember having a birthday party, and someone bought me a Disney jigsaw puzzle. I remember a holiday at the seaside: my dad bought me a kite with a picture of a spaceman on it. I remember running away from home, and getting as far as Wharton's Farm before it started to get dark and I realised I was better off with my mum and dad." As he'd recalled these things, he'd been

331

looking down at his hands. Finished with his recollections, he looked up, slightly embarrassed at how personal some of these revelations had been. "I can remember lots of things, Claire, but I couldn't say with any certainty what year they actually happened in. Some of those might have happened in nineteen sixty-four, but I couldn't tell you which ones."

Glances passed between Claire and the others. He didn't know what they signified, and decided it wouldn't make any difference right now if he did.

"What if I asked you about Forest Farm?" Claire still.

He shrugged. "What about it?"

"It doesn't trigger any memories?"

"No it doesn't." He was beginning to feel impatient, wondering why she was reluctant to simply get to the point.

As that thought crossed his mind, her eyes locked on his.

"You're right," she said. "It's time to stop asking questions, and start explaining things."

Had she picked that up just from his tone? He studied her face carefully, but her expression offered him no clues.

"This might seem a bit long-winded," she said, "but we need to explain everything to you properly."

"Why? Are you worried I won't understand it?"

"No. You just won't believe it." The words were spoken evenly. The lack of stress or emphasis ensured he would take notice of what she had to say.

"The Sullivans owned Forest Farm for three generations, going back to the end of the last century. Before that, the family worked land in this area for hundreds of years."

"They weren't ones for travelling then."

Ignoring Martin's remark, Claire went on. "By nineteen

332

sixty-four, the farmer was Phil Sullivan. Do you remember *him*?"

He didn't, but the name was familiar. And then he realised where he'd heard it recently.

"Are you going to tell me about him committing suicide?"

"So you *do* remember him?"

"No, but Ian McLean was telling me about how he killed himself years ago." Even as he said it, he recalled more of the conversation they'd had in the pub the previous evening. That was why nineteen sixty-four had seemed familiar. Ian had told him Phil Sullivan had shot himself that year. "Something about finding his wife in bed with…" He racked his brains, trying to summon up the details. "With his son-in-law?" he said at last, pleased that it was coming back to him now. He noticed Adam nodding in response to his words. "But wasn't there some doubt about whether it really was suicide or not?"

"It was suicide." Adam's interjection was quiet but firm.

"Didn't his wife top herself a couple of years later?" There were at least three winces at his choice of words, including one from Claire. He noted that and resolved to think more before speaking.

"Betty did kill herself, yes," Claire confirmed. "It was a very bleak time for the family."

"I'm not surprised," Martin said. "And, to be fair, it sounds like both of them over-reacted. But surely she didn't really expect to have an affair with her son-in-law and there be no repercussions?"

"She didn't," Claire said.

"She didn't expect there to be no repercussions?"

"No. She didn't have an affair."

"So she wasn't found in bed with her son-in-law?"

"It's not as straightforward as that." Claire grimaced, as if she was recalling the incident herself. "Someone else was involved." She fixed her gaze on Martin. "And now they're back."

THREE

"Please tell me you're kidding." Martin looked around the faces staring intently at him, clearly waiting for a reaction.

"What do you mean?" Adam seemed puzzled by his comment.

"You don't seriously think *I* was…" He tailed off, recalling his resolve to think before speaking. "I mean, I was *eight*. I hadn't even reached puberty."

Realisation struck Adam first, and then, like dominoes falling, horrified looks appeared on their faces.

"No, no!" Adam again. "That's not what Claire meant. No one else had sex with Betty." His familiar use of the first name struck Martin as odd. Both brother and sister had referred to her that way now, and it seemed strange coming from people who would have barely been teenagers when the woman died. "I'm afraid we can't get away from the fact that it was Ray."

"Ray?"

"Ray Smith, the son-in-law."

"Ah. So if they did…" he hesitated, then realised Adam had been blunt enough, "…have sex, what do you mean when you say 'someone else was involved'?"

Glances passed between Adam and Claire, as if to say: "Do you want to do this, or shall I?" It seemed Claire got the short straw.

"They were being controlled."

"What? Blackmailed?" He thought back to the implication of the look he'd been given a few moments ago. "And you think *I* was responsible? I was only…"

"…Eight," she completed for him. "Yes, I think we all got that." The warmth of her smile surprised him. They all seemed so serious about whatever it was they were trying to tell him. Yet she'd seen humour and used it lightly. "Don't worry, Martin. No one's blaming you."

He thought about his family, and wondered if that was true. Was it possible that the things Claire was going to tell him might shed some light on why they rejected him? She didn't give him time to dwell on that.

"There was no blackmail. When I say they were being controlled, I mean someone physically forced them to do it." She paused and thought about that. "And even that's not quite right," she said, clearly frustrated with her inability to explain things.

"Perhaps we should go back further," Adam suggested. "Maybe we need to fill Martin in with who we are."

Claire nodded her agreement and treated Martin to another smile. He liked them.

"We're sentinels," she said simply. When he didn't interrupt with a question she went on: "Our job is to wait and watch for the ravens gathering. Because when they do, a man comes to this place. And when he comes, he brings pain and misery with him. The last time the ravens gathered was in nineteen sixty-four."

"He's not a regular visitor, then."

She ignored his flippancy, and brought his attempt at humour to a sharp end: "About once every twenty-five years." She nodded at the baffled look on his face. "This has been going on for a long time. And this is where you're going to have to trust me, because I'm going to say a few things now that won't make sense at first. So just bear with me."

Apart from the fact that he'd been brought here against his will, Martin couldn't think of any reason not to trust her.

"You used irony when you made the remark about him being a regular visitor."

"More sarcasm than irony."

The look on her face told him he was pushing boundaries unnecessarily. He shrugged sheepishly.

"He *is* a regular visitor. Just not in the way you meant. He's been coming here since long before Ravens Gathering existed."

"Bearing in mind your comment that your job is to watch for the ravens gathering, I take it the name isn't a coincidence."

"I'm sure not, though I couldn't tell you who first gave it that name. Certainly, it's been called that since before the Domesday Book. And there were sentinels here long before that."

"Okay," he said at last. "Let me get this straight. You're telling me that you've been here for centuries and your sole purpose in life is to watch out for this guy who pops up here every twenty-five years?"

Claire smiled. "I think I need to flesh out that explanation," she said. He got the impression she was humouring him, but he liked the smile anyway.

"Firstly, the sentinels are part of the Order. The Order itself is not based at Ravens Gathering. *Kindness Farm* is an outpost, if you like, with just a few of us acting as sentinels. Most members of the Order live at the Refuge in France."

"Well, the climate's better," Martin said lightly.

She cocked her head and looked at him. The message she conveyed was for him to shut up. But the method told him she was amused, in spite of the circumstances.

"It is at the moment," she said. "But we didn't make a choice based on the weather. The point I'm making, Martin, is that the location of the Refuge has nothing to do with why we are here in Ravens Gathering.

"The Order's purpose is to protect the continuity of humanity and the Earth. That probably sounds somewhat extreme, but I can't think of a clearer way to explain it. We've existed for as long as there has been what you might call intelligent life."

"Might?"

"Well, intelligence tends to suggest rational thought, and there's not actually too much of that out there. We're more emotional than we like to think, and more intuitive than we realise."

"So by 'we' I take it you're including yourselves as humans?"

"Don't doubt that for a second," Adam put in sharply.

"For now, though," Claire continued as if she hadn't been interrupted, "let's stick with the concept of intelligent life, even if it's only as a form of shorthand."

Conscious of Adam's interjection, Martin just nodded.

"I don't propose to give you a full history of the Order, but there are some things that might help you to appreciate what we're about. For instance, our connection with the Source has helped to define us."

The question was begging to be asked.

"What's the Source?"

"The Source is an energy that runs through all of us: humans, animals, plant life... Every organism, every cell, has the Source inside it, connecting us all. It even exists within things we consider to be inanimate, like rocks and earth and the air we breathe. Without it, nothing would exist on the planet."

"Are you talking about God?"

"Not in the sense you mean. For most people God assumes a creator that cares. The Source is a part of Creation, but it makes no judgement about our actions, or the consequences of them. It's indifferent. It's just there.

"As humans we're unique. We think, we rationalise..."

"But only in a limited way," Martin reminded her.

She smiled, and he enjoyed the moment.

"True," she said. "But compared to every other creature on the planet, we at least have the capacity to be rational. Not that it always leads to good things happening. Humans are very complex."

Ain't that the truth.

"But somehow this... Source... is connected to your Order?"

"Yes. Though, as I've mentioned, it's connected to each and every one of us anyway. But the connection with the Order is very strong. We open ourselves up to it and it flows through us."

Intrigued, Martin asked: "And what does that feel like?"

Claire shrugged. "If I was to explain it to you properly, I'd have to understand what it felt like to live without it, and I've never known anything different."

"Then how do you know you don't feel the same as us ordinary mortals?" Martin was careful not to make his tone too mocking.

Without warning, she reached out and touched his hand. A tingling sensation erupted through his arm and up to his shoulder. He jolted backwards, breaking the contact, and the tingling stopped. Before he had time to react, her hand was on top of his again. This time, there was nothing more than the warmth of flesh on flesh.

"What was *that*?" he murmured, almost breathless. Everything had happened so quickly, he hadn't had time to process how he was feeling.

"The Source passing through me to you. Don't be afraid of it. It won't do you any harm. It can't, because it's already inside you anyway. The difference at the moment is that it's dormant."

"Why?"

"Because you don't *know* it's there yet. Like most people, you haven't opened yourself up to it."

"So are you saying only people who are in this... Order... are open to it?"

"Oh no! There are lots of people in the world who *feel* it. They don't understand what it is, necessarily. Some think it's a connection to God, or they have a particularly spiritual leaning, or just feel at one with nature. So we're not unique in feeling it. We just have a better understanding of what it is."

"And that's because the Source is somehow linked to your Order?"

"It's more a case that we have studied it in depth and incorporate it into our lives. There are elements in this world, Martin, that you can't begin to imagine, and the Source has provided us with exceptional gifts, both physical and metaphysical. They're gifts, but they carry with them a responsibility."

"What kind of responsibility?"

"A responsibility to protect humankind from destroying itself."

FOUR

For a moment, Martin stared at Claire. He wasn't sure what he wanted to see in her face. Maybe an impish grin to let him know the whole story was a wind-up. Instead, she simply looked back at him, her expression earnest. He sensed she wanted him to accept what she was saying, but would understand if he didn't. There was no desperate neediness there, no wild-eyed mania. He turned to look at the others. They were all sitting back and watching, curious as to the outcome.

"Are we really that much of a threat to ourselves?" he asked at last.

"More than we realise."

"When you say 'we', do you mean we, the Order, or we, the human race?"

"Right now, I mean the human race. We constantly strive for more: more money, more possessions, more convenience, more things to make our lives *easier*. So we build things, and then build replacements that are better. In the process, we use up our natural resources, poison the world we live in, and generally give ourselves even more to strive for in the future. And that's without taking into account the evil that lurks inside us."

"All of us?"

"Each and every one. We have the capacity for good and

bad. Both are in there, and it's up to us to decide which path to lean towards. Do I really need to give you examples of the evil men do to each other?"

Martin shook his head. He hadn't needed to come home to find evil: it was in the news every day of the week, from the raw brutality of domestic violence to the slaughterhouse of war.

"So we're steadily destroying ourselves," he said thoughtfully. "And you jump in and avert disaster at every turn."

"No. That's not our job." She smiled at the look of bewilderment on his face. "If it was, we'd have headed off Hitler and Stalin and Pol Pot and every other psychotic madman that ever existed. We aren't here to save every individual from harm. We only act if there's a threat to the survival of the human race or the existence of the Earth itself."

"So how does that fit in with what's happening in Ravens Gathering?"

"I said earlier that the farm is an outpost of the Order, that we are sentinels. Our job is to watch for a man who is a potential threat to both. That might seem a bit extreme as we are only talking about one individual, but he has a unique characteristic. He can travel through time."

"What's he called? The Doctor?"

Clearly, Martin's humour was lost on them. They all looked puzzled.

"We don't know his name," Claire said earnestly. "For ease, we refer to him as the Raven."

"Okay," Martin said, deciding he needed to take some control of the conversation before it became too weird.

"Tell me, then, how does he get about? Is it an old fashioned Police Box or a DeLorean?"

More puzzled looks.

"Do you mean, how does he travel through time?" Adam asked.

"Yes."

"He has an amulet that is directly connected to the Source. It gives him the ability to travel through time. Fortunately for us, he doesn't understand exactly how it works, so he doesn't know the full extent of its powers."

"How come?"

"Because he stole it."

"And presumably it didn't have an instruction manual with it." Martin was thinking aloud and didn't expect a response. "So he can travel through time with it?"

"Yes. But that seems to be all he can use the amulet for. So when he does travel, he always finds himself in the same place."

"Which is why he keeps turning up in Ravens Gathering," Martin said. "And that's why you guys are on watch here."

"That's right."

"I think you'd better explain some more about this Raven."

Adam nodded to Claire. It was clearly time for her to pick up where she left off.

"I'd better just explain a bit more about time travel, because it's a difficult concept to appreciate. The principles seem straightforward enough. You move from one time to another. But there are nuances that are sometimes hard to comprehend. For instance, the Raven comes from a time around three hundred thousand years ago. We don't know how old he is, but suspect he's probably in his thirties or forties. But, because he's travelled in time, he's actually lived for longer."

Martin frowned exaggeratedly. He wanted her to elaborate, but didn't want to speak again.

"Let me give you an example. You're thirty-three." He hadn't told her that, but he realised that, with his repeated claims to have been eight in nineteen sixty-four, she didn't need a degree in mathematics to work it out. "Let's say you make a jump forward in time by a hundred years. Then you stay there for a year, before coming back to the current time. How old do you think you'll be?"

It felt like a trick question, but he went for the obvious answer anyway. "Thirty-four?"

"You'll have lived thirty-four years, but you won't have physically aged at all. While you're out of your own time, you can't age. In practice, it's not as precise as I make it sound. Time will have elapsed in your absence. Not at the same pace, but it does go by. We don't understand why that is, or how it happens. There's no science to this."

That'll disappoint a lot of writers, Martin thought.

"It seems to be the Source's way of ensuring that you don't accidentally populate the same moment in time twice. Because that would be weird, wouldn't it? Meeting yourself."

That would be weird?

"So every time he travels forward in time, he does age, but only by the period he is gone from his own time. Does that make sense?"

He nodded, urging her on with his eyes.

345

"What that means, then, is that the Raven could have lived the equivalent of several centuries, but is physically still a relatively young man. Does that make sense?"

Martin nodded slowly. He was pretty sure he'd taken it all in, but planned to ask questions at the end if he was still unsure.

Beside him, Martin was conscious of Mason shifting in his chair. They'd been sitting for three quarters of an hour now, and Mason was a big man. He guessed it could get very uncomfortable for him. The others seemed to be as captivated by Claire's explanation as he was, and were sitting stock still. Even though they'd surely already heard it, there was no lack of interest.

Claire went on: "If you're clear on that, the next thing to consider is why the Raven keeps coming forward in time. You remember I talked about there being a capacity for good and evil in each of us?" As Martin nodded, she continued: "In practice, most of us tap into both at different times in our lives. Some find a strong leaning towards one or the other, and that leaning can be enhanced by exposure to the Source.

"We haven't been able to properly identify the Raven within his own time. But what we do know is that he was able to tap into the Source."

"Like you guys," Martin put in.

"Yes. Like us, he is a sorcerer."

"A sorcerer?" Martin made no attempt to conceal his incredulity. "Are you joking?"

"Where do you think the word sorcerer comes from?" Adam asked. "It means someone who is able to use the Source."

"Which means," Claire added, "he has the ability to connect with the rest of the natural world. Not in a way that's all-seeing, all-feeling, but if he wants to control another human, animal, or even a flock of birds, he can do."

Recognising the sincerity of their words, Martin's feelings were already shifting, and the implications of their explanation made him uneasy. "But he *is* a human being?"

"Oh yes. Flawed in many ways, like the rest of us. He's not invincible. We know that for certain. But that doesn't mean we should underestimate him. Back at home, we know he was already very powerful before he stole the amulet. But he's greedy and wants more power. Discovering the ability to travel in time has the potential to give him that. Do you understand how?"

Bearing in mind that everything she'd told him so far was news to him, Martin hadn't had time to work that much out. He shook his head.

"Can you imagine taking a Chieftain tank three hundred thousand years back in time?" She paused to let that one sink in.

It took a few moments for Martin to think that through. "Jesus Christ!" The idea was horrifying. "He'd destroy anyone and anything he came across. History isn't my strong point, but I'm guessing weaponry wasn't too well developed back then. A few spears, maybe a bow and arrow?"

He was treated to Claire's warm smile. She was amused at his ignorance, but he was comfortable with that.

"Some societies were a little more advanced, but the point is the same. Nothing could destroy the tank."

"You made that sound as if it actually happened."

"It did. In nineteen sixty-four. Though we didn't appreciate that was what he'd done until after the event. We were too late to stop it going."

"In fairness," Adam added, "we couldn't really intervene anyway. We already knew about the tank in advance. The Order has records that refer to it, so we knew it would have to go back. We can't change what's already happened."

"We also can't let him know we're on to him," Claire continued. "As you've probably gathered by now, we know what his plans are, and we know that he will eventually die in his own time. But there's still a risk that he might have transported some equipment to other points in history, with the potential for devastation there. It might not be caused by him, but by some other person stumbling on to it and using it. For that reason, it was felt by members of the Order that, as an extra safeguard, he needed to be monitored."

"For three hundred thousand years?" Martin couldn't keep the incredulity from his voice.

Adam responded with a modest smile. "Possibly longer. It took us a long time to find him. We didn't know where he was based geographically, so we didn't know where to look for him, either then or in future times. It's fair to say that the Order had its work cut out for it."

"We only narrowed him down to this area about seventy thousand years ago." It was Claire again. "Of course, I'm generalising about the timing. When you're dealing with numbers this big, being out by even a few thousand years doesn't make a lot of difference."

"So a group of us moved out here," Adam came back,

"and we've been watching over the area since. At first, his visits were very sporadic. There could be gaps of a thousand years or more between sightings. And we probably missed him on some occasions. It took us a while to realise the ravens were a sign that he was coming.

"We think he started coming more often when he realised that the technology was changing more rapidly. For centuries, armies had fought with weapons that were essentially just variations on swords, spears and glorified hammers. Then we started to see widespread use of gunpowder, and with that came various types of guns and bombs. The internal combustion engine sent developments into overdrive. More importantly for him, he could travel further.

"You see, one of the major limitations for the Raven must have been his ability to travel. He can tap into the Source, but that doesn't mean he can fly or simply transport himself through space. So he was restricted by how far he could physically travel from this area.

"We all know now that gunpowder, for instance, was widely used in China centuries before it came to Europe. But we didn't know it until relatively recently. And if *we* didn't know it here in Sherwood, how would he know? But we had trains appearing in the nineteenth century, and we're pretty sure he used the railways to go to different parts of the country. We suspect he even travelled over to mainland Europe for a while."

"*Suspect*? Weren't you following him?" Martin's earlier resolve had disappeared.

"No. We never do. Our aim is to be aware of when he arrives, and when he returns. And whether he has anything to take back with him. Remember, if we get too close, he might realise what we're doing.

"But do you see what I'm getting at? There have been more technological advances in the last two hundred years than there have been in all of the time that has preceded them. So we think he'd realised this, and become more focused on his search for weapons he can use in his own time."

"Do you know what else he's taken? Besides the tank, I mean?"

"Not everything," Adam said. "Not with any certainty. But we do know he took some guns with him. Those seem to have been taken back in the nineteen thirties, so are probably next to useless beside the tank."

"And whatever else he picks up on his next visit," Martin added thoughtfully.

"Which is already happening."

"Hence the comment Claire made earlier," Martin deduced. "That he's back. The person who was responsible for Betty Sullivan..." He just caught himself in time. "... having sex with her son-in-law."

"That's right. But this time there's something different. This time you turned up as well."

FIVE

Martin was conscious of them all studying him carefully. They were obviously looking for something. The problem was, he hadn't got a clue what it was.

"I don't know what you're talking about."

There was no immediate response. All five of his roommates simply continued to look at him. It was Jennifer who broke the silence. She had barely spoken since he'd arrived, so he'd assumed she was only there because she was Adam's wife. He adjusted that assumption rapidly.

"You're lying." The words should have been spoken with a degree of petulance, like they came from some bratty teenager who couldn't get her own way. Instead, her words were a simple statement of fact.

He opened his mouth to respond, but realised his, "No I'm not!" *would* sound like a bratty teenager's petulance. So he held back for a moment, collecting himself, all the time aware of Jennifer's eyes on him.

She'd been pretty much in the background and, like Mason and Croft, left Adam and Claire to do all the talking. It was clear now that her role was to observe, and he guessed she'd been doing that diligently. It was also apparent that she wasn't in the habit of taking prisoners.

"Tell us the truth, Martin."

Somehow, he didn't think she was going to give him

the option. Although he hesitated for a moment longer, he realised that it was actually a relief to finally share what he'd been experiencing. And after everything he'd just been told by these guys, they were hardly likely to fill the room with mocking laughter.

"The truth is I can't explain exactly why I'm back in Ravens Gathering. Something drew me back." He paused, expecting one of his hosts to jump in with a question, but, having done her job, even Jennifer was waiting patiently for him to carry on. "I've always had dreams, ever since I was a child. Well, pretty much the same dream, really. It comes and goes. It's not there all the time. In fact, there was a point when I didn't have it for two or three years. But I suppose it's always been there in the background.

"Anyway, it became more regular earlier in the year. At first it was a couple of times a week, but it built up quite rapidly until it was there every night. I can't explain what changed. There was no detail in the dream that seemed different. I just had a strong sense that it was calling me home. And that's why I'm here."

This time when he paused, Jennifer must have sensed his unwillingness to continue.

"Don't stop there. Tell us everything."

He shot her a look, but she didn't seem inclined to back off.

"While I've been here, I've been up to the clearing in the woods at the back of Forest Farm. The dream always ends there, and when I arrived in the village it seemed like the natural place to go. So I've seen the ravens."

"They aren't the only ones," Adam said, "but the clearing is the focal point." Martin was conscious that

Adam was watching him expectantly. Though what he was expecting to see was still a mystery.

"It was creepy up there. I felt threatened, even though they were just birds. And there was something else I felt while I was up there. Obviously the familiarity. Apart from the dream, I played up there when I was a kid. But there was a sense of loss as well, a kind of melancholy. It only started to lift when I came away, but it's still not gone completely, and the last time I was there was early this morning."

Glancing around the room, he knew he had their attention, even though what he was describing was pretty humdrum compared to time travel and talk of an ancient order. He also saw sympathy. It wasn't obvious in all of them, but it was definitely there in Claire's eyes.

"Then there've been some strange things happening in the village. I've not been involved, but as I became aware of them, there was a sense that I was somehow connected." A terrible thought occurred to him. "If this Raven could force people to do things, is it possible he could have taken control of me? I mean, maybe if he did…"

Adam leaned over and rested a reassuring hand on his forearm.

"If the Raven made you do something that would normally horrify you, he'd make sure you were aware of it. He seems to gain strength from negative feelings. If you can imagine, in the modern day what Betty and Ray did would still cause a shock. But, rightly or wrongly, we live in a more tolerant society now compared to the early sixties. Back then, it would be hard to imagine the scandal it would raise, not to mention the emotional upset for everyone involved. The Raven would have taken the emotional pain as a kind of psychic energy. It would make him stronger. That's why he forced Betty and Ray together."

"So what you're saying is, if I'd killed that dog and stolen the van, he'd have made sure I was conscious of it. That way, he'd be able to feed off my guilt."

"Not to mention your anger and frustration at not being able to stop what you were doing. So, no, you can be confident that you weren't directly involved."

"But I was connected?"

"You say you were, so only you can know for sure."

"How, though?"

Looks passed amongst the members of the Order. Martin didn't know what they signified, but it was clear they were keeping something from him.

"A few minutes ago, Jennifer told me to tell the truth. It's obvious there's something *you're* not telling me. Truth goes both ways, you know."

"We're not trying to hide anything from you, Martin." It was Claire. "Having said that, there are things you need to discover for yourself."

"How long do you think this one will take?"

"Just a few seconds. I think this one is worth you taking a crash course in."

From the tone of her voice, he suspected he wasn't going to enjoy the crash course.

"You said your dream ends in the clearing."

"Yes."

"Can you tell me who's there?"

"Will it make a difference?"

"I think so."

"Okay." He bowed his head, thinking for a moment,

354

trying to bring the faces into his mind. "Well, my parents are there. And so are my brothers and sister." He hesitated, then corrected himself. "Actually, no, Colin isn't there, just Matt and Janet."

With his head down, he didn't see the pained expressions cross the faces of the three Hawthorns.

"Some other families are there. The Salthouses, the Paynes, the Dakins and the Wheelers." He frowned, trying to picture them all. "Actually, they're not all there, either. None of the younger children are there." He looked up as it struck him. It was something he'd never noticed before. "This isn't a dream, is it? It's something that really happened."

"We'll come to that soon," Claire reassured him. "Just think about who else is there."

The image of the clearing grew in his mind. He could see the tree trunks flickering in the glow of firelight. Families were mingling, parents and children together. They were moving around rhythmically, as if dancing to some unheard beat. Sweat rolled down their faces, though whether from their exertions or the heat of the fire that blazed in the centre of the clearing, he couldn't tell. And standing amongst them all was a stranger.

"There's a man. He's tall and thin. Dark hair. Long. His face is pale. He's got dark, staring eyes." Lost in the images of the dream, he suddenly felt the urge to pull out of it. He still didn't understand everything he'd seen. Maybe didn't want to. His eyes re-focused, coming to rest on Claire's face.

"That was him, wasn't it?"

Inexplicably, there was sadness in Claire's eyes. They

355

even looked a little watery. She nodded, apparently unable to trust herself to speak.

"I was there, wasn't I?" he persisted, looking at the others for help now, since Claire didn't seem able to verbalise.

Beside him, Adam swallowed hard and nodded. He cleared his throat, coughing out some of the emotion he was feeling. "You were," he agreed.

"So I saw him in nineteen sixty-four."

"And he saw you," Adam said. "From what you've explained, I'd say he must have formed some kind of psychic connection with you in those few moments. What caused it is anyone's guess. But since then you've been dreaming about him, and when it was time for him to come back, you were drawn here too. Just like the ravens."

"What does that *mean*?"

"Honestly, we don't know."

"Well what do the ravens do? Do they help him in some way? Are we going to see something like *The Birds*?"

Perhaps predictably, he was met with blank stares. But he tried again just in case.

"You know, the Alfred Hitchcock film? Tippi Hedren, Rod Taylor?" He shrugged. "You're just not movie fans, are you?"

Mason and Croft shrugged back, but they were smiling at him as if they had a joke to share. Their roles as heavies were long past.

"You're right about the movies. We don't really have any interest in that or in television. We're aware that they're there, but we have more important things to deal with."

"Only once every twenty-five years," Martin pointed out.

"At the moment," Adam reminded him. "But with even faster advances in technology, he could start coming more often. Our vigil has to be a hundred percent."

"Fair enough. But what about the ravens? What do they do for him?"

"In our experience, they seem to act as watchers for him. They act as his eyes and ears. Other than that, we can only speculate. It just seems that they're drawn to this area when he is due. When he leaves, they go too."

"So I could be acting as his eyes and ears too?"

"If you were, you'd know about it."

"How can you be sure?"

"It's happened before. Trust us on this, Martin. We've been dealing with him for long enough. We've seen connections made where he is aware, and where he isn't. If you don't know, he doesn't. And we've been watching you since you arrived in the village. We know the signs, and you aren't displaying them."

"Is there a chance that could change?"

"It's possible, but we'll cross that bridge if we come to it." Adam looked at his wife. "Has he told us everything?"

"Everything he can," she said.

"Good." He smiled amiably at Martin. "Now we need to tell you what we want from you."

SIX

He'd been half expecting it, but was disappointed all the same. Over the past hour or so, he'd begun to feel safe amongst these people. It'd felt as if they were there to help him, even if it was only to understand what had been happening to him. But deep down he'd known they'd want something from him. When he'd been asked for help from the police earlier today, he'd kicked back. Over the years, that had become his natural reaction. This time, in spite of the apprehension he felt, he realised he was looking forward to helping.

"The van from the Post Office was hidden in one of the barns at Forest Farm last night," Adam said.

"I know. The police found tracks there this afternoon. But how do *you* know?"

"I followed you to your parents' house last night." Adam showed no sign of embarrassment over this and, oddly, Martin felt no sense of grievance at having his privacy invaded. He was more interested in where the explanation would take them. "After you'd gone in, while I was waiting for you, I saw the Raven. He came out of the vicarage."

"What was he doing there?"

"Difficult to say for sure, but we suspect he's using the vicar and his wife to help him." He must have seen some puzzlement on Martin's face, because he elaborated.

"There are certain things he doesn't seem to be able to do for himself yet, especially when it comes to the advances in technology we've talked about. We're pretty sure he can't drive, for example."

Martin couldn't help himself. He snorted a laugh. "I'm sorry," he said. "It just seems ludicrous that we're running scared of this bloke who can travel through time and has designs on building up a power base built on fear – but he can't drive yet."

"You have to bear in mind that, in the grand scheme of things, driving isn't significant," Adam pointed out. "Besides, since the advent of the motor car, he's probably only spent the equivalent of a couple of weeks around them."

"That doesn't mean to say he couldn't control one if he wanted to," Mason added. "He could tap into the Source and use the energy flowing through a vehicle's individual parts to make it move. But it's a lot less draining to control flesh and blood. He'd also get an energy boost from all of the negative emotions passing through the person he's controlling."

"Exactly," Adam agreed. "Which is exactly what he did last night. He was on his own when he left the vicarage. He had things to do. But eventually he came back and fetched Simon."

"Simon?"

"The vicar. He took him to the Post Office, and they stole the van. Obviously I couldn't get too close, so I didn't see exactly what happened. But they were in there longer than it took to break in and steal the van. I can only assume some of that time was taken up by the Raven forcing Simon to torture the dog." He looked meaningfully at Martin.

"Like we said earlier, he wouldn't have done it himself. He'd have fed off the loathing and shame and anguish that a man of the cloth would have experienced in carrying out such a barbaric act."

There was silence in the room for a few moments as they all let that thought sink in. Then Adam continued.

"Simon drove the van up to the farm. Obviously, I didn't see everything because I was on foot. But I saw them turn into the farm entrance, and later I saw them come back on foot. After they'd gone back into the vicarage, I went up to the farm and looked around. That's how I know the van was in the barn."

"It's not there now, though," Martin told them.

"We know," Claire said. "We're pretty sure he's used it to go to another part of the country. But he'll be back."

"How can you be sure?"

"Because his home is on this same spot three hundred thousand years ago. And it's a lot easier to cover distances in a motor vehicle on tarmac roads than it is over the sort of terrain he's got to deal with there. He'll want to go back from the village. Besides, he's done this before. Betty Sullivan was his driver twenty-five years ago. And on previous visits he's taken others, either to drive him or guide him through the intricacies of contemporary activities like buying rail tickets. Every time, he's come back. And, having chosen the barn to hide in last night, the chances are he'll hide it there again when he comes back."

"Which, presumably, is where I come in?"

"It isn't a coincidence that you're staying at Forest Farm," Adam said. "Something drew you there –"

"My dad was working there."

"– and something made the McLeans invite you to stay there."

"I think that might have had something to do with Tanya's interest in blokes, to be honest."

In most environments, he would have expected to see knowing smiles from the men. What little reaction he saw suggested pity more than anything else.

"These are all factors, Martin," Adam went on. "And you could probably point to the troubles within the McLean marriage as well as the financial difficulties they face as being issues that support those factors. But it does beg the question as to why everything should fall into place now."

"Coincidence?"

"If the Raven returns to the farm, you can decide for yourself whether it's a coincidence or not."

"So what do you want me to do?"

"Just be alert. And let us know if the Raven returns. That's all. Don't confront him, don't try to intervene. We just need to be aware."

"And what will you do?"

"Hopefully we do nothing. But we've got John and Ed here to help, and we can get others if we need them."

Martin looked at Mason and Croft in turn, before looking at Adam again. "You made that sound as if they don't belong here."

Adam gestured to his wife and sister. "Normally there are just the three of us. John and Ed got here this morning."

"From France?" Martin asked, surprised that they'd been able to get there so quickly.

"Yes. You saw them arrive."

The surprise turned to confusion. "I'm sorry?"

"You were here when we all came back?"

The confusion evolved rapidly into bewilderment. "What are you talking about?"

"You were here, weren't you? We saw you."

That was true, he realised. He had been at the farm this morning. And they'd appeared from nowhere. He thought he'd hidden himself well, but then he recalled Adam saying "Welcome back," when they'd first arrived in the Land Rover. He clearly hadn't hidden himself well enough. Or maybe no amount of hiding would have kept his presence away from them. Adam's words started to make a kind of sense to him as other things began to click into place.

"Wait a minute. Did you say, when you all *came back*?"

"Yes. Claire and Jennifer and I had been to the Refuge. We thought it was best to report everything in person."

"So you didn't just telephone?"

"We don't have a telephone."

"And you definitely haven't had time to fly over and back again. So how do you do it, then?"

"We have ways…" Adam deliberately tailed off.

"What, a kind of 'Beam me up, Scotty' arrangement?"

Unsurprisingly, none of them seemed to know what he was talking about, but in spite of that, he guessed he was on the right track.

"You've got something in that barn that allows you to travel to this Refuge, haven't you?"

"Something like that," Adam agreed. "But let's not dwell on that. The main thing is that we've got access to more help if we need it."

"And do you think you will need it?"

"We should all pray that we won't."

PART FOUR

FAMILIES AND
HOW TO SURVIVE

ONE

Yesterday had been a long day. Productive, but long. Roads were confusing to him, dark tracks that seemed to go on endlessly, jostling vehicles crowding them in a way he didn't remember from his last visit. The journey had taken much longer than he expected, but he'd quickly realised the vicar's navigational skills were little better than his own. Even so, he knew he couldn't manage it by himself, not over such a prolonged period of time.

Arriving at Aldermaston in the afternoon gave him a chance to survey the village and surrounding countryside. Then, when it was dark, he'd used the Amulet to travel a thousand years into the past. He didn't know how long ago the Atomic Weapons Establishment had been there, so he played it safe. They drove a mile and a half across open grassland before returning to 1989, and the inside of a building within the AWE. Having bypassed the external security, completing the rest of their mission was relatively straightforward.

Even so, he'd been exhausted by the time they returned to the vicarage. There he'd slept, grateful for the soft warmth of the vicar's bed. Physically re-charged, he'd then needed the psychic re-charge. Terror, abhorrence, frustration and guilt provided that for him in abundance. Energised, he was looking forward to tonight.

On previous visits, he'd spent much longer. Sometimes weeks and months had passed as he learnt what was on offer. And usually what he learnt had given him only limited advantages. But this had to have been the quickest visit yet, and surely he had the greatest prize. They called it a bomb. He didn't know what that meant, but he'd seen enough to understand what it could do. There had been vague references to it last time he was here, so he knew it had potential. Now he knew more. The vicar had been able to show him pictures of its effects, and described the devastation caused by the two bombs dropped nearly fifty years earlier. He couldn't pronounce the names of the places mentioned, and he didn't really consider them important anyway. What was important was the death toll. Curiously, there didn't appear to be any definitive numbers mentioned in the notes Cantor had been able to obtain for him. But with the lowest figures for one site being in the region of sixty thousand people and the other being ninety thousand, it was clear that the power this afforded him was beyond anything he could have previously imagined. For a start, he'd never encountered populations in his own time that came close to these numbers. So if he set one of these devices off, it would virtually guarantee that anyone and anything within a radius of a few miles would be destroyed. Even more importantly, the pain and suffering caused would generate massive amounts of psychic energy for him to tap into, boosting his personal power beyond anything he'd experienced before. Added to that, the after effects on survivors in a wider area would mean a continuing flow of energy to him for years to come.

Such was his thinking, and thus the cause of his

excitement. What he had yet to consider fully was how he was going to benefit from this death and destruction without putting himself in danger. In one sense, that didn't matter. He had time on his side – literally. So he could consider how to resolve that issue later. The main thing was to have one of these bombs in his possession. And the thrill of that knowledge coursed through him, together with the anticipation of what he would find as he went still further forward in time.

Of course, he knew he couldn't go too far forward. Although he didn't know when it would happen, he'd been warned there was an end coming to the world. The cause was unknown to him, but it seemed reasonable to assume the ever increasing power of the weapons he was discovering would have something to do with it. With each leap in their development, he felt sure he was getting closer to that time, and as the rate at which their destructiveness escalated, he grew more cautious. His journeys forward in time grew shorter. There was no scientific calculation made, just a natural wariness. The sheer scale of the devastation this bomb could inflict suggested that time was very near. Already he was contemplating a reduction in the number of years before he would return to the village. Maybe ten would be a safer option. Or maybe he should satisfy himself with the arms he had managed to accumulate so far.

In spite of his abilities, he was only human. When he learnt of the amulet's existence, it came from the lips of a desperate creature who had managed to travel to a point where the Earth had already torn itself apart. What would be the point in going that far? He'd used these trips through time to gather tools that would give him greater power at home. Of course, there appeared to be advantages to living in other periods of history, and he didn't rule out returning to some of them. But there was something strangely comforting about the familiarity of his own time. Not that he needed to make any decisions right now about whether he should return to Ravens Gathering in the future.

Tonight, he would take the bomb home with him and add it to the growing collection of weapons he was accumulating. Before he did that, he needed to make his presence felt in the village. He knew he already had, but only in small ways. He'd been drip-feeding his malevolence to the general population since he arrived here three days ago. It was the norm for him. The locals would be irritable, argumentative and malicious. Conflict would arise, and bloom outwards, much like the mushroom clouds he'd seen moving images of. And all he had to do was pause outside their homes and make those mental deposits.

Of course, he was also responsible for more obvious trauma. The tractor that had injured Peter Salthouse had been under his control, as had Simon Cantor when he butchered the dog.

The village was stirring, its misery rising. But tonight he would take things to the next level. Tonight he would have a reunion. He had acquaintances to renew, and the horror those people would feel should create more than enough energy to sustain him for several weeks to come.

As he walked up the track towards the barns, he was aware of the ravens. Some hovered overhead. Others perched on nearby fencing. There was no order to them yet, but that would come later when they all gathered at the clearing.

Beside him, the vicar stumbled along, filled with the anguish of having watched helplessly as his wife was raped. For now, he was needed. The bomb was too heavy for them to carry into the woods, so Cantor would drive the van to the clearing. Once it was in place, he would send for the old acquaintances. They would join him in the clearing before he returned home.

Everything was going according to plan. Until he reached the old outbuildings.

TWO

The significance of the truck didn't strike him at first. There was a large open space outside the buildings, and it didn't seem unreasonable for it to be used to park a vehicle. It was when they opened the door to the old barn that he realised something was wrong. For a start, there was no sign of the van. Which meant there was no bomb.

Even though he knew the barn must be empty, he wasted half a minute or so roaming around it, peering into dark corners. He knew it wasn't possible for the van to feel fear or, driven by that sensation, to sneak into the shadows and hide. Nevertheless, he searched, and with every passing second he felt tension rising inside himself. His breathing grew heavy, the sound more pronounced in the enclosed space.

Where was it?

He'd picked this place because it was abandoned. The farmhouse was occupied, but it was clear the building was unused – a fact confirmed by Cantor. So how would anyone know about it?

Tension had already evolved into anger, which in turn was becoming a burning rage. After all the effort he'd expended, the energy he'd used up to get them into Aldermaston. It had left him drained, barely able to control the vicar for long enough to get them back here. And for what purpose? He was furious, desperate to find the source of his frustration so he could lash out at it.

No one knew about this hiding place. No one except him and Cantor.

It was a thought that brought him up sharply.

Cantor!

Rational thought was gone. The fact that the vicar had been secured in his own cellar all day was a detail that escaped him. He withdrew his knife from the sheath at his belt, turning as he did so. The blade plunged into Cantor's stomach, and the sensation provided him with a release similar to the one he'd felt less than an hour ago with the vicar's wife. He felt wetness on his hand, and the slickness spurred him on. The rage poured out of him as he ripped and slashed and tore at the man of God he had possessed over the past few days. Even when he fell to the floor, all life draining from him, the Raven continued to stab, stopping only when he heard the door open wider.

Although there was no obvious indication anyone was there, he knew it hadn't been a gust of wind that widened the gap between door and frame. The movement had been too precise. And, more importantly, he could smell them. Sweat and fear are a potent combination.

Wiping the blade, he slipped the knife back into its sheath and stood up straight.

Two. He was sure there were two of them there. One on either side of the gap. The door itself was to the right of him. He stretched out his right arm, hand open, feeling air, heavy with latent energy, flow across his palm. Curling his fingers, drawing the Source in, he felt an intense surge of power build up, then twisted his hand outwards, palm directed at the door, and pushed. The distance between his hand and the door was a good twenty feet. The effect was as if he'd used a truck with a battering ram attached to the front of it. In an instant, the door exploded, splintering outwards, tearing into the soldier who was standing on the other side of it. He felt the soldier's pain, fed on it. But only for a moment. Then all life expired from him. Fortunately, the other soldier must have seen enough in the dim light to know that his colleague had been literally torn apart in the blast. The Raven tasted the revulsion and terror that came from that quarter. Already, he was striding towards the doorway, his right hand directed at the wall shielding the survivor. His movement gave him momentum, just as his anger did, and the energy he was drawing from the frightened young soldier. From fewer than ten feet, he let loose another blast, punching a hole in the brick wall. Naturally, it wouldn't break as easily as a wooden door, but the hole was about two feet square and at chest height. He heard the scream from the other side of the wall, and the clatter of something metallic hitting the ground, together with the unmistakable heavier thump of a body.

When he stepped out of the building, he could see the vague outline of a man lying down. It was misshapen, partly due to the section of wall lying across his upper torso, and partly because of the fact that his torso was flatter than it should have been. Black liquid pooled at his side.

He didn't need to see the soldier's eyes to know he was afraid. That fear was pulsing out towards him. Fear of death, fear of further injury, fear of the pain that was already more intense than anything he'd ever felt in his life.

Even – and this was something the Raven couldn't begin to comprehend – fear of letting his comrades down.

"Pathetic fool," he muttered. He had no intention of inflicting any further damage to him. To do that would kill him, and the Raven couldn't feed off a dead man. He walked on, heading for the track. Not that he knew where he was going to go, or what he was going to do exactly. But he knew that staying here would serve no purpose.

There were lights on in the farmhouse. He could see them over the wall between the house and the track. Maybe the people inside could enlighten him about how the van and bomb had been discovered. And, more importantly, where it was, so he could go and retrieve it. He closed his eyes, allowing his mind to focus on the house and the other minds in it. It took a few moments for him to find them. One was dormant – sleeping, he supposed. The others were in different parts of the house. He felt conflicting emotions coming from one of them. A little more pain for him to draw on.

Then the thoughts changed, and he heard them as if they were being spoken in his own head.

What a relief they'd managed to move the bomb and take it back where it had come from.

The bomb had gone back! All that effort gone to waste. Rage bubbled up inside him. Like a toddler unable to get its own way, he lashed out. Gathering energy from the air around him, he directed it in blasts at the part of the house from which those thoughts had come.

THREE

A howling wind accompanied the trashing of the bedroom. It came from nowhere. Certainly there was no obvious source – no window open, no hole in the wall. Regardless of its origin, it seemed in keeping with the clothes straining against their hangers in the wardrobe.

Martin was shielded from the worst of it as he crouched just outside the room. Freaky gusts slapped his cheeks, but he felt safe there – unlike Ian and Tanya, who were still laying on the floor. From this angle, Martin could see only their feet and ankles. They thrashed and jerked as the furniture exploded around them. It was impossible to tell whether they were reacting to the crashes and bangs, or whether glass or heavy furniture was dropping on them.

He wanted to call to them, but realised it was just a basic need to make contact. Nothing practical could be gained by it, especially as the shrieking of the wind meant it would be difficult for them to hear him.

What could he say anyway? *Don't worry. It'll all stop when the Raven gets fed up.* He didn't believe it for a moment. So he'd be lying, which wouldn't offer any real comfort to them. Not that Tanya would have a clue what he was talking about. And even Ian might not completely understand.

Last night, Ian had been brought in on some of what was happening. It wasn't planned, but then he hadn't banked on Ian being with him if he found the missing van. Quite rightly, he'd wanted to call the police as soon as they came across it. The problem was, Martin knew he had to get in touch with Claire, Adam and the other sentinels. That was what they'd asked him to do. Of course, if anyone else had come up with the yarn they'd spun the previous night, he'd have laughed at them. But there was a certainty about them, and an indefinable sense that he could trust them. So, if their story was true, he couldn't let them down. Because if he did, he'd also be letting the rest of the village down, and God alone knew who else – whether in the present, the past or the future.

How did you convince someone else, though?

As they'd headed back from the barn to the house, that was the question running through his mind. He kept opening his mouth, ready to say something, but filled with doubt about his ability to get the message across. It wasn't as if he could just make a quick phone call either. *Kindness Farm* didn't have a telephone. So they'd have to drive over, which would mean delaying the call to the police even longer. Martin didn't have a problem with that, but he couldn't see Ian going along with it unless he had a good reason. Scratch that. Unless he had a good and *plausible* reason.

It was like last minute revision, or not telling your mum about breaking her favourite ornament until she's just about to discover it for herself. You put it off until you don't have any other choice.

That was why they were at the kitchen door before Martin finally started talking.

"I know you've only known me for a day or two, but would you do me a favour before we call the police?"

Ian paused, his hand on the door knob. "You *know* something about this, don't you?" He said it as if he didn't want to believe it, and Martin was encouraged by that.

"I do, but not in the way you think," he said hurriedly. "We haven't got time for me to give you a full explanation," he went on, aware that a full explanation would probably only lead to Ian questioning his sanity. "But there's a group of people nearby who are watching out for this."

"That's right. The police." There was a sarcastic edge to his voice.

"You know I don't mean them. These guys are… Well, they're kind of like the police. I suppose you could say they've been on a long-term stakeout, waiting to catch the bloke who's responsible for stealing the van."

"Bearing in mind that the van was only stolen yesterday, how long term has this stakeout been?"

That would be a hard one to sell. He ducked it.

"It's not the van, it's the bloke who stole it. They've been waiting for him to turn up."

"And what are they going to do with him when they find him?"

Probably an even harder sell, Martin realised. Ian was clearly assuming he was talking about people who'd make the Krays look like Mary Poppins. On that basis, he might be relieved to hear that they didn't want to harm the thief. But he'd also be somewhat sceptical.

"They just want to talk to him."

"About?"

Martin could feel his story – such as it had been – falling apart. "I can't tell you," he said weakly.

"What's your involvement?"

The change of tack, while more than reasonable, threw Martin.

"How do you mean?" He was stalling, trying hard to think of something credible as an answer to Ian's question.

"I mean, how come you know about all this? Have you really just come back from the Canaries, or are you part of some gang and you've just been sent here to help with a job?"

"Why would a gang send me to my home village to do a 'job'?"

"I don't know. But then, I don't really know much about *you*, do I, Martin?"

In spite of the intensity of his words, he still managed to keep his voice low. Both of them had. Somehow it didn't seem appropriate to be speaking in normal conversational tones when they were outside at this time of night.

Holding his hands out submissively, Martin shrugged. "Look, I know this sounds off the wall. In part that's because I haven't got time to explain everything to you. And I know it's a lot to ask you to trust me on this. But I really need to let these people come and have a look before the police get here."

"What are they going to do? Bring sniffer dogs so they can try and follow the trail he's left behind?"

"I doubt it."

"Then what?"

Martin racked his brains, trying desperately to think of some way of explaining things to Ian that might just make sense. As he did, he became aware of an engine noise. Not unusual in a farming community at that time of the morning. But it was getting closer. He turned to look behind him as Ian looked over his shoulder. Light flickered on the track leading up from *The Barns*. The beams grew bigger, filling the ground on the other side of the gate. They briefly saw the shadowy outline of the front of the vehicle, then the lights turned into the yard, blinding them.

As the Land Rover pulled up, the driver killed the lights, but left the engine running. It took a few moments for his eyes to readjust to the darkness. Tiny stars exploded across the backs of them, gradually dying out. When they were gone, Adam was standing in front of him, Claire and Mason were just behind.

"What the hell are you doing here?"

"Claire will explain that to you in a minute, Martin." Adam studied Ian carefully for a moment. His scrutiny was met with silent hostility.

"The van's here," Martin said impatiently. "He wants to call the police."

"That would be the right thing to do," Adam pointed out.

"Yeah. But not yet. I was trying to explain why he needed to give me time to call you in."

"Difficult job." Adam clearly understood the struggle Martin had experienced. He glanced at Claire. "I'll enlighten Mr McLean while Martin shows you what he's found."

She nodded agreement, then took Martin by the arm and headed back towards the gate. Mason stayed with Adam, presumably to give Ian an added incentive to stay put and listen.

They were almost at the gate before Claire said anything. By then, they were pretty much out of earshot of the others.

"There's obviously something very special about you, Martin. I don't know why, but you seem to have picked up some psychic abilities." A flash of teeth reflected in the dim light. Martin hoped it was a natural accompaniment to the light-hearted tone. "Obviously, we realised you had the link to the Raven, but we hadn't appreciated you'd connect with one of us as well."

"What do you mean?"

"You woke me up."

His natural instinct would normally have been to make a smutty remark. Instead, he felt awkward. Back at *Kindness Farm*, he'd begun to take more care of what he said in front of her, and this was an extension of that. Feeling self-conscious, he tried to keep his words to a minimum.

"How?"

"I felt your anxiety."

"I've been feeling *anxious* since you kidnapped me."

She ignored the reference to kidnapping. "Not *this* anxious. Your stress levels shot up about twenty minutes ago."

Was it really only twenty minutes since he'd heard the van? "And you could feel that?"

"It's a bit more tenuous than that. More a sense of it than a complete experience. But I did also catch glimpses of things you were seeing as well." They had reached the barn. She turned and gestured to the shadowy walls around them. "All of this. Flashes of the track." She paused, looking him squarely in the eyes. "You saw him, didn't you?"

Martin opened his mouth to respond. He hesitated, not sure what to say. A part of him felt embarrassed at not pursuing the Raven. Even though they had made it clear he was only to report to them, there was still the concern that he might have seemed cowardly. And he didn't want Claire to think less of him.

"You did the right thing."

He stared at her.

"If you'd gone after him, you'd be dead by now." He felt her hand on his shoulder. She rubbed it gently for a moment, comforting him.

"Is there anything else you can see?" he asked warily. "In my head."

The surrounding darkness made it difficult to see clearly, but Martin thought she frowned. "No images at the moment." Her hand stopped moving, squeezed the top of his arm. "There's a lot of pain, though."

He looked down, frightened of what he was feeling.

"I'll do what I can to help," she said. "If you want me to."

His sense of gratitude surprised him. He looked back up. "Do you think you can?"

"For some reason, we've made a connection. It might help, or it might get in the way. Who knows? For now, though, it acts as an extra layer of protection for you."

There'd been a softness in her voice and – he was sure – in her eyes. Maybe something else could happen between them. An unfamiliar optimism began to grow within him, and he was surprised it didn't diminish when her expression hardened and she nodded towards the barn door. "Now, let's go and find out what he's been up to."

By the time they returned to the yard, Adam had done his job with Ian.

"That's two of you in one night," Adam remarked

quietly to Martin as they approached. "Can't remember that happening before."

So Ian had been made aware of the existence of the sentinels. But he didn't fully understand about the Raven. In the short time Adam had been with him, it had been impossible to give him a full appreciation.

Now, as wardrobe doors thrashed about, threatening to tear themselves off their hinges, as curtains ripped away from their fixings and across the room, Martin hugged himself against the doorframe, filled with a need to connect with Ian. For the first time in many years, he acknowledged his loneliness. He'd spent more years on his own than he cared to remember, even before he'd left the village, but the sense of loneliness had been suppressed. Crouched only feet away from this couple he'd known only two days, he wanted desperately to be with them.

And then it was over. The few clothes that had managed to cling on to the rail in the wardrobe flopped down. The curtain pole rattled to a stop. A vase that had been rocking on the edge of a chest of drawers rattled to a rest. For a long moment there was silence.

Remaining bent over, Martin scuttled across the room, broken glass crunching under his feet.

Ian's jacket was powdered with glass and pieces of mirror. Incongruously, a sock lay at an angle between his shoulder blades, a flimsy pair of panties had folded themselves around his elbow, and a single shirt sleeve lay across the backs of his thighs. Tanya's left leg was exposed, from mid-thigh down. He could see it between Ian's legs, and it had been slashed and torn, blood running from some of the wounds. The reassuring thing was that it wasn't gushing. Apart from her leg, Ian seemed to have done a good job of shielding her. The only other blood on show was coming from Ian's right ear. His shirt collar was splattered with bright red stains.

Martin reached down and shook Ian's shoulder. With hindsight, the flinching response was only to be expected.

"It's okay," Martin soothed. "It's only me. But you've got to get up. We've got to get out."

At the sound of his voice, Ian seemed to slump, tension easing out of him. Presumably the relief at the familiar sound rather than the content of his message. As he relaxed, though, Tanya grunted.

"Get off me, you bastard!" She sounded panicked rather than angry, and it did the trick. Ian scrambled to lift himself off her, and was immediately conscious of her nakedness.

"Look the other way, will you?" he snapped at Martin.

But Martin already had, and was grabbing loose items of clothing from the bed and shaking the glass out of them. He glanced back only to make sure that anything he tossed over to them went in the right direction. Then he pulled the duvet off and flipped it over and on to the floor. It wasn't a fool proof solution, but it should protect Tanya's feet from most of the fallen glass.

That done, he turned to check their progress. Tanya had pulled a pair of lightweight trousers on. They were white and already streaked with blood. Ian was handing her a sweatshirt. Both of them were trembling.

"Come on!" Martin urged. "We've got to get out of here!"

Tanya looked up at him, confusion on her face. The fact that her breasts were exposed to him didn't seem to bother

her in the slightest. He suspected that would have been the case regardless of the circumstances. If those circumstances had been somewhat different, Martin might well have taken time to admire the view. But embarrassment would have made that a short time.

"What the hell just happened?" She sounded stunned, distant.

"I'll explain later. Right now, we've got to go. You can finish dressing while we're going."

"Where?"

He shot a look at Ian. "Just bring her, will you?" The Raven was nearby. He had to be the cause of the destruction in the room. Martin didn't know how or why, but he couldn't think of any other explanation. So they needed to get as far away as possible.

It was clear that shock had hit Ian as well. He looked at Martin, but his gaze was unfocused, almost as if he had just woken from a dream. The sharpness he'd demonstrated when he'd told Martin to look away was gone now. His wife was still half-naked and now he was virtually oblivious to it.

Martin stepped towards them, and gripped Ian's left arm. He didn't feel comfortable about touching Tanya.

"Now, Ian! We haven't got much time."

In truth, he didn't know how much time they had. For all he knew, the Raven could have already moved on, gone to cause havoc elsewhere. He didn't want to bank on it, though. There was the chance that his connection with Claire had kicked in and the sentinels were aware. But he'd already worked out why that wouldn't help them. The Sentinels had to keep their presence hidden from the

Raven. So they could only show themselves if he wasn't there. Which meant he couldn't rely on them riding in like the cavalry to save him at the last minute.

"Haven't got much time for what?" Ian asked. He didn't sound quite as vague as he looked. Martin could only hope the stupor was wearing off.

He started to pull Ian forward and gestured at his right arm. "Get Tanya! We're going!"

Ian planted his feet firmly and resisted. "Where?" he asked.

And from behind him, Martin heard a voice. It sounded strained and awkward, as if it was struggling with the language. But that didn't disguise the menace that came with it.

"A very good question. Where *are* you planning to go?"

FOUR

Collins was wedged between John Mason and Ed Croft. They were on the back seat in the Land Rover. He got the impression they'd done this before.

In the front were Adam and Claire Hawthorn. Everyone had been introduced politely and they were on first name terms, in spite of his concerns when he'd seen them all coming out of the barn. They *had* been tooled up, but any thought they may be a potential threat to him had been set aside as quickly as their weapons. When they'd seen him in the yard, Claire had told everyone to put the guns and clubs down. Then she'd walked forward on her own. Her intention was clearly to reassure him, and he'd been impressed at how smoothly she'd handled it. Within minutes, they were all gathered in the farmhouse kitchen, Jennifer putting the kettle on and organising mugs.

Of course, they didn't want to answer any of his questions. Not that the questions were the ones he originally intended to ask. Their mysterious appearance from an empty barn opened up a whole new line of enquiries. But everything he asked was deflected in such a skilful way that it took him several minutes and almost half a mug of tea before he realised what they were doing.

They nodded politely and would respond courteously, and sometimes at length. But when they finished speaking, he'd realise they'd revealed nothing. It was artful and, frankly, impressive. He made small talk while he considered how to break down the politeness barrier. And drank more tea.

As a group, they were clearly at ease with each other in a way that went far beyond anything Collins had experienced before. The fact that three of them were related might have been offered by some as a partial explanation. But Collins had enough understanding of family lives to know that friction was a more common component than peace and tranquillity. There was an underlying tension among them, but he sensed it was connected to some outside factors, and nothing to do with their own relationships. Their outward calm gave the impression of an unnatural stillness that had the potential to give him the creeps. Yet, strangely, didn't.

At least it didn't until Claire suddenly jolted upright.

It wasn't a subtle movement. Everyone saw it.

"What's wrong?" Adam asked, but there was something about his tone that suggested he already had an inkling.

"Martin." It was all she said, and then they were moving, picking up their weapons as they went.

"Jennifer, you stay here," Adam said. It wasn't an order, but Collins knew *he* wouldn't have argued. "If we're not back within the hour, go to the Refuge." He turned to Collins. "You can come with us. This might answer some of your questions."

Collins followed them out to the yard. He started for his Cavalier, but Mason grabbed his arm and steered him towards the Land Rover.

"You'll be safer with us."

The idea he might not be safe hadn't been too prominent

in his mind. He'd been thinking about Martin Gates. It hadn't been a massive leap to connect him with the 'Martin' Claire had referred to. The fact he was being referred to *here* only added to the confusion he was feeling. He knew he should be asking questions. He just didn't know where to start. And things were moving so rapidly, he didn't have time to sit back and consider everything. He liked to work in a logical manner. True, he was quite capable of throwing himself into action if the situation arose. Probably not as much as he would have done ten years ago, but he was confident he could still handle himself. Nevertheless, his strength was in analysis. He liked to gather the facts together and connect the dots. Right now, there seemed to be dots flung far and wide and he hadn't got time to work out whether any two of them might join up.

Adam drove. They were heading towards the village.

Claire twisted in her seat to face him. She looked very serious.

"We haven't got a lot of time, Inspector, so I won't explain everything now. If you need to know anything at the end of all this, I'll fill you in afterwards. Right now, we need you to trust us."

In spite of the fact they seemed to have appeared from nowhere, and there was a strange quality to them that he couldn't explain, he couldn't think of a reason not to trust them. Still, he was curious.

"Why do you need me to trust you?"

"Because we need *you* to help us."

He waited for the rest.

"We can't be seen at *Forest Farm*. But we think Martin is in danger, so we need someone to go and help him."

"Why can't you be seen?"

"That's what I'd need the time to explain."

He glanced at the men on either side of him. "Am I going to get a choice in this?"

She smiled back at him reassuringly. "They aren't there to threaten you, Inspector. Their job is to protect you."

They were in the village now. The Land Rover passed the opening that led to the farm.

"We're going in the back way," Claire explained, seeing the puzzled look on his face. "It attracts less attention. We'll be there in a few minutes. I need to know whether you'll help or not."

"What difference would my presence make?" Collins asked. "There are already soldiers up there. Surely they'd be better equipped to help."

"That would be true if they knew what to expect."

As he asked the next question, he wasn't sure he wanted to know the answer. "What should they be expecting?"

FIVE

Still stunned from the battering he'd taken, Ian struggled to focus for a moment or so. He was confused at Martin's demand that they leave. In spite of having just been assaulted by the contents of his bedroom, the very fact that it was his bedroom and therefore familiar to him offered some comfort.

There was also something familiar about the man standing in the doorway, though that offered no comfort at all. And when he realised why, he felt violated. It wasn't the man himself. It was what he was wearing. The clothes were Ian's. He remembered wondering where the jacket had gone only a day or so ago. Now he knew. This bastard had been in his wardrobe and stolen it, together with the rest of the clothes he was wearing. Only the shoes weren't his, and he guessed – correctly – that the only reason for that was because the stranger's feet were too big.

"Who the hell are you?" he managed at last. Even as he spoke, he was struck by the fact that Martin hadn't said anything since the newcomer had arrived. Surprising when you considered that he'd been very vocal up to that point.

The stranger wasn't paying attention to Ian, though. Instead, he was looking intently at Martin.

Ian knew the look. It was one he'd seen before – and probably used himself. A look that said *I think I recognise you. But I'm not quite sure.*

Martin had his back to Ian, so he couldn't see whether the expression was mirrored, or if it suggested that he recognised the stranger. When Martin took a couple of tentative steps backwards, Ian thought he might have a clue.

"I know you." Although it was a statement, there was still a hint of a question, as if the man was still unsure. The wrinkled forehead suggested he was struggling with his memory.

In another situation, Ian might have assumed the stranger was distracted, possibly even vulnerable. He had no sense of that here. The eyes may have been on Martin, but he was aware of being watched. It was more a feeling than anything, but he had no doubt that if he made a move of any description, the man would take it all in – probably even anticipate it.

And there was menace there as well. If he did anticipate a wrong move, he would intercept it with violence. The eyes were dark and cold, bereft of emotion. There would be no compassion. He would do what was necessary, regardless of the consequences for others.

The world Ian had thrived in could be cut-throat at times. But all that was at stake in business was money and reputation. No one got physically hurt. This man was capable of going well beyond hurting people. Ian recalled the description he'd been given of what had happened to the Payne's dog. At times over the last day or two, he'd wondered whether Martin had been responsible. Not now. The cause of the Labrador's death had been pure evil. And pure evil was standing in the bedroom doorway now.

"You're a Gates." He smiled and nodded to himself

as the connections were finally made. If there was any humour there, it was unquestionably dark. "How are your parents?" The question was laced with malice.

Ian had to raise his hand to stop Martin walking back into him.

A mocking smile acknowledged the effect he was having on them. His eyes shifted and looked over Martin's shoulder. Ian realised he was looking at Tanya.

"Brazen," he commented. His eyes slid back to Martin. "Just like your mother."

There was a tension in Martin's shoulders. Ian recognised it because he was feeling it himself. An outraged anger at having a loved one spoken of in those terms, mixed with a sense of helplessness because you know the stranger has all the power.

Instinctively, he reached out to put his arm around Tanya.

"Fool." The stranger let the word hang in the air for a moment. "You want to protect her, and yet she has done nothing but betray you."

He felt Tanya tense under his arm. But this wasn't anger or outrage. His stomach suddenly felt hollow, an aching void, as he realised why. He was aware of her looking at him, but he bowed his head. He didn't want to see the guilt in her eyes, and he didn't want to see the triumphant mockery on that creature's face.

It shouldn't be a surprise, he tried to reason with himself. He had suspected it for long enough. That didn't make the pain any easier though. Her semi-nakedness made matters worse, of course. She still hadn't pulled the sweatshirt on. He knew that she, like him, had been frozen by the appearance of the man in the doorway. So it wasn't that she was deliberately flaunting herself. But it was still maddening to think that the slut was showing her breasts off like that. Far from wanting to comfort her, right now he could have happily slapped her.

Which brought him up short. He'd never felt like that. No matter how angry he was about anything she'd done, not once had he been inclined to lash out physically. Verbally, yes, but even that had been pretty low-key in the grand scheme of things. Right now, though, he wanted to strangle her.

Even as the thought passed through his head, he snatched his arm away. The urge had been almost overpowering. It would have been so easy then to slip his hands around her throat, and pay her back for all the times she'd been unfaithful. All the times she'd worked late, or stopped over at a conference, or been out with "the girls". The lying bitch! And he'd known it all along. Deep down, he'd known she was cheating on him, whoring around, laughing at him for being such a mug…

"You are right to be thinking that," the stranger said. "She has used you. She deserves to pay for what she has done." He spoke firmly, evenly. His diction was wooden, like a foreigner trying to get to grips with the language. But the words were compelling, pushing him.

Ironically, they also brought Ian to his senses. Keeping his eyes fixed on the pieces of shattered glass in the carpet between his feet, he began to breathe deeply. Slowly, he began to refocus. He knew Tanya's infidelity was real. He knew she'd betrayed him sexually, and probably in other ways too. He also knew in his heart that their marriage had

392

been over a long time ago. He'd fought that, pretended to himself that everything was all right or, even if it wasn't now, he could make it all right. But it wasn't, and it never would be. So they had to move on with their lives. Causing her physical pain wasn't going to solve that. Feeling those urges had been alien to him. He hadn't understood why he felt that way, though he'd been willing to give in to the compulsion. Then the stranger had spoken and he'd realised where the impulses had come from.

Clenching his fists, he looked at the sneering face across the room.

"You might as well give in to it. If you do not, I will do it for you."

"No you fucking won't!" Ian leapt forward, shoving Martin aside. The distance to the doorway was a little over ten feet away. Around three paces. He managed only one before he was lifted up and thrown backwards. The chest of drawers behind him stood about waist high. He cleared it, smashing into the wall and the edge of the window frame, the impact jarring his whole body. His head snapped back against the wall and he slumped, sliding sideways off the top of the chest and landing in an untidy heap on the floor.

He could feel consciousness slipping away. The sounds from the rest of the room were growing distant. Fingers stroked his face, a hand gripped his arm. They felt light, feminine. He was glad she'd come to tend him. She may not have been the best wife a man could have, but he knew there was goodness inside her.

"Do not bother with him." The voice sounded as if it was in another room. "He will be dead soon enough. As will you." There was a pause, a slight shift. Ian thought it was because he was slipping deeper into unconsciousness, then realised the stranger must have turned his attention to Martin. "As will your family, Mr Gates." Darkness overcame Ian. The last words he heard were: "Tonight we will finish what we started."

SIX

When he'd heard the voice, Martin had known it was the Raven. The possibility of him turning up was the reason he'd been urging Ian and Tanya to get out of the room. But the voice was the clincher. The slow, careful way he used the language, together with the harsh coarseness of the sound. It seemed like a cross between the husky rattle of a long-term smoker and the hoarseness of a football fan who's spent an intense ninety minutes on the terraces. There was no mistaking the voice. If you'd heard it before, you'd recognise it again. And he did. Twenty-five years after he'd last heard it.

He knew what the Raven would look like before he turned. It had been a hazy image in a dream for so many years. But now it was vivid in his mind. The voice alone was triggering memories. They were surging up, pouring uncontrollably into his consciousness. After such a long time, the face should have been an indistinct blur. Instead it was more familiar to him than his own father's had been. Then again, Patrick had aged fifteen years since he'd last seen him. The Raven hadn't aged at all. For him, only days had passed since he'd last been here.

Images from the woods flashed behind his eyes. Darkness, interspersed with flickers of firelight. Orange flames, half hidden by the trees that lay between him and the fire. Up ahead was the unknown. He was frightened, yet compelled to go on.

Clothing was scattered on the path. He knew that was inappropriate. But he was eight years old. He couldn't begin to comprehend why they were there, or why he knew there was something wrong. At first, the discarded clothes were spaced far apart. As he came nearer to the clearing, their appearance was more frequent. And not just a single item at a time. Two or even three would materialise out of the darkness, dropped in a heap on the ground. One pile included a man's shirt and a skirt. He didn't stop to examine the underwear that peeked out from between the two garments. The quantity of clothes struck him as odd too. Certainly there were more there than his parents, brother and sister could have brought with them on their own. He lost count of the pairs of trousers he'd seen, and the dresses and skirts, not to mention the wide and varied range of underwear.

They were in the clearing. He knew the clearing well. It was a safe place to come if you wanted to play. Some older lads had set up a rope swing to one side. They'd tied a section of branch to the bottom of it. Depending on how brave you were, you could use it to sit on, legs either side of the rope, or you could stand on it. There was a hollow in the ground over there, so you could climb on to the branch easily, then launch yourself out into space. It gave a sense of danger, but you knew you were safe really. Martin had spent hours up here. Using the swing, making dens, playing hide and seek. Sometimes he came with his mates, but he was just as happy up here on his own. Firing make-believe guns at make-believe bad guys. He was the Lone Ranger or

Robin Hood. But, like any other little boy, always the hero.

He didn't feel heroic now. Creeping through the woods, his only illumination coming from the fire in the clearing. And around the fire were others.

In the bedroom of the farmhouse, he flinched as he recognised Mrs Payne. She and her husband had moved to the village a year or so earlier to take over the Post Office. He didn't know how old she was. When you're eight, everyone over the age of twenty is old. So seeing her naked had come as a shock. She was standing apart from the others, swaying gently as if she was listening to music, her hands were gently caressing her breasts and stomach. Another figure came into view. It was a man. He reached out and cupped one of her breasts in his hand, then squeezed it. As he turned, Martin recognised Mr Salthouse, who worked on one of the other farms in the village. Mrs Payne reached down with one of her hands. Martin followed the movement with his eyes and was astonished to see Mr Salthouse's erection. He hadn't realised that could happen. Mrs Payne began to stroke it.

Movement to the left caught Martin's eye, and he looked over, grateful he didn't have to watch any more of that. He didn't know what was happening, but it didn't seem right, whatever it was.

Without realising, he'd continued to move towards the clearing, even as he felt stunned at what he'd seen the postmistress doing. It was by moving forwards that the others had come into his line of vision. He had a relatively unobstructed view of the clearing now, and could see there were easily more than twenty people in it. Almost all were naked. Every face he saw was a familiar one from the village.

There were others there whose faces were concealed from him, either looking in another direction, or because they were lying down. The lying down was disturbing to him. Because they weren't lying on their own. And in reality, they weren't just lying. They were moving, rhythmically, parts of them rising and falling. He felt ill. A heavy ball was growing in his stomach, a weight that he would only come to understand twenty-five years later. Fear and horror combined.

Overhead, the trees rustled in the light breeze. And something else rustled as well. The birds he'd seen over the past few days. Gathered together now to watch their master at work.

His father was standing next to the only stranger in the group. Martin knew him now. Patrick's face was a picture of torment as the Raven spoke to him. From this distance, Martin couldn't hear a word, but his father's expression told him enough. His cheeks glistened, though whether it was sweat or tears Martin couldn't tell. The pair of them looked to the side, and Martin followed their gaze. With a jolt, he realised his mum was lying on the ground. He could see her face because her head had been propped up somehow. Her feet were pointed towards him, legs apart. He saw two pairs of hands on her body… God! He couldn't bring himself to think about it even now, a quarter of a century later. She turned her head to one side, and he saw another erection was close to her face.

"Brazen," the voice cut through his thoughts. "Just like your mother."

Martin was paralysed by the horror of what he'd just replayed to himself. He didn't remember that from the dream. It had been reality. He felt anger towards his mother. *How could she do that?* She was always so prim and proper, and there she had been... The thought didn't bear completion. He also felt angry towards the Raven. His sneering voice goaded him, forcing him to confront memories from the past. He wanted to lash out, to punch and kick the bastard until his head was nothing more than pulp. But he knew he wouldn't be able to get close to him. Even as his attention turned to Ian and Tanya, taunting them, Martin sensed the creature's power. The frustration at his own impotence burned inside him.

Thankfully the images had dissolved, interrupted by the Raven's voice as he poked and prodded Ian with his words. Martin tried to focus on what he was saying. Not because he wanted to hear it, but to distract himself from the conflicting emotions that raged inside him. Because the scene he'd just recalled was all the more terrible when he thought of how badly his mother had treated him as a child. He'd been pushed aside, especially after Colin was born. Pushed aside, but not forgotten. Deliberately avoided. Was it so she could focus on her other needs?

For more years than he could remember, he'd pretended he was hardened to it, that he didn't care. But a child's rejection by his parents does affect him, and the pain never goes away.

"She has used you," he heard. "She deserves to pay for what she has done."

The words were about Tanya, but they felt so relevant to his mother. *Yes she does*, he thought. *And so do the rest of them.* He'd come home because he felt the dream was calling him. But he'd also hoped there could be reconciliation. Now he knew the only thing that would give him satisfaction was revenge. Ostracised and abandoned, his departure greeted with indifference, that was no way to treat your own child. He deserved better than that. Especially from a whore and a husband who stood by and let her get on with it.

"You might as well give in to it."

Again the words were aimed at Ian, but Martin accepted them himself. It was time to do what he should have done years ago. His rage was becoming a steely determination to make his family pay for the pain they'd caused him. Each and every one of them.

Then Ian was pushing past him and shouting at the Raven, the shove breaking Martin's train of thought for a moment. He didn't really care any more what happened here. Tanya and Ian weren't his problem. He just wanted to get out and pay a visit to the family cottage. Even the sight of Ian flying backwards as if thrown by an invisible giant didn't affect his dedication to the job he wanted to complete.

He stepped forward, and the Raven's head snapped in his direction. Martin stopped. For some reason, he'd assumed the Raven would sense his purpose and support it. After all, he was here to cause chaos and mayhem. Anything Martin had planned would only add to that. But the dark eyes glittered with hatred and malevolence, his expression leaving Martin in no doubt that he'd better remain where he was.

Behind him, he heard a series of thuds as Ian's body landed on the floor.

Apparently satisfied that Martin wasn't going anywhere, the Raven returned his gaze to a point on the other side of the room.

"Do not bother with him." Although he hadn't been aware of any other movement, Martin realised Tanya must be with Ian. He didn't look back to confirm it. Instead, he remained focused on the Raven. "He will be dead soon enough. As will you be." The long dark hair swayed slightly as he turned his head to look back at Martin. "As will your family, Mr Gates. Tonight we will finish what we started."

Martin opened his mouth to speak. Part of him wanted to protest. He wanted to deal with his family. To let someone else kill them would only deprive him of the opportunity he was craving. But another part of him wanted to know what the Raven meant. What had been started that needed finishing?

As he hesitated, uncertain which of these ideas needed to be vocalised first, there was a crashing noise from downstairs, followed by the sound of excited voices.

SEVEN

Adam had parked the Land Rover a quarter of a mile down the track. Its dark green paintwork blended well with the trees he'd pulled in between. From there, they'd continued on foot until they were within sight of the farmhouse yard. Then Collins was on his own. Claire had made it very clear on the ride over that they would only step in as a last resort. And bearing in mind that she'd previously indicated his life might have to be sacrificed, he couldn't help wondering just how bad things would have to be for them to consider it necessary to show themselves.

True to her word, Claire had told him very little. If anything, he felt there were even more pieces missing from the jigsaw than he'd previously thought. And there was a major credibility gap. As a man who dealt in facts and evidence, her claim that they'd just returned from France when he saw them emerge from the barn seemed far-fetched. Sure enough, it had been empty when he'd been in there only minutes earlier, but that didn't mean to say that he hadn't overlooked some hidden door or hatch that might have led to a basement of some kind.

She admitted her reluctance to reveal this to him on the basis that she didn't think he'd believe her. But then she'd gone on to say that the presence of a portal – she'd actually used that word – in the barn was nothing compared to the supernatural powers possessed by the man who'd stolen the bomb.

At which point he'd wanted to know how she was aware of the bomb. More had been revealed. The fact that they'd asked Martin to help them and, when he found the stolen van, they'd gone to *Forest Farm* to inspect it before the police had been called. And that Ian had been to visit them with an update after returning from the police station that afternoon. That surprised him. Of the three people he'd interviewed today, Ian McLean seemed like the most trustworthy. He would've been the last person he'd have expected to pass on everything he'd learned during the course of the day.

It was Ian's visit that had prompted them to return to the Refuge – whatever that was. They'd reported everything they'd learned and sought guidance from their colleagues. Not that she'd disclosed what that guidance was to Collins. Instead she'd tried to impress upon him how important it was to be wary of the man they called the Raven.

The yard was barely illuminated. Cracks of light from behind curtains added almost as much as the dim glow from the lamp outside the kitchen door. Shadows shifted under a low breeze. Beyond the house itself, there was more light. It seemed to be coming from the direction of the old barn where they'd found the van. That was at odds with his own understanding of the Army's game plan. He'd been led to believe they were going to leave a small force there. But, on the off-chance that the people responsible might come back, that force was going to be discreet. They didn't want to scare them off. The brightness of the lights suggested they'd given up on that idea.

He decided he'd be better off if he was close to the house. If anyone was to suddenly appear, he'd be less visible there. As he moved diagonally across the yard in that direction, he heard a rustling noise above him, and looked up. Along the rooftop he could see the silhouettes of what looked to be dozens of birds.

The McLeans' vehicles were parked on the other side of the back door. Their shapes weren't very clearly defined, but well enough for him to know he was unlikely to bump into them. He made his way along the wall until he reached the kitchen door. The window was a couple of feet beyond, and a subdued glow around the edge of the curtains told him the light was on. He waited, watching carefully for any sign of movement inside. A minute passed very slowly. The second minute went slower still. He knew that still might not be long enough, but he was impatient to move on.

Taking the door handle gently in his hand, he turned it slowly, careful not to make a sound. Though, as he eased the door open, he did wonder why he'd bothered to be so cautious.

EIGHT

"Stay where you are!" the Raven hissed. He glared at the three people in the bedroom as if to underline his words.

Satisfied for the moment that they weren't going anywhere, he stepped backwards out on to the landing. His movements were cautious. Not because he was afraid, or because he was concerned about forewarning the new arrivals that he was on to them. They must have realised the noise they were making would alert everyone in the house to their presence. It was more that he was surprised. After all, why would anyone be stupid enough to think this was the way to defeat him? There was that, and also he wanted to make sure the occupants of the bedroom stayed where they were, so he was keeping his eyes on them as well as trying to see down the stairs.

Which he couldn't. They were too far away. He checked to make sure no one had moved, then turned and strode across the landing.

When he had entered the house, he'd come through the back garden. The door opened into the hallway, a good portion of which was beneath the landing. And that was where the noise seemed to be coming from. He couldn't see anyone at the foot of the staircase, so he took a step down and leaned over the banister hoping for a better view.

As he did, there was a blast of gunfire and the carpet on the landing was shredded, splinters of wood bursting up from it.

NINE

Sergeant Boyd was twenty-three. Too young to have fought in the Falklands, or any other major conflict for that matter. Two tours in Northern Ireland had seemed to present him with an opportunity for some action, but contrary to the popular view of the media, only small parts of the country could be classed as truly dangerous. He'd spent most of one tour looking tough with a gun in the city centre because the shoppers needed protecting, and another tour had been spent acting as liaison with the RUC. It had been interesting work, and had no doubt helped him get his stripes, but he'd never seen any real action.

To find two of his men had been killed was both shocking and – though he'd never admit it to anyone else – exciting. At last he'd have the opportunity for some action. And, looking at the state his men had been left in, he was in no doubt that he and the rest of his squad would be facing some stiff competition.

Torrance had still been alive when they'd found him. Fortunately, that had barely lasted long enough for them to watch him gasp and expire. Boyd knew he'd regret thinking it was fortunate later, but the reality was that there'd been nothing they could do for him, and to simply watch him suffer would have done no one any good.

So they'd left the two bodies and formed a huddle in

the shadows of the outbuildings. His men had looked to him for guidance and he'd quickly begun to formulate a plan. When they'd been left behind, his CO had been satisfied eight would be enough. Now there were just six of them. The obvious thing to do was to split into pairs and start the search for whoever was responsible for the deaths of their comrades. But whoever *was* responsible had easily dispatched two men, so pairs might not be such a good idea.

Their best chance was to work as a single unit, though that carried with it the risk they'd head in the wrong direction. As it was, three pairs would be limited in the scope of their search. But Boyd reasoned that the intention had been to retrieve the van, and with the van no longer there, the murderers – it had to be more than one – must have simply left. Which meant they'd almost certainly gone back down the track to the main road.

So that was the plan. Until one of his men noticed a curtain jerking unnaturally in one of the bedroom windows of the farmhouse. His attention had been caught by flashing as the curtain let out spasmodic glimpses of light.

They went in through the garden. The curtain had settled down, and everything seemed to be peaceful. Boyd had hesitated, not sure what to do. If they went charging in now, and it was just the owners participating in some horseplay, it could get very uncomfortable. Not just tonight, but later when the official complaints started coming in. They'd even started backing away from the house as he considered his next course of action. Then they heard a raised voice – "No you fucking won't!" – followed a moment later by a series of distinct thuds.

Decision made.

The door was locked, of course, so it took them a few moments to break it in. Not as easy as they made it look on telly, and a lot noisier. Because they didn't know how many they were up against, Boyd's tactic was essentially to go in making as much racket as possible. With any luck it would startle and maybe even frighten the people they were after. The fact they were likely to be terrorists also meant they'd use the shoot first and ask questions later approach. He might not have seen any action in Northern Ireland, but he knew damn well that 'shoot to kill' was official policy, and he had no qualms about using it now.

Inside, they'd found themselves in a large hallway. The staircase was to the right of them, but they couldn't see the foot of it because it was facing the wrong way. Overhead, they heard the creak of floorboards. Boyd gestured to two of his men to follow him. He was going for the stairs. In the meantime, he wanted covering, and hopefully they could take a few of the bad guys out at the same time. He pointed to the remaining three, then lifted his finger so it was directed upwards. As he ran for the stairs, the hallway was filled with the roar and chatter of machine gun fire.

TEN

Martin remained standing in the same spot after the Raven moved away from the doorway. He half expected to see the pale face reappear around the door frame to catch him out, and daren't move immediately. He strained his ears, listening for the creak of footsteps on stairs. If he heard that, he would try to escape. The blast of gunfire came first.

In front of his eyes, the floor erupted, the carpet bursting upwards in spurts that seemed to cover the whole of the landing. If the Raven had been in the line of fire, he'd be dead by now. And if he hadn't, Martin realised, he wouldn't be able to get back to the bedroom without being hit by the spray of bullets. He'd already worked out there was only one escape route. Even so, he looked around him, searching for an alternative in that crazy way you do when you aren't thinking rationally.

Outside the room, the roar from the guns dimmed. He guessed one of them had stopped firing. The volume of shots told him it must be the Army downstairs. He'd known a group of soldiers had been left behind to watch over the barns. What had brought them in, he didn't know, and frankly he didn't care. He was just glad they were here.

There was another blast, though that seemed to come from a point to the right of the doorway rather than below.

It didn't matter. He was moving now, heading for the window.

Tanya was cradling Ian's head, stroking it with more tenderness than he'd thought she was capable of. His initial thought was to just get out on his own. Although it didn't feel as urgent as it had a few moments ago, he still had a strong desire to get to his parents' cottage. They'd treated him like shit since he was a child. He couldn't let them get away with that. And if he stayed here much longer, he was likely to be caught in the crossfire, which would eliminate any chance of getting his revenge. But seeing Tanya and Ian made him hesitate. Was it really fair for him to just leave them here?

Behind him, the gunfire slackened for a few moments and he heard some metallic clattering downstairs. Then the volume cranked up again, shutting out all other sounds.

"We've got to go!" He'd bent down and was shouting into Tanya's ear.

Her reactions were slow. She seemed to be in a daze, but Martin didn't have time to be calm and understanding. He gripped her arm and tried to pull her to her feet.

"What are you doing?" she demanded, resisting him.

"Getting us out of here!"

"What about Ian?"

Good question. Martin's head turned rapidly between the window and the unconscious figure on the floor. If he could get Ian to the window, how was he going to get him out and down to the ground without killing him or – at best – leaving him seriously injured? He let go of her, and headed for the window. A glance at the door told him the Raven was still preoccupied.

The window frame was about eight feet across, and divided into three individual panes of glass. In the centre was a fixed pane, which was maybe five feet wide. On either side of it the other two opened outwards. He opened the nearest one and peered out into the darkness. As his eyes adjusted, he could make out that there was a garden. It was predominantly lawn, with flower borders. Paving stones formed a pathway that ran diagonally across the lawn, disappearing into gloom. Directly below was a patio area that extended maybe six or eight feet. There didn't appear to be any furniture there to cause additional hazard. He estimated the drop to be about twelve feet. If he went out backwards and held on to the ledge with his arms fully extended, his landing would be reasonably safe. Getting an unconscious man out was a different matter altogether.

Somewhere in the house, he heard an agonised scream. The bursts of gunfire stopped. For a moment, he was afraid the Raven had killed all the soldiers. Then he heard more shots. These were spaced out more, as if they were going for accuracy now rather than spraying bullets indiscriminately. He hoped they were successful, but he doubted it. As if to underline that thought, he heard a strangled cry, closely followed by rapid firing.

Whatever was happening down there, he realised he had to move swiftly. He glanced to his side. Tanya was staring up at him. She still had a dazed look about her, but he could see it was clearing, and with that clarity came fear.

He hesitated a moment, his gaze passing quickly between the open window and the couple on the floor. If he left now, he'd probably get away. He could let the Sentinels know what had happened, and they could decide what to do. It would almost certainly be too late for the McLeans, but there was a bigger picture here. That was how the Sentinels would approach it. But could he live with himself afterwards?

Tanya had shown herself to be hard-headed from the first time he'd met her. She was in control of her life and took what she wanted. He'd seen her for what she was straight away. And yet here she was, desperately afraid but clearly unable to leave Ian behind.

Something shifted inside him. Knots had been forming in his stomach. At least, he assumed they must have, because he was suddenly aware of them loosening. Tension eased and interior barriers began to fall away.

Bending down, he took Tanya's hand. "We have to go," he said softly, his voice barely loud enough for her to hear.

ELEVEN

Unarmed and unprepared, Collins had done what every right thinking man would do when the machine guns had gone off. He'd thrown himself back out into the yard, slamming the door behind him. Even with the door shut, the racket was more than anything he'd experienced before. In nineteen seventy-seven, he'd been involved in foiling a raid on a security van. A sawn-off shotgun had been fired at him from close range. Fortunately, the shooter was panicking and the blast went wide. But the noise had reverberated in his head for days after. That paled into insignificance by comparison to the din coming from the farmhouse.

His first thought was to return to Adam, Claire and the others. But they'd sent him here knowing he'd be in danger, so he didn't imagine he'd be met with much sympathy. Instinctively, he wanted to call for back up, but he didn't have a radio with him. Even if he had, he suspected this whole thing would be over before any assistance arrived.

So his options were limited. He could go back into the house, but that would be suicidal. Or he could go around the house and see if there was a safer way in. Or he could head for the other side of the yard and run down the track to the village. There, he could knock on doors until he found someone who'd let him use a phone to call for help.

If he did that, he'd have to hope he got there before the Hawthorns caught him, or whoever was shooting the hell out of the farmhouse.

He jogged to the gate that led out to the track. There, he cursed his own sense of duty and turned left instead of right, heading up towards the old outbuildings. Earlier in the day, when he'd gone up to see the crime scene, he'd noticed there was access to the back of the house through a garden. The garden itself was surrounded by a high wall, but there was a gate. And it was open when he reached it. Looking through, he took a moment to take in the scene in front of him.

At ground level, he could see flashes of light coming from what could only be an open doorway. Those flashes were accompanied by the cracks and bangs he recognised as gunshots, though by now they were more sporadic than they had been.

On the first floor, slightly to the right of where the doorway was, curtains had been pulled back and a window was open. Martin Gates was there with Tanya McLean next to him. The house was a good hundred yards away, but he could tell from their body language that they were hesitating. And he could understand why. It was potentially a long drop if they just jumped out. Without thinking, Collins ran across the lawn, veering away from the doorway. There was no point in risking being hit by a stray bullet.

As he reached the patio, he saw Tanya's legs were half way out the window.

"Let her out as far as you can!" he called up.

Martin's head appeared, squeezed between the window frame and Tanya's shoulder. He peered down for a moment, squinting into the gloom. Apparently recognising Collins, he gave a curt nod then disappeared again. As he did, Tanya began her descent. There was little finesse about the operation. As soon as her upper body was clear of the ledge, Martin let her drop as rapidly as his arms would allow. Then Collins was gripping her legs, steadying her, and pulling her down. He took her weight as Martin released her, and helped her to the ground.

She turned and gave him a puzzled look. "Inspector?"

But he didn't have time to respond. Another pair of legs was slipping over the window ledge. He gently pushed her to one side, further away from the door, and reached up.

From inside the house, he heard a sickening yell, filled with pain and anguish. The gunshots had fallen away now. There was an occasional crack and pop, but it sounded as if there were only two or three guns in play. What he didn't know was which side had them.

He caught hold of the feet and worked his hands up the legs, steadying them as he had with Tanya. Then she was alongside him, helping to take the weight. Even with her assistance, he was surprised at how heavy the body was. Then he realised it was her husband, and he was out cold. They dragged Ian away from the house. He knew it was necessary to keep the patio clear if they were going to help Martin down.

They were laying Ian down on the grass when there was a crashing noise to one side. He looked up to see a soldier lying face up, half in and half out of the doorway. His face was battered and bloody. The features were still recognisable, but only just. Blood poured from his forehead and nose. His eyes glittered briefly in the half light. For a moment, Collins felt they were looking at him. Then the body was jerked back into the house. The soldier opened his mouth to scream, then the back of his head bounced against the threshold and he was gone.

From just beyond the doorway, Collins heard a squelching sound and then silence. The guns had stopped. Above him, he heard heavy breathing from exertion, and in the sudden peace of the night, it seemed to reverberate around the garden and the house. He watched the doorway, terrified that whoever – or whatever – was inside would be able to hear Martin's breathing and would come to investigate.

Further inside the house, he heard footsteps on wooden floorboards. He strained his ears, trying to gauge whether they were coming nearer or moving away.

A sharp slapping nearby made him jump. He leapt back, further on to the lawn, hoping to God that he was far enough away. There was a blur of movement in front of him, then he felt a hand on his shoulder.

"Come on!" Martin said urgently. "Let's go!"

TWELVE

Two of the soldiers were dead. The others would join them, but it would take a while. Their injuries had left them completely disabled. There was enough pain to make them suffer, not enough for them to black out. And they knew they were dying. The misery they were experiencing fed the Raven.

He'd been distracted by the intruders. Inflicting that level of suffering took concentration. But now, as they lay helplessly on the floor or – in one case – hung from a coat hook on the wall, his attention returned to the people upstairs in the bedroom. As he started up the stairs, he was still basking in the afterglow of the destruction he'd just wreaked in the hallway. So it took a few moments for him to realise something was amiss. He was nearing the top of the stairs when he realised what was wrong. Then he was moving hurriedly.

Reaching the doorway, his eyes only confirmed what his more reliable senses had already told him. They were gone. And they weren't visible from the window either. With the light on in the bedroom, he couldn't see anything further than half way down the garden. He knew they were out there, but moving away rapidly. With an effort, he could probably catch up with them. It was a tempting idea. But he knew he had to think. Simply giving chase might give him an immediate release, but there was more at stake than capturing those three. After all, in the grand scheme of things, how important *were* they?

The one called Gates offered an opportunity to add to the torture he'd already inflicted on that family. It would be entertaining to compound the suffering they'd all endured. Entertaining, and nourishing at the same time. Just as it would have been if he'd been able to play with the other two. Although it was less than an hour since he'd satisfied himself with Jessica Cantor, this new woman had her attractions. He was sure he could have managed some form of sexual encounter with her. The more degrading the better. They would both suffer.

But those needs had already been served by the intervention of the soldiers. Their torment had given him enough energy for now.

So the only reason to go after the others was to stop them from bringing more people back. Maybe more soldiers. The Raven didn't know how easy or difficult that would be, and he certainly didn't have time to find out.

Reluctantly, he accepted that it was time to go. His plans had been thwarted. How or why he didn't know or understand. And he was pragmatic enough to realise there was nothing to be gained by looking for enlightenment. He had failed for now. But he had time on his side. He could return home now. Or he could travel to another point in time. Maybe even a year from now, when all the fuss had died down, and everyone would assume it was all over. He could come back and start all over again. A year from now for everyone else, but the blink of an eye for him.

He reached inside his shirt and fingered the object resting against his chest. He could go this instant.

Something stopped him, though, something that hovered at the edge of his mind. He couldn't tell what it was exactly. Gates's face kept popping into view, but he couldn't yet make a connection.

Standing by the window, he hesitated. Which wasn't like him. He was used to decisive action.

A raven swooped down and landed on the lawn. It stood facing him, looking up as if waiting for orders. Another joined it, then another and another until they formed a large shadow in the middle of the grass.

Less than a week had passed since the last time he was here in the village. Only a week. He'd recognised the man as a Gates, and yet he wasn't really sure he'd been there. The family were there, father, mother, son and daughter. Of course the boy was twenty-five years older, but he'd expected him to look older than he was. Not a lot older, to be fair, and maybe that was why he was confused. There had been another boy, though. He'd come later. Perhaps it was him.

Time was on his side, but he knew he still had to make a decision.

When he'd planned this trip, he had always envisaged how it would end. In one respect, the ending was to be the highlight. It would be tinged with regret that he hadn't succeeded in bringing the bomb back with him. But to him it seemed appropriate to, at the very least, get the pleasure he deserved by forcing others to experience unbearable pain.

It was time to go. And as the thought passed through his mind, the lawn erupted as a hundred birds rose up in unison, before scattering in smaller groups, carrying their master's invitations to his celebration.

THIRTEEN

The Land Rover was cramped with eight people in it. Mason and Croft were sitting on the floor in the back. Ian and Tanya were squeezed on to the back seat together with Collins. Martin was in the front, squashed up against Claire. Adam had turned the vehicle around and they were heading back down the track.

For a short time, they travelled in silence. When they'd come out of the darkness behind the farmhouse, it was clear that Collins and the others were desperate to escape from something. You didn't need to be a rocket scientist to work out what that something was. And the Sentinels knew that if they were discovered by the Raven, all their efforts over the millennia would have been wasted. Collins had opened his mouth to speak, but Adam had gestured for him to save it till later. Then they ran, leading the way back to the Land Rover. Even getting in needed no verbal communication. The Sentinels knew instinctively where they needed to be, and the others were happy to be pushed into place.

They were passing the barn conversions before anyone spoke.

"I wanted to kill my parents." Martin sounded bewildered. He was staring ahead, through the windscreen, but he was seeing other images in his head. The fear on his father's face when he'd visited him and Matt at the barns. His mother sitting quietly in the cottage the other night, looking so much older than he ever imagined she would. And her glistening body lying on the ground, waiting to be used. Colin bouncing into the pub like a child. Matt's animosity towards him. Janet's refusal to look at him when he saw her. This was his family, and only one of them accepted him. The one he thought he knew the least. And surely the only reason Colin accepted him was because he was too simple to know otherwise.

So of course he was angry. They'd rejected him when he was just a child himself. And now he was back they'd made it clear they didn't want him around any more. They were cold, heartless bastards, and they didn't deserve to have him in their family. Yes, he was angry, and he had every right to be angry. But he didn't want them dead.

He felt Claire take his hand, and that simple gesture broke the dam he'd built over the years.

More than twenty years' worth of bottled up emotion burst out. The pain of rejection, of missing his parents. Now *there* was a concept that hadn't even occurred to him. He'd missed his mum and his dad. Even though they'd been there in person, they'd not been there for *him*. His loneliness and emptiness. All of it came pouring out. There was no pricking behind the eyes and a gradual build up. He sobbed, grieving for the loss of the family life he knew he should have had.

Claire put her arm around him.

FOURTEEN

When children fall over and hurt themselves, they cry. They let the pain out in a short, sharp burst. In that instant, adults are convinced they're suffering the most intense agony. And yet, sometimes only moments later, they can be laughing and playing as if nothing ever happened. The natural inclination is to assume they were making a lot of fuss about nothing.

On the other hand, when adults hurt themselves, they hold it in, not wanting to make a fuss. And they don't. Not at that moment. Instead, they spend the next several hours, days or sometimes even weeks moaning about the incident. They cling to the suffering.

Sometimes it's good to let it all out. Sometimes it can be healing.

FIFTEEN

Claire held Martin close to her for several minutes after the sobbing died down. It felt natural to be this close to him. He'd turned towards her while he cried, and his head rested gently against her breast. Strangely, she found it almost as comforting as she knew he did. Her hand rested on the back of his head, holding him in place. She sensed his need for succour and instinctively wanted to provide it.

They were in the village now, passing the row of cottages where the Gates family lived. The Post Office was just ahead of them. As they approached it, four figures appeared. They came out on to the pavement from the driveway at the side of the shop. In the dull glow of the streetlights, they were little more than silhouettes. Claire didn't see them because she was focusing on Martin. But she did notice the Land Rover was slowing down. She looked over Martin's head at her brother.

"What's happening?"

Adam was concentrating on his wing mirror. "The Paynes," he said. "All of them have just gone out."

"*All* of them?" Claire couldn't keep the shock from her voice. "Are you sure?"

"I don't see who else it could have been." Adam looked across at her. His expression was grim.

"What's going on?" Collins asked. He had lots of

questions he wanted to ask, Claire knew. To have held off this long was commendable. It showed his humanity. He'd allowed Martin his reaction, but now things were changing again. Unfortunately, they still didn't have time for detailed explanations.

"Don't know for sure," Adam said. His tone was flat, emotionless. Claire recognised it. For most of their lives, they were able to enjoy a peaceful existence. They worked and laughed and generally got on with life. But they never lost sight of their purpose. So among the work they did they trained. They were proficient with a wide range of weapons, from swords to clubs to guns. Their nature took them towards peace. Having to take action, or confront the effects of the Raven's actions, meant they each had to make a mental shift. Adam's technique was to shut down all his emotions. She knew now that, until the Raven was gone, Adam would appear cold and ruthless. Only afterwards would he open himself up. And then he would suffer. How long that lasted would depend on what he had to endure. It might be days, or weeks or months. She hoped not too long.

The village boundary was coming up ahead of them. Adam swung across the road into an opening that led into a field. Then he reversed back out and turned towards the village centre again.

"Come on," Collins urged, "tell me what's happening."

Up ahead on their right was a small housing estate. It had been built in the nineteen fifties, a mixture of semi-detached bungalows. As they neared it, three shadowy figures emerged and began walking into the village. Seeing them, Adam pulled into the side of the road. He let the engine idle as he watched them.

425

"Who are *they*?" Collins again. "And why are they so interesting?"

"It's the Salthouse family."

Martin raised himself from Claire's breast. "The Salthouses?" She watched him rub the tears from his face as he looked through the windscreen, his eyes following them as they passed *The Major Oak*. "What are they doing?"

"He's doing it again," she murmured, more to herself than anyone else.

"Who's doing what again?" Collins asked, his voice filled with frustration.

It was Martin who answered. "He's calling them up to the woods, isn't he?"

Adam nodded. "It means he's going, though. We can just let him get this over and done with, then he'll be gone."

With her arm still around Martin, Claire knew her brother was right. But she also knew it would leave even more devastation in the village. And she wasn't sure how Martin would cope with the aftermath. She squeezed Martin's shoulder, trying to communicate to him that she would do everything she could to make him feel better.

In a way, she'd half-expected the response she got. Martin shrugged her arm away. His head swivelled between brother and sister, taking them both in as he spoke.

"You can't let him get away with this."

"Get away with…?" But Collins didn't complete his question.

"We can't expose ourselves," Adam said. "We've already explained this. If we do, he'll know we're on to him."

"We can't intervene," Claire agreed, though with less certainty.

426

"You selfish bastards!" Martin said angrily. Then he was pushing against Claire, reaching for the door handle. "Here! Let me out."

"What are you going to do?"

"I'm going to stop him."

"You can't."

"Why not?"

She didn't answer.

He looked deeply into her eyes. "Something else happened up there twenty-five years ago, didn't it?"

"Why do you say that?"

"Because I *am* angry at the way I've been treated by my family. But I also know how this Raven creature made me feel. He made me want to kill them. And if he could do that to *me* in a matter of a few minutes, what did he do to *them* that made them treat *me* like *that*?"

Claire looked down, unable to meet his gaze. "I can't tell you, Martin."

"Can't or won't?"

"If I tell you, it won't make sense." She looked up again, hoping he would forgive her one day. "Sometimes you just have to experience it for yourself."

"Like having kids?" Collins chipped in helpfully from behind them. "People can tell you everything they know about what it's like to be a parent, but until you experience it for yourself, you can never fully understand."

"Probably not the best analogy," Claire said, "especially as I've never had children. But the principle's right."

The Salthouses had disappeared from view now. Martin gestured to the door. "Time's moving on. Will you let me get out?"

427

Beyond him, Adam sighed. "I'll take you up there," he said, and Claire was surprised at how relieved she was to hear his words. "But it's just to save you some time. When we get there you'll be on your own."

He shifted into gear and pulled out again.

SIXTEEN

"If the Raven's preparing to leave, it stands to reason that he won't have followed us," Adam said. It sounded to Collins as if he was thinking aloud. "If he's on foot, the fastest way to the clearing from the farmhouse is along the path Martin took when he first got here. So we'll be safe to go back up the track we've just used."

"That's the way Ian took me to the clearing," Martin said.

"I should be able to get you quite close without the Raven knowing you've got company."

They passed the row of cottages at the edge of the village. Two of the front doors had been left open. Light from the hallways spilled out on to the street. Collins saw Martin's gaze rested on the houses until they were past.

"Who lives there?" he asked no one in particular.

"The Dakins," Claire said gently. "And Martin's family."

"Look, I know you don't want to tell Martin what's going on, but can you at least fill me in on what he already knows?"

"In all honesty, Inspector, you wouldn't believe us if we did." The voice came from behind him.

He turned in his seat. Squeezed in with the McLeans, movement was awkward, so he couldn't adjust his position well enough to see the man who was speaking. Low down on the floor and with the streetlights casting moving shadows as they passed by, both men seemed to be little more than dark and blurry outlines.

"What do you mean?"

"Do you believe in sorcery?"

"Are you telling me this is about witchcraft? Are we about to interrupt some kind of pagan ceremony? *Wicker Man* kind of stuff?"

"I think that proves the point," the voice said.

For a moment, Collins thought the comment was directed at him. Then he heard the other amorphous form respond. "I think you're right."

"Are you two taking the piss?" He was finding this more than just a little annoying, bearing in mind that it wasn't that long ago when he'd risked his life to help Gates and the McLeans to escape – and at the insistence of these four people from a farm that didn't appear on the map.

"And he's definitely not going up to the clearing," the first voice added conversationally. "Too much anger."

"What the *fuck* are you talking about?"

Beside him, he felt Tanya McLean flinch. He suspected more at the tone than the words themselves. He was sorry for that. She'd already gone through a bad experience, and he didn't want to make it worse. But the blokes in the back were talking in riddles and sounded as if they were making fun of him. He was happy enough to be the butt of a joke in the right circumstances, but as far as he could tell, at least half a dozen soldiers had been killed within the last hour and an atomic bomb had been stolen in the last twenty-four. Leaving aside the death of the dog, he suspected there was more yet to be uncovered, none of it pleasant. The brutality and the ruthlessness of whoever was responsible should be enough to have them all on guard and pulling together as a team. Not taking the bloody *piss*!

One of the men leaned forward, his face materialising in the half light. He could see it was Mason and, as he spoke, Collins realised he'd been the first to speak.

"Forgive me, Inspector," he said calmly. "It wasn't my intention to upset you. But you have to know that the creature we are facing tonight…"

"I didn't notice *you* doing much of the facing," Collins snapped irritably.

Mason raised his hands in a gentle gesture of supplication. "I was speaking figuratively, Inspector. I'll try to choose my words more carefully."

Collins slumped back against the door. "Fuck!" he said, though it was more of a mutter. Mason's composure was frustrating, yet it had also knocked the legs out from under his anger.

They'd turned off the main road now, and the light from outside had virtually disappeared.

"I wanted to make a point, Inspector, and I went about it the wrong way. Any one of us here in this vehicle has the possibility of coming face to face with that creature." Collins felt Tanya pull away from him. He suspected she was looking for comfort from her husband, though as he was still unconscious he could only be effective in the same way as a teddy bear would be against the bogey man in the middle of the night. "It feeds off anger. And rage. And hate and pain. Any negative feeling you have, Inspector, will make you less effective. You know that from your own experience. If you're resentful, or jealous, or bitter or angry, you can't function as efficiently. When you go up against criminals, you give them an edge if you're suffering from any of those emotions, don't you?"

Mason paused, but Collins didn't respond. Just waited.

"Experiencing those feelings doesn't just give the Raven an edge. He feeds off it. Your weakness makes him stronger. It's what you might call a double whammy. That's why we can't let you go in."

"You can't stop me," Collins protested.

"Yes we can," Mason said with a confidence that left Collins in no doubt that he meant it. "But it would be better for us all if you simply accepted what I am saying as fact."

"That this...Raven...that you keep referring to is basically some kind of supernatural being?"

"Something like that."

Years of police work had put him up against all kinds of villains. There were some things he'd witnessed that he couldn't take home with him. Those memories had to be stored in a separate compartment in his mind, locked away where they couldn't get out and scramble his brains – and his life – for good. And there were times when he did wonder whether the bastards that had committed those crimes were truly human at all. But they were. The evidence showed it. Whatever it was that had caused them to visit so much violence on others – and the shrinks had plenty of factors they could throw in to explain their behaviour – in the end they were just nasty people. And so was the Raven.

That didn't mean he shouldn't be treated with caution. But an armed response unit sounded like a more effective solution than trying to stay calm.

"You're not going to go along with this, are you, Inspector?"

Up ahead, they caught the first glimpses of the converted barns. As they did, the headlights suddenly went out. Distracted by that, Collins didn't notice Mason lean a little further over the back of the seat, his hand outstretched.

SEVENTEEN

Cutting the lights made sense, although it puzzled Martin for a moment. They were getting closer to the woods, and Adam wouldn't want to warn the Raven they were on their way. What surprised Martin was the fact that Adam didn't slow down. There was some light coming from one or two of the barns, but not enough to provide a clear view of the track ahead of them. In spite of this, the Land Rover eased through the bends effortlessly. Martin peered at Adam, trying to work out how he was doing it, but in the darkness he couldn't make out his features at all. Then they were turning off the track and passing between the trees. The engine note changed as Adam shifted down the gears, careful to keep the revs down. No point in turning the lights off, Martin supposed, and then announcing your presence with a roaring engine. They slowed down as they negotiated the trees. More often than not, Martin was only aware of them as they appeared in the side windows – and sometimes not even then.

Behind him all was quiet. He didn't know what had happened to Collins, but guessed Mason had decided to shut him up for a while.

He leaned closer to Claire. "I'm sorry about earlier," he said, keeping his voice low. It seemed strangely intimate. Though the idea of intimacy was strange to him anyway, he realised.

"Don't worry about it. I do understand." She'd turned her face towards him. He knew because he felt her breath on his cheek.

"I wish *I* did."

Her hand touched his, squeezed it gently. "You will." She didn't make it sound as if his understanding was something to look forward to.

Resting his head against her shoulder, he reflected on the roller coaster of emotions he'd experienced in the last hour or so. After years of resentment – albeit suppressed – how was it that he suddenly cared so much about his family? He thought he'd come back for an explanation, or possibly revenge. And less than an hour ago, he'd been desperate to exact that revenge. But now he just wanted to save them from whatever fate the Raven had in store. His only doubt was whether he was up to it.

Mason's words to Collins kept going through his mind. The chances were that he would be angry or frightened or any of those other negative emotions. If that would only serve to make the Raven stronger, what chance would he have against him?

The Land Rover slowed some more, then Adam turned it sharply to the right and stopped.

"That's as close as I dare take her," he said. "Ideally I'd like to turn around so we're facing the other way, but I don't even want to show reversing lights."

Martin looked past Claire through the passenger window. In the distance there was a faint orange glow. It flickered, as fires do.

Adam placed his hand on Martin's shoulder. "You're on your own now," he said flatly.

435

Claire opened the door. It creaked in the stillness of the night, but no demons came rushing out of the darkness to attack them. Martin followed her out, and was struck by the chill in the air. He hadn't been aware of it earlier. Then again, he and Collins had been running and carrying Ian between them. Stepping out from the warmth of a vehicle filled with seven others made it more noticeable.

They walked away from the Land Rover, towards the firelight. He felt Claire's hand in his. It seemed right.

Starlight shone down through the trees, offering limited illumination. It was enough for him to see her face, though. She looked concerned. He hoped it was for him.

"I don't know what to do," he said. It was an admission he didn't want to make in front of the others. Somehow he felt safe with her.

She lifted her hand to his face. "You will when you get there." She said it with a confidence he certainly didn't feel was warranted. Yet he took strength from it.

"Will you be here for me when I get back?"

A sad look crossed her face. "That could be very complicated, Martin."

He grinned and, for a moment, he looked the image of the cocksure surfer dude he'd cultivated over the years. Nodding his head in the direction of the clearing, he quipped: "And you think this isn't?"

It took a moment. She hesitated before smiling back at him. Then she hugged him and told him what he wanted to hear.

EIGHTEEN

They'd parked about half a mile from the clearing. In daylight, he guessed it would have taken him about ten minutes to walk to it. After tripping over several fallen branches and tree roots, he decided against trying to match that.

The high he'd felt when he left Claire fell away rapidly. As he made his way through the woods, he was reminded of the dream. Or rather, the memory of that night in nineteen sixty-four. No clothes to find this time. But he knew that was only because he was following a different path. There were similarities, though. The trees partially illuminated by the moonlight; the scurrying of creatures on different sides of him; the occasional glimpse of birds in the branches. And, up ahead, the glow of the fire growing larger as he moved nearer.

Before long, he began to wonder how much was reality, and how much was the memory. The sensations he felt were identical to those he'd experienced during twenty-five years of nightmares. Apprehension was an understatement, terror an overstatement. He knew there was physical danger. The Raven was more than capable of killing him. Or worse. But he wasn't concerned about that as much as he was about what he was going to find when he reached the clearing. Which was how he'd felt before.

The difference this time was that he'd already seen some of it.

In spite of that, just as he had when he was eight, he kept on, slowly but surely making his way towards the fire. Still a few hundred yards away, a gust of wind blew in his direction, and he momentarily felt the warmth of the flames. Sound came with it. Muffled voices. They sounded subdued. A product of the distance or the Raven's control over them? He couldn't tell.

He could see movement, silhouettes and shadows shifting around the flames. His throat seemed to tighten. It was the prospect of what he might see. The image of his mother laid out on the ground flashed into his mind. He made a conscious effort to push it aside. But it shot back in as soon as he relaxed. She'd been in her thirties when he'd seen her like that. A disturbing enough vision. What if she was like it again? He didn't know her age, but knew she must be around sixty. She looked older though.

Then the humour kicked in.

What the fuck am I thinking? Her age isn't the important thing here. She's my mum!

And he couldn't help himself. He chuckled. Just for a moment. But it was enough. It broke the spell. The image of Anne Gates submitting to a sexual act was banished from his mind. At least until he reached the clearing. The thought sobered him, but the images stayed away.

Even though there was no wind, he began to hear sounds from the clearing. Voices again. A few words he couldn't make out. Muted and brief. There was no dialogue. More like instructions being given. And there was the crackle of burning wood, and the rustle of leaves.

He guessed they were on the ground and being pushed around by feet moving through them.

The trees suddenly seemed to part before him as if they were being pulled aside by some supernatural power. Startled, he stopped moving, and as he did so the trees did too. It was an optical illusion, he realised, a result of the angle from which he'd approached the clearing. But it meant he had an unobstructed view of the fire now. Figures seemed to be dancing on the far side of the clearing. He could make out their heads and shoulders over the top of the fire. As they turned, swaying in time to music only they seemed to hear, the firelight reflected off their naked skin.

Reluctantly, he stepped forward again, forcing himself nearer. The gap between the trees opened still further, revealing more of the clearing. He saw the Raven. Because he was dressed, he stood out from the others. He'd discarded the clothes he'd been wearing at the house, but the new ones were familiar to Martin. In this light, it was impossible to tell the colour. Everything he had on was dark: the long cloak, the shirt, trousers and boots. The only lightness came from the pale face, which currently looked very self-satisfied, and from a chain that hung around his neck, its links flickering with reflected firelight. Something dangled from the chain, but from this distance Martin couldn't make it out.

A few moments passed before he realised he was focusing on the Raven to avoid having to look at everything else. He was now less than twenty yards from the edge of the clearing. There was nothing in the way to obscure his view. Swallowing hard, he braced himself.

He'd assumed that seeing his mother performing a

sexual act with someone else would be his worst nightmare. As he took in what was actually happening, he realised it would have been a blessing. With all his senses reeling, he was oblivious to the Raven's attention turning towards him.

NINETEEN

It had been a disappointing day. But now it was time to move on. He had things to do back home, and he wasn't going to achieve anything here at this time. For now, he would use these people to build up his energy levels. He didn't need the energy to travel, but he knew he might need it when he got back.

He stood to one side of the fire and watched the spectacle before him. Naked bodies obeying his every command. Not that he said a word. His will was stronger than that of all the other people in the clearing combined. Effortlessly, he bent their minds, twisting them into shapes they couldn't possibly comprehend. Much to his amusement – and their horror.

And now the revulsion they felt at their own actions flowed into him.

The Salthouse family. Their eldest daughter, Monica, had been here last time, and they were remembering her now, the grief tearing them apart. Images of her hanging in a barn. She'd only been able to find binding twine. Her strangulation had been long and painful. Their other daughter, Teresa, was with them tonight. Nearly thirty, she was on her knees at the side of her mother, trembling because she already knew her fate and, no matter how much she wanted to, she couldn't scream or cry for help.

To add to their pain was the guilt over Peter, still lying in hospital, kept alive with machines and a continuous flow of morphine. The son who was conceived at a similar gathering twenty-five years earlier.

The Payne family. Helen contained within a circle by her parents and sister, Linda. They were holding hands and dancing around her, flesh rolling and bouncing as they moved; their faces screwed up as they hurled abuse, calling her names that were incomprehensible to her. They were shouting over each other, so most of their words were incoherent. Yet she had a sense they were blaming her for them being there, even though they seemed to be doing this of their own free will. Naked and profane, leaving her bewildered and frightened. She wanted to push her way out of the circle, but was held in place by some invisible force.

The Walker family. Frank and Elizabeth locked together as their daughters looked on. The girls stood on either side, their faces clearly expressing their disgust at what they were witnessing. Hard as they tried, they couldn't close their eyes, hadn't so much as blinked since it began. Elizabeth's gaze was drawn to Catherine. The poor girl was sobbing, her hands raised to her face, but not enough to cover her eyes. Elizabeth knew why. The Raven wanted her to see the webbed fingers, and experience the shame that went with them.

The Dakin family. Tears coursed down Derek's cheeks. He'd lived with humiliation for a long time. He'd understood that his wife hadn't been in control of herself when she'd conceived Ronald. On a rational level, he could acknowledge it. Especially as he himself had committed unspeakable acts that night. But those acts lived on only in the memory. Ronald's birth was a permanent feature of their lives, a living, breathing reminder of what had happened. And his disability only served to underline it. So he'd never been able to forgive Joyce. And that was why she swallowed the painkillers. *His fault.* And he'd been left to bring up the little bastard. He looked at him now. Ronald was facing him, and slightly to one side of him stood Stephen, Derek's son. The first-born. He hated them both, resented their very existence. Without warning, they both reached out and grabbed him, each one taking an arm. Startled, he instinctively tried to resist, but all his energy was gone. Then they were pulling him and, with a shock, he realised they were taking him towards the fire.

The Gates family.

Matthew had tried to resist the call when it came. The "caw" of the Ravens had triggered something buried deep in his mind, and he'd instinctively known what it was. As if expecting to be clutched by a *Star Trek* style tractor beam, he'd thrown himself on to the sofa and stretched himself out, grabbing one of its arms with his hands, and gripping the other with his toes. Now, standing in the clearing, he'd been feeling stupid about that from the moment he'd let go and stood up again. But maybe that was good. Because, if he focused on that embarrassment, maybe he'd forget the true source of his shame.

He looked at his mother, and knew that wasn't going to happen.

Colin was confused. That wasn't an unusual state of affairs for him, but he recognised this was really something very different. For a start, he wasn't used to seeing his parents naked. Nor, for that matter, had he regularly seen either Matthew or Janet in a state of undress. And then there was everyone else up here. He'd gone to school with some of these people. But in all those years of schooling, he'd never seen Catherine or Helen without clothes on. He might have seen Ronald in the showers after PE, but he wasn't even sure about that. PE hadn't been one of Colin's strengths. He never seemed to understand the rules. So he was excused more often than not. Anyway, it was definitely odd to see them like this. It was giving him a peculiar feeling. There seemed to be a strange tension coming from between his legs. He saw his mother lying on the ground, her private area towards him. Curious, he began to move towards her.

The Raven felt the torment pouring out of them, absorbing it and letting it wash over him. It was like swimming under a waterfall, both relaxing and stimulating at the same time. A time to savour. Then he felt a new stab of pain from the edge of the clearing and he turned to see Martin watching. The look of horror gave the Raven an additional surge of energy. Having a witness to events was going to give the experience an extra, delicious edge.

TWENTY

Images came spilling into Martin's mind, a montage he would have preferred to be less graphic. Especially as he was faced with more than enough explicit stuff from where he was standing. But the combination of memories and real-time spectacle gave him context. It wasn't pleasant, but it made sense at last.

His mind had suppressed the true horrors, hidden them from him. The dreams had tried to express them, but still hadn't been enough. And maybe, in a way, his mind had done him a favour. In truth, he would have preferred not to know.

But now he did, he could do something about it.

He'd been angry earlier, and afraid his anger would only serve to help the evil creature responsible for this atrocity. Instead, he instinctively felt a completely different emotion. Claire had been right. Now he was here, he knew exactly what to do. He began walking again, crossing the last few yards to the clearing.

Ahead of him, he saw Colin dropping to his knees in front of their mother's feet. Matthew had moved beside her and was looking down. Nearer to Martin, his father was standing with his back to him. Patrick was behind Janet, his hands apparently roaming over the front of her body, touching places no father had a right to.

Martin reached them in three strides. He rested his hand on Patrick's shoulder, making the older man jump. When he turned to see who'd touched him, his face crumpled, and Martin recognised the reaction for what it was. He pressed his mouth against his father's ear.

"I know you don't want to do this. He's making you do it against your will. I forgive you."

Patrick began to tremble as tears flowed freely from him. Janet felt the change in movement, and looked over her shoulder. When she realised Martin was there, her face reflected her terror. Martin touched her cheek gently. She flinched as if she expected him to strike her.

"I am so sorry," he said. "I won't pretend to understand exactly how you're both feeling right now. But, believe me, I do know you're not responsible. I forgive you." He put his arms around their shoulders and squeezed them, hoping they'd feel the love he felt for them both in that moment.

Then he let go and moved on. Matthew and Colin were with their mother. When he stopped next to Matthew, all three became aware of his presence at the same time. The reactions from Anne and Matthew were predictable. Colin's was tragically comic. Looking up from what he was doing, he beamed at his brother. His expression was like that of a small child about to go on a fairground ride for the first time: a mixture of pride and apprehension.

Dropping down into a crouch, Martin avoided looking at his mother's body. He rested a hand on his younger brother's head and ruffled his hair playfully. It didn't seem appropriate under the circumstances, but he needed Colin to feel good about himself.

"I will always be proud of you, no matter what," he said carefully.

He looked away, turning his attention to Matthew and Anne. "And the same goes for both of you. Now I know why you treated me the way you did. You were embarrassed and ashamed. God knows, if I'd experienced this, I'd've felt the same. You must've been scared shitless I'd remember it all. Or maybe you thought I did remember it and just wasn't saying anything. I'm sorry you've had to go through this. I know it's not your fault. I forgive you all. For this, and for every time you've hurt me. Because you were really trying to protect yourselves. And I guess you were also trying to protect me too."

"Oh, Martin, I'm so sorry," Anne said, her voice quavering.

"I know you are. But really you have nothing to be sorry about."

"Bloody hell!" Matthew said abruptly.

"What's wrong?" But even as he asked, Martin realised his brother was looking downwards. Following his gaze, he felt relief wash over him.

Then they were laughing, the two brothers rocking backwards. Colin knelt up to watch them, puzzled by the sudden change of tone. He wanted to join in, but didn't understand the joke. Then Matthew pointed to Colin's groin and he looked down to see his own flaccidity. He still looked as if he didn't understand why it was funny, but started laughing all the same.

Looking around him, Martin reached out and patted both brothers on the shoulders. "I've got to help the others, but remember that I love you." He gazed into his mother's eyes for a moment. "All of you."

He stood up. The Raven was still standing in the same place. He was staring at him, a mystified look on his face. Martin smiled and nodded as if in greeting, which caused his frown to deepen.

The family nearest to him were the Paynes. He didn't have fond memories of them. They'd never made him feel welcome in the shop. For the first time, he was beginning to understand why. They'd seen him that night in 1964. They knew he'd seen them, and they were afraid of what he might say. To them or to others.

Only a few paces and he was alongside Mr Payne. After all these years, they'd kept him at such a distance he'd never even heard him called by his first name. The realisation saddened him. Both for himself and the Paynes.

"You have no need to fear me," he told John Payne gently. "I know this isn't your doing."

His gaze turned to Mrs Payne, who seemed to have recovered herself sufficiently to make an attempt to cover her breasts. He focused on her face, not wishing to cause her more discomfort.

"I'm here to help," he said simply. Her lips trembled, yet they curved upwards slightly at the corners. As tears began to flow, he knew they were accompanied by a sense of relief.

There was a more urgent need just beyond the Paynes, though.

Derek Dakin hadn't aged well, but looked sufficiently similar for Martin to recognise him. He also recognised imminent danger when he saw it. His two sons were only a few feet away from the fire, and it was clear from the way all three were struggling what their intentions were.

A quick glance around told Martin that there were dangers for the others too, but this one was more serious. He didn't run. That might startle people, and he didn't know what the implications of that might be. It also might prompt the Raven to take some action. So he walked towards the Dakins, trying to hurry without being too obvious.

"Is that Steve?" he asked conversationally, as he approached them. The older Dakin brother looked over his shoulder. "Didn't you used to go to school with Matt?" Having grabbed his attention, he wanted to distract some more, so he gestured towards his own brother, still kneeling on the ground a few yards away.

Stephen Dakin's eyes widened as he realised who was speaking to him. Martin closed the gap and rested his hand on Stephen's naked shoulder. "I know what's happening here, Steve. And I know what happened last time. You have nothing to be ashamed of. It's not your fault. You're being made to do this, just as you were made to do things before. I've forgiven my family for everything they've done. You should forgive yourself. And let your dad have the chance to forgive you too."

"He's had his chance," Stephen said sharply.

Martin nodded his understanding. "Perhaps he has," he said, and rested another hand on Derek's shoulder. "But perhaps you needed an outsider to forgive you first. Is that right, Derek?"

And Derek collapsed, all resistance falling away. The sudden change caught the brothers by surprise, the dead weight pulling them all down to the ground in a heap. They were still close to the fire. It wouldn't take much to push Derek on to it.

"What do you think you are doing?" a horribly familiar voice demanded from close behind him, and Martin felt his stomach lurch.

TWENTY-ONE

The Raven watched in amusement as Martin entered the clearing. He had sensed his shock, and knew it could only get worse as he understood the full extent of their shame. Everyone else in the clearing was immersed in misery. And most of them had already been here before. So they *knew* how depraved and sickening their actions were going to be. This member of the Gates family hadn't been actively involved last time. He may also have been too young to understand. His reaction would undoubtedly be one to savour.

So he left Martin alone, letting him get close so he could fully appreciate just how debased his family's actions were – which would intensify his responses, and thus increase the Raven's energy levels further.

That was the intention. But the opposite had happened instead. The effect was marginal at first. He didn't realise anything was wrong. True, it was strange that he didn't get a surge of power when Martin stood alongside his father and sister. He assumed there was a delayed reaction. But then he watched as Martin moved on, surprisingly relaxed as he crossed the short stretch of ground to his mother and brothers. Even then, he focused on how Martin would respond when the full implications of his mother's behaviour sank in. Would he understand that what she was about to do would be with someone who was both her son and grandson?

Then the younger brother was kneeling up. The Raven didn't immediately concentrate his efforts on forcing Colin to carry on. He was too puzzled for that. And still feeling puzzled when Martin stood up again, especially as the anticipated burst of energy was still not forthcoming. Instead, as Martin stepped away from his family, he experienced a jolt, and was suddenly aware of feeling physically tired. The abruptness of it left him dazed for a moment. He'd never known this to happen before.

Looking for a reason, he cast his eyes around the clearing.

Nigel Salthouse was turning to his daughter. Neither of them seemed enthused about what was going to happen next. So that was good.

The Payne family were still gathered in a circle around Helen. He didn't notice that their voices weren't raised as much as they had been.

Catherine Walker was still peeking over the tops of her webbed fingers as her father continued to abuse her mother.

Patrick and Janet Gates were still close together, but they weren't touching any more. He was aware of Martin talking in the background, but his attention was fixed on father and daughter. Patrick reached out to Janet, but it was simply to put a paternal arm around her shoulder.

The Raven felt as if he'd taken a body blow, something that hadn't happened to him since he was a teenager. A lot had changed since then. He had mastered sorcery in its truest form, and controlled legions in his own time. His powerbase continued to grow, and grow more rapidly with the use of weaponry from the future. Today, with the loss of the bomb, he'd experienced his first failure in many years. It was a setback, and he would get over it. Already, he planned to return, and soon. Then he would be back on course with his plans.

But this was something else again. His control over the people in the clearing was slipping. And he realised now that it was slipping because his own psychic strength was being sapped.

The rest of the Gates family were getting up. Martin had moved on to the Paynes. The other brothers were on their feet, and helping their mother. Patrick was leading his daughter towards them. Incredibly, they were all moving of their own free will.

He had the capacity to reach out with his mind, invisible sensors that stretched like tentacles in any and all directions he wanted to. He used them now, searching for answers. *Why was he suddenly losing his power? How much control did he still have?*

For the first time since adolescence, he felt fear. Fear of losing control. Fear of the unknown. And that was exacerbated when the sensors reached the Gates family. As they made contact, he felt his energy drain still further. Instinctively, he snatched the sensors back.

When they touched the Dakins, he was relieved to feel no further drain. But he was aware that they were regaining some control over themselves. He tore his eyes from the Gates family, and saw that Derek Dakin was actually struggling against his sons now. Before he had not been able to. They were already so close to the fire. It wouldn't take much for them to throw their father on to it, and if they did that, he could open their minds to the awfulness of their own actions. That realisation could be enough to generate the boost he needed.

In the few moments it took for him to cover the ground between them, somehow the Dakins had collapsed into a heap. He stopped a few feet behind Martin.

"What do you think you are doing?" he demanded.

There was a pause, as if Martin was collecting himself, and then he turned and looked the Raven in the eye.

"I've come to help my family," he said evenly.

The Raven recalled their first encounter.

As the families had performed for him, sickening themselves with their violations, he'd been aware of a presence just beyond the reach of the firelight. He'd sensed youth, aware of its fear and confusion. There was enough suffering within the clearing to feed him. Even so, he'd let his sensors reach out, searching for the child. And when they found their target, they wrapped themselves around him like the fingers of an enormous, invisible hand. Then they pulled him into the clearing.

Strangely, the reward he was looking for came from a different source than he expected. The boy's fear did increase, but the surge of energy he experienced came from the others. It took a few moments for him to understand what had happened, and then only by trying to imagine how he might feel if he was a mere mortal like them. They'd been feeling shame before, carrying out perverse and wicked acts that were beyond their own comprehension. And those acts were being witnessed by others. If there had been a saving grace, it was that the only witnesses were equally guilty. Only now they were being watched by an innocent.

Greedily, the Raven had grabbed the boy and held him close, turning him around, ensuring he saw every detail, forcing him to watch the villagers' humiliation.

This was the same boy. A man now. Yet the images he'd seen today had still been shocking to him. The Raven realised that somehow he had managed to suppress the memories. He didn't understand psychology. Where he came from, it hadn't been invented yet. But he knew the mind could play strange tricks, so he knew there was no point in dwelling on what had happened since his last visit. He was more concerned about what was happening now, and why his powers were draining away.

He pointed to the sprawl of bodies by the fire. "*They* are not your family."

A shrug. "What can I say? I offered a bit of help and it became a habit." Martin's eyes lifted and focused on something over the Raven's shoulder. "Looks like things aren't working out the way you wanted them to."

Spinning round, he saw the Payne family had broken their circle. The terrified girl in the middle seemed to be looking for somewhere to run, but one of the other women put an arm round her. Beyond them, Nigel Salthouse was on his knees, sobbing. His wife and daughter were reaching out to him reassuringly.

"My guess is, he's asking for forgiveness." The words came from behind him. "You might want to consider that yourself sometime."

The Walker girls were handing clothes to their parents, who were now sitting side by side, shaking their heads in a mixture of disgust and disbelief.

"You did this." The Raven's voice was low, but the

menace in it was still strong enough to carry. As he turned to face Martin, he knew his words had been heard. He could see the apprehension in his eyes. Automatically, he expected to feel a small surge from his reaction. That was what always happened. He fed off it, and it grew inside him. Not this time. The realisation was shocking to him. He couldn't rely on his psychic power or energy to help him. Worse, a lot of his physical energy had been drained away as well. He had no advantage here. What he did have was rage.

He launched himself forward, his hands curled into claws aimed at Martin's face and chest. Martin jerked sideways, so one hand missed him entirely, and the other scrabbled ineffectively over his right shoulder. Even so, the weight of the Raven's body smashed into him, and the two men fell to the ground, landing dangerously close to the edge of the fire. Nearby, the Dakins got to their feet and backed away.

As they landed they bounced, throwing the Raven to one side. Martin rolled away from him, and scrambled to his knees. The fire blazed a couple of feet to his right. The Raven was a similar distance from the fire, and about five feet away from Martin. He too had reached his knees. Very warily, they both rose to their feet, each of them braced for an assault from the other. The Raven went first.

It had been some time since he had been unable to draw on other resources. Reliant solely on his own physical strength and fighting skills he had learnt and half-forgotten over the years, his approach was haphazard but brutal.

TWENTY-TWO

In spite of Martin's preference to walk away from a fight, there were times when you had no choice. After his beating by the jealous boyfriend and his mates, Martin had realised similar situations might crop up again. Next time, he wanted to be more prepared. So he'd joined a Dojo and thrown himself into the world of martial arts. Wherever he moved, one of the first things he did was find a new place to practice. It became one of the few constants in his life.

When it came to combat, he'd learnt about the two most dangerous weapons he had: his knees and his elbows. Judicious use of these weapons could bring a fight to a rapid end, something he'd experienced on two occasions since then. Though, to be fair, on both occasions, his opponents had been at least slightly inebriated, and almost certainly had no formal training.

This opponent was neither drunk nor untrained.

TWENTY-THREE

Lunging at Martin, the Raven threw a punch at his face. He was aiming for the nose, aware of how painful and debilitating a broken nose could be. It was also likely to bleed profusely, and if the others saw the blood, it might give them cause for doubt and fear. But Martin's arms swept across his body, his left forearm deflecting the punch as his right fist thrust towards the Raven's chest. The sorcerer didn't have time to move out of the way. Instead, he deliberately relaxed his body, rolling backwards to minimise the effect of the blow.

Martin took the opportunity to take a couple of steps to his left, putting some distance between himself and the fire. *A possible weakness?*

Righting himself, the Raven didn't hesitate. He knew he needed every advantage, and giving his opponent time to plan his next move wouldn't help. Instead, he swung his left fist, causing Martin to lean back in the direction of the fire. As his hand swept past Martin's head, he lashed out with his right leg, catching him across the upper thigh. Something flashed in Martin's eyes, a combination of pain and anger. For a moment, he felt hope that there might be something to feed on.

He watched with amusement as Martin took three rapid steps backwards, keeping himself out of range. *Maybe this wasn't going to be so challenging after all.*

He was wrong.

As Martin came forward again, he was aware of the sense of anticipation from the people around them. Not concern for the man who was trying to save them. For reasons he couldn't understand, there was no sign of doubt. Instead, he felt as if they were trying to transmit their own energy to him to give him more strength. He moved back himself, preparing to block whatever was coming. At the last moment, Martin twisted to one side, his body rotating as he did so. Caught out, the Raven lowered his guard for a moment as he tried to work out what was happening. Even as he did, he saw Martin's left elbow heading for his face. He jerked back so it missed his nose, but felt a tooth loosen as it connected with his jaw.

Even as he tasted blood in his mouth, a punch landed under his rib cage. Although he was too late, instinctively he'd raised his hands to protect his face and, in doing so, exposed his abdomen. Still in motion, Martin had brought his right fist up. The angle was awkward, so the impact wasn't as great as it could have been. The shock effect was enough, though.

Momentum took Martin on, so he was now behind the Raven. Spitting blood, the sorcerer turned to face him. Rage coursed through his veins, fuelling a desire to punish. But it seemed he wasn't the only one with that desire. And, even though it was tempered by what was clearly a cold fury, Martin's desire was stronger.

A flurry of kicks and punches struck the Raven before he'd completed his turn. Blows to his thighs, shins and flanks. They came in hard and fast, yet deliberate. Nothing glanced off. Every time there was contact it hurt. He found himself reacting, all control lost as he tried to fend off each attack. A foot caught him on the inside of his thigh. It was tender, but it also made him realise there were other tender spots Martin was getting close to. He focused his efforts on protecting his lower abdomen.

Almost as soon as he did, Martin dropped back, giving them both a little space. He didn't have time to consider why. Martin leapt up and forward, his right foot connecting with the Raven's chest. Trying desperately to keep his balance, his arms flailed around him, as if flapping them would hold him upright. Back on his feet, Martin shot forward, spinning around as he did, his back bumping into the Raven's chest and stomach. Focused on trying not to fall over, the elbow driving into his solar plexus was as unexpected as it was painful.

Martin shoved the Raven back before he had a chance to grab on to him. Already he was turning again. Bent over, the sorcerer didn't see the kick coming until it was too late. The pain he'd felt in his gut evaporated as piercing agony exploded between his legs. He collapsed to the ground, landing on all fours and panting desperately.

His anger towards Martin was intense. He was filled with an urge to lash out at him. He wanted a weapon that could inflict awful damage to him, lacerating him, punishing him with unbearable pain. But winded and experiencing an ache that radiated out to encapsulate his lower torso and upper legs, he could only dream of what he would like to do. In this state, he was in no position to even throw a punch.

He cast an eye around the clearing. It was a place that had given him so much pleasure. The rituals had changed over time, but the objective had always been the same. Now he could see the various families were huddled together in different parts of the clearing. Each family remained apart from the others, but all seemed to be doing something remarkable: they were healing.

It had been a mistake bringing the boy into the clearing. More accurately, his mistake had been to hold him so closely. In those few minutes, as he fed off the energy from the others, somehow he must have shared a part of himself with the youngster. They'd formed a connection. It had happened before, but in the past he'd been able to use it to his advantage. Perhaps if he'd appreciated this early enough, he could have done the same this time. Instead, it had worked against him.

Even as he realised it, he felt yet more of his energy slip away. He slumped forward submissively, resting his head against the ground. From the corner of his eye, he could see Martin's boots only a few feet away. They could strike him at any moment. It was a wonder to him that they hadn't done already. With his hands no longer supporting him, he lifted his right arm.

Somewhere off to his right and behind him, he heard someone call out.

"He's reaching for something inside his cloak!" It was a warning, alerting Martin to the danger that he might produce a weapon. As his hand encircled the metallic object hung from his chain, the Raven smiled to himself at that thought. He wasn't going to produce anything. Quite the opposite.

The last words he heard were: "Bring your hands out where I can…" And then he was gone.

PART FIVE

MEN ARE FROM MARS

ONE

DI Collins was at his desk. In front of him was the report he'd compiled for the MoD. They'd taken the investigation over. Apparently it was no longer a police matter. He'd assumed the Army would be taking charge, so was surprised when he was confronted with uniforms from the Air Force. They were sitting across the desk from him now. Air Marshal Buxton and Group Captain Rowland.

The Air Marshal was in his late forties. Slate grey hair, clean shaven, and pale-faced. He looked as if he spent far too much time indoors. Rowland looked younger, but that may simply have been because he led a more active life. His hair was slightly longer than you would normally expect of a military man, a feature Collins didn't overlook. He was broad, but in good shape.

Buxton's rank alone told you he was in charge, but he sat back and let the Group Captain do all the talking. Collins was aware of being observed as Rowland gently interrogated him. The door was closed.

"I understand you have no recollection of Saturday night?"

"It's a bit hazy."

"How do you mean?"

"Well, I remember working here late, but I don't remember leaving or getting home."

"But you did go home?"

465

"That's where I woke up Sunday morning."

"Has your wife been able to throw any light on this *haziness*?"

Collins knew what he was implying, and he didn't like it. But he also knew he was severely outranked and that these guys could pull strings he didn't even know existed. So he had to put up with it.

"She doesn't know what time I got in. But she's used to that. It goes with the territory."

"And what time did she go to bed?"

"She's not sure, but not earlier than eleven."

"So you got in sometime between eleven and…?"

"Around eight the next morning. That's when she woke up."

"Any idea what time you left here?"

"No. The last person to see me was the Desk Sergeant, and he reckons that was between seven and eight Saturday night."

"Potentially thirteen hours unaccounted for then?"

Glances were exchanged. Collins wondered if they were debating whether to have him committed or not. Buxton nodded for Rowland to continue.

"What do you know about events at Forest Farm?"

"I take it you mean on Saturday night?"

"Of course."

"Nothing more than you do." He tapped the report. "Everything I know is in here."

"I'm sure I'll enjoy reading that later. For now, though, give me your take on what happened?"

"Well, to be fair, we were only called in after the Army found their men dead."

"But you went up to the farm. What did *you* make of it?"

"It was a massacre. Whatever hit those boys, they didn't have a chance."

Rowland frowned. "*What*ever?"

Collins looked at him blankly. "I'm sorry?"

"You said 'whatever'. Not whoever."

He shrugged at the pair of them. "Well, frankly, it did look as if they'd been attacked by machines, not people."

More exchanged glances.

"Any indications as to who might be responsible?"

"Not really."

"Interesting choice of words."

"All right. No obvious suspects."

"What about the McLeans?"

"Can't see it myself."

"With respect, Inspector, that's hardly concrete evidence. Were they at the farmhouse?"

"No. They said they'd found the events of the previous night too disturbing, so they stayed with friends."

"Have the friends confirmed that?"

"Yes."

"And who are they?"

Collins glanced down at his notes. "An Adam and Jennifer Hawthorn."

"Locals?"

"They live at another farm nearby." He lifted a page to check the details. The name struck him as odd, and yet strangely familiar.

Rowland was moving on. Collins got the impression he was going through the motions anyway. The McLeans weren't likely suspects.

"Didn't they have a lodger with them?"

"That's right. A bloke called Gates."

"Where was he?"

"Under the circumstances, he moved out as well. His family live in the village, and he stopped with them. Apparently their sofa was a more attractive option than staying at the farm."

"And presumably his family have corroborated that."

"Yes."

The Group Captain sat back in his chair and looked up at the ceiling thoughtfully. Collins took the opportunity to look at Buxton, but he seemed more intent on his wing man than anything else.

Dropping his gaze, Rowland asked: "And what about Scene of Crime? Did they find anything?"

It was tempting to be flippant and ask: "What, besides all the blood and gore?" But Collins thought better of it. He still had to provide for his wife and boys.

"Nothing that jumped out at us. No traces of any weapons other than the ones the soldiers were carrying. There were fragments of clothing all over the place, but if you'd seen the state of the master bedroom, it could take months or even years for us to work out what fabrics came from where." He paused and shook his head as if in disbelief. "There was one strange thing though. There were bloody hundreds of fingerprints, which is hardly surprising given the number of bodies we had going in and out of that place last weekend. But we did find a match."

"Well why didn't you say so before?" This from Buxton, who suddenly leaned forward. Collins half expected him to

468

produce a swagger stick and start waving it at him while he demanded an explanation. "This could get us our man."

"I doubt it, sir. The fingerprints were on record from two separate murders, but the killer was never identified."

"Still, it might help us."

"I doubt it. The murders took place in nineteen thirty-nine."

TWO

They took his report with them. He'd typed it himself. No carbons. Just as instructed. Any other records about the events in Ravens Gathering were now in Rowland's briefcase. The case was closed as far as Westfield Police were concerned. Still, the Superintendent would be pleased. One less thing for him to worry about. For a small town, they had enough crime on their hands.

It wasn't in his nature to let things lie, so Collins was surprised at how relaxed he felt about it all. His reaction puzzled him, but not enough to make him feel any more concerned. Frankly, the MoD were welcome to it. There was something strange about the whole situation. Especially the fact that they hadn't seemed interested in why Simon Cantor's body had been found on the farm, or why his wife had been raped and her mutilated body left to rot at the vicarage. At least, not during their interview. But they'd taken the paperwork for that as well.

As he watched them walk away from the building, he was struck again by the fact that the RAF were involved. It was Friday now, and the Army had been buzzing around the farm incessantly since last weekend. So why the sudden change?

Sometimes the answers come when you least expect them. No matter how hard you wrack your brains, you can't make the connection. Even for a copper like him, who was used to lateral thinking.

The boys were watching *Raiders of the Lost Ark* when he arrived home that evening. Collins was vaguely aware of the video playing in the background as he wandered back and forth around the house. After swapping his suit for something more comfortable, he set the table while his wife finished making dinner. The TV was at the far end of the lounge-diner. Indiana Jones was telling the pretty girl in the white dress to close her eyes. Collins wasn't much into fantasy and adventure films, but he'd sat through *Raiders* a few times with the boys. It had been good to share the experience with them. They were getting older now, though, and weren't really interested in sharing things with their parents.

When he came back with the condiments a short while later, the scene had changed. He stopped a moment and watched it as the missing connections began to form. It was the warehouse filled with crates. He wondered if that was where his report would end up. Or somewhere like it. Locked up with the other records he'd handed over to Rowland. And then he made the lateral leap. *Raiders* was a Stephen Spielberg film. But a few years earlier he'd made another film: *Close Encounters of the Third Kind*.

As the end credits started to roll, he startled his boys by laughing out loud.

THREE

Autumn felt as if it was beginning to settle in. A week or so earlier, it had been sunny and he'd been making favourable comparisons with the Canaries. Now it was cooling, and he wondered whether he'd be able to handle it. He'd spent a long time in warmer climes. Even so, he wasn't going to stay cooped up indoors. It might be cold, but at least it wasn't raining.

He'd walked a lot over the last few days. The woods and farmland still gave him enough variety to stop him from getting bored. Not that he was focused on the scenery. He needed the exercise to counteract the tension. Things were better with his family, but it was going to take time. After years of them fearing he might remember what he'd seen in nineteen sixty-four, in some respects it had been a relief that it was now out in the open. But that didn't mean it was going to be easy for any of them. They were talking to him now. Only short bursts, though, and it was upsetting for them and for him. So he walked, and they coped with their feelings in whatever way felt right for them.

Counselling would probably have been helpful, but that wasn't going to happen. So his mother cleaned, and his father drank, and Matthew worked on his car, and Janet sat in her room and read. Colin, of course, didn't seem too perturbed by the experience. For now, though, they kept him at home, filling his head with other things: Disney videos, picture books, jigsaws, Lego, toy cars. All designed to overlay the images from the previous Saturday. When he went out into the village, they wanted other memories to come spilling from his mouth.

The previous Saturday. A week ago today. In some senses, it felt like a lifetime away. In others, it was as if it had happened only moments ago.

Without realising it, he'd strayed on to Kindness Farm. He recognised the track he'd used to leave the farmyard the week before. A part of him wanted to walk past it. Another part of him – the part that suspected his subconscious had really brought him here – urged him to step off the footpath he was on and visit the Hawthorns. The track was only visible for twenty yards or so, then it turned and disappeared from view between two mounds that rose perhaps fifteen feet above it. From here, he knew he was safe. He could hesitate all he liked, and they couldn't see him from the farm yard.

It was a small comfort to him as he wrestled with his feelings. He hadn't seen the others since just after dawn last Sunday. They'd remained hidden from the rest of Martin's family and the other villagers in the clearing. The shame and distress they were all feeling would only have been exacerbated by the appearance of the Sentinels. He'd spotted Adam and Claire briefly as he led his family from the clearing. Their presence reassured him, and he felt sure they'd only revealed themselves to him. After that, his focus was on getting everyone home.

Clothes were retrieved. Probably not all, but enough to allow people to dress with sufficient decency to be seen on Main Street. Not that the street was teeming with witnesses in the early hours of the morning. But it gave them all some comfort.

As his own family settled in, kettle on and something stronger available for those who wanted it, Martin had excused himself and stepped outside. He didn't understand how he knew they'd be waiting for him, but he did. They were in the front garden of the vicarage. A hedge concealed them effectively from the road. There was no sign of the Land Rover.

Both of them looked grim. Adam nodded towards the vicarage.

"He was here. There's nothing anyone can do, but we'll make sure the police are alerted."

"Without exposing yourselves?"

Adam smiled, though there was little humour in it. "He's learning," he told his sister.

Martin was very conscious of Claire watching him. She nodded her agreement. "He's definitely learning. You did well up there." He had a sense that she was holding back.

"Yes you did," Adam said. "We can't thank you enough."

From the street, he heard a diesel engine drawing near.

"That'll be Croft," Adam said. "He took Ian and Tanya back to our place."

"How are they?"

"Ian's conscious again and Tanya's still in shock. They're both going to need looking after. But we can do that."

"What about Collins?"

In spite of the circumstances, Adam grinned. "He'll be okay. Mason's taking him home."

"Is *he* conscious then?"

"No."

"How does Mason know where he…?"

"Let's just say we have our ways."

"What do you think will happen when he wakes up?"

"Collins? Don't worry about him. He won't remember a thing."

Martin raised questioning eyebrows.

"Again, let's just say we have our ways."

On the street, they heard the Land Rover pull up, then the back of it appeared in the gateway as Croft reversed into the drive.

"We've got to go," Adam said. He gestured across the road. "You've got a lot to do over there. And it's probably a good idea if we're not seen together just yet. So we'll keep our distance for a while. We'll be in touch when the time is right."

He nodded in what Martin took to be an attempt at reassurance. Beside him, Claire did the same, but she seemed more distant than Martin had hoped. A few seconds later, they were gone, the Land Rover heading back to *Kindness Farm*.

Back in the present, his hesitation made the decision for him. Adam strolled into view from the direction of the farm yard. He was dressed for work, but there was no sign of tools. When he saw Martin, he smiled.

"I thought it might be you," he said cheerfully. He offered no further explanation and Martin knew there was little point in asking.

Reaching him, Adam patted him on the back. "It's good to see you. Out for a walk?"

"Yeah," Martin said mechanically. He felt awkward at being caught like this. He was also unsure how the Sentinels would be towards him anyway. After all, they'd achieved what they wanted, and he'd begun to suspect he'd simply played a useful part in their game.

Adam must have seen something in his demeanour. He gestured towards the path that led away from the farm yard. "Let me join you. We've got a lot to talk about."

FOUR

"How're you getting on with Norma?"

Startled, Martin stopped walking. They'd only travelled a few yards.

Adam laughed. "You might not have seen us, but we've been keeping an eye on you."

"Worried I might start talking about what you're doing here at the farm?"

"No. Just making sure you're okay."

They started walking again.

"Do you think I *am* okay?"

"It's relative, isn't it? You've got a way to go yet but, considering what you've been through, I'd say you're doing okay. So. Are you settling in at the pub?"

"You make it sound like I've picked Norma as my soul mate and we're planning to live happily ever after."

"She's a lovely woman, but I don't think she's your type."

Martin was tempted to ask what Adam thought his type might be, but decided against it. "It's just a place to stop for a while. The cottage isn't really big enough for Matt and Janet to be living there, let alone me as well." Matt had called on Norma Sunday afternoon and cleared the way for Martin to get a room. She hadn't been too enthused at first, but now things had quietened down in the village and

477

he'd been nothing less than the perfect guest, she'd come around.

"It probably seemed odd finding your brother and sister still living at home."

"It did," Martin agreed.

"But you can understand why now."

He didn't say anything, just nodded slightly. It was still difficult to accept that his younger brother was also his nephew. Colin's slowness made him vulnerable, and it was a parent's natural instinct to be protective of their child. So Matt needed to be there. As for Janet, he guessed she'd been violated as well. Fortunately, she hadn't fallen pregnant, which was probably a great relief for everyone. But the psychological effects had been harsh, not least the damage to her self-confidence. They'd been through a terrible trauma, one that none of them could cope with alone. Nor could they share it with anyone else. Especially not the family member who'd seen it all happen. In time, he hoped it would all make sense.

Adam must have sensed the direction of his thoughts. "I won't pretend to know how it feels to be in that situation, and nor should you. Unless you've experienced it yourself, you can't. But you've done the most important thing you can. You've accepted them, and they know that you don't blame them."

"What about the other families?"

"What do you mean?"

"I don't know. I feel they need help. Some of them might even need medical attention after what happened on Saturday. But where will they go for it?"

"They can't go anywhere. The shame's too great."

"Do you think they'd accept help from me?"

"Don't you think you'll have enough on with your own family?"

"Probably. But not forever. And at the moment, they need to be left alone some of the time as well. I could be using that time to do something for the others. Even if it's helping with the funeral arrangements for the Salthouse family." Peter had died earlier in the week. The trauma to his body had been too much for him. There were some who would consider it a blessing, but Martin wasn't going to make that judgement. He knew the family were grieving.

Adam bowed his head as he considered Martin's suggestion. "I can't tell you what to do about Nigel's family, or any of the others for that matter. Only you can decide. All I would say is, listen to your heart."

"My heart's telling me to try."

"Then that's what you must do."

The path they were on came to a stile, and beyond that it went into woods. They continued to talk as they climbed over and carried on walking.

"You're not planning on going back to the sun then?"

"Not just yet." That was a subject he didn't want to talk to Adam about. Time to change the subject. "Was there a lot of gossip in the village? You know, back when the babies were born."

"Gossip? You mean because there were so many at one time?"

"That could have just been coincidence. No, I meant about the fact that there was something wrong with them all."

"It was unusual, and I'm sure the families involved were very conscious of it. But you have to bear in mind that not all of the conditions were obvious immediately. Colin, for instance, just seemed to be a late developer for quite a few years. Peter's leg was shorter, but not noticeably so when he was a baby. And Ronald's deafness wasn't diagnosed until he was nearly two. The defects in the two girls were more apparent. But then it wasn't that long since the scandal of the Thalidomide babies, so some people might have thought they'd got off lightly."

"Still, it's well known that inbreeding causes defects. Surely a few tongues wagged."

"They probably did," Adam agreed reluctantly. "Fortunately, they weren't wagged too loudly, so the families were spared that particular humiliation." He paused a moment, clearly pondering what they had been talking about. "Of course, if there had been that kind of talk, it would have all been wrong, but there's not a lot you can say to enlighten the ignorant."

"What do you mean, it would have been wrong?"

"Well, it's true that the incidence of physical and mental defects is higher when there has been –" Adam smiled "– as you so delicately put it – inbreeding. But the reality is that the incidence is still incredibly low. The chances of it happening to five families from the same village is hundreds of thousands to one."

"So what happened here then?"

"Well, unfortunately, there was a case of incest that came to light here during the nineteen thirties. I can't prove it, but it seems likely that the Raven became aware of it when he paid us a visit in nineteen thirty-nine. The scandal would have still been talked about. I know the family concerned were almost lynched at one point. That kind of reaction would have been just the sort of thing he'd have got a kick out of."

"That still doesn't explain how five pregnancies resulted in five defects."

"He's a sorcerer, Martin. The Source could be described as many things. It could be nature, or God, or some infinite intelligence that guides us. Whatever you believe about any of those things, the Source is something that runs through us all. We all have the ability to tap into it, but sorcerers have a greater ability than others. The Raven caused those defects deliberately, so he could intensify the sense of shame, and present the families with constant reminders every day. That's something else I can't prove, but it's also the only possible explanation."

"So my mum and Matt have probably blamed themselves even more for Colin being retarded."

"Not a nice word, but accurate nonetheless. And, yes, it only added to the pain they felt, which was exactly what the Raven wanted."

"But why couldn't you tell them. It wouldn't have solved everything, but at least it would have made them feel better about something."

Adam look uncomfortable about that. They walked several paces before he answered. "You already know the answer to that, Martin. I know it seems harsh. But we have to consider the bigger picture."

"The needs of the many outweigh those of the few."

"Very well put."

"I think you've got Spock to thank for that one." Even

as the puzzled look crossed Adam's face, Martin flapped his hand in a dismissive gesture. "Forget it. What were you going to say?"

"Well, I was going to try to put things into perspective. And I could do that by comparing the suffering caused by famine and brutal dictatorships in Africa. But that would be unfair. Physical suffering and mental suffering are quite different. Then again, I could point out that the world has a population of over five billion right now. In that context, what's the suffering of a handful of people in a little village in Nottinghamshire? And that would be getting closer to the truth. Because the proportions are actually far more significant. You see, if the Raven can go back in time with the kind of weaponry he's trying to, we won't be concerned with the fate of the world's current population. We'll have to take into account the populations that would have existed over many tens of thousands of years.

"Sacrifices are being made all the time, Martin. Bigger sacrifices for smaller causes. That doesn't mean it's easy for me to watch your family suffering, or the Paynes, or the Dakins..." He tailed off. Martin could tell that the recollection was genuinely upsetting for him.

They walked a little further into the woods as Adam collected himself.

"I'm sorry," he said at last.

"That's okay. You don't need to say any more."

The path twisted and turned through the trees. They followed it for a while in silence, each reflecting on their own thoughts. It was Martin who spoke first.

"How're Ian and Tanya?"

"They've recovered from the shock. Fortunately, they have no idea what happened in the clearing, so it's just the experience at the farmhouse they've got to come to terms with."

"Have they been back?"

"Ian has. The Army allowed him in just long enough to pick up some of their things. I don't think Tanya wants to see the place again."

"I got the impression she wasn't too enamoured with the place in any case."

"No. She's talking about moving back down south. I think she wants to be with her family."

"What about Ian?"

"He's not part of the plan. But they've talked about it together and with Jennifer. She's very good at helping people."

Martin hadn't spent much time with Jennifer, so he wasn't in a position to agree or disagree on that point.

"It's strange. I really got the impression they were becoming closer."

"In a way, they have. They've set aside the niggles and petty annoyances that had built up between them. Without those in the way, they've been considerate of each other and loving. But it's loving with care, not passion. We can all tell that they're sad about it, but they know it's the right thing for both of them."

"Must be difficult."

"It is, and it will be. But they're both strong people, and at least they know it's something they've agreed on."

"Still, it seems odd that Tanya's heading back to her family. She never struck me as being family orientated."

Adam stopped walking for a moment. They'd reached a fork in the path, but he took the opportunity to look at Martin appraisingly. "Would you have thought that you were family orientated?"

Martin shrugged. "Probably not."

"How do you feel now?"

"Like they're the most important people in the world to me."

"Family always are." Adam rested his hand briefly on Martin's shoulder. It was strangely affirming. Then he pointed to the left-hand path. "Let's go this way."

The path took them upwards. It wasn't steep, but the incline was consistent and went on for some time. Sunlight filtered down through the leaves and branches overhead, so they could see the pathway ahead of them. Martin didn't recognise where they were, but he was more interested in anything Adam had to tell him.

"What are Ian's plans?"

"He doesn't have any yet. He'll probably have to stay for a while, until the farm's sold."

"That could take a while. It was on the market for long enough before he bought it."

"Possibly, but I understand the Ministry of Defence are interested in buying it."

"What on Earth for?"

"Quite the opposite I imagine."

Martin shot him a puzzled look.

"Because the Army can't explain what happened, they've turned to the RAF. And they've turned to the RAF because they have a department that investigates extra-terrestrial activity."

"They think it was *aliens*?"

"I'm sure they won't admit what they're thinking to anyone, but it sounds like the MoD is willing to explore that option further. And to do that without interruption, they'll need to own the site."

"So Ian's money worries could be over."

"That's probably an overstatement. The Government isn't noted for its generosity. But it should make it easier for him to move on. What's more important is that he's been in touch with his children."

"I didn't know he had any."

"Let's just say he's not been the most attentive father."

"How did it go?"

"Not well. But he's not going to let that put him off. He knows he's at fault, and it's going to take a lot of work to put things right. He's learnt a lot about himself in the last couple of weeks."

"He's not the only one."

The incline was getting shallower, and the top was coming into view. Beyond, it looked as if the trees were pretty much on a level.

"Has Tanya given any indication when she'll be going?"

"No. I don't think she's ready to leave yet. She needs to build her confidence back up first. Right now, she needs to feel safe, and *Kindness Farm* is providing that for her. It's always been that sort of place."

"Is that why it's called *Kindness Farm*?"

"I can see why it might look that way, but no. In a way, it's a bit of a joke. We might have a serious job to do, but we enjoy a bit of humour. Even if it's black humour."

"Black humour?"

"Yes." The path had levelled out now. Adam stretched his arm out, pointing to their left.

About a hundred yards away, Martin could see the clearing.

FIVE

They were standing almost directly opposite the place where he'd entered the clearing a week earlier, so it took him a few moments to realise what he was looking at. The ashy remains of the fire were the giveaway. Other than that, there was no hint of the evil work done at the Raven's behest. Instead, the area seemed completely benign.

"Notice anything different?"

It took Martin several long seconds. He allowed his eyes to rove across the space, searching for something specific that would explain the difference in atmosphere. Obviously there was daylight, but there had been daylight when he'd come up with Tanya.

"The ravens," he said at last.

"The ravens," Adam agreed. "They gather before their master arrives, and stay together for as long as he's here. Do you know what they call a gathering of ravens?"

Martin shrugged. It had never crossed his mind that there was a name for it. "A flock?" he guessed.

"Some people refer to it as a murder, which isn't technically correct. A murder refers to a gathering of crows. With ravens it's an unkindness."

It wasn't the funniest joke in the world, but Martin could see the humour in it. "So *Kindness Farm* will be here to counter the unkindness when it arrives?"

"Assuming it comes back."

They were walking again now. The path would have taken them away from the clearing, but Adam had stepped off it and was leading Martin towards the pile of ash.

"Don't you think it will?"

"I'm optimistic. We know that one day he will be defeated in his own time. We just don't know how far into the future he gets before that happens."

"And when will we know?"

"I'd love to be able to answer that. The pattern he's followed has been to appear at more frequent intervals. The last few times, those gaps have been twenty-five years so, if we follow that line of thinking, logically we should know around 2014. He could be back sooner, though. He didn't get what he wanted this time, so he might come back for it in the next year or two."

Martin shook his head, not sure whether to be impressed or confounded by the scale of the work the Sentinels were involved in.

"How do you cope with that?" he asked. "Knowing that this creature might materialise so many years from now, but equally he could turn up tomorrow?"

Adam stepped into the clearing and waved a hand at the debris that lay there. Remarkably, the tyre swing was still intact. The fire hadn't come close to it.

"We know what he's capable of. If we let down our guard, the consequences could be catastrophic."

"And yet you don't know who they would be catastrophic for. Or when it might happen."

"It's what we do, Martin."

"Don't you ever tire of it?"

"I can't even comprehend why anyone would think like that. The Order is committed to protecting mankind. This just happens to be the task we are assigned to at the moment."

"And when will that assignment end?"

"That's not our decision, but I suspect we'll have another fifty years or so of it."

Martin was very conscious of a humorous glint in Adam's eye. He got the sense that he'd made the comments deliberately, and was waiting to see what the reaction would be.

"I'd heard there was a bit of a pensions crisis, but I hadn't realised it was that bad. I take it what you're really saying is that you're here for the rest of your life."

"No I'm not. How old do you think I am, Martin?"

"I don't know. A bit older than me, I suppose. Nearly forty?"

"I'm seventy-nine."

He deliberately left that hanging between them.

"So when you mentioned the events in nineteen sixty-four…"

"I was there, Martin. I saw you. So did Jennifer. So did Claire." His eyes were fixed on Martin's face, studying him carefully.

A lump seemed to have lodged in Martin's throat, cutting off his voice. Adam had no reason to lie to him. And, while what he was telling him would have seemed outrageous at any other time, in the context of what he had learned over the last week or so, this was only a minor surprise. He swallowed hard.

"How old is Claire?" Suddenly, it was the only important question he could ask.

"She's seventy-five." The humour had gone from Adam's eyes, replaced by a sadness that Martin couldn't get a handle on yet.

Claire was old enough to be his mother. At a push, she might even be old enough to be his grandmother. For the first time in his life, he'd thought he'd made a real connection with a woman. The hang ups he'd developed about sex made some degree of sense to him now. Even so, he knew they wouldn't just go away. And yet, somehow, he'd felt sure Claire would understand, that she'd be the one to help him move on. More than that, though, he had felt there was potential for a real future together.

"It's a tough one to get your head around, isn't it?" Adam said, but Martin wasn't sure how to take it.

"Are you immortal or something?"

"No. Far from it. But we do live longer than other humans. Three hundred years is a fair average."

Three hundre... He couldn't even contemplate the rest of the thought.

She'd already been alive for over forty years when he was born. In nineteen sixty-four, she'd watched him as an eight-year-old, and she'd been fifty. No wonder she'd been reluctant to commit when he'd been preparing to leave her by the Land Rover last Saturday. She had leaned in close and told him to come back in one piece. And she'd said it with a tenderness that made him believe she felt the same way about him as he did about her. Now it seemed she'd just been playing with him, getting him in the right mental state to go and do the job they wanted him to.

He felt crushed at the deception. Perhaps more so than he might have done at another time. But there had been so much progress made with his family. For the first time he could ever remember, he'd wanted to be close to them, wanted to stay in the village. Her betrayal had thrown that idea aside. Right now, all he wanted was to get as far away from the village as he possibly could.

Then Adam said something completely unexpected.

"You need to talk to her. She's very frightened at the moment."

"Frightened? What's she got to be frightened of?"

"Of losing you. With everything that's happened to you. With the…" He hesitated, apparently struggling to find the right words. And apparently failing. "With the situation of your mother and brother having sex, and knowing the same happened between your father and sister, she knows that any relationship the two of you had could be a reminder of that."

"What?" He looked at Adam incredulously. "Are you *mad*? Why would I think that? It's not as if she looks as if she's old enough to be my mum."

"All right, let's take that point as read for now. What about how you're going to feel when you're in your seventies, and she still looks as if she's in her thirties or forties?"

That stopped him for a moment. Right now he was young and virile. Well, he assumed he was virile. For the two of them to be together now would be perfect. But how *would* he feel in forty years' time? When she was still looking young and beautiful, and he was heading for the knacker's yard. More importantly, how would *she* feel?

"Think about it," Adam said gently. "It might not work out. Away from the unusual events you've been through together, you might find the attraction isn't there in the same way. But if things do get serious, you need to understand what you're letting yourself in for. And when you've thought about it properly, you need to talk to her."

EPILOGUE

A faint drumming beat its way into his dreams. He didn't know how long it lasted. That is the way of sleep and dreams. Not long, he guessed as he woke. The shift from sleep to wakefulness was swift. That hadn't changed.

It wasn't drumming. Just a rhythmic tapping sound. He pushed the duvet aside and got up, crossing to the window. The moon was out, and there was no cloud cover at the moment to dim the light. In the distance, he could see trees swaying gently in the breeze. The raised land around them shielded the farmyard from most of the effects of the wind. Even so, he could see a loose end on a sheet of tarpaulin was flapping. It was covering a tractor they'd had to move out of its normal shelter in a barn. A series of metal rings were embedded in the edges of the tarpaulin. He guessed one of them was repeatedly connecting with the tractor's body as it lifted and fell.

Now he knew what it was, he realised it was only barely audible. Most people who were awake wouldn't have noticed it. Anyone else would have slept through it. He looked back at the bed for confirmation.

In the half light, he could only make out the outline of her body. It was unfair, because even that wasn't truly clear, not with the bedclothes draped over her. But he could still see the gentle rise and fall of her chest. She was asleep, undisturbed by the tarpaulin or him getting out of bed. He guessed she must be used to it by now.

He couldn't see her properly in this light, but he could see her in his mind. As attractive now as she'd been when he first met her. Which was more than could be said for him. He wasn't in bad nick for his age, he supposed. But the blond hair was almost gone, replaced with grey. At least he hadn't started losing it yet. And his skin wasn't as smooth as it used to be. Working the land had taken its toll on his face and hands. But she still loved him.

That had been his greatest fear. She would grow tired of seeing his old face when hers remained youthful. Now he knew her love could see beyond that, and his fears were different. He was fifty-nine now. Still young by modern standards. But he was more than half way through his life. Way more. Yet she was barely a third of the way through hers. By the time he died, she still wouldn't have reached the halfway point. He hoped she wouldn't waste the rest of her life mourning him. She would smile at him when he broached the subject, tell him to focus on their time together. And he did, most of the time. But he wanted her to be happy, and he couldn't bear to think of her otherwise.

The children would help, of course. They were still teenagers, but – ironically perhaps, given their likely longevity – they had matured well. There was none of the selfishness he saw when he went out into the rest of the world. Though that may have been down to their limited exposure to what was laughingly considered to be society. They still had no TV or computer. Their time was spent together as a family. They worked the farm, they laughed and played and learnt the lessons they needed to learn.

Occasionally, they would travel to the Refuge. Adam and Jennifer had returned there when it became apparent that Martin and Claire would settle down together. The farm didn't warrant two families, and they were ready to start their own as well. Patrick and Anne spent time with their cousins and other members of the Order, and benefitted from the wisdom and guidance the Elders had to offer.

So Martin had no concern that they would abandon their mother in the pursuit of personal happiness. They knew they could find that by just being who they were and caring for others around them.

In the middle of the night, alone with his thoughts, he allowed himself to feel melancholy as he watched the outline of his sleeping wife.

Outside, he heard a rustling sound. Pushing the curtain back again, he looked out. Clouds had rolled over, so the yard was darker than it had been a few moments ago. On the roof of the stable block, he could make out silhouettes of birds. They hadn't been there a few moments ago. The roof itself was higher at the back, angling down as it ran to a point overhanging the doors. There were three birds there, perched on the top. As he watched them, he felt a chill go through him as another one landed alongside. Then another, and another.

Twenty-five years, Adam had told him. That had been twenty-six years ago. He glanced over at Claire, still asleep, still oblivious. Then he thought of the children. What if the Raven was able to call on them as part of the Gates family line? It wasn't a thought he considered often. But it was there, at the back of his mind.

495

He noticed the light through the curtains brighten, and look outside again.

They were pigeons. He had to suppress the laughter. The relief felt ready to burst out of him.

His family was safe. In his heart, he knew they were out of the danger zone when 2014 had passed into 2015. But you never stop worrying about your family.

A MESSAGE FROM THE AUTHOR

Time is our most precious commodity, so I really appreciate the fact that you've given up some of yours to read *Ravens Gathering*. With that in mind, I do feel a bit cheeky asking you to give up some more, but I hope you'll bear with me just a little longer.

I learnt many years ago that the best way to build success in business is by word of mouth recommendation. This is as true for authors as it is for any tradesman or professional. The simplest form of recommendation is to tell your friends and family (just don't include spoilers). What's less obvious is that readers do read reviews by other readers. At the moment, the most accessible places for reviews are Amazon and Goodreads, but I will update my website with details of others as I become aware of them.

Of course, not everyone feels comfortable writing book reviews, but they don't have to be lengthy critiques. Very often, a couple of sentences are plenty. Even so, if you are unsure about what to write in a review for any book, I have included links on my website to articles that can help.

Ravens Gathering is not intended to be a one-off book, although I don't anticipate there being a sequel (as such). Two of the characters appear in books I am currently working on, and I expect at least one more to show up in another I'm planning. So if I've piqued your interest, and you'd like to learn more about me or my books, please do stop by at the website and feel free to send me a message.

www.graemecumming.co.uk